'Told with a wit honed by the Arctic winter and a story that lures you in with the perfume of the Finnish forests, this is Wes Anderson meets the Coen Brothers in rural Finland … a book I will never forget' Matt Wesolowski

'An original and darkly funny thriller with a Coen brothersesque feel and tremendous style' Eva Dolan

'This was a truly beautiful book – deliciously dark, thought-provoking, and gorgeously written. It gave me chills, and not only because of the endless snow and cold. I see why Antti is so revered in Finland' Louise Beech

'Right up there with the best … offering a sympathetic, politically engaged investigative journalist and a profound concern for the environment' *Times Literary Supplement*

'Tuomainen's spare style suits the depressing subject and raises a serious question: how do you find hope when law and order break down?' *Financial Times*

'Both a thriller and a dark, laugh-a-minute journey that will keep you hanging on to the end. The story of a man investigating his own death has been done before but not with such gusto' Maxim, Jakubowski, Crime Time

'A tightly paced Scandinavian thriller with a wicked sense of humour and a bumbling ne'er-do-well at its centre' Matt Grant, Foreward reviews

'At my first smirk I almost felt guilty; should I be laughing? … Further occasions of raised eyebrows and blurts of laughter escaped, so I relaxed and really settled in to this fabulously entertaining read. Antti Tuomainen has hit just the right notes, and I can picture Jaakko and the other characters lighting up the big screen. Devilishly dark humour abounds in *The Man Who Died*, paired with an absolutely cracking storyline, earning a tremendous thumbs-up from me' Liz Robinson, LoveReading

'The comparisons with *Fargo* are apt, for *The Man Who Died* shares the same black humour and is populated by similarly hapless characters. Reading the book, you just know that the story is going to end badly for some, and part of the fun is trying to guess who will come to the stickiest end' *Nudge*

'It's dark, humorous and darkly humorous. *Palm Beach Finland* is a destination you'll want to have on your literary boarding pass this summer!' The Book Trail

'I loved the subtlety of the humour in *The Man Who Died* and this has been perfected once more for *Palm Beach Finland*. Characterisation is brilliant, the description of the landscape as chilling as a Finnish summer and the story … This is one summer vacation you won't forget in a hurry. Loved it' Jen Med's Book Reviews

'Like a summer breeze, swimming in and out of the muddy water with witty remarks, spot-on comments, and an attention to detail that make this trip to the ocean a million times worth it, the author hits the mark and provides a unique and unforgettable tale of dreams' Chocolate 'N' Waffles

'The writing is clever, it's electrifying and utterly brilliant. This is an author you want to watch out for; each of his books is a joy to read and usually renders me speechless at the level of inventiveness woven throughout the plots' The Quiet Knitter

'All books have to end, even narratives as good as this, but it's so well crafted that the dénouement fully satisfies, as well as provokes thought. This remarkable novel is truly extraordinary, a gem of a thriller, beguilingly and well written, lively and thoughtful!' Shots Mag

'It might not be the classic dark and gloomy noir but delivers enough drama, danger and killing to keep you on your toes, and remind readers that the most stunning forest in the middle of summer can hide very dark secrets indeed … The book is a joy to read' Crime Review

'I have to say, despite this being crime fiction, it has humour thrown into the mix. Quite dark humour really, which was a distinct change for me. I'll definitely be reading some of Mr Tuomainen's other novels!' Crime Book Junkie

'Jaakko follows the trail around town as he investigates, coming across a whole bunch of fabulous characters who wouldn't be out of place in an episode of *Fargo*. Layered and oh so very dark, and exactly the way I like it. Superb' Espresso Coco

Orenda Books
16 Carson Road
West Dulwich
London SE21 8HU
www.orendabooks.co.uk

First published in the United Kingdom by Orenda Books, 2018
Originally published in Finland by LIKE Kustannus Oy, 2017
Reprinted 2019, 2022
Copyright © Antti Tuomainen, 2017
English language translation copyright © David Hackston, 2018

A catalogue record for this book is available from the British Library.

ISBN 978-1-912374-31-1
eISBN 978-1-912374-32-8

Typeset in Garamond by MacGuru Ltd

Orenda Books is grateful for the financial support of FILI,
who provided a translation grant for this project.

FINNISH
LITERATURE
EXCHANGE

For sales and distribution, please contact *info@orendabooks.co.uk*

WARNING

The following is based on real events and real people.
Nothing has been changed. In Finland,
the sun shines all year round.

GROUCHO: Then let's get down to business. My name is
                        Spaulding.
CHANDLER: Roscoe W. Chandler.
GROUCHO: Geoffrey T. Spaulding.
CHANDLER: What's the 'T' stand for? Thomas?
GROUCHO: Edgar.

—Marx Brothers, *Animal Crackers*

'There will be killing till the score is paid.'

—Homer, *The Odyssey* (trans. Robert Fitzgerald, 1961)

PART ONE
DREAMS

It was an accident. An unfortunate turn of events. It was a misunderstanding, a delicate imbalance between push and shove. And thus the neck broke like a plank snapping in two.

◉

They met opposite the sign. Kari 'Chico' Korhonen was the first to arrive. He tried to look as though he wasn't waiting for anyone, but this proved unexpectedly difficult. Chico tried to look at the sign as though he was seeing it for the first time, as though he were walking past and just happened to glance to the side. Ten steps towards the shore, a quick look to the right:

PALM BEACH FINLAND
It's the hottest beach in Finland.

A flinch, as if he'd forgotten something, then ten steps back towards the city, a look to the left:

PALM BEACH FINLAND
It's the hottest beach in Finland.

To Chico, the change was as mind-blowing as the arrival of colour television. Jorma Leivo, the beach resort's new owner, seemed to have flicked a giant colour switch. In only two months, what was once known as Martti's Motel had transmogrified into Palm Beach Finland, as though an earthy grey egg had hatched to reveal a brightly coloured, sweetly singing bird.

Chico liked the new colour scheme: turquoise, pastel blue, pastel pink, pastel green. The entire resort, which Jorma Leivo had also renamed and completely rebranded, was shrouded in a garish glow:

the buildings by the shore, the restaurant, the chalets and changing
booths, the shop, the windsurfing rental facilities, even the pizzeria. Everything gleamed with a thick coat of fresh paint. The sign
itself measured twenty metres by five metres; passers-by were positively blinded by its bright neon colours, its monolithic lettering
and slogan. Given its location, it was probably visible as far away as
Tallinn. The beach was dotted with similarly gaudy sunshades, the
specific purpose of which was a matter of some discussion. The con-
tinuous wind and near-freezing water kept the deckchairs stubbornly
empty. Along its other side, meanwhile, the beach was edged with
a brave new row of trees, which Chico enjoyed strolling past. Palm
trees, freshly planted. Plastic, of course, but still.

Life was changing. It was about to begin.

What else could this possibly mean?

Moreover, what might this mysterious meeting with Jorma Leivo
hold in store?

Never mind that their first encounter had come about because
Chico had been caught pickpocketing. It was an accident, pure
and simple. Chico had been watching a podgy woman wobbling
towards the water; he'd sauntered up to her handbag, pinched a few
lunch coupons and returned to the lifeguards' post, where Leivo was
waiting. He didn't listen to Chico's excuses about a sudden cash-
flow crisis or how problematic high-season prices had become for
the locals, but said soon afterwards that he – Leivo, that is – might
have use for a man of action with a bit of nous. A man just like
Chico. And when Leivo mentioned that when you spend your time
fumbling about with fivers you miss out on the big bucks, Chico
had seen the gates opening before him. Breaking through was always
about luck, about chance, he knew that. He'd read the biographies,
he knew how Eric Clapton and Bruce Springsteen had started out
and…

'Sorry.'

Chico turned. Robin's brown eyes met his.

'What are you sorry for?' asked Chico.

Robin looked at him. Robin's entire head was covered in what looked like an even black rug a millimetre thick. It was impossible to tell where his stubble began, where his hair ended, where exactly his face was. Nor was there anything to suggest that Robin was a cook, that he worked in the pastel-blue restaurant on the beach: formerly The Hungry Herring, now Beverly Hills Dining.

'I thought it wouldn't matter if I turned up late, seeing as we're supposed to be meeting here by chance and we're pretending we don't know each other. I thought I'd say sorry and ask if you had the time.'

'But if you know you're late, then you know what the time is,' said Chico. 'And we do know each other. Leivo said this is all top secret, so best not to attract attention. Let's do as the boss says.'

Robin turned his head, looking in turn at the shore and the town. 'I can't see anyone. Nobody can see us either. We can go.'

Robin was a reliable guy, thought Chico, even though he was one sandwich short of a picnic. Besides, Robin was a childhood friend. If you've known someone your entire life, then you know them through and through, right? It was seven minutes to seven, and they set off to meet Jorma Leivo.

◉

Judging by his hair and eyes, Jorma Leivo could have been a mad scientist from the silver screen: his crown was bald, straggles of fair hair curled upwards and sideways, and his blue eyes stared with such intensity that before long you had to look away. In other respects he looked like the men in the clothing catalogues from Chico's childhood. Leivo was trussed up in an extremely pink shirt and a bright-white blazer with shoulder pads that by any standard would be considered over the top. He was sweating profusely and spoke in a voice that was at once gruff and gently encouraging. Chico thought the overall impression was of an international businessman. This was a good sign.

'Nothing too serious,' said Jorma Leivo as he looked at them both in turn. 'A smashed window, a rainwater barrel knocked over, a fire in the shed, a stolen bicycle, someone pisses through the letterbox. Be creative. Little things, annoying things. Preferably every day. Preferably so that each little annoyance is followed by a larger one. You understand the principle. A steep curve that keeps rising and rising.'

Chico waited.

'I need that house and the plot of land signed over to me within the month,' Leivo continued. 'The sooner this happens, the better. A month is the absolute limit. You start today. Any questions?'

Chico tried to look as though he had these kinds of discussions all the time. He leaned back, as relaxed as he could under the circumstances, crossing his right leg over his left.

'We're professionals in our own field—' Chico began.

'What field's that?' Leivo interrupted.

Chico looked at Leivo. He should have tried to say more. Now he only had an answer to the next question. Now he…

'That's classified information,' Chico heard from beside him. Robin had spoken. He had spoken the way he usually spoke: as though a tape with random soundbites had started playing within him. Leivo glanced at Robin and leaned backwards. He looked as though he was about to ask quite what Robin meant. Chico couldn't allow that to happen; he had to turn the truck before it reached the cliff edge.

'What kind of fee did you have in mind for this, Chief?' asked Chico.

Leivo looked back at him.

'*Chief?*'

'Well, I thought I could call you Chief, seeing as you're the boss.'

'Am I?'

Chico thought about this for a moment.

'It's hard to talk with staff about who's the boss,' he began and instantly regretted his words. 'And vice versa, I guess.'

Leivo laid his hands on the table, and opened and clenched his fists.

'Listen, this is off the record. I'm only your boss when you're in the lifeguard hut,' said Leivo, looking first at Chico, then at Robin: 'And when you're in my kitchen. Let me be very clear: this job has nothing to do with your other duties.'

Chico could smell the fresh paint on the walls. For a moment a deep silence engulfed the pastel-pink room.

'I only pay for results,' said Leivo. 'The fee is five grand.'

Chico changed position, uncrossed his legs and crossed them again. He wanted only two things: first, he didn't want to show how much that sum of money meant to him – it meant everything – and second, he needed Robin to keep his mouth shut.

So it looked like the big four-oh wouldn't come to represent Chico's failure after all. He would make it. He was thirty-nine years old – but what did it matter? It was meaningless. Because this time next year, he would be in full swing. Eric Clapton was seventy, B. B. King was still performing at the age of eighty-seven. A debut record next year, club gigs, sports halls, stadiums, T-shirt sales, merchandise. Chico would catch up with Eric before his fiftieth birthday party, where a young English woman, her breasts tattooed and gleaming would…

'That sounds reasonable,' he said eventually.

'Of course, it's for you two to share,' said Leivo. 'That's the full amount.'

'Five thousand divided by two is two thousand five hundred,' said Robin.

Two thousand five hundred euros wasn't quite enough for a bona fide, brand-new custom-designed Les Paul guitar, Chico found himself wondering. Not enough for the kind he had strummed in the instrument shop, the kind he so desperately wanted to get his hands on.

'It's up to you how you split the fee,' said Leivo. 'What's most important is that we understand one another. We never had this conversation, and you have never done whatever it is you're about to do. I don't want to hear anything about it. I have never paid you anything, you have never received any money from me. And now, this meeting is over.'

Leivo stood up. Chico did not.

Leivo looked at him, almost with a note of impatience. 'Is something unclear?'

'In a situation like this, isn't it usual to provide some kind of down payment?' asked Chico.

'Without seeing any results first?'

Chico glanced at Robin, who seemed to be staring at his knees. At least he was still sitting.

'A down payment is like a retainer,' said Chico and felt a not insignificant amount of pride at his choice of words.

Leivo was silent for a moment, then pulled his wallet from his jacket pocket. 'What kind of retainer are we talking about?'

Chico tried to conceal quite how unaccustomed he was to talking about such sums of money.

'Five hundred,' he said. 'Per head.'

'Very well,' said Leivo, and just as the sense of victory was about to burst out of Chico, he added: 'I'll pay you a hundred each and we'll call it a deal.'

Leivo pulled four fifty-euro notes from a thick wad and handed them across the table to Chico. Chico acted instinctively. He leapt up from his chair and grabbed the cash. It was only then that he realised how flustered he became at the mere sight of money. It had that effect on him. There was nothing he could do about it.

The bills felt ever so slightly damp.

◉

The property in question was situated at the end of a magnificent peninsula. On either side of the peninsula was a beautiful sandy beach, and looking from the mainland the beach rose gently to the left and ended in a broad, thick area of forest, on the other side of which, completely hidden from view, was the area that belonged to Palm Beach Finland. Chico knew that Jorma Leivo had already come to an arrangement about the purchase of this land.

Chico and Robin lay on their stomachs beneath the pines and stared at the house. Darkness had fallen.

'What's Leivo got against Olivia?' asked Robin in a whisper.

'Nothing, I suppose,' Chico whispered back.

'So why does he want us to piss through her letterbox?'

'We're not going to piss through Olivia's letterbox.'

'So what are we going to do then?'

Chico didn't have a chance to answer. Lights came on in the ground floor.

Olivia had come home. To be completely accurate, Olivia had come home a few months earlier, immediately after her father's death. He had suffered a massive heart attack while out in his kayak. The wind had carried him into the children's swimming area and he had frightened the kids, hunched over, his face stiffened into a permanent smile and an oar jutting upwards in his hands. Someone had taken a picture, which Chico had later seen. The day after his death, Olivia Koski had returned to her former hometown, alone, and decided to stay. Alone.

And now: lights in the window, a human shadow on the wall.

Chico wasn't the kind of man to operate without a plan of action. He picked a hefty-looking stone up from the ground and showed it to Robin. Robin took the hint, and picked up a stone of his own. Chico explained the plan, which had probably been in existence since Neanderthal times: run up to the house, throw the stone, run away. On the count of three. At two, Robin sped off, and Chico followed him. They ran through the woods and into the yard, and threw the stones at the same time. The illuminated downstairs window shattered. Chico and Robin were about to round the corner of the house and disappear back into the woods when they heard it. Something between a squeal, a gasp of pain, and a shrill cry for help. They stopped in the darkness of the yard, stood on the spot as though turned to pillars of salt. Again, the same sound.

'I told you we should have pissed through the letterbox,' Robin whispered. 'It doesn't hurt anyone, and it's fun.'

Chico tried to think. This wasn't part of the plan.

'We're going to have to…' he began but didn't know how to continue. They would have to do something. Something. 'We have to make sure nothing bad has happened.'

The same sound again, this time followed by knocking and banging.

They turned, quietly paced along the wall of the house to the veranda, walked up the steps and opened the door. The veranda, complete with a sofa and all the trappings, looked pleasant and empty. The sound was coming from deep inside the house. Chico walked in front, Robin close behind him.

The glass-fronted internal door creaked when Chico opened it. Startled, he clenched his teeth together. He stopped and sensed Robin tight up against him. The light was coming from the right. Chico could see cupboards and furniture typical of any kitchen. He listened carefully, but now everything was silent. No sounds, no knocking, no banging. Again he took a few steps, towards the kitchen door, and when he reached the doorway he stopped and peered inside.

A tiled floor, a dark wooden countertop, cupboards, the broken window. But more importantly: blood. Blood and shards of broken glass. Everywhere. A pool of blood right beneath the window. Droplets and spatter everywhere. A red streak across the white fridge door leading…

Right here.

Chico could taste the electric whisk in his mouth. He was falling backwards – he knew that much. He tried to stay upright but his legs weren't quite in the position he'd imagined them, so he simply spun on the spot.

And as he fell, everything around him was bright and then darkening, like a series of disparate images: long dark hair, a face covered in blood, Olivia's slender figure in black jeans and a black polo-neck jumper, the white plastic shell of the electric whisk as it reflected light from the spherical lampshade above.

As Chico came crashing to the floor, he saw Robin peer into the kitchen, just as Chico had a moment before. And just like him, he too got a whack from the whisk, this time on his temple. Robin fell to his knees in the doorway as though begging to be let into the kitchen.

Chico's surprise was tinged with annoyance: they are worried about her, they come into the house to check she's all right only to get whacked in the face with a bloody kitchen appliance. Now Chico heard footsteps, and he guessed what was coming but didn't have time to do anything about it. Large black spots still obscured his field of vision. The whisk struck him like a bear's paw: it was painful and dizzying.

'We only came to help,' he whimpered.

But Olivia wasn't listening.

She had already turned round. The whisk rose into the air and came down like a guillotine. Robin remained on his knees despite the blow. Chico's ear felt like it was on fire, and a searing pain ran down that side of his head.

They had to get the situation under control.

Chico grabbed the table for support and pulled himself to his feet. The dark figure was approaching. Chico leapt forwards. He caught Olivia by the thighs, making her lose her balance. He hollered at Robin to grab hold of her. They toppled backwards towards Robin, and he lunged for them. The whisk fell from Olivia's hand.

Olivia ended up lying on her stomach on the floor. Chico was holding her by the legs, while her head was under Robin's armpit. Chico was shouting instructions. They struggled to their knees. She was light. It turned out there was some use for Robin's stubbornness after all; his grip on Olivia didn't flinch.

Chico's plan was the third he'd had that evening: they would take her outside, into the fresh air; they'd talk about it and sort things out, Chico would repay the cost of the broken window. Their down payment would cover it. Of course, paying damages like this wasn't exactly in the spirit of their agreement with Jorma Leivo, but needs must.

Running away is out of the question, he told Robin, she knows who we are. Robin looked as though he understood what Chico was saying.

With some difficulty they struggled to their feet. The body dangling between them was wriggling, grappling, lashing out. Chico took a firmer grip and shouted at Robin to hold tight. We'll take her outside.

Robin nodded, turned to get into a better position. Chico did the same. He shifted his weight to the other leg, shouted 'Now' and tensed his muscles. The pool of blood, in which Olivia had been lying face-down and where Chico now stood in his Adidas trainers, was fresh and slippery. He lost his footing. As he stumbled backwards he instinctively tightened his grip. At the same moment Robin, with Olivia's head still under his arm, yanked them towards the front door.

The crack was like a dry plank snapping in two. Olivia's body went limp. Robin was still carrying her headfirst into the yard. Chico was holding on to her legs, and staggered to his feet in the pool of blood. Chico bellowed at Robin, shouted at him to stop and let go. Chico let go. Olivia slumped to the floor.

Chico clambered to his hands and knees. Robin was standing in the doorway.

'I've never seen her like this,' said Robin.

Talk about stating the bleeding obvious, thought Chico. He took a few cautious steps towards Robin, then brushed the body's long dark hair back from its face and wiped one of the cheeks with a sleeve of the T-shirt, just enough to make out its features. The skin on the gaunt face was strangely white and taut, and the eye staring intensely at the tall skirting board in front of it was bright blue, the ear was small, the moustache thin and the goatee on the chin narrow and black, as though etched in pencil.

For once Robin was right. Chico had never seen Olivia like this either. The reason was clear: it wasn't Olivia.

TWO WEEKS LATER

1

It seemed that other people always thought that the great challenges and pains of a divorce were their business too. Everyone wanted to share their experiences, tell you what had happened to them and how they had got through it.

Jan Nyman always found these situations stressful: he couldn't simply say he wasn't interested (though he categorically wasn't interested), he didn't think there was anything particular for him to 'get over', and he didn't have a bad word to say about his ex-wife, Tuula. Quite the opposite. But his boss had now decided to stick his oar in, and given that he'd invited Nyman into his office, and sounded agitated and officious on the telephone – *Come straight to my office, do not pass the cafeteria, do not go to your desk* – all Nyman could do was grin and bear it.

'Maiju and I went on a week's therapy retreat once,' said Muurla after explaining that he too – naturally – had experience of divorce. 'To try and get our relationship working again. There were six other couples there too – people on the brink of divorce; people who should have taken a hint, run as fast as they could in different directions and never tried to do anything together ever again; people who shouldn't even wait for the bus together, let alone drive out into the middle of nowhere to open up old wounds. We arrive at this farmhouse after an infernal drive – four hundred and twelve kilometres of non-stop argy-bargy – and as soon as we get there the women start going nineteen to the dozen over the welcome drinks – chaga tea, or whatever they call it; tastes like earwax, smells like your granny's armpit – regaling us with all the gory details of their sex lives, so by this point we all know that Jari can't get a hard-on and his wife has started sleeping around, and I liked it, she says, and the blokes are just sitting right there listening, their ears red with embarrassment, the floorboards creaking, and by now the chaga tea is stone cold. The camp was run by some softly spoken lad who didn't join the rest of the men in the sauna. I thought it must have been a status thing, like he wants to keep at a distance from his clients while all the time he's watching us, staring at us, looking as though he's about to lose hope with us: his face red, his lips pursed tight, a twitch in his temple. He didn't like it when the rest of the men decided to have a game of volleyball, didn't like it one bit. He stood further off in the bushes, wouldn't come near the court. Then on the fourth day it was my turn to heat the sauna, and I'm walking to the sauna with an armful of good dry logs when I hear this moaning and grunting from the changing room, and I look inside and there's one of these husbands – not flaccid Jari but some city-slicker type – lying on his stomach on the bench while the softly spoken instructor guy is doing him up the backside so hard his cheeks are shaking. Shirt still on, top button done up, the lot. I put the logs back on the pile, go back to Maiju, give her a kiss on the cheek and say let's just file the sodding papers and be done with it. The drive home was relaxed and we're still good friends to this day. It's a pretty ordinary story, really.'

Muurla seemed to be gathering his thoughts. Nyman thought it best not to comment on the story in any way, not even with a *yes* or a *right*. He glanced outside.

The Vantaa offices of the National Bureau of Investigation were on a plot of their own, and the southwest wall, on the third floor of which was Muurla's office, looked across the street into an undeveloped greenfield site the size of a football pitch. It was so green, so grassy, so neatly edged with small birch trees that Nyman thought of his summer holiday. He still hadn't taken it. That said, by looking at him you might say his holiday was well under way: new white trainers, relaxed, baggy jeans, a flannel shirt in red and grey, a few day's stubble accentuating the dimples in his cheeks, his dark, longish hair still wet and tangled from the shower. This was what he normally looked like – according to Tuula, he was a cross between a country singer and a long-distance runner. He was neither. He was the best detective the Undercover Unit had, and he imagined that might be the reason he was sitting here now. He looked up at his boss, who seemed to have returned to the here and now.

'There's the case file in its entirety,' said Muurla, clasping his fingers together and placing his hands on the table as though in prayer. 'It's online too, so you can read it there. Here's the short version: a body turns up in a small town. Local investigation, no results. Regional investigation team in and out, no results. The case is a mystery.'

Nyman looked at the man sitting behind the desk. His face resembled a broad antique sofa, its leather worn and lumpy. Muurla had been his boss ever since he had joined the undercover team after years in the Violent Crimes Unit of the Helsinki police. He didn't know anything about Muurla's background, he didn't even know how old his boss was; true to its name, the Undercover Unit operated on a strictly need-to-know basis. He must have been closing in on sixty. Nyman liked working for Muurla: he was only interested in results, he wasn't cocky and he didn't offer advice or guidance. Of course, that might have been because he had very little to offer in that department. Nyman preferred not to think about that option.

'There must be something else to it, if they want us to investigate,' said Nyman. It was a question.

'They think it was a professional job,' said Muurla. 'At least, they *should* think so. There's still a lot we don't know, but it looks like this: there's a man in the house, either invited or uninvited, some other people arrive, either invited or uninvited, they all either know one another or they don't, and their actions are either premeditated or spontaneous, but the long and the short of it is that one of them ends up with a broken neck. Your regular Joe Blogs couldn't do something like that, and certainly not the owner of the property – a woman who might be involved in this, but then again might not. She's been interviewed on numerous occasions since and she's stuck to the story she told the police the first time: she arrived home to find the house trashed, and on the floor was a man she'd never seen before. We can't confirm any of her story, except that she was elsewhere at the time of the incident. But whether or not she knew about what was going on in the house is a different matter, and if she did know, how was she involved?'

'And the *modus operandi* suggests a professional hit?'

'Yes,' Muurla nodded. 'As you'll see from the case file, the victim was badly beaten first, then killed in an exceptional and very physical manner that would require great skill. According to the coroner, this kind of job requires two people who know what they're doing. This isn't something an amateur could pull off. The victim has to be in exactly the right position. This requires knowledge of anatomy, timing, cooperation, maybe even a familiarity with martial arts – and we're not talking about yellow belts here. Black ones, for sure. And there's something else: nothing was taken from the property. They turned up, did the job, and left before the owner returned. So everything else might be a distraction – the property might have been trashed afterwards for show. And there's one more factor to complicate matters…'

Nyman waited. Muurla leaned against his desk and edged his elbows forwards one at a time, cautiously moving closer to Nyman.

'There was some confusion when everything kicked off,' he said, his grey eyes boring ever deeper into Nyman. He was used to this by now: this was the way Muurla looked at someone who was about to be sent out of the office door and asked to do something utterly impossible. 'After hearing the original call to the emergency services, the police assumed the situation in the property was still ongoing. So a squad barged inside and shook the guy who'd broken his neck, naturally thinking he was just another local nutcase who had taken a cocktail of modified drugs, thrown some rocks around, smashed a few windows, broken in, messed the place up and passed out. Everyday stuff. Anyway, in doing so this group of boy scouts really messed up the crime scene. What's more, there's some renovation work going on in the property at the moment, so you can imagine it's been like Central Station in there. And so, to put it politely, the forensic investigation has been, shall we say, challenging, and the criminal investigation has been conducted manually, old school, as my son would say. Talking of offspring, it's probably a good thing you two don't have any children, what with the divorce and everything…'

'Who am I?' asked Nyman before Muurla could go any further. Nyman felt he must have heard at least four hundred different divorce-related anecdotes over the last month, some pretty tenuous and far-fetched, and none of which remotely resembled his own situation.

'Your name is Jan Kaunisto,' said Muurla and tapped a plastic folder on the desk. On top of the pile of documents was a brand-new Finnish passport. 'A maths teacher. On summer holiday.'

'Excellent,' said Nyman, and he could hear as he spoke quite how dry and laconic the word sounded. His tone of voice notwithstanding, he was pleased that this time he was able to keep his own first name. It helped when getting used to his new identity.

'There's a month's wages and holiday pay in your account,' said Muurla, opening the plastic folder enough to show the documents beneath the passport. 'And here's a debit card. You can sort yourself out with whatever else you need – telephone, that sort of thing. Any questions?'

'Plenty, but the case file will probably answer most of them.'

Muurla slid the folder across the table to Nyman. They looked at each other. 'Do you want to hear my theory?'

Nyman remained silent. Muurla took that as an ardent *yes*.

'This woman has recently met a man,' he began, folding his arms across his chest in a way that made him look closer to retirement than Nyman had previously thought. 'But this man turns out to be something quite different from what he appears. She realises he's not going to leave in a hurry. She knows people around town, so she hires a couple of bruisers to take care of things. These guys do what they've been paid to do, then they stage – or try to stage – the scene to make it look like a break-in or a fight.'

'Then what?' asked Nyman.

'What do you mean?'

'If the woman hired some professionals, as you suggest, they'll be back. These kind of people never go away, they take you for every penny you've got. They always come back, and when they can't use you anymore, they make sure no one else can either.'

Muurla thought about this for a moment.

'It's just as well you're going to be there, then,' he said. After a further moment of contemplation, he nodded again, not at Nyman but seemingly at something only he could see. 'Mark my words, the woman's pulling all the strings.'

2

Olivia Koski was walking round the house with a man in a baseball cap. The man was rotund and spoke like a gushing water fountain. Olivia thought it best to stay alert, though, as at some point in the man's stream of consciousness he might say something relevant. A moment earlier the man had introduced himself as Esa. It was like the moment a stylus touches a record and begins to play. Now the record was in full swing, and so was Esa. The brand-new yellow-and-brown van he'd arrived in bore the words KUURAINEN AND COMPANY – PLUMBING SOLUTIONS, so Esa must have been either Kuurainen or Company.

At the southern wall of the house Esa stopped and turned to face Olivia. His arms dangled at his sides; he raised his eyes slightly to look at her and had to squint into the bright midday sunshine. He looked like a little boy carrying out an important task.

'This is where I'd run it,' he said. 'The main water pipe, that is. Hot and cold. How long have you been having trouble with the water?'

Olivia thought of her father, her father's father, and his father before him. Sincere, wise, good men, whose fingers and thumbs had belonged to some of the most impractical hands in the history of humanity.

'Since the tens.'

Esa chuckled.

'Not the 2010s, the 1910s,' Olivia explained.

Esa's chuckles came to an abrupt end. He looked at the ground and returned to talking endlessly.

'I'd dig here, lay the pipe along here, renew the lot, inside and out. What's the water like at the moment?'

Olivia didn't have to think long about the pressure or quality of the water, all she had to do was think back to her shower that morning: the shampoo that she couldn't rinse from her hair, the wriggling around, the eventual chattering of her teeth.

'Freezing cold,' she said. 'And I can almost count the number of droplets.'

'It's on its last legs alright,' Esa nodded, and Olivia could tell the contractor could barely hide his enthusiasm. 'This needs sorted urgently.'

'How urgently?'

'Hard to say. The plumbing could conk out next week or the next time you flush the toilet. And seeing as there's little to no pressure – and saying you deposit something bigger than normal – there's no telling whether it'll go down or not. Not that I'm suggesting you would, Mrs Koski – you cut a slender figure, so maybe you wouldn't – but say you have a buffet lunch one day or you're having a bit of trouble downstairs, then—'

'Miss.'

'Sorry?'

'It's Miss Koski,' said Olivia. 'People called Mrs are generally married, though given my age…'

Olivia tried not to show quite how exhausted she was. The last two weeks had been even tougher than the weeks and months before that, which, with all the funeral arrangements, were rough enough to start with. Had she bitten off more than she could chew? It wasn't the first time she'd thought this. Here I am, she thought, standing in my garden, listening as a perfect stranger waxes lyrical about my bowel movements.

'Water,' said Olivia. 'I want running water in my house. That's why I called you.'

'Exactly,' said Esa. 'We have to decide whether to go for a full pipe refit or whether to concentrate on this area here.'

'A full refit?'

'We'd be talking seventy grand.'

This was nothing particularly new. Olivia had never built or renovated a house, but she'd had plenty to do with builders and decorators. It was one of those areas of life in which you could suggest, agree and promise absolutely anything to absolutely anyone, and nothing ever had to be factually correct – it never had to arrive on time, never had to work or reach completion. Not to mention whether the sum of money Esa had pulled out of a hat had anything to do with the scope of the job at hand – or whether it would be enough.

'Let's concentrate on this area,' said Olivia.

At this, Esa clearly tried hard not to look disappointed. But his disappointment lasted only about a second and a half. Like most men in his trade, after the initial setback he started fishing for money from a different angle and didn't seem to worry himself unduly over how abstract or generally impractical his suggestions were.

'You'll appreciate, even that is quite a big job. This is an old house, with old structures; it's a challenging project. Sourcing materials, renting machinery...'

'And?'

Esa folded his arms and looked as though he was adding it all up. Olivia couldn't say what went through men's heads at moments like this, but it couldn't possibly have anything to do with the value of the work or materials. The final results always proved otherwise.

'Fifteen thousand.'

'Euros?'

Esa stared at her, again looking like he was weighing it up in his head, and nodded. 'Euros.'

Olivia paused. 'Why is it a sum like that sounds as though half of it is made of Scotch mist? The kind of sum a professional tradesman plucks out of thin air and throws at a woman who lives by herself and who knows little about the ins and outs of drainage, plumbing and ventilation, in the stereotypical and all-too-predictable hope that because she's a woman she won't understand anything of this most manly of manly subjects?'

Esa said nothing. Either the sunlight had struck his cheeks and brightened them or the redness was radiating from inside. He looked baffled, perhaps even a little agitated. The wind rustled in the trees.

'Stereo-what…?' he began quietly.

'That's right,' said Olivia. 'The question is, why?'

Esa looked askance at Olivia, his face tilted slightly to one side.

'Why? Why indeed,' he said. 'It's not Scotch mist. Ten thousand. That's my final offer.'

Olivia waited for a moment, then gave a nod. She wasn't planning on telling him that this figure was almost precisely ten thousand more than she currently had in her bank account.

'I'll email you a written quote,' he said. 'Once it's been accepted and the down payment received, we'll get to work. But you realise this is unprofitable work for us, we almost have to pay the clients to let us dig up their gardens…'

All the way back to his van, Esa muttered to himself about how everyone was taking him to the cleaners: women, the taxman, subcontractors – and now his customers. Olivia had heard it all before and didn't pay it any attention. She chose not to ask Esa how happy he would be if all the people he'd mentioned suddenly disappeared, leaving him to potter around in peace, without hindrance or distraction, to dig up gardens and lay drainage pipes without the interference of women, the taxman, subcontractors and customers. It would surely be the kind of bliss that only a man could understand.

Upon arriving at the van, Esa turned in a semicircle – literally spun on an axis – squinted his eyes again and looked at the house. He looked like he was pondering something. Olivia knew what he was imagining: a set of shiny new windows.

'Yep, this place certainly needs touching up here and there,' he said, with more than a little dose of payback in his voice.

Olivia said nothing. She was waiting for Esa to get into his van and drive off. Eventually he clambered inside, started the engine and swerved out of the yard. Olivia felt like shouting – something, anything, at anyone.

It was a small town. Everybody knew what had happened. Or

rather, nobody knew *what* had happened, but everybody knew exactly *where* it had happened.

⊙

And there it was. Her kitchen, which was beginning to look almost the way it used to.

For three whole days her kitchen had been like a movie set: broken glass everywhere, things strewn all around, *her* things, every surface red from the fingerprint powder, and on every surface imaginable, both vertical and horizontal, police marking tape and the dried blood of the unknown victim. Naturally she'd asked the police who this man was, or rather who he *once* was, but to her surprise the officers, especially the last two to visit, had asked her the very same question. Needless to say she'd been unable to answer, and so they all appeared to be in a situation in which nobody knew anything about anything.

But somebody must know. All Olivia knew was that it wasn't her.

Scouring the floor had been an operation in its own right, that and making sure she'd picked up every piece of broken glass from between the floorboards, from the table tops, the chairs, the counters. There were even pieces of glass in the bread bin. The peppermill was covered in blood.

After the initial shock – when she had returned from town to discover the man, run out into the yard and made that garbled call to the emergency services – she had taken the events in her stride with a calm that surprised her: after all, she was living in a house in which a man might have been murdered. Perhaps it was the shock of her father's recent death from which Olivia was still suffering, a relative had suggested.

Was she suffering?

When the news of her father's death had arrived, she'd cried for a week and regretted not having spoken to him more often, or not having spoken about the things they should have spoken about, without having an idea of what those things might be. Then the feeling passed and she realised she had spoken to him quite enough and that her father wished her all the best, just as he had done when he was alive. That was it.

And that's what this was all about. Right here in this kitchen, this house.

Which reminded her of money, yet again, of the way things had always gone – always! – and always for exactly the same reason.

She had been engaged twice and married once. Both relationships had lasted almost exactly eight and a half years. On both occasions she had been the one who eventually said, *Enough is enough, Kristian / Marko.*

She'd often wondered whether there was something seriously wrong with her, something that flared up every eight and a half years, but as often she wondered whether the greatest success of these relationships was that it was only her money she ended up losing.

Kristian: a photographer who had once owned a camera – but didn't any longer. Olivia was young, *very* young. Kristian had temporary complications when it came to money and inspiration. At that point his complications had already lasted twenty-nine years. Olivia had listened, stroked his head, consoled him, and carried on studying, though she eventually dropped out of college because one of them had to work and pay the rent for their home and the office space they rented in the same building and for which Kristian still hadn't fetched his own set of keys, until one day Olivia came home from work, sat down on the sofa she had paid for and said to her boyfriend as he sat through a zombie-film marathon (Kristian's idea of hard work) 'This isn't working…'

Marko: owner of an office hotel situated in a place nobody could ever find and where nobody wanted to work. Marko spent all night sitting in the director's office looking out at the lights of the nearby industrial area, drinking room-temperature *salmiakki* liquor and waiting for the phone to ring. Perhaps he was still sitting there, still waiting for the phone call that never came. Olivia had dropped the keys next to the bottle of liquor on Marko's desk. Marko was tapping the computer's mouse with his forefinger and running the cursor over the empty reservation diary when Olivia said 'This isn't working…' and walked out of the door. Soon afterwards she started sharing a one-bedroom flat in Kallio with her former classmate Minna, and there she had lived until she moved back here, to this house.

Conclusion: men are an expensive hobby. They can be charming, funny, rude, stupid, bright as a shining star, dull as the handle of a hammer, handsome, not so handsome but still perfectly okay, trustworthy or untrustworthy, and everything in between, but whatever you do, whoever you meet: keep hold of your wallet.

And so here she was: thirty-nine years old, witty if necessary, with long dark hair beneath which was a brain that at its best was quick and practical, though it didn't have such a great track record when it came to men. She'd been told on more than one occasion that she was broad-shouldered, strong-legged, slender, long-nosed, magnificent, with a slightly exotic suntan, a handsome woman, and that her eyes weren't just brown but nut-brown. In the course of her life she'd made her fair share of mistakes, and for those she took full responsibility. She didn't hate anyone or anything and she wasn't embittered; she was penniless and marginally desperate. But there was one possession she planned to hold on to, because in that possession she saw a turning point, a new opportunity: she would not give up this house; she would renovate it, turn it into a home for herself, no matter how many dead men turned up in the kitchen.

Perhaps this was the secret to her sense of calm.

Olivia Koski leaned against the sturdy wooden doorframe a moment longer. Between the kitchen and the hall was a short corridor of sorts, so short in fact that it was more like an elongated doorway. From the wall nearest the yard jutted an empty hook. Olivia looked at the hook again, and in particular at the darkened area on the wall beneath it. As she'd cleaned up the apartment she'd found everything else, but not the artefact that had been hanging on that hook and that had belonged to her father and his father before him. She didn't understand why anyone would steal it. Assuming it had been stolen.

The brightness of the day lit up the house, cleaned the kitchen, lightened her mind. There's no reason to panic, she tried to convince herself.

Surely?

Every now and then the house creaked, gave a dull thud, and she took fright. It was all to do with the dead man in her kitchen, of course. For a few chilling seconds she imagined there was somebody in the house, then she relaxed again. This was a safe place, that much she'd learned. Safe, but certainly not without its problems.

The drainage pipe, which her father – a dreamer and unofficial record holder for the world's most impractical human being – had never afforded a single thought, would last. It wouldn't give up on her. Not before she could get her hands on ten thousand euros. A moment ago she'd imagined she was only missing just over nine thousand, but that was premature, wishful thinking. After paying her bills she would need to find ten grand exactly.

She looked at the clock on the wall and gave a start.

Her shift started in fourteen minutes. She'd accepted the first job she'd found, the only job on offer. It was badly paid, the working conditions were always changing, and her colleagues behaved strangely, especially these last few weeks. But the worst of it was the uniform. At first it had seemed just awkward, and the feeling hadn't gone away, though Olivia had hoped it might.

Maybe, she thought once more, maybe today will feel different.

Maybe today I won't feel like a cut of meat on display, like a nudist at the South Pole.

She walked into the hall, took her uniform from the clothes rail and held it in her hand. No, the feeling was still there. Olivia undressed and stood in the middle of the hallway, as naked as the day she was born, for that's what her uniform felt like. She took a deep breath, picked up the outfit, pulled it on and flicked the rubber straps over her buttocks hoping it wouldn't feel the same as yesterday.

It did.

She looked at herself in the mirror. Even if she were to close her eyes, she thought, she would still see that bright-yellow text. It was worth a try. A quick blink, a moment of darkness – and true enough, for a brief moment she didn't see the text.

But at the same time, for a few chilling seconds, she saw the figure of a man walking towards her, as clearly as if it was happening in broad daylight, somewhere out in the open, on the shore perhaps. The man raised his hand as if in distress.

Olivia opened her eyes, out of bewilderment more than anything. The man disappeared, as did the cold.

The text on the front of her bathing costume seemed to suggest more than just the resort's new name. Olivia stood in front of the mirror a moment longer.

It felt better to keep her eyes open.

3

A man with impossibly aerodynamic hair, and surrounded by a stifling cloud of aftershave, introduced himself as resort manager Jorma Leivo, then turned his back. Following him, Nyman realised he was walking directly through a series of fruit bushes. Resort manager Leivo gestured towards the shore with his right hand, which was half hidden by the sleeve of his white blazer.

'The beach is up there with the best,' said Leivo. 'Whatever they've got in St Tropez, we've got too, only better: canoes, pedalos, rowing boats, surfboards, Optimist dinghies, deckchairs – brand-new deckchairs; a hundred and twenty of them. You'd better reserve one before they're all gone. Okay, it looks like there's only one in use right now, but it really depends on the day. Volleyball, tennis, mini golf. Three holes, so Tiger Woods would approve. Dancing classes – our instructor's been to Mexico, so we're talking world-class salsa. There's the restaurant offering à la carte and all kinds of delicacies, plus seafood, pizzas and craft beers you can't even get in Germany. Happy people. It's a top-notch beach experience for a five-star clientele. The sky's the limit round here. If everything goes to plan, next summer we'll be opening a casino, a Moulin Rouge-type place, tits and windmills – tasteful, classy – and after that a helipad for VIP guests, movie stars and Formula One drivers. The shopping mall isn't ready yet, it's still in the design phase – something for the ladies, you know. You don't have to be rich and beautiful to spend money. The waterfront shop is open. *It's the hottest beach in Finland.*' Leivo turned around just enough to give Nyman the decisive nod that concluded his monologue.

'Palm Beach Finland,' said Nyman, looking out to sea, trying to keep up with Leivo's voice and smell.

'That's right,' said Leivo. 'My idea. It's my beach too, of course, but who's counting?'

'This place used to be called something else.'

'Ah, but it wasn't up to this standard.'

'What standard was it?'

Leivo stopped and turned again. He reached out his left hand and pointed with his forefinger. At the end of his forefinger, about a hundred and fifty metres away, was a large – no, giant – neon sign, its text gleaming.

'That, my friend, is the future,' he said.

Nyman read the text on the sign.

'Right.'

Leivo gave Nyman a look of satisfaction. They continued on their way. The sun was high in the sky, the day was at its warmest – which didn't mean it was warm: the wind whipped waves against the shore, and the beach was almost empty. The sea was blue and expansive. At these latitudes, thought Nyman, it gets warm only about seven and a half times a year.

'And what do you do for a living, may I ask?' said Leivo.

'I'm a maths teacher.'

'Ah, long summer holidays,' Leivo mused. 'That's nice. It being summer and all that.'

Nyman couldn't tell whether Leivo was joking or whether, like so many people, he was simply talking without truly listening to himself. Nyman noticed the rivulets of sweat trickling down Leivo's face. They ran from his forehead and down his cheeks until they reached his neck, where they stopped at his shirt collar. Some of the sweat dripped from his chin onto his white blazer. Perhaps the resort manager had been drinking heavily, thought Nyman, and now his body was detoxifyng itself. That would explain the aftershave, which could have masked the smell of a paper factory, but Leivo didn't look as though he had been on the booze. Quite the opposite. The man was effusive, perky and energetic. And his perspiration couldn't have had anything to do with the temperature. Nyman could feel the wind penetrating his shirt, turning the skin along his arms to goose bumps.

His thoughts were interrupted. They appeared to have arrived.

There were six chalets in total. They were all painted in bright colours, each glowing in its own garish way: turquoise, pink, mint green, purple, violet, baby blue. They stood in a straight row, tight against one another on a thin strip of pine forest, and their microscopic white-painted verandas all faced the sea. Nyman noted the signs above the doors and read them: *Castillo, Zito, Trudy, Gina, Switek* and his own chalet, *Tubbs*.

'You're in luck,' said Leivo and opened the door of the mint-green chalet. He handed Nyman the keys. 'This was the last one. Think of it as a direct flight to Miami, a piece of bona fide Florida. Five-star views. International quality, but for the discerning Finnish taste. These chalets are going like hot cakes. As we agreed, you can book one week at a time, and on the first day of every new week you have the option of booking for the next. You should take advantage of that; people queue for weeks to come here.'

Nyman glanced at the adjoining chalets. They looked quiet. He couldn't see any cars parked nearby, no towels drying on the railings, no beach equipment on the veranda or propped against the walls.

Jorma Leivo reappeared in his field of vision. 'All reserved,' he said. 'Advance bookings.'

Leivo gestured in a new direction, to the other side of town, towards the end of a peninsula that from this distance looked green (the trees) and brown (the soil). Nyman couldn't make out any houses, let alone people.

'We'll be expanding, of course,' Leivo explained. 'We're going to have a marina and luxury accommodation for gold-star customers. The cards will be ready soon, a thousand euros a piece; worth their weight in gold, let me tell you. Why go to Spain when you could come to…'

'Palm Beach Finland,' said Nyman, sensing Leivo expected him to finish the sentence.

Leivo nodded with gusto and handed something to Nyman. Nyman took it: a square, bright-pink parcel.

'I didn't have time to blow it up myself,' said Leivo, and to Nyman's ears this was the first time he'd sounded genuine. 'It's a pink flamingo. Every guest gets one.'

'Thanks,' said Nyman.

Leivo seemed thrilled. 'It's to create the right mood. And you should keep it. You can have plenty of fun with it. Do you want me to blow it up?'

Nyman thought of asking him to do this, but at that moment Leivo's pocket began warbling an eighties disco hit. Leivo took his phone from his blazer, looked at it, furrowed his brow, and for a moment he seemed to forget all about Nyman. Nyman duly noted this. Then Leivo snapped to, rejected the call and put the phone back in his pocket. He raised his eyes to Nyman again and smiled. The smile was in line with everything else he had presented: it didn't seem to know whether it was in the right place or not. If there was a right place at all.

'The chalet names,' said Nyman, though he saw Leivo was making to leave. 'Where's *Crockett*?'

◉

Jan Nyman watched Jorma Leivo as he walked off; he noticed that his blazer was clinging to his upper back, but in a slightly higher place than he imagined was normal. Nyman shivered with cold. It was chilly despite the bright sunshine.

Judging by the hour and fifteen minutes he'd spent at this resort so far, he couldn't quite imagine it replacing St Tropez as the number-one destination for the rich and famous, or that vast flocks of tourists would descend on this beach anytime soon, but who knew what could happen? He'd witnessed stranger things. And he didn't want to come to any rash conclusions. He had a suspicion – thinking about the case file he'd read on the bus and train journey – that far too many rash decisions had been made without him.

He stepped inside the chalet Leivo had left open and instinctively closed the door behind him.

The chalet comprised a single room, about twelve metres square. Opposite the door stood a bunk bed, the kind in which Jan Nyman had last slept approximately thirty years ago. He claimed the lower bunk for himself. The left-hand wall featured a miniature kitchen and a miniature bathroom – to the extent that the tiny plastic booth with a showerhead directly above the toilet could reasonably be called a bathroom. The kitchenette included a sink, a fridge, a coffee machine, and a selection of IKEA cooking and dining implements stood propped in the draining cupboard. Through the window, situated on the right-hand wall above the dining table, he could admire the straight, light-brown trunks of the surrounding pine trees.

Nyman looked around. Not exactly Nice or the Ritz Carlton, but it was considerably more comfortable than outside in the wind. And it was perfect for his purposes.

He placed the contents of his large sports bag in the wardrobe attached to the end of the bed: T-shirts, socks, underpants, smart shirts for evenings at the restaurant, swimming trunks, shorts, a woollen jumper for chilly evenings, and his favourite flannel shirts and jeans – two pairs of each. He would have made a pot of coffee but he had no filters, and nothing to put in them for that matter. He flicked through the investigation reports and case material on his iPad and found what he was looking for.

The photographs were taken without the subjects' knowledge. Obviously. Even so, some people always looked as though they were posing for the camera. Perhaps it was a sign of the times: we took so many photographs of ourselves that we were always contorting our bodies in every conceivable direction, just in case someone took a snap. Many of the people in the photographs were in swimming costumes. It was understandable in the circumstances.

He already recognised most of the subjects. There was Jorma Leivo, and his modest criminal record – small-time fraud and a few accounting misdemeanours from ten years back; a few years later one count of threatening behaviour; and almost immediately afterwards an exceptionally feeble attempt at driving under the influence with a blood-alcohol concentration of only 0.06%, driving within the speed limit on an isolated road in the middle of nowhere – the man whose shirts seemed soaked with sweat from one day to the next, regardless of the time or weather. Nyman paid particular attention to the men photographed in the woman's company and tried to commit their names and faces to memory. After suspicions arose that she might have had something to do with the body discovered in the house, the local police had naturally started following her too.

Many of the images were of the woman on the beach with her colleagues. First Nyman looked at the photographs of her colleagues. One of them was a Hollywood-handsome guy who looked like a surfer and who always seemed to have his hands in his pockets. No matter whether he was wearing shorts or long trousers, one of his hands always seemed to be engaged in a casual game of pocket pool. Like most handsome men, his expression was somewhat empty, and yet mysterious and timid: *Who am I, I don't understand anything, am I looking in the right direction?* He didn't look like a professional hit man, but who could say for sure? People are full of surprises.

One photograph differed from the others. It was the most recent image, taken only four days ago, and it was the last in the pile. The photographer had returned home on the same day as the investigators.

In this image the surfer was standing close to the woman, and his expression had a sense of feeling – tension, thought even, as he looked at the woman with something clearly approaching despair. Perhaps despair was too strong. But then again … Nyman stared at the photograph a moment longer. Regret?

Perhaps these two were in some kind of relationship and the surfer dude had screwed things up. The hand's permanent residence in his pocket suggested the man let his little surfer do most of the thinking; it might even have decided where the rest of his body ended up at any given time. In his professional and personal experience, Nyman surmised that concentrating the decision-making like this generally led to full-blown tyranny and rarely resulted in a happy ending.

Nyman continued to flick through the photographs. If the woman *did* know something, if she was the key to the case, he would need both direct and indirect access to her. He went over the names again, attached them to faces and tested himself on them. A while later all his answers were correct and he gave himself full marks.

He was about to put his iPad to one side, but stopped.

Nyman wanted to see where the woman had been when these photographs were taken and how she appeared in them.

Perhaps these two matters would tell him more about who she really was.

4

Holma was dangling the man from the balcony when the phone rang. He'd been meaning to change his ring tone for a while; this one attracted far too much attention, and besides at the time it was only supposed to be a joke, a facile, ancient hit by a white rapper, and a slogan that, by now, felt like a physical thumping in his head.

Holma was holding the man by the knees. The man was hanging in the air, his back pressed against the railing of the balcony, his arms flailing and his head twitching as though he were dancing upside down. The top-floor balcony was in a row of grey concrete towers on the eastern side of Helsinki's Merihaka district. Across the bay rose the coal mountains of Salmisaari, and a cycle path ran along the pavement below. From this vantage point the two looked almost equidistant.

Ice, ice, baby.

This was the nature of ring tones; you remembered them when the phone rang and forgot about them as soon as you'd answered. Until you heard it again and … It was an endless cycle. That said, there weren't many people who knew his number. People who called him did so for a good reason, which meant they called him very rarely. And so, thinking about it more reasonably, it was no wonder that a ring tone, which had seemed funny after a night playing pool and drinking a few pints with the boys, was still on his phone.

Holma felt the phone vibrating just above his heart. Tightening his grip on the man's legs, he reached his fingers into his jacket pocket but couldn't quite get to his phone. His fingertips just about touched the narrow strip of fabric at the top of the pocket, but the phone was deep inside, lying slightly on one side.

Ice, ice, baby.

Wasn't there a setting somewhere to limit the number of times someone could keep the phone ringing?

Holma tried to put himself in the caller's position. If he'd heard the ringing tone twelve times, would he allow it to ring a thirteenth time? What was the probability that someone would pick up on the twentieth ring? Not very high, he thought. More than that, Holma started to question his own judgement. Had he given his private number to someone who didn't really understand how phones worked, who didn't appreciate telephone etiquette? And all the while his phone continued ringing and vibrating.

Again he tried to slip his hand into his pocket. But it was no use.

Holma looked across at the heaps of coal. The sun was beating down, the coal mountains gleamed like black icebergs. Holma had a tendency to imagine things and conjure up elaborate scenarios that in the light of day he could no longer see or understand. He imagined the large power station rising up behind the coal mountains was an ice hall where the rink was black and where people played and sat in the dimness and everything was dark … But where would be the fun in that? And wouldn't…?

Ice, ice…

Holma relaxed his grip, straightened his arms, snatched his phone from his pocket and answered. He might have heard a distant thump, a splodge, something faint, but by that point the phone was already at his ear and it might have been simply the sound of crackling from the satellite. The voice at the other end was old and familiar.

'Bad news,' said the voice.

'Tell me that first,' said Holma.

A pause.

'I just got off the phone with a copper I know. The subject came up when we were talking about … something else.'

The voice knew people in the police force. Holma was aware of that. He waited.

'Your brother Antero. Dead. Murdered. It's a bit of a mess.'

Antero, the black sheep of the family. Everything Antero touched ended in disaster. If Antero had tried to rob a local supermarket, he'd have shown the cashier his loyalty card in the process.

'For some reason it took time to identify the body. It all happened two weeks ago. Some small town. Local police have been all over it, but so far they've come up with nothing.'

The voice gave the name of the small town, mentioned the name of the person in whose house Antero had been found with a broken neck. The voice gave the address, said something about a kitchen and an electric whisk, but Holma was still suffering the after-effects of that ring tone. The chorus was lodged somewhere far inside his brain. It was stuck so firmly, its roots so deep, it smothered everything else.

'How are things there?' the voice asked.

Holma took a step forwards, looked over the balcony railing and down to the cycle path below. Far beneath him the man looked as though he had lain down on the pavement to sleep.

'All calm.'

'Do you want to take a few days off?'

Holma hadn't given the matter any thought. But it made sense.

'Might do me some good.'

'I'll get someone to take care of anything urgent. Give me a ring when you want to come back. These things can be upsetting.'

Upsetting maybe, but when it came to Antero, it was only a matter of time.

'I don't want anyone working while they're not one hundred percent. Recharge your batteries, focus on things that perk you up, and you'll come back more motivated than ever.'

The voice hung up.

Holma returned indoors, glanced around. Everything was as it should be. He placed the preprepared suicide note on the table and left. On the way down to the ground floor he thought about things.

Focus on things that perk you up. The words rang in his ears. Holma thought of Antero, their shared beginnings, carjacking on a summer's night, their first tentative break-ins and clumsy robberies. Learning things together.

Holma smiled at his reflection in the lift mirror. He had other reasons for this than faded memories. He wasn't worried about being seen in or around the building. He knew that his features often caused people problems. It was to do with the symmetry of his face: nothing stood out, nothing stayed with you. When he was younger, people said it was hard to recognise him at all. At the time he'd felt bad about it, and he'd strangled the woman who'd said so just enough that she knew she'd insulted him.

Youth.

Golden memories.

Their first time:

A clear autumn evening, the leaves of the trees glistening. Holma and his brother have been given their first official gig, and they're driving through the town. They have been hired by a renowned criminal. Their brief is to remind an actor living in the pricey southern suburbs of Helsinki about a substantial outstanding debt. They gain entry to the actor's home. It's easy enough. The actor is drunk, and the smell and stubble reveal that he's probably been drinking for a while. It's about two in the morning and the actor automatically assumes they've come to deliver his pizza. Do we look like delivery boys? asks Antero. You look too stupid even for that, the actor replies. Naturally Antero takes exception to this comment. He lunges at the actor and the two of them fall wrestling to the parquet floor. Holma looks around. This was the kind of penthouse he would have dreamed of living in – if only he'd known it existed. He'd never seen anything like it before: white-painted walls with high ceilings, bay windows almost as deep as the vaults at the Suomenlinna Fortress, the floor covered in broad, lacquered wooden boards, in the corner of the large room a decorative fireplace that Holma later learns to call a ceramic stove. There and then Holma decides that, one day, he too will live in a place like this. The actor is powerful. He tries to roll on top of Antero, and eventually succeeds. A moment later the actor is straddling Antero's chest, his knees pinning Antero's arms to the floor; he slaps Antero round the face, saying nasty things about him, debasing him. Holma has to admit that some of what the inebriated actor says is rather funny and apt. Holma remembers hearing the word *improvisation* in the past; one of his teachers must have used it. The actor starts improvising. Holma listens for a moment. He turns and steps into the kitchen, and admires that too. Bright white cupboards and countertops, the legs of the table and chairs gleaming and metallic. He tries to imagine what it would be like to eat breakfast here, or any meal for that matter. He rifles through the drawers, finds a knife with an extremely sharp blade – its tip like a needle and its blade only widening slightly on its long, long journey to the handle; a knife whose formal purpose is a mystery. He returns to the living room and thrusts the knife up to the hilt in the actor's neck just as the doorbell rings. The actor bows slowly across Antero's body, as if after a performance. Antero's face is glowing like a tomato set on fire. The doorbell rings again. Holma puts his forefinger to his lips, and Antero understands to keep quiet. Holma goes to the door. The pizza has been prepaid. He carries the steaming box into the kitchen. They eat the pizza before driving back through the autumnal city.

The lift reached the underground parking lot and Holma awoke from his reverie. He walked to his car.

Only two weeks and two days ago Holma had told Antero it was time for him to become more independent, time to do something for himself. It seemed his brother had taken that advice quite literally.

Holma sighed. Either way, Antero was family. And if anyone so much as snapped a hair on the head of someone in his family, then…

He clicked open the car doors.

5

'Why are we meeting him out here?' asked Robin. He took a few steps, walked in a full circle and said out loud something that Chico knew only too well.

They were at the bottom of a quarry, standing right at the edge of a small pond.

Robin was running through things, thinking out loud: 'Thirty shrimp casseroles, seven o'clock. Dessert: sorbet and strawberries. Chop organic strawberries for thirty.'

Chico didn't answer, but he understood Robin's predicament. He understood it only too well.

The last two weeks had been a blur. But they had stuck by their decision. Keep calm and carry on as if nothing had happened. Or as if almost nothing had happened. There was only one problem: their faces looked as though they had had an unfortunate encounter with a brick wall. Or an electric whisk.

The solution to this came from the glam rock of their youth, from the only rock group they had played in together; the only group in which Robin had ever played: they had started wearing make-up again. For the first few days they had needed an embarrassing amount of powder, eyeliner and mascara. *No fucking way, it's Alice Cooper*, people said in bars. Chico couldn't explain that he wasn't actually an Alice fan, though he made an exception for the legendary *Billion Dollar Babies* album. A few days later they went through a shorter phase, emulating The Cure and Robert Smith, before finally reaching this last, more modest approach, along the lines of the veterans of hard rock still alive today: eyeliner, a touch of mascara, a few dabs of powder to distract from the darker areas around the eyes and the swelling across the eyebrows.

Chico pulled at his T-shirt. There wasn't anything necessarily wrong with his Eric Clapton T-shirt, he knew that, but it was too tight. Everything felt too tight.

Chico looked around: a circular and allegedly deep pond at the edge of the quarry, the car they'd borrowed, Robin's mother's plum-blue Ford Siesta parked at the water's edge, young birch trees and ragged bushes along the light and brown embankments, pines standing tall as if keeping watch, and above it all a bright sun that didn't yet warm them.

Robin was stressed, Chico could see it. He was disappointed too. Robin had great plans for that money, Chico knew that only too well. Dreams and plans. And in one way or another they all involved Nea.

Nea was one of the lifeguards – Chico's colleague and the brown-est white person Chico had ever seen. She was also the most scantily dressed person he'd ever seen. On many occasions Chico had felt like asking Robin what he planned to do about his infatuation, other than stand paralysed with awkwardness and let out a low, mumbling sound every time he saw her, staring at her shining brown skin, of which there was so much on display that even Chico had to double-check that she was wearing at least some clothes. Thankfully, however, he'd never got round to asking.

For a while everything had seemed fine, but now they'd slid back to square one, maybe even further than that. *Palm Fucking Beach Finland*, thought Chico as Jorma Leivo finally appeared at the end of the dirt track.

Leivo drove his car right up to them, forcing them both to take a step backwards and pushing them towards the edge of the pond. Leivo opened the door, stepped out of the car and stood at its front corner, almost as wide as the bonnet of the Pajero itself. Chico guessed Leivo had deliberately cornered them before the conversation could get under way.

'Two weeks,' said Leivo and stared at them with those frightening blue eyes of his. 'Two weeks, and nothing to show for it.'

It took Chico a moment to understand quite what Leivo meant. Surely he couldn't be serious.

'Well, the situation—'

'The situation is that you two haven't been doing what I asked,' said Leivo.

Chico shook his head. He wanted to refute what Leivo had said, but couldn't quite believe he'd heard right.

'But we're at work every day,' he said.

'Damn right you are,' Leivo snapped. 'And I pay your wages. I'm not talking about that. We have another agreement, one that we've shaken hands on. And the matter is now more urgent than ever.'

Chico was about to say something – he wasn't sure what – when he heard Robin's voice beside him.

'We killed the dude, accidentally yanked him in different directions.'

Jorma Leivo started bellowing and raised his hands to his ears. 'I didn't hear that,' he said, now even angrier than before. 'I don't know anything about that. I just…' Leivo lowered his hands. 'For crying out loud. I'm paying you to do a job, and it's your job to actually do it. Is it really that complicated? Am I working with a pair of complete idiots or what?'

'Maybe,' said Chico. He was responding to Leivo's previous observation, but now it sounded as though he was unsure of his own idiotism. He didn't care. What he saw here was the opportunity to negotiate. 'It's not that simple. I mean, it actually *is* quite complicated. You see, we've only been paid one instalment, for one job.'

Gotcha.

Jorma Leivo looked at him. Thank God Robin was keeping his mouth shut. Leivo cleared his throat. 'And the police?' he said.

Chico waited for Leivo to continue, but he didn't.

'They don't know what happened,' Chico nodded. 'It's obvious.'

Leivo looked at him. What was going on in Leivo's eyes? Why were his blue eyes glowing like that? Were they about to explode?

'Not for now,' he said, now strangely slow and clear, as if he were talking to a child. 'But what if someone told the police what had happened?'

Chico could feel Eric Clapton shrinking on his chest. Eric and the guitar, his grip now tighter than before.

'Here's what I suggest,' said Leivo, still speaking slowly. 'I suggest you take care of your job – both jobs – and then, once everything's been taken care of, we can think about your remuneration. You've got exactly two more weeks. It must happen within two weeks. I need her signature on the dotted line. I don't know how clearly I need to spell this out, but you have two options: the local nick or a simple job that needs sorting. I don't want to know what went on in the house, and this meeting never happened. This conversation never happened either.'

Leivo paused. Either the boughs of the pine trees were humming, thought Chico, or the sound was coming from somewhere deep inside him. Leivo turned to look at Robin.

'Two weeks,' he repeated.

'Two weeks is fourteen days,' said Robin.

Jorma Leivo got into his car, reversed a few metres, stopped and seemed to be weighing up his options: as if he might either accelerate towards them and dump their bodies in the pond, or turn the car. For a moment the Pajero stood on the spot, then the bonnet began to turn. Chico could breathe again; he took a few steps forwards, a few steps away from the edge of the water, just in case.

◉

Robin was driving. Chico was sitting next to him, watching the landscape shudder and shimmer past. It was late summer.

Yet another summer. That greenness that lasted only a moment, the sun that rose so high that eventually it had to get its own back. And boy did it get its own back. For a full six months it wouldn't show its face. And so another year had passed, another whole year of life.

The guitar he had almost held in his hands.

The debut album he had almost released.

Chico thought of Eric Clapton. He knew Eric had had his fair share of tragedies, his own difficulties, but … nothing like this. No matter how hard he tried, Chico couldn't imagine Eric Clapton sitting in his childhood friend's mum's car – one that looked like a yoghurt pot, the air heavy with the scent of vanilla Wunder-Baum warmed in the sunshine – blackmailed into violence with the threat of a prison sentence, and all because he'd slipped and pulled when he was supposed to remain upright and push.

Suddenly it all felt quite surreal.

He couldn't imagine Eric Clapton in a situation like this because Eric would simply never get himself into a situation like this. I mean, what did a super-rich international rock star know about situations like this in the first place? And right then, as though a playlist featuring all of Eric's most compelling blues renditions had suddenly started spinning inside him, he heard everything with new ears, mortal ears, and Chico had to ask himself: how did Eric know how to play the blues, how to sing it? What did he actually know about the blues?

The feeling was new and confusing, it turned the songs upside down to reveal everything that lay behind all that masterful guitar playing, and for a moment Chico couldn't see anything no matter how much he fumbled in the darkness for his mentor. The sensation passed as quickly as it had arrived, Chico was once again in the car with Robin beside him. It was a huge relief, but a seed of uncertainty had become lodged in his mind.

Chico realised he had come to doubt even Eric Clapton.

6

The bright-blue beach hut was a long row of white-framed doors and windows, and served as a boatshed, a warehouse, a coffee shop and a grocery store. Jan Nyman stopped at the fridge in the grocery section and took out a bottle of Dr Pepper, paid in cash and sat down on the broad terrace outside. The chair felt warmer than the air temperature.

Nyman was happy with his new shorts. Their dark brown went well with his red-and-white checked short-sleeved shirt, and a pair of light-brown sandals rounded off the maths-teacher-on-vacation look perfectly. The sea glimmered in the afternoon sunlight – no longer with the intense midday glow and not yet the golden mirror effects of late evening; this was a languid light, stretching out across the water as far as the eye and sails could take him. And speaking of sails, Nyman looked at his phone, still in disbelief.

It was true, though:

You have been enrolled in a windsurfing class for beginners. Starts Tuesday 9 a.m. Register at the West End. That's right, the West End. You can't miss it.

Nyman sipped his chilled drink. Of course, he thought, Muurla had forgotten to mention something essential. And this, if anything, was essential. He would not be windsurfing though. He would go to the West End, whatever that meant, and would switch to a team sport – beach volleyball if there was nothing else on offer. If you wanted to get to know people, team sports were the best. On a previous case he'd joined a floorball team while trying to track down a guy dealing in growth hormones. He never located the man, who was wanted for involuntary manslaughter, but he'd made many new friends to whom he couldn't give his real name and whom he could never meet again. But that was another case.

Nyman looked up. The West End was opposite him, situated on the other side of the almost deserted beach: a bright white sign and turquoise lettering told him this was the place. Next to the sign was a pink building with two shiny plastic palm trees on either side of the front door.

Nyman stood up and walked off, taking the most direct route across the beach. It was a mistake. In an instant the sand forced its way into his sandals and started chafing his feet. If he was this unaccustomed to beach life, how could someone even begin to believe he wanted to take up windsurfing? Nyman stopped, took off his sandals and was surprised at how warm and soft the sand felt against his bare feet on such a chilly day. The feeling was pleasant, and it made him stop and look around. Buildings in garish colours, a large bright sign, of which he could only see a sliver. He stood there for a moment, enjoying the feel of sand between his toes, the sensation of his brain processing powerful sensory stimuli. It was a brief moment. Nyman started walking again, and after a second or two could barely remember why he had stopped in the first place.

He arrived at the pink door of the pink building, opened it and stepped inside. At first he could see only outlines, but his eyes soon grew accustomed to the dimness.

And he did not cancel his windsurfing course after all. It was all because of the woman behind the desk.

Long dark hair, long regal nose. A tall, magnificent woman.

Olivia Koski.

'I've come to register for the beginners' windsurfing course,' Nyman continued once he'd introduced himself. 'The group that starts tomorrow at nine.'

'That's right. Nine o'clock means we're in the water at nine. Before that we carry the boards down to the shore and make sure the sails are in order. Do you want to rent a board or have you brought your own? We sell boards too – new and second-hand.'

Her brown eyes were striking; the photographs didn't do them justice. Her voice was friendly, very pleasant indeed.

'I'm a complete beginner,' said Nyman. 'I've never even stood on a surfboard, let alone actually gone surfing. What would you suggest?'

Olivia Koski looked at him, her eyes almost level with his. Nyman was one, maybe two centimetres taller, but his posture was hunched – relaxed, as Nyman might have preferred to think – and Koski was standing slightly higher on the uneven floor. The office was empty, except for this woman wearing only a swimming costume. It must be a protocol thing, thought Nyman. Few people would wear a one-piece swimming costume to work out of choice.

'Let's start by finding you the right board,' said Olivia Koski.

The boards were stored in a locked shed outside. She opened the wide doors facing out to sea. Nyman looked at the woman's shoulders, her arms, her back: exercise and sunshine, and a long, light-coloured scar starting behind her right shoulder and disappearing midway down her back. They stepped inside the shed, and Nyman saw more sails and surfboards than he'd seen in his entire life. Olivia Koski glanced at him, sizing him up.

'Five foot eleven, one hundred and sixty-seven pounds?'

'Five foot eleven and a half, one hundred and sixty-three pounds.'

'The Distance Runner,' she said and tapped one of the boards. 'This is the one.'

'How long have you been windsurfing?' asked Nyman keeping his eyes firmly on the board he'd been allocated, his voice carefree and chatty.

'Thirty-nine years,' said Olivia Koski.

Nyman looked up.

'My father,' she explained. 'He was always in the water, one way or another. Swimming, windsurfing, canoeing, diving. I used to accompany him – as far back as I can remember.'

'Are you from round here?'

'Originally,' she replied, staring past Nyman and out to sea. 'I was away for a long time and came back when … Are you buying or renting? I'm sorry, my thoughts were … somewhere else.' The woman gave a melancholy smile, her brown eyes finally settled on Nyman's face. 'A beginner, you say?'

'Completely.'

This time Olivia Koski looked at him more closely, and to Nyman it seemed this was the first time she truly paid him any attention.

'I'd rent this one,' she said. Now she sounded as though she was choosing her words carefully. 'Not just for a day, but for a while longer. Think of it as reserving the board for yourself in case you take a liking to it. This board is top of the range, but we can talk about the price. So if you're planning on sticking around for a while…'

'At least a week.'

'Then I'd rent this one for a week, and if, or rather, when, the windsurfing bug hits you like a bolt from the blue, I'd buy it at the end of the week.'

'So windsurfing hits you like a bolt from the blue?'

The woman smiled, but her smile stopped short. 'I'm not the best judge of people, but I know a thing or two about windsurfing, so in that respect…'

Nyman nodded. 'Let's do that. I'll take the board for a week.'

The woman seemed to be waiting for something. Nyman didn't know what.

'People normally ask for a discount,' she said eventually. 'And failing that, at least they ask the price.'

Nyman smiled. 'It seems I really am in vacation mode.'

Again she looked as though she was taking stock of him. 'We have hourly, daily and weekly rates. One hour is thirty euros, a full day is ninety euros, and a week is three hundred and sixty. The longer the rental period, the cheaper it is per hour, so you get a week for—'

'For the price of five days.'

Koski looked at him even more closely than a moment ago. 'Four days.'

Nyman did the arithmetic again and smiled. 'Four, of course,' he said.

Olivia Koski continued by explaining that he could take the board with him immediately if he wanted or he could leave it here, right here, and collect it in the morning. Tomorrow morning would be great, said Nyman and explained he had other plans for the rest of the day. The woman said that would be fine and suggested they move into the office to sign the paperwork. She closed the shed doors, clicked the lock shut, and together they walked back towards the office.

Koski walked in front. Nyman tried not to look at her backside, but looked all the same.

'Can I ask you something?' he said, then realised he was addressing her buttocks and raised his eyes. He didn't want to be one of those men, though all men are *those* men. 'Palm Beach Finland...' he began and hadn't managed to formulate the rest of the question before the woman replied.

'The name is new, the place is old,' said Koski and glanced behind her. 'The new owner painted a few walls, put up a sign and renamed the place. He wants to give it an international feel and appeal to foreign tourists.'

'How's that going?'

The woman stopped. They were about to take the wooden steps up to the deck outside the office. She turned and looked at Nyman from above. Her brown eyes flickered.

'The name has three words,' she said. 'And the last of them is *Finland*. If you're looking for a holiday in the sun, do you really think this is top of people's list?'

Nyman filled in the rental forms and paid the deposit, ninety euros. Or to be more correct, Jan Kaunisto filled out the forms and paid the deposit. Nyman followed events from over his shoulder. He was still thinking about the way Koski had talked about the resort's new name and the idea of booking a holiday in the sun. Again he glanced at the woman's swimming costume, the text printed across it. He looked around.

'Do you know any nice places to spend an evening round here? Where can I go to meet people?'

'People?' asked Olivia Koski. 'You mean women?'

Did Nyman see something in her eyes? Maybe not. Maybe he was just imagining it.

'A nice little place, food, drink, open late, somewhere that's popular with the locals.'

'You're from Helsinki.'

It wasn't a question.

'I was born there,' said Nyman. 'And I've lived there all my life.'

'Well, welcome to whatever this place is calling itself today. There's nowhere to do all of those things, but if you combine a few places maybe you'll find what you're looking for. I'll show you on the map.'

The map was a colourful sheet of printed A4. At the top were the words PALM BEACH FINLAND. The map was not in any proportion. His green chalet, Tubbs, was as big as an entire neighbourhood at the bottom of the map. And the edge of that neighbourhood looked like it opened out into the desert. Nyman looked at Olivia Koski's hands. Crosses appeared on the map, places acquired names. Everything was within walking distance, and when he asked, Olivia Koski assured him she wasn't a regular customer at any of these establishments.

'But you work here,' said Nyman.

'No, no, no,' she said. 'I'm a lifeguard, as you can see from the uniform. I'm just standing in for a colleague. Something came up.'

'I mean in general,' said Nyman and nodded towards the beach. 'You work here.'

The woman leaned a forearm against the desk and looked at Nyman.

'A girl's gotta do something for a living,' she said.

7

Holma had already resolved to shoot his satnav and the woman who lived inside it, who constantly took him down ever smaller roads before changing her mind again, when he saw a sign on the side of a barn advertising the best pizzas within a hundred-kilometre radius. Holma didn't particularly want a pizza, but the pizzeria was in the right direction, only eleven kilometres away. He was sitting by himself in his black BMW 530i, which was gleaming from a recent clean, with his unregistered Glock 17 on the dashboard. He could have silenced the satnav once and for all, but settled simply for switching it off.

The silence was refreshing. He could hear his own thoughts again. He liked them. He'd heard that some people didn't like examining their own thoughts too deeply, but Holma certainly wasn't one of them. He enjoyed listening to himself.

Genuinely. Objectively.

He often thought – and this too was a thought he had developed himself and which amused him for its aptness – that other people would be knocked for six if they had thoughts as good as his. They would have understood more, seen things with more clarity; they would have been capable of the same kinds of observations as him. Of course, when he did try to help people, this wasn't the case, and it caused no end of misunderstandings.

He genuinely didn't know why though. Holma only gave people advice when he could see that they needed it. Of course, he identified a lot of need around him, but that was mostly to do with the original state of affairs: the fact that his thoughts were, undoubtedly and with complete objectivity, like finely polished diamonds. And he wasn't selfish either; he always did his best to amuse and enlighten people with his opinions, only to receive a cold shower in return. That irritated him, though he didn't show it. Even he was only human. Perhaps, for want of a better word, more *imposing* than others, but human all the same.

He didn't consider himself a genius, a number of specialised skills notwithstanding, but he did think he suffered from an ailment that afflicted many Renaissance people like himself. He was an all-rounder. That was it. An all-rounder.

It wasn't his fault that so much human activity overlapped with his particular skill set. He had phenomenal mental capacity, so why should he be forced to hide it? Why should he be ashamed of his own exceptional character? Why – and now he could feel another aphorism coming on; another apophthegm to add to his growing collection, which he'd long thought should be published in a handy self-help manual for the masses – why hide your light under a bush, as they say, when the bush will simply catch fire and burn all your wisdom to ashes ... In fact, was it a bush or a bushel? As proverbs went, it still needed some refinements, but there were plenty where that came from, and he would share them all for free, for only the price of a book.

The car arrived at a T-junction. The road headed both left and right. The signpost in front of him gave distances to towns he had never heard of and with which he decided never to acquaint himself. Having said that, to the left of the signpost was one sign that caught his attention. He hadn't heard of the place before, but the English-language slogan, the bright colours and the palm trees looked like just the thing that would have attracted Antero.

Antero, his little brother. Different mother and different father.

It was complicated. They were adopted, they had different biological parents, but they were family. For the most part. His adopted father had disappeared while he and Holma were on a father-and-son camping and canoeing trip. Holma never got to know his new father; he was about to move out when the guy appeared in the hallway, and, besides, by that point Holma didn't feel the same sense of attraction towards his adoptive mother. The feeling had worn off, as the prison psychiatrist would tell him much later.

Antero was backward, in so many ways. It was their primary-school teacher who managed to put this in the nicest terms, when she said Antero was a searcher. He was an admirer too. He worshipped Holma and wanted to be like him, but nobody could be like him.

Holma overtook the slower motorists in front, heard the tooting of horns as he passed, something that happened every time he tried to overtake when he shouldn't. People didn't appreciate that he had the situation under control.

The landscape began to change. He felt the proximity of the sea and loosened his tie.

Though his visit was somewhat melancholy in nature, there was a positive way of looking at it. A holiday. He hadn't had a holiday in a long time. He could combine his investigation into Antero's misadventures with a spot of sunbathing.

He might even meet a local beauty on the beach. They might look at those palm trees together, and she too could listen to his proverbs. They might get to know each other a bit better. He liked that. More precisely, he liked people getting to know him.

He had so much to give.

8

Olivia Koski was sitting in front of Jorma Leivo. The windows behind Leivo's head looked as though they were ablaze: the sun struck the bonnet of the SUV parked outside and bounced up into the office making both of them – the car and the office – look newer and cleaner than was really the case.

'Fine,' said Olivia and waited.

She thought about what she'd said, how she had answered the question *How are things?* Wondered whether she could still retract it, add something like *All things considered...* but decided against it. She felt extremely uncomfortable sitting in the office in only a swimming costume and a pair of trainers, especially as the man behind the desk had wrapped himself in a bright-blue shirt and white blazer, was bathing in the powerful light, and had adopted a tone of voice somewhere between creepy sugar daddy and aggressive street peddler.

'Good to hear,' said Leivo. 'And thanks so much for stopping by head office.'

Olivia smiled. It wasn't a genuine smile, but then again, neither was Jorma Leivo's *thanks so much.*

'It's nothing.'

'We haven't had a chance to chat much. It's a shame. I think of myself as a hands-on leader, and I lead by talking.'

Leivo paused. Olivia didn't know what to say. Was she going to have to chit-chat with him? Hopefully not.

'It was a frightful thing, what happened in your house,' he continued. 'Most unfortunate indeed. A dangerous man – let's be honest, a criminal – forces his way into your house. It makes you think. What's happening to the world, who can we trust, where can we feel safe? Can you ever really feel safe living in a remote little town? And,

perhaps more to the point – and I don't mean this to be demean-
ing – as a woman alone in a remote little town, can you feel safe? Is
anything worth risking your life for? Not to mention what might
happen to the value of property round here once people learn we are
being targeted by the most depraved serial rapists. I'm sure you've
been thinking about all this yourself.' Leivo's expression showed that
he was going to continue regardless of what Olivia replied.

'I admit I've thought about it,' Olivia said. It was the truth.

'Let me recap, just in case,' said Leivo. 'As we know, nowadays the
value of many remote properties in bad condition is only theoretical.
There is such a thing as use value, but it's economical jargon that…'

That I won't understand because I'm a woman, Olivia thought to
herself.

'…that we don't need to get ourselves bogged down in right now,'
Leivo continued. 'Because we can talk about the matter at hand,
about what's on offer. Because we can assess the current situation and
see what we can do about it. By that I mean doing what is sensible
and safest.'

Jorma Leivo leaned forwards, carefully placing his hands on the
table as though he were testing to see whether the stove was hot or not.

'Let me tell you, it's a good thing you weren't at home when that
man turned up to assault you, to torture and murder you in the most
brutal fashion. He thought he could get away with it because the
house is so isolated and worthless—'

'Worthless?' Olivia asked, her tone neutral, not at all offended,
but her interest piqued.

Leivo looked confused. It was hard to say whether his confusion
stemmed from her question or the fact that he'd been interrupted.

'What I mean is that after this sadist – the first one we've had
round here, but you can bet he won't be the last – after he'd destroyed
your house—'

'He messed up the kitchen,' said Olivia. 'I've cleaned it now.'

'That's right, rapid response,' Leivo nodded. 'In other circumstances
I'd applaud you, if only such extremely brutal, sexually-motivated

murders with all their twisted ritualistic characteristics weren't so commonplace in this country.'

There was no point trying to end this conversation by herself, she thought. Leivo would get to the point when it suited him. Or once he had composed himself. Olivia could simply focus on being there. Even that was hard work.

The rule stipulating that during working hours all employees had to wear their work uniform – in Olivia's case this meant a swimming costume made of cheap fabric and bearing a logo that harked back to the 1980s – caused discomfort for at least two reasons: the fact that people saw her wearing it at all and the weather being what it was. It was generally cold, and men's eyes generally wandered somewhere other than her face.

Leivo inhaled slowly, his head angled slightly backwards, his chest expanding. He looked like something pulled from the depths of the ocean, gasping for air.

'I want to meet you halfway,' said Leivo. 'I see this shaping up into a classic win-win business opportunity. It's a business term that means—'

'I know what it means,' Olivia interrupted and noted how profusely Leivo was sweating.

The light streaming in from behind him revealed the beads of sweat appearing on his cheeks. Olivia could see Leivo mentally processing the matter before putting it into words.

'I want to buy your plot,' he said.

Olivia stared at him. 'What plot?'

'The plot with your sex-murder house on it.'

'Even though it's apparently worthless?'

'The house is worthless,' Leivo nodded slowly, as though something were gradually dawning on them both. 'But the land—'

'Why?'

The question stopped Leivo in his stride. He looked at Olivia for a moment. 'Well,' he stammered. 'One small step for man…'

Olivia waited, but Leivo didn't complete the sentence.

'I don't know what you mean.'

'We're expanding.'

Again Olivia waited.

'We?' she asked.

'Palm Beach Finland. I'm offering you the chance to get involved.'

'I think I'm already quite involved,' said Olivia and looked down at the logo written across her chest. 'I've already surrendered most of my clothes. How will selling the house make me any more involved?'

'Not the house, the plot,' said Leivo. 'You have to look at the bigger picture, see things that don't exist yet. In three years' time we'll be the number one resort among the rich and famous. Stunning women, just like yourself, handsome men just like … people from all over the world; boats, yachts, each bigger than the last, their sails wider, their keels deeper.'

Olivia began to realise where Leivo was going. The beach-side plot she had inherited was the key to the bay which, because of its depth, would allow almost any size of boat to moor there. Her plot of land included part of the small peninsula extending out into the bay and a crucial stretch of the shoreline, which could be connected to a future marina. Yes, she owned a beautiful stretch of beach, the end of a peninsula, but the most important part of this deal was the plot itself – and it was that plot Leivo was trying to get his sweaty hands on.

'We'll have rows of bungalows – Florida-style bungalows, the biggest and the very best, each with their own private beach. It's a luxurious little touch. You can moor your yacht at your very own jetty. None of those poky Finnish summer cottages; these will be villas.'

'I already have a villa,' said Olivia.

'Modern villas,' said Leivo. Olivia wasn't sure whether he'd heard her or not. 'The kind of villas with panoramic windows, open terraces, real *architecture*.'

Olivia decided not to ask what Leivo meant by the last word.

'In what way would I be involved, exactly?'

'By selling the plot, you would accumulate capital which you could then use to buy shares in our future limited company.'

Leivo had clearly been practising this spiel.

'And what if I don't sell?' asked Olivia.

'Why wouldn't you?' Though Leivo was clearly trying his hardest, a sense of urgency had entered his voice.

'I have a dream too,' said Olivia. 'And it involves my hundred-year-old house. I inherited that house from my father. I plan to renovate it, from its foundations right up to that small, rusted weathervane at the top. Then I'm going to live in it.'

Olivia didn't add that she'd already made plenty of bad choices in her life, and always as a result of listening to men who always had suggestions that always involved her money. Men were like a playground slide: you got to the bottom and realised you'd lost your wallet. She'd had enough.

Leivo's expression, which Olivia had difficulty making out – the sunlight, Leivo's hair and clothes, the oddly bright walls in the room, all put her off balance – now seemed darker, sterner.

'The future…' Leivo began and again seemed to think hard about how to continue. 'It's coming whether we like it or not.'

Leivo might have had other thoughts about the future, about tomorrow, next year, but Olivia wasn't interested. She didn't care. In fact, she hardly spared a thought for her uniform any longer, that or the imbalance of power between the two parties involved in this negotiation. So she said exactly what was on her mind.

'I'm grateful for this job. I wish your company well. This company and the future company. But I'm not selling. Neither the plot nor the house. It is mine and it's going to stay mine. If it's all the same, I'd better get back to the watchtower.'

For a moment Leivo seemed lost for words.

'Of course,' he nodded eventually. 'Work before pleasure.'

Olivia stood up. Leivo did the same. They looked at each other. Olivia in her swimming costume and trainers, and across the table the large sweaty man who paid her wages, painting doomsday scenarios in his teddy-bear voice. But the situation was different now from when Olivia had entered the room.

'Bye,' she said.

'Bye,' Leivo nodded.

Olivia had already turned when she heard a voice behind her.

'You could still change your mind,' said Leivo. There was a sense of determination in his voice, she thought. It sounded strange. Leivo continued. 'You never know, you might come to see things differently.'

◉

The remainder of the day in the lifeguards' tower: too much wind, too few events, too many thoughts.

A stubborn collection of clouds glided at a snail's pace across the grey sun and refused to break up. Why was it always windy on the ground, but in the sky nothing ever seemed to happen? Olivia fetched her hoodie to keep herself warm, pulling the hood tight over her head.

She looked at the handful of people on the beach and thought about what she'd told Leivo. It was almost as though she knew exactly what she was doing, as though she knew how to do it. Jesus Christ. She didn't know what she'd do if something unexpected happened. Whatever it might be. She'd used all her savings on a hurried paint job, her monthly salary was enough to cover the property tax, insurance, the water bills, the road maintenance, the rubbish collection, the electricity, phone, internet, food, trainers ... but nothing else. Lifeguarding wasn't exactly the best paid profession. As for the other things Jorma Leivo had hinted at – murder, rape, torture, and God knows what else – Olivia couldn't deny that the thoughts keeping her awake in the early hours had recently been the stuff of horror movies. Think rationally, Olivia would tell herself at such moments, this was just a one-off, random, inexplicable event. There was no threat to her. And yet a shiver ran the length of her body now, from the soles of her trainers to the top of her head. Stop it, she told herself, serial killers like that don't roam around sleepy towns like this.

It was three-thirty. Chico appeared at the foot of the watchtower.

Olivia still found it hard to call Kari Korhonen 'Chico'. She always thought of him as Kari. She still saw a young dreamer with a guitar slung over his shoulder. He was now slightly older than before, of course, but this older Kari still looked like a dreamer and still carried a guitar. Olivia wasn't sure exactly when Kari had become Chico, or why, for that matter. Perhaps it was for the best. And perhaps she should accept it and call him Chico. It suited him better: the shades, the Bermuda shorts, the tattoo on his lower abdomen with calligraphic text running through it in such small and ornate lettering that in order to read it you'd have to bend down so close that your mouth would be positioned quite literally…

Which Olivia was not planning to do but which Chico may have imagined was the whole idea behind the tattoo. They hadn't spoken much since Olivia had come back to town. There was no particular drama; they'd never been especially close and their shared job didn't require much communication. Of course, it had all come as something of a surprise – the fact that Olivia had found herself working in the same place as Kari Korhonen, who at the age of eighteen had said he would never work for The Man. At first they'd wondered whether this was an abbreviation for a mysterious company with which Kari had had a run-in, but he eventually explained what he meant. To him, The Man was the system, the machine. And now they both worked for it – in matching swimming costumes.

As Olivia descended the steps she realised her legs were stiff, as though she'd been sleeping in an awkward position. Chico was swinging his arms around, presumably to keep himself warm. Olivia couldn't see his eyes, they were obscured behind a pair of almost-opaque sunglasses, and his head was turned towards the sea.

'What's up?' Olivia asked at the bottom of the steps.

Both of Chico's arms were moving and he seemed to start. The sunglasses briefly turned in Olivia's direction.

'What d'you mean?' he asked.

'You're on time. This is the first time in about two weeks that we've changed shift and you're actually waiting at the bottom of the tower.'

'I couldn't sleep.'

Olivia looked at Chico and recalled how the girls in their class used to say he looked like Patrick Swayze. They did share a certain something, once you factored in the passage of time and the parochial *je ne sais quoi*.

'It's almost three-thirty in the afternoon,' said Olivia.

'What? Right. I've been awake all night. Again. Stress.'

'Too much work,' she smiled but wondered whether that was too sarcastic. Given his next question, however, Chico most likely hadn't been listening to her.

'How are you doing?' he asked. 'Olivia?'

Olivia was taken aback. For two reasons. Chico had never before asked her anything personal – except the compulsory questions after she'd moved back. *Are you seeing anyone? Any ex-husbands? Kids in care?* Besides, now he really seemed to be trying hard. His tone sounded genuine.

'Thanks for asking, Chico. I'm fine. I can't seem to get used to this uniform. Today I had a little chat with the boss and I completely forgot to mention it. Either that means I secretly like it or I simply don't remember I'm wearing it when … I'm wearing it.'

Chico turned his head.

'You talked to the boss? Leivo?'

'Jorma Leivo, the guy that owns this place.'

Olivia looked into Chico's sunglasses. His hair was wet and tousled, perhaps from the shower.

'What did he say?' asked Chico.

'Told me about his plans,' said Olivia and waved her hand in an arc through the air. 'Palm Beach Finland.'

'His plans?'

'He wants to expand,' she said, then decided that Chico didn't need to know the details of the discussion she and Leivo had had about plots and houses. 'But we knew that already.'

Chico's arms were trembling. 'Quite a wind.'

Olivia looked out to sea. Grey clouds, slow, heavy waves. She remembered that she still needed to go to the supermarket and the hardware store.

'I've got to go,' she said. 'Renovations – you know how it is.'

'How's it going…? The renovation?'

Olivia shrugged her shoulders. 'It's not cheap.'

Chico nodded, but not in keeping with Olivia's answer. His internal rhythm was altogether different, far more agitated. 'Right. Money.'

'And I need lots of it,' said Olivia.

Chico nodded again, then stopped. 'D'you remember when we used to spend all summer on this beach, all night, sitting round the bonfire playing the guitar?'

Olivia tried to get an impression of what was going on behind those sunglasses, but she couldn't see a thing.

'That was twenty years ago,' she said. 'I was always cold, and biding my time until I could get out of this town for good.'

Chico said nothing. He climbed up to the watchtower and sat down.

◉

Jan Nyman took a plastic kitchen chair outside and tried to sit on his veranda for a moment and take in the scenery, the scent of the pines and the fresh, salty sea air. But it proved impossible. Within a few minutes the wind had achieved its goal and penetrated his jeans and flannel shirt. And so, as the sun set in the west, painting the sky in shades of light pink and brown, Nyman was left with two options: either he could take his iPad and walk to the restaurant on the beach or he could sit at his small kitchen table and read the information he'd requested and which had just arrived in his inbox, then walk to the restaurant and enjoy dinner with a clear, or at least semi-clear, conscience.

He plumped for the latter.

What he read was largely what he'd been expecting.

The bank-account information was a week and a half old. Everybody was broke: Jorma Leivo, the Surfer Dude aka Kari Korhonen, and Olivia Koski. None of them had a penny to their name. Life could be like that, as Nyman knew only too well.

The surfer's finances were fairly consistent, in that his account resembled a dead man's pulse. Nyman paid attention to the seasons. During the winter it seemed that his wages were paid in the form of unemployment benefit from the Department of Social Security, and during the summer he was paid by the resort, which operated under a variety of trading names. The surfer never appeared to have very much money at his disposal, and it never seemed to be spent on living expenses. His money went on … What *did* it go on? The vast majority – almost all of it – was withdrawn from the ATM in cash. This might be interesting, then again it might not. It seemed he had been blacklisted by lenders years before. Perhaps he didn't want to tell them everything he was doing with his money.

Jorma Leivo and his business ventures were a world of their own. His current account might as well have been covered in cobwebs – he quite simply never used it. His company, on the other hand, had numerous accounts in three different banks, and the movement of funds between banks and accounts was lively to say the least. So lively, in fact, that Nyman decided to send the complete details of Leivo's financial operations to an acquaintance in the fraud department and quietly ask him for a favour: to follow Leivo's accounts in real time.

The favour wasn't entirely legal. Leivo wasn't officially the focus of the investigation. Nobody was. Officially. Nyman had run into problems like this before in his role as an undercover agent. And it often meant that he had to operate under the radar and in many directions at once.

Nyman wrote an email, explained that he knew and understood

that he was asking for something for which he had no authority, that he was instigating the action and it was entirely his own responsibility. If the fraud investigator was ever asked about it, he should say that Nyman told him he *did* have the relevant authority and that Nyman's superior had given him free rein. Which was sort of true. Muurla knew that his undercover agents used all means possible to achieve their goals and that oftentimes those means wouldn't stand the light of day; but he would never accept a fishing expedition quite like this. That said, Muurla purred like a cat when his agents brought him results, Nyman knew this from experience. He uploaded the attachments and pressed *Send*.

Olivia Koski's financial situation was the worst of all. It was dire. Even the surfer had more money in his account. Okay, it was only a tenner here, a tenner there, but still. The last of Olivia Koski's money seemed to have been spent paying off a significant insurance bill. An old, wooden house: the sheer size of the building's insurance made Nyman shudder. Earlier in the year there had been a few thousand euros in the account, but it had all disappeared in the last two months. The largest individual purchases were at a number of high-street hardware stores.

The account's total balance at the last statement: eight euros and three cents.

◉

So it's come to this, Olivia thought to herself. She had just bought a large pot of white paint on credit.

She placed the pot on the floor in the hallway and turned towards the kitchen. She hadn't switched on the lights, the setting sun cast horizontal beams through the house, changing the colour of the walls, the size of the rooms, their depth. The blackness of the shadows.

The horrors Jorma Leivo had hinted at began to come to life again. An intangible danger – the feeling that something terrible could happen at any moment. An imminent threat.

It's all in my imagination, she thought. All of it.

Perhaps her fears had begun resurfacing because she was tired, and because of the simple fact that she'd started living on credit again. Though it was a small sum of money, it reminded her of the past, of failed times. It was something she never wanted to relive.

One of the many things she never wanted to relive.

Bad men, decisions delayed, dreams dashed, hasty solutions born of her own pennilessness. Maybe that was why Leivo's fearmongering gave her goose bumps.

Someone had broken into her house. God knows what he'd been meaning to do…

Olivia had instinctively assumed the man must have been a burglar. A burglar who got into an argument with his accomplice or accomplices, and met a messy end. It had never occurred to her that she might have been the target. What if she wasn't safe in this house after all – a house in which she had always thought she was secure?

She had lost her appetite – didn't feel like stepping into the kitchen to put some supper together. She turned and saw the pot of paint in the middle of the floor. She was far too tired to start painting anything. She wanted…

She wanted…

Olivia moved the pot of paint and placed it by the wall, took off her clothes, walked past the large hallway mirror without looking at her reflection and went into the bathroom. She stepped into the bath and turned on the tap.

And nothing happened.

PART TWO
IMPLEMENTATION

1

'I'd rather not kill anyone else.'

Chico glanced around nervously and tightened his grip on his beer bottle. 'Shut up,' he hissed.

They were sitting in their regular spot, the table at the far end of the local pub. A few metres away the jukebox glowed in neon shades of pink and light blue, thirsting for more of Chico's valuable coins. Rather, normally it thirsted. But not now.

'How can I answer the question if I shut up?' asked Robin.

'Give me a sensible answer,' said Chico. 'Don't start talking until you've thought it through.'

'I have thought it through. I don't want to kill people, that's all.'

'Okay, just don't say it out loud.'

Robin appeared to do as he was told. Chico took a deep breath.

The incident that Robin was referring to made Chico feel strange – a vague sense of queasiness, an odd emotion that seemed tied up with his own mental processes. He'd never experienced anything like this before, but it was simply too hard to think about what had happened. Not like back in school, when he had to remember something complicated, but because the mere thought of what they had done didn't seem to fit into his brain. Either that or it kept turning and churning, changing form and shifting from side to side. And so, whenever the events in Olivia's house started to resurface in Chico's mind, he focussed on thinking about something else entirely. He made lists, all the while trying to forget the doubts he'd had in recent weeks. The top-ten guitar solos ever. Eric Clapton's top-ten guitar solos. Eric Clapton's top-ten guitar solos from the 1970s. Eric Clapton's top-ten guitar solos between 1970 and 1972…

'"Layla",' thought Chico and sipped his beer.

It tasted good, though the best-before date had passed years ago. Chico knew the barman, knew how to enjoy quality imported beverages on the cheap, and knew that everybody ended up a winner despite all the pedantic regulations, or perhaps because of them. He couldn't decide which.

'We have to do something,' he said, once he could no longer stand the cacophony of wailing guitars in his ears.

'As long as we don't…'

'Of course not. Forget that for a minute. It was an accident. I've said so a thousand times. Shit happens. Last night I watched some American documentary about a guy with two heads.'

Robin stared at him. 'Did he kill someone?'

'What?' Chico asked, incredulous. 'No. But he had two heads.'

Chico could see that Robin didn't follow.

'It's just chance, isn't it?' he said. 'A freak of nature.'

'A two-headed man,' Robin nodded. 'A man with two heads.'

Chico could see the metaphor was still eluding Robin. Then again, perhaps Robin didn't need to understand everything. Chico stared ahead and contemplated things, picking at the label on his bottle. It seemed the beer had expired in 2014. Did it have a funny aftertaste after all? He looked at Robin.

'Two weeks,' he said. 'You heard it yourself. If we don't come up with the goods, Leivo says he'll tell the police what we did.'

'What if we just do what he wants?'

'That's what I'm trying to explain,' Chico sighed.

'What was it he said the first time we met him, back in his office?'

Chico looked at Robin with fresh eyes. He couldn't tell whether Robin was secretly wise or simply a first-rate, dyed-in-the-wool, out-and-out idiot, but what did it matter when every now and then, completely out of the blue, like a bolt of lightning from a clear sky, he remembered something as though it were recorded on tape, repeated it out loud and helped sharpen Chico's thoughts, Chico, of course, being the dynamo of the two.

'Robin, you're a genius.'

'Thanks, man,' said Robin, clearly confused.

Chico imagined Robin probably didn't hear compliments like that very often.

Robin's cheeks reddened slightly. 'Sometimes things just, you know, pop into my head,' he said modestly.

Chico clinked his bottle against Robin's and took a long gulp. The beer definitely had an aftertaste, something cheesy. But it was a fair cop: if you want a bottle of premium Dutch Pils for one euro in a small Finnish town, you have to compromise somewhere. Chico was a businessman too, he understood how capitalism worked. Or was this socialism? No matter, there was something old, sticky and cheesy about the beer, but it only cost one euro a bottle, and at that price it meant he could sit in his favourite bar, even when he was virtually penniless, and think about ways to get his hands on larger sums of money. Capitalism or socialism?

And now an opportunity appeared to present itself.

'Tonight,' said Chico. 'We'll sort it out tonight.'

Robin looked surprised. The smile prompted by Chico's compliment disappeared from his face in a millisecond. Robin stared at the bottle in front of him.

'I can't make it,' he said.

'Why not?'

'I just can't.'

'Robin,' said Chico. 'Why not?'

A short pause, filled only with a sharp click from the billiard table at the other end of the room.

'It's talent night,' Robin said quietly.

Chico leaned back against the wall of the booth. He thought for a moment. He thought about two things. The first was talent night; the second was Robin.

'What are you performing?' Chico asked and realised there was a note of something approaching dread in his voice. 'I mean, what talent are you going to … demonstrate?'

'I'm just watching,' Robin replied quietly, lowering his head.

'Watching what exactly?'

Robin looked at him and swallowed. 'Nea will be on stage.'

Chico thought about this for a moment.

'And what's she performing?'

'I don't know. She's on stage at half-ten.'

'So Nea invited you, did she? You personally?'

Robin lowered his eyes. Now he spoke even more quietly than before. 'She posted on Facebook that she was doing it.'

'You two are friends on Facebook?'

'I sent her a friend request.'

'When?'

'December.'

Chico looked at Robin and waited. Robin had said all he was going to say. Chico pushed against his cushioned seat and leaned forwards across the table. Let it go, he thought, this isn't important.

He was about to take a gulp from his bottle but noticed a yellowish fleck floating in the liquid. The fleck looked almost alive and seemed to be twitching about on the surface. He pushed the bottle away. He desperately needed some money. He was tired of this; tired of drinking this nasty fondue of a beer, tired of playing on a cheap replica guitar. He wanted a fresh beer and a genuine, custom-made Les Paul.

Now he knew how to get his hands on both.

'We'll be finished before talent night,' said Chico. 'I'll pick up some matches at the bar.'

2

Jan Nyman became aware of movement and noise in the next-door chalet. He was sitting at his miniature dining table, and now realised his back was stiff so he stood up. He'd been reading for a few hours. It was time to leave.

He drank two glasses of water, put on the lighter of his two flannel shirts – the one in green and light-blue check, pulled on a pair of navy-blue jeans, slipped his iPhone into his front pocket and tied the laces on his red Converse All Stars. He looked at himself in the mirror, adjusted his hair, considered shaving but decided this wasn't the time: he was a maths teacher on holiday, and he wanted both to feel and look like one.

Nyman stepped outside.

The wind buffeted him as it had before, but it was a beautiful evening, almost serene. The sun was setting slowly, its soft brush gilding both the sky and the sea. The air was fresh and smelled of a giant salt bath. Nyman looked towards the neighbouring chalet. Behind it he could see the back of a shining black car, one of the new BMW models, the 520 maybe. A towel in migraine-inducing stripes was hanging over the railing like a flag planted on conquered territory. Nyman locked the door of his chalet, then, as he turned he heard the door of the neighbouring chalet opening.

On the veranda Nyman saw a man in swimming trunks: light-skinned, his face hard to make out – it was as though his features had melted in the evening sun; the shades and contours had all combined. A man of about forty, a year or so older than Nyman, his upper body muscular, which made his legs seem all the scrawnier, as though he'd been going to the gym regularly but stubbornly avoided working out his thighs. And the oddest detail of all: his choirboy fair hair, which would have looked adorable on a twelve-year-old, but which made a man of forty look as though he'd come down with the last shower. The man noticed him.

'Hello,' said Nyman. 'Evening swim?'

The man said nothing, but simply turned to face Nyman. His black swimming trunks were small and tight. Too small, too tight.

'What do you mean?' he asked eventually.

Seeing as you're wearing a pair of kids' swimming trunks.

'It's a nice evening for it,' said Nyman. 'The sun should keep you warm.'

The man looked up at the sky. Very well, thought Nyman. You can either continue this silly game, he said to himself, or you can do what you're supposed to do. The man only looked at the sky for a second, two at most.

'Been here long?' he asked. The voice was in fact surprisingly friendly.

'Only a day,' said Nyman.

'Holiday?'

'Damn right.'

'Me too,' said the man. 'Long overdue.'

Nyman decided to make good use of the situation. He took a few steps towards the neighbouring veranda and reached a hand across the fence. It was one of the single most effective ways of gathering information that had ever been invented: a quick and surprising introduction.

'Jan Kaunisto,' said Nyman.

The man held out his hand and smiled. 'Esa Koljonen.'

The two shook hands. Judging by what was happening in the man's eyes, in the areas around his eyes, and from his movements and the grip of his hand, Nyman decided that the man's name either was Esa Koljonen or it wasn't.

They exchanged a few words about the weather, about summers in general, and once the man seemed to warm to their conversation – and especially to the sound of his own voice – Nyman wished him a pleasant evening.

He left the man on his veranda, walked into the town and quickly arrived at the so-called beachside boulevard, a street whose official name was Shore Street. Once on Shore Street Nyman hesitated for a moment, then chose a bar based on name alone. If the resort was called Palm Beach Finland, why shouldn't there be a bar named Hawaii? Later that evening Bar Hawaii would be home to talent night.

The bar was half empty, and cosy, perhaps even a little claustrophobic. The ceiling was low and the bar counter long. The principal design material appeared to be bamboo. To the left of the bar was a row of booths, each with a covering of leaves and branches that provided extra privacy but made the room feel even smaller. At the far end of the bar were a jukebox and a fruit machine, their lights flashing in exotic colours. The stage appeared to be right next to the entrance.

A small sign on the bar counter revealed that talent night was due to start in an hour and fifteen minutes. Nyman ordered a bottle of beer from the female bartender – clearly a seasonal employee, as she struggled to find everything – and was about to take a sip when he saw a familiar profile in the mirror: long dark-brown hair and a long, slightly noble nose.

Olivia Koski was sitting by herself.

◉

The background music was soul, a classic number – a velvet-voiced man imploring his listeners for some sexual healing. Nyman wondered whether he should wait for the song to end; in the worst-case scenario, Olivia Koski would think he had selected this song from the jukebox and was now turning up to instigate a healing procedure of his own. Nyman had seen plenty of men working themselves up to approach a strange woman, but invariably they prepared far too much: the right song, the right flowers, the right position of the planets … dream bachelor, wedding march, twin children, erectile dysfunction, a shared plot in the cemetery, all condensed into a single second. Of course, he'd seen other kinds of men too, men who stalked their prey like big cats: lying in the long grass then hungrily springing into action, their jaws wide open – *Fancy a shag? Why not, bitch?* – and ending up drunkenly consoling each other at the end of the evening: *Mate, you never let me down.*

Nyman took a sip of beer and glanced again in the mirror. Olivia Koski didn't appear to be paying the slightest attention to what was going on around her. The velvet-voiced man continued his song. Nyman picked up his bottle and walked towards Olivia Koski's booth. The wine glass on the table in front of her was almost empty.

'Hi,' said Nyman and held out his hand when he realised Olivia didn't recognise him. 'Jan Kaunisto. I rented the Distance Runner board from you today. Can I get you another glass of wine and join you?'

Olivia seemed to be thinking about something, then held out her hand. 'Maybe. I'm Olivia. That's maybe to the glass of wine. Let's see once I've finished this one.'

Olivia gestured towards the other side of the table. 'Be my guest,' she said. Nyman slid into the seat and looked at the woman sitting across the dark wooden table. Her hair was wet; he caught the scent of floral shampoo. The ceiling in the booth was low and the lamp attached to the wall emitted a soft, pallid light which might or might not have been its desired effect. Nyman felt as though they were sitting in a den or a tree house.

'So, talent night,' said Nyman. 'Are you watching or performing?'

Olivia glanced at him, perhaps slightly amused. 'I came here for a shower,' she said and nodded towards the bar. 'You don't happen to know anything about plumbing renovations, do you?'

'The only time I ever experienced that was in an apartment block,' said Nyman and shook his head. 'It took longer than planned and ended up costing more than it should have.'

'Brilliant. That cheered me up.'

'I must admit I didn't really follow it very closely. I was working away from home at the time. Are you getting a renovation done?'

'Hopefully,' she said, then shook her head. 'Maybe. I don't know.'

Nyman waited.

Olivia stared at her glass, then eventually raised her eyes. 'So you're not a plumber and you're not a windsurfer. What exactly do you do?'

'I'm a maths teacher,' said Nyman.

'Long summer holidays.'

'Everyone says that.'

'It's true though, isn't it?' she asked and sipped her wine.

Nyman took a gulp of beer. 'What's up with your pipes?' he asked.

'They're a hundred years old and they've given up the ghost. I need to replace them. But I haven't got…'

Nyman waited.

'Let's talk about something else.' Olivia pushed her glass away and looked Nyman in the eyes. 'What brought you here?'

Nyman looked at Olivia, at those brown eyes. When he was dealing with criminals, lying always came naturally to him – he lied systematically, automatically, without giving it a second thought. But right now there was something about lying that disturbed him. He decided to add at least an element of truth to everything he said. Maybe that would make it feel less wrong.

'A friend told me about this place, said I might have an interesting time.'

'Did your friend say why?' Olivia asked.

'Well, I guess it had something to do with the location by the sea. I'm not sure. And he particularly recommended windsurfing, which is something I've never done before.'

'He didn't mention anything about a strange occurrence here a few weeks ago?'

Nyman tried to look puzzled. He might even have succeeded.

'I feel like everybody knows about it,' said Olivia.

Nyman continued to feign an element of confusion. He was trying his best.

Eventually Olivia put him out of his misery. 'You'll hear about it sooner or later. A dead man was found in my house.'

'What, just like that?' asked Nyman, quite sincerely.

'I don't know if it was just like that,' she said, and Nyman listened carefully to her tone of voice, trying to judge how she spoke about the event, what she stressed, what she said and didn't say. 'Someone smashed the windows. There was a fight in the kitchen. Well, in fact I don't know whether there was or wasn't, but the kitchen was trashed. Then, somehow, a man died. I arrived home that night and found him there. The police think he was probably murdered. They're looking into it. I've no idea what conclusion they've reached, because they never tell me anything. I don't know why. You'd think they would keep the owner of the property up to date. Maybe not though.'

Okay, thought Nyman. Impossible to make any judgements based on this.

Olivia glanced at him. 'You don't seem very shocked,' she said.

'That's quite a homecoming.'

'It was terrible,' she said, her voice neutral. 'And there's something else, something I haven't told anyone else.'

Nyman sipped his beer and waited.

'It's a bit embarrassing,' said Olivia.

Nyman made a hand gesture to indicate that her secret was safe with him. And it was, assuming what she was about to tell him didn't involve a criminal element. *Go ahead*, Nyman tried to smile at her.

'I'm not entirely sure about it. I'm not sure why I'm telling you this. It's about my father and grandfather. I think the thief must have taken a backscratcher from the wall between the kitchen and the hallway.'

'A backscratcher?' asked Nyman.

'My grandfather was a fisherman. He wore long johns from the beginning of August right through until Midsummer – basically all year round. He didn't have many pairs of long johns – in fact he probably only had one. As you can imagine, during the winter they started getting a bit itchy in certain places. So my grandfather got himself a backscratcher which he hung on a hook between the hall and the kitchen and which he used to solve his little problem. He used it for decades. Once my grandfather died, my father started using it. Why would anyone steal something like that?'

'Are you sure it's missing?'

'I've cleaned the ground floor from top to bottom many times. I don't know why I told you this.'

'Sometimes it's good to talk about things,' said Nyman.

Olivia leaned her head back slightly and looked at Nyman almost from above. 'But you knew all this before. The bit about what happened in my house, at least. I always notice when people know about it. They look at me differently from other people. I doubt they do it on purpose, but it happens all the same. *She's the one with the body in her kitchen.* Something like that.'

Nyman nodded, but not too enthusiastically.

'I did hear something,' he said, relieved that at least in this regard he could tell the truth.

'I knew it. The other option is that you've seen so much brutality in your career as a maths teacher that the thought of bodies in people's kitchens doesn't disturb you in the least.'

'Oh, it always disturbs me,' he said.

And when it was Olivia Koski's turn to look puzzled, Nyman explained what he meant. He told her about his deployment in Afghanistan – two tours as a peacekeeper in Mazar-i-Sharif. He didn't go into details. Still, it felt good talking about himself. Naturally he left out the bits about his years in the Violent Crimes Unit, the citizens of Helsinki who over the years he'd seen turn up dead in every imaginable way.

'And what then?' asked Olivia.

'After Afghanistan? I came home, went back to college, met a woman.'

This was all true. In its own way.

'But you're on holiday by yourself?'

Nyman couldn't discern anything flirtatious in the question. It was simply a question.

'Divorce,' he said. 'She's a very nice woman. I haven't got a bad word to say about her. But we haven't got anything in common. With hindsight I think we met each other at a time when both of us wanted to get married to someone, so we ended up marrying each other.'

'Sounds better than my relationships. Engaged twice, married once. I was going to say we had nothing in common either. But in my defence, I should say the two men had a lot in common. For instance, I ended up supporting both of them.'

'That's modern,' said Nyman.

Olivia might have smiled, he wasn't sure.

'But it's been a while since then,' she continued. 'I came back here a few months ago. My father passed away…'

'I'm sorry to hear that.'

'Thanks.' Olivia paused for half a second, then continued. 'I inherited a house where the plumbing has stopped working. The place needs a complete renovation. I've done lots of small things myself, but I've been putting off the bigger jobs until I win the lottery.'

'You play the lottery?'

Olivia shook her head. 'No, I don't believe in that kind of thing.'

'What, chance?'

'The lottery isn't chance. It's torture. Chance is the idea that you might find a good bloke, but it's not like the choice you make on lottery odds, which would be like choosing between all the men on the planet, all three and a half billion of them. You choose from an insanely small group of men that you get to know in the course of your life. And I don't mean in the intimate sense. Let's say there are seven of them. Two are hopeless cases – I'm an expert on them. Then there's one that's tidy round the house, but he's no good because that's all there is to him: he doesn't make a mess, but that doesn't exactly count as a personality feature. Then there's one interesting guy with whom everything seems to be going well, but who one day stops calling you. Then there's one that turns from a prince into a

frog the minute you kiss him, though there's no physiological explanation for it. Then there's … Wait a minute.'

'You've got three left.'

Olivia shook her head.

'Two,' she said. 'Of whom one is the product of my imagination,
in the sense that he's the first man I ever kissed, back then we were
fourteen and I haven't seen him since, and he doesn't look like Brad
Pitt but sits lounging on the sofa stroking his double chin while he
waits for a nice sandwich and for death to pay a visit.'

'Then there's only one left.'

'And that's chance.'

Nyman looked at Olivia Koski. She moved her glass on the table.

'It's empty now,' said Nyman.

Olivia looked at her glass.

'That can't be chance.'

3

Chico caught sight of an ancient lawnmower. It was right behind the door they had broken. He inhaled the smell of cut grass and petrol. Robin was behind him at the door of the small shed.

They had taken a different route from last time, waited hidden among the trees and watched Olivia step out of the house, take her bike and cycle off. It had all happened in a matter of seconds. Olivia's movements were quick and expressed a sense of purpose.

They'd waited almost another half an hour, though the house had remained dark since Olivia had left. But you could never be too careful; Chico had learned that much. He wasn't necessarily worried about the prospect of there being an insane burglar in the house again, but caution was everything. And the foundation of success in business was to avoid any conflicts of interest. Chico wasn't entirely sure what this meant, but he'd once heard a man in a suit saying so at a vitamin sales event.

Chico stepped aside and Robin slipped in. Chico aimed the beam of his torch at the lawnmower.

'Over there,' he said.

Robin said nothing.

Chico explained the plan: lawnmower into the middle of the yard, match into the petrol tank and run. The message would be loud and clear and, even better, it would be only a warning. Not a catastrophe like a trashed kitchen or a murdered hippie. A clear message. And the money would appear in their account. Well, not exactly in their account. Chico didn't want to have to explain the sudden cash injection to a beady-eyed official at the social-security office; they always took more than a passing interest in his financial affairs, one devious way or another. And all because he…

Chico stopped himself before his thoughts became too agitated.

He always seemed to get himself worked up if money was close at hand, if there was even the idea that he was about to get his hands on some, if he'd been promised it or at the mere sight of cash. His heart began to pound and his whole body broke out in a sweat; his face and the top of his head started to burn up.

Chico took a deep breath, inhaled the pungent odour of the shed – a mixture of mildew, old equipment and something else he couldn't identify – and shuddered as he thought about the vole fever you could catch in sheds just from breathing in mouse shit; well, not the shit itself, not the actual faeces but the … What was it? Not the smell but the little specks it gives off – things that float in the air. What was it you even called something like that? A faecal molecule…?

He had to pull himself together, focus his thoughts, regroup.

'Do you understand?' he asked both Robin and himself.

'Good plan,' said Robin.

'Thanks,' said Chico. He was beginning to think so too now he could see more clearly.

Chico let the beam of his torch pan across the shed: everything from canoes and wheelbarrows to rakes and sleds, every imaginable form of clutter accumulated over the decades. Chico moved the light back to the lawnmower. He crouched down, unscrewed the cap on the petrol tank and nudged the lawnmower with his foot. Good, he thought, plenty of gas. In his left hand he held the cap, in his right the torch.

'Okay,' he said to Robin, still looking around in the torchlight, scanning the dark recesses and the piles of junk to locate any rodents, any evidence of poo. 'Take the matches out of my pocket.'

Whatever happened next happened so fast that Chico didn't have time to open his mouth. Robin's fingers moved with the dexterity of a pianist. The fingers slid into Chico's front pocket and pulled out the box of matches – everything happening in the same seamless, lightning-quick movement. Why right now, Robin? His fingers opened the matchbox, struck the match and chucked it into the petrol tank. It all happened so smoothly that though Chico saw it happening out of the corner of his eye, he didn't have time to utter a single word.

For a brief, whooshing moment he saw everything in the shed illuminated in bright light. He made a mental inventory of its contents. It was understandable, as his feet were glued to the spot. He guessed that what he was looking at now would be the last things he saw in the world. The heat was unbearable.

Finally he moved.

The world was whirring.

He felt his face burning up as he collapsed in the yard. The firm, recently cut grass felt cool – so wonderfully cool – against his face, and by now he didn't care how much rodent poo entered his lungs, it was much better than…

He rolled onto his back as soon as he could.

At some point he might even have lost consciousness.

The entire shed was in flames. From the angle at which Chico was watching events, it could have been a large house on fire. It was disappointing to note that the shed truly was the size of a small house. The flames reached up to the edge of the sky.

4

'Dreaming,' said Olivia. 'At some point it starts to feel harder than actually doing something.'

Nyman had asked what had made Olivia decide to stay here, to take on the task of renovating the dilapidated old house. And as he'd guessed, it wasn't just about the house and its plumbing.

'I mean the kind of dreaming that says everything is possible, that it's just a matter of time before something amazing happens or something inside you changes,' said Olivia and shook her head. 'That there's plenty of time and all doors are still open to you. They're not.'

'I'm slowly beginning to learn that.'

'How old are you?' she asked.

'Thirty-nine.'

'Exactly.'

Nyman didn't plan on asking how old Olivia Koski was. He already knew: thirty-nine. Three months younger than Nyman, to be precise. Instead he asked quite what she meant.

'Either you know what I'm talking about or you'll never know,' she said. 'When you think about it, how many times can you start over? How many times will you get another chance? I don't want to be cynical or pessimistic, but the answer is: not many. But really, I can only speak for myself. I don't know if it's the same for you. If you're a happy, recently divorced maths teacher who just wants to learn to windsurf, then you've already achieved everything you set out to achieve. But I haven't. And time seems to be speeding up. Only yesterday I was twenty. I'd better get a grip.'

Olivia sipped her wine. The soul classics continued: now the same soft-voiced man was singing about how he wanted to *get it on*. With these songs in the background Nyman felt an element of awkwardness when he looked deep into Olivia Koski's brown eyes. When the man with the velveteen voice started singing something along the lines of *understand me sugar* and *stop beatin' round the bush*, Nyman had to avoid direct eye contact. And not just because Olivia Koski seemed natural and attractive in an unapologetic way, as if she felt at home here – as if she felt at home wherever she went. That's it, he thought. You can see the life in her; you can sense how alive she is. Exactly. But the real reason for his awkwardness was that…

'This is pretty heavy stuff,' said Olivia, bringing him to. 'Maybe it's just the effects of what happened today, what happened recently…'

Nyman shook his head.

'I'm happy to listen as long as you like,' he said. 'I can't exactly claim I haven't been thinking the same kind of the things recently.'

'Do you ever dream of being something other than a maths teacher?'

'Definitely,' said Nyman.

'What then? You must have goals and dreams?'

'Can I tell you a story about my ex-wife?'

'Who could it possibly hurt?' said Olivia.

'We were getting married either that day or the day after,' Nyman began. 'She said something to the effect that one dream was about to come true and there were still so many wonderful dreams waiting their turn. Something like that. Then she asked what my dreams were. I thought about it for a moment and told her I didn't have any dreams. She said she'd never heard anything so depressing. We could have signed the divorce papers there and then, filled them out in advance. But the point is I didn't mean anything bad by it, and I didn't even consider it a very depressing thought. Quite the opposite, actually.'

Nyman took a sip of beer. Olivia Koski watched him, fascinated by what he was saying … maybe.

'I'd just come back from Afghanistan,' he continued. 'I thought to myself, I'm privileged: I'm a white man, I've still got both arms, both legs, a brain of some sort, I was born in Finland, I live in Finland. I was only talking about myself and the point I'd reached in my life, but I couldn't dream about anything. When it came to myself, I thought everything was about action. I tried to explain the difference between these two concepts. I tried to explain I was in a position where dreaming was just about putting things off and constantly coming up with new excuses, and said that if I really wanted to do something, I could start working towards it there and then if I wanted to.'

'What did your wife say?'

'My future wife,' Nyman corrected her. 'She said that maybe she didn't know me as well as she'd thought, then asked if I could set off that very minute to a paradise island somewhere in the Pacific and lie down on a white sandy beach.'

'And you answered…?'

'I'd just wiped the last remnants of Afghan sand from my eyes. I told her I never wanted to see another grain of sand again and that as a free man in his twenties I didn't find the idea of lying on my back in the sun much of a dream, let alone a life goal, something to strive towards, and that I never wanted to lie in the sand again, no matter whether it was white, red or brown – unless it was to avoid machine-gun fire. My wife-to-be – my ex-wife-to-be – said maybe we should have had this conversation earlier.'

Olivia looked him in the eyes. Nyman couldn't quite read her expression.

'You said what you thought.'

'I don't know if it was worth it. But it was the truth.'

Olivia tasted her wine, replaced her glass on the table.

'Do you always tell the truth?' she asked.

Nyman was about to answer, was about to open his mouth – to say what, he didn't yet know – when Olivia Koski's phone rang. It buzzed against the table. Olivia picked it up and answered. Nyman turned towards the bar, to give her a sense of privacy.

'Yes, I am,' Nyman heard Olivia say. 'Yes … What? Excuse me, what? Right away. Yes, right away.'

The call ended, Nyman could sense it though he didn't hear anything resembling a goodbye. He turned to Olivia, but she was already on her way to the bar. She said something to the waitress, who gave an affirmative nod. Olivia returned to the table, looking both agitated and as though she was lost in thought.

'I've ordered a taxi. It's on fire.'

Ten seconds later they were standing in front of the bar waiting for the taxi. Silence. Once both of them were sitting in the back seat of the taxi and the journey was sufficiently under way, Nyman plucked up the courage to speak.

'Where is the fire?'

'At my place. In the yard.'

Nyman knew of dozens of cases of a washing machine or dryer catching fire and gutting entire apartments in Helsinki.

'Did you leave any appliances switched on?'

Olivia shook her head.

Nyman recalled the photographs of the house and the garden.

'What about the sauna?' he asked. 'Were you heating the stove?'

Nyman instantly realised he'd made a mistake. Of course, he thought, how am I supposed to know she has a sauna in the yard?

Olivia turned slightly. The evening sun lit one side of her face, while the other remained in shadow. Nyman decided not to say anything else. He was certain he could feel Olivia's gaze on his face.

They arrived at the end of the path leading up to the house, and the taxi slowed.

A fire engine had parked sideways across the path; the taxi stopped ten metres behind it. Olivia dashed out of the taxi, leaving the door open, and disappeared behind the fire engine. Nyman stayed behind and paid. The taxi driver said something about smoke detectors. Nyman closed the door. He walked around the fire engine, and at that moment saw a local police patrol car and two men in police T-shirts and baseball caps standing in the middle of the yard.

In the bright flashing lights of the fire engine, the police stood staring at the smoking ruins, watching the firefighters at work. The air was acrid, bitter, as though the embers of a thousand bonfires lay smouldering all at once.

The firemen then sealed off the area and made sure there were no isolated fires that might cause the blaze to spread into the woods or the house itself, which Nyman now saw for himself for the first time. It really was impressive – and in a truly terrible condition.

Olivia was already talking to the chief of the fire department, who was gesturing towards the pile of charred ruins. From the photographs in the case file, Nyman knew that only a moment ago on that same spot there had been a rectangular, red-painted wooden shed, which, judging by the hefty brick chimney stack, probably included a sauna big enough to fit an entire family. Nyman wanted to speak to the fire chief too.

Having said that, he wanted to avoid the police officers, but it seemed he might be too late. One of them – grey beard, metallic-framed glasses, blue eyes, fifty years old, give or take – had already spotted him and was walking slowly but surely in his direction.

'Seen anything of interest?'

Nyman glanced at the policeman. Play dumb, he told himself.

'Has there been some kind of fire here?' he asked.

The policeman did not respond.

'Got any ID on you?'

Nyman pulled his passport out of his back pocket and handed it to the man. The policeman looked at him and opened the passport. 'Mind if I take a picture?' he asked.

'No problem,' said Nyman and the policeman took out his phone and snapped a photograph of Jan Kaunisto's new passport.

'I know everybody else here,' he said as he handed Nyman the passport.

'I'm with her,' said Nyman and nodded in Olivia's direction.

The officer paused for a moment.

'Holiday,' he said eventually.

Nyman guessed it was probably a question.

'Yes, got here yesterday.'

'Alone?'

'Yes.'

'And you found yourself a woman straight away?'

'Yes.'

'A woman whose house burns down almost immediately.'

Nyman looked to his right.

'The house seems fine, thank goodness.'

'Is that what it looks like to you?'

Nyman thought he understood the man. They were local police officers who still hadn't got to the bottom of the homicide in Olivia's house. Which, in turn, was why he had been sent to wrap up the matter. And here he stood, outside that very same house, being informally interviewed by that very local officer, unable to tell him just what an extraordinary set of coincidences was at play here.

'Looks like it could do with a bit of sprucing up,' said Nyman.

'A bit of sprucing up, that should do it,' said the officer.

'Can I go?' asked Nyman, already taking a step forwards.

'Where are you staying?'

'Palm Beach…'

'The holiday resort,' said the officer. 'If we have any questions, we'll find you there, I take it?'

'Unless I'm out windsurfing.'

The officer looked him up and down. 'A windsurfer.'

That was a question too, it seemed.

'Not properly,' said Nyman. 'I'm a beginner.'

'And a pyromaniac? Beginner or professional?'

Here we go.

'I was with her,' said Nyman, nodding again towards Olivia, and thought of the man in the adjacent cottage with his microscopic swimming trunks. 'And there's a witness who will tell you I was at my chalet before that.'

'A witness?'

'Isn't that what they say?'

'If we suspect you of committing a crime, we might talk about witnesses.'

Nyman didn't reply. The officer stared at him for a moment longer, then turned his head, which Nyman understood as permission to walk away.

The officers of the Violent Crimes Unit at the Helsinki Police also investigated arson cases, and sometimes his own investigations had involved establishing where a fire had started. It had been a while, but the nature of fire hadn't changed, and Nyman had experience with many different kinds of fires.

The chief fire officer was a dark-haired, chubby-cheeked man with short, powerful limbs. He looked like an energetic young wrestler. Nyman came to a stop beside him. They were standing approximately in the middle of the yard, facing out to sea, with the house behind them and the soaked, gleaming, smoking ruins in front of them.

Nyman glanced around.

Olivia had gone inside the house, the police were standing by their patrol car at the edge of the yard, and the senior constable still had an eye on him. Nyman looked at the chief fire officer. He was clearly a man of action. With a man like that Nyman decided he could be direct.

'Looks like a powerful blaze,' he said. 'If she wasn't heating the sauna, the source of the fire must be elsewhere. Any electricity cables running out to the building?'

The fire officer gave a matter-of-fact nod. 'There's electricity in the sauna changing room, over there,' he said and pointed to the right-hand edge of the foundations. 'But electricity doesn't catch fire by itself. You need an electrical appliance too. And there weren't any. You'd be able to see where it melted. Over there is what's left of an old motor, and that means there might have been petrol in it. But petrol doesn't catch fire by itself either. And the other factor is how quickly the fire spread.'

Nyman knew what that meant. 'It wasn't smouldering for hours, like a cooker or a coffee machine might – warming things evenly over time.'

The fire officer shook his head. 'No, a sudden explosion, more like,' he said. 'And it happened right there in the middle where there's neither a sauna stove nor electrical appliances. It seems odd.'

'Why's that?'

The fire officer looked at him. 'There are millions of sheds in Finland. How many have you seen explode? All of a sudden, completely by themselves?'

5

Holma was genuinely confused. He was even slightly agitated. He took a sip of beer, read through the rules on the small sign by the bar and raised his hand. The waitress noticed him and walked down to Holma's end of the counter. He watched her approaching, and when she was right in front of him he gave her a full, beaming smile.

'Talent night,' he said and turned the sign so that the text faced the waitress.

She looked at him, not the sign, and pulled a pen out of her pocket.

'That's right. You want to take part?'

'No.'

'Another drink then?' she asked.

Holma looked down at his glass. He had only drunk a third of his beer, so he shook his head. The waitress stared at him. Holma couldn't tell whether her expression was quizzical or not. Maybe she always looked like that.

'I've read through these rules,' he said. 'There's a mistake.'

'A mistake?'

Holma pointed to the first section at the top of the sign. 'It says here, only one talent per performer.'

The waitress glanced at the sign. 'So it does,' she said. Her voice sounded uncertain. 'I haven't read it. Lasse came up with the rules.'

'Who's Lasse?'

'The owner.'

'Is Lasse here?'

'No.'

'So where is Lasse?'

'I don't know.'

'When will Lasse be back?'

'His next shift's on Tuesday.'

Holma looked at the woman. In other circumstances he would have made the conversation quicker, he thought. But that would require some privacy, and something sharp and sufficiently weighty.

'So who can I talk to about the mistake in the rules?'

The waitress was still holding the biro, clicking the nib in and out. She glanced behind her, then turned back to Holma.

'Me, I suppose.'

Holma nodded and gave her another quick smile.

'You make sure to tell Lasse about this, okay?'

She nodded. 'Sure.'

'There are some people…' Holma began and decided he should aim for utter simplicity. 'There are some people with more than one talent.'

The waitress said nothing.

'There are people,' he continued, 'with lots of talents.'

The woman was silent. She looked like she was listening.

'And there are some people,' he added, 'who have so many talents that they could perform all evening, moving from one talent to the next.'

She looked at him.

'So,' said Holma. 'On Tuesday, I want you to tell Lasse you need to change the rules.'

The woman said nothing. Then she nodded. 'I'll do that.'

'Thank you,' said Holma.

The waitress walked away, giving him a quick glance over her shoulder. Holma offered her the broadest smile he could muster.

He didn't believe her. She wouldn't tell this Lasse anything at all of what he'd said. Holma had seen the same thing a thousand times. People were untrustworthy. Behind his smile, Holma was furious. He tried to calm himself by thinking about what he'd done a few weeks ago to a woman who turned out to be a police informant. He'd taped her mouth and hands, left her dangling by her tied legs from a pull-up bar, and closed the door behind him – naturally without asking whether anyone was likely to come home any time soon or whether anyone else had keys to the apartment.

His mood lightened.

The power of positive thinking, he reminded himself.

He sipped his beer, turned to face the stage, and then he saw her.

◉

Personal Fitness & Super Dancing by Nea.

Holma read the pink-and-black sign several times, and still couldn't tell whether he knew what it was all about. But still: Nea – that part was easy to understand – had started some form of public aerobics class. The soundtrack was dance music, new and rhythmical, the lyrics something about a giant snake, an anaconda – there was much sighing, much moaning, a woman singing while speaking, speaking while singing, her voice a whistle, a whisper, a nasal drone. *Ohmygosh, lookatherbutt.* Holma knew what she meant. What a great butt it was. The singer repeated it a thousand times. An excellent choice of music.

Nea was dressed in what looked like a wrestling outfit with about as much fabric as there was cardboard in the coaster beneath Holma's pint glass. She was nubile, she had a sense of rhythm: jumping, gyrating, shunting, shimmying, pumping, pushing, grunting and grinding. She smiled throughout her routine, her white teeth gleaming like a row of miniature spotlights.

Holma thought of Pamela Anderson and the leather-clad Finnish celebrity of yesteryear playing the violin in a squatting position, and the two merged in his mind to produce an image of Pamela running in the waves of the Pacific with a Stradivarius in her hand.

Nea resembled one or both of them, but she was more tanned. Quite a lot more tanned. She was very tanned indeed. She was the most tanned white person Holma had ever set eyes on. He drank his beer, and his feet seemed to latch on to the beat of their own accord.

He'd dreamed of meeting a local beauty, and it looked as though his dreams had, at least in part, come true.

Nea seemed to have accepted the rule about one talent per performer. When the music stopped, she took a bow so deep that for a moment she entirely disappeared from view. When she reappeared she gave that broad smile again, dazzling at least half of the customers. Holma clapped his hands together and continued clapping as he walked towards talent night's dead-cert winner: *ohmygosh, lookatherbutt.*

◉

'Did you take any pictures?' asked Nea, the delicious, half-naked, tanned angel, once they'd sat down. Holma had offered to buy a bottle of champagne, but Nea replied that she'd just lost so many minerals that she needed a super smoothie to maintain her protein balance and plenty of zinc because it was good for the skin. Holma thought about this for a moment, processed everything he heard, shook his head in answer to the question about the photographs, and smiled. Nea looked at him with her bright-blue eyes set in her glistening, orange face like a pair of tropical fish in shallow water.

'Shame, I could have Instagrammed them,' she said.

Holma had no idea what she was talking about.

'You're the clear winner,' he said. 'Are you sure you don't want some champagne?'

'Problems with my magnesium,' she said and shook her head. 'It doesn't absorb properly. And alcohol has such a terrible effect on your B and D levels, your immune system suffers, your iron balance, everything. Anyway, it's protein time, thirty grams every two and a half hours – that's right now: papaya, soya, whey, amino acids…'

Holma smiled; he didn't understand a word. Nea squeezed thick green liquid into her mouth from a plastic bottle, swallowing in long, cumbersome gulps. Holma sipped his beer. It seemed to slip down his throat much more freely.

'I'm Sampo,' said Holma after placing his pint on the table. It wasn't his real name, of course, but under the circumstances it felt just right.

Nea looked at his outstretched hand, then held out her own. Her nails were long and shiny.

'Nea,' she said.

They shook hands. Holma didn't feel inclined to let go, but eventually released his grip.

'I'm on holiday,' he said.

'Here?'

He thought about this for a moment.

'Yes. Here.'

'I'm leaving.'

'What, now?'

'No, not now,' said Nea and rolled her blue eyes. 'Soon.'

'Why?'

'Oh, come on,' she said. 'You saw my show.'

'It was the best performance all evening.'

'You haven't seen the others yet.'

Holma glanced at the stage. The performer immediately after Nea was a middle-aged man with a beard. He was standing at a tall round bar table, frantically gluing matchsticks to one another, building something abstract. A woman sitting right in front of the stage was the only one of the approximately twelve customers in the bar actually watching the performance. But she was watching it all the more closely. All of a sudden she began barking instructions at the man: 'Cut, cut,' she hollered as though she was watching a football match. 'Cross! Press! Hold!'

Holma smiled at Nea. 'Where are you going?'

Nea shrugged her shoulders. Holma followed the movement of her bare limbs and liked what he saw more with every passing second.

'Somewhere,' said Nea. 'Somewhere I get a bit more respect.'

Holma tried to think of a place where Nea might get the respect she wanted. He couldn't think of any.

'What's stopping you?'

Nea looked at him. Holma got the distinct impression Nea was taking stock of him.

'Money,' she said.

Sometimes good ideas appear out of nowhere. Sometimes they require a muse. This time it was a combination of the two.

'How much?'

'How much what?'

'How much money do you need to get out of town?'

Nea glanced first right then left. She pushed her empty plastic bottle to one side – Holma thought it looked more like a storage box or a small bucket than a drink container – and leaned her elbows on the table. Holma found it hard to look anywhere except the spot where her wrestling singlet gave way under the pressure from her breasts. He forced himself to look at those blue, tropical-fish eyes.

'Loads,' said Nea. 'Like, megabucks.'

They sat in silence for a moment.

'What's that in numbers?' asked Holma.

Nea nodded.

'Well…'

She continued nodding. 'I don't know…' More nodding. 'At least…' The nodding suddenly stopped, as though Nea had reached her destination. 'Ten grand.'

The woman in front of the stage was wildly clapping her hands. The man proudly presented his matchstick structure. Holma thought it looked like a banana. Or a gondola. The Eiffel Tower. He leaned forwards.

'Can I speak in confidence?' he asked Nea.

'You want to tell me a secret?'

'It could be a secret. Our secret.'

Nea sat quietly and waited for him to continue.

'There was a tragic death here a while ago. A man broke into a house and…'

'I know,' she said. 'Some kind of Hannibal Lecter, they said, a real sicko, he was going to rape her.'

Holma thought of Antero. If there was one man in the world who didn't resemble Hannibal Lecter, it was Antero.

'And the man died in that house,' he said.

'She's my colleague, you know,' said Nea. 'The woman that lives in that house.'

Good, thought Holma and nodded. 'I'm a lawyer representing the deceased man's family. We are prepared to offer ten thousand euros for information that leads us to the guilty party so we can wrap up this case.'

'Ten grand,' said Nea, and thought about it for a moment, her eyes gazing somewhere into the distance. 'Wow.'

On the stage a red-haired woman was tying a length of white rope between two timbers, apparently with the intention of walking along the rope or performing some kind of acrobatics. Given her advanced stage of inebriation, the performance was sure to be an interesting one.

'That's the amount you said you needed, right?' said Holma and smiled.

'I don't know…'

'But, if you happen to hear anything, discover anything…'

Nea straightened her back. Holma saw how her muscles shifted, tensed beneath her skin. Like a predatory cat preparing to launch into a gallop.

'Aah,' she sighed.

'Looks pretty heavy, that big sports bag of yours,' said Holma with a smile and saw out of the corner of his eye that the woman who had climbed up on the rope was now thrashing her arms in the air, then she disappeared from view. He heard a crash. 'I can give you a ride home if you like. My new black BMW is just outside.'

6

Cold, cold, cold.

Jan Nyman stood in the morning chill of the water and listened to the instructions. Standing still was easy, and in fact almost unavoidable, and there were several reasons for this. Despite his wetsuit, he was freezing cold. The water in which he was staggering up to his waist surrounded him like congealing jam. The sensation must have had something to do with his wetsuit, which made the water feel like something other than water, and Nyman wasn't sure whether he liked it or not.

The sun was given no chance of warming him. Clouds hung in two layers: lower down was a thin gauze the breadth of the horizon, and above that a grey wall, so dense and massive that it looked almost solid. Nyman squinted and looked up above the boughs of the trees; he could have been forgiven for thinking it was October.

The day resembled others like it – days when Nyman started doing something only for the weather to let him know what it thought. He recalled his wedding day, which was supposed to be filled with spring light. Instead, hailstones rattled down from the April sky, sharp and heavy, like tiny Swiss Army knives cutting at their cheeks as they tried to pose for the photographer.

Last night's events disturbed his concentration too. He had waited for an opportunity to speak to Olivia Koski, but she hadn't given him the chance. Olivia had come out of the house and into the garden, spoken to the fire chief one more time – Nyman hadn't caught a word of their conversation – then simply wished him good night. *Thanks for the taxi, maybe see you tomorrow.*

Nyman could read between the lines. He took the gentle hint, left the yard and walked back towards the centre of the small town, then on to the resort.

That morning he'd woken in his neon-green chalet with a blocked nose, and he suspected Tubbs might be riddled with mildew.

The third factor causing him a degree of chill was what he knew in general and what he knew about Olivia Koski in particular. She was penniless. Olivia had used the last of her savings to take out a substantial insurance policy covering both the house and all the buildings in the yard. Soon after signing the policy, the plumbing in the old house had given up the ghost. Olivia had told him this herself. Then, within only a few hours, the insured outhouse – a shed complete with sauna and various other contents – burned to the ground. And Olivia Koski was conveniently and verifiably somewhere else at the time.

Nyman knew that even if it was later proven that the fire was started deliberately, there would be no way of proving that Olivia had started it. It simply wasn't possible; the timing was off. The fire had spread very rapidly. According to the fire chief's initial assessment, it had started and spread from a location where there was neither an electrical point nor any source of an open flame, such as a sauna stove, a hearth, an oven, or a washing machine that might have caught fire; and in Nyman's experience, such a fire could only have been started on purpose and *in situ*.

That said, the fact that the fire was lit deliberately meant that Olivia Koski either did know about the fire or she did not.

Under different circumstances Nyman might have thought nothing of it: saunas burn down and barns explode all the time. Finns rarely express their emotions, but when they do, they really mean it. He might have thought it was just bad luck that Olivia Koski had been the target of a prank or petty vandalism, someone calling in an old fishing debt or a jealous, hapless lover taking revenge after being spurned.

But this was the same yard where a man had been murdered only two weeks earlier. And now it had been ravaged by a ferocious blaze. The distance between the two locations was thirty-five metres. What was the likelihood that events of this nature could take place both inside and outside the house without the owner's knowing anything about them? Pretty slim.

If Olivia Koski really did know nothing of either incident, she would be understandably confused. But she didn't seem confused. And if, on the other hand, she did know about it, she must have had connections to people who ... had carried out her instructions, which in turn meant that Olivia Koski was leading an operation aiming at ... what exactly?

Nyman kept his hands on his board, palms down, and stared at the back of his hands. They looked the way they did in November when he'd forgotten his gloves: ruddy and slightly shrunken. He tried to sense his other extremities, recalled a simile involving a shrimp with an eye infection and quickly thought of something else.

◉

Jan Nyman wasn't a natural windsurfer. More to the point, he didn't have the faintest idea who in God's name would be. The board was a three-metre stretch of hell: both light and wobbly like a cork in a wine bottle, and stiff and unyielding like a strip of pavement the same length. The wind was always coming from the wrong side of the sail, no matter where he tried to position the stretch of white-and-red fabric. What's more he unfailingly seemed to lean in the wrong direction. He either fell on top of the sail or ended up underneath it. He conceded that it would be best to listen to his teacher's advice instead of thinking about other matters, about work.

His teacher – a friendly young man who didn't hesitate to grab Nyman by the buttocks and press his thumbs deeper than Nyman thought was entirely necessary to maintain his balance – guided him through the basics until they both agreed that was enough for one day. They looked at the large black-and-white clock on the wall of the pastel-blue beach house and wearily nodded at one another.

Nyman didn't quite manage to thank the teacher. It might not have been possible at all. His face was frozen stiff and there was a distinct sensation in his backside – as though someone was diligently trying to advance further than necessary. Who knew windsurfing was a full-on contact sport?

Nyman carried his board into the shed, shivered with cold and looked out to sea.

A grey-blue sheet of cloud, a few Optimist dinghies with small white sails that looked almost like optical illusions, a solitary swimmer in a woolly hat slowly progressing with a calm breaststroke. Nyman knew the beginning was always like this, that it felt like you couldn't get the hang of anything. It happened every time he started a new case; the first few days always seemed futile, yet they were unavoidable. They often contained something that later turned out to be important, something that in a new light ended up explaining what simply hadn't made sense before. And now, for the moment at least, it seemed as though Olivia Koski was pulling the strings behind the scenes, as Muurla would have put it. And that meant Nyman would have to get close to her again.

He tugged his wet hair into some semblance of order.

He wanted to be honest with himself.

He would have tried to get close to Olivia Koski regardless.

7

Olivia Koski tried to stop her head exploding. She could feel the fuse slowing catching. She listened.

'At the end of the day,' came the woman's voice, 'it's a matter of the length of your employment, your current income and collateral. And, to be honest, none of these meet our criteria. So for that reason we will be turning down your loan application today. It's nothing personal.'

'Whose income, whose employment and whose collateral are we talking about?'

'Excuse me?'

Olivia knew this was pointless, every bit as pointless as the conversation she'd just had with the insurance company: *We won't cover arson attacks of this kind until we receive final confirmation from the police regarding the cause of the fire, and that usually takes around six months.*

'You said it's nothing personal, and yet you refuse me a loan on the grounds that I've only just started my crappy job, my income is a joke, and the house I could use as collateral – which I own – is falling apart at the seams and there's no running water.'

'I'm sorry,' said the woman, before asking gingerly: 'No running water at all?'

'I can still flush the toilet,' said Olivia. 'But I can only dream of having a shower.'

'As long as the drain still works, there's always hope.'

Olivia stared outside. Was that a car pulling up in the yard? She took the phone from her ear, listened for a moment but couldn't hear anything. She returned to her conversation.

'Is that the bank's official position? As long as the drain still works, there's hope? What happens once the toilet stops working and the shit quite literally hits the fan? Should I jump out of the window?'

Yes, there was a car outside, an expensive-looking one. Olivia walked from the hall into the living room in order to see better. Either the car was brand new or it had just been washed. Out of the car stepped a blond man whom Olivia didn't recognise. She realised she was only wearing a T-shirt and her underwear.

'Of course, the bank doesn't have a...'

'An official position when it comes to faeces,' said Olivia. 'As long as there's hope.'

'Well, how should I put it...?'

The man was standing in the yard and looking at the house, turning his head from side to side, clearly eyeing up the yard too. Olivia turned and walked into the bathroom.

'Thank you for your help,' she said into the telephone. 'After my morning coffee I'll try and produce something really hopeful and send it to you for assessment.'

She threw on her dressing gown. It instantly felt wrong. She was half naked and defenceless. At the same time it felt like a pointless thing to worry about. Except, of course, for the fact that there was a strange man at the door – and what was her experience of strange men in recent weeks? She pulled her dressing gown tighter round her body.

This dressing gown felt like one of the few things she could still trust. It was a large, sturdy, soft, warm friend that she had bought herself as a present when Kristian had forgotten about her birthday for what was to be the last time. God, she thought. It's come to this. My dressing gown is a friend – in a house where I can't even have a shower. She dropped her phone into the gown's deep pocket and tied the belt. She wondered whether to get dressed instead, but ended up asking herself why she should do anything at all.

She walked to the door and saw that the blond man was already making his way up the steps.

Strange features, she quickly thought to herself, then a second later decided perhaps he didn't have strange features after all – no, not strange at all, perfectly normal. Normal in an odd, cold way. Eventually her eyes fixed on his hair. His hairstyle might have been fashionable at some point. No, upon further reflection it had never been fashionable. It was only then that Olivia noticed the man's beaming smile, which looked more like a muscle exercise than an expression of benign friendship.

'Olivia Koski?'

Olivia looked at the man. Not exactly a chainsaw murderer, at least not at first glance. A black suit, a gleaming white shirt, no tie, shiny leather brogues.

'That's me,' she said.

'Excellent,' said the man. 'My name's Wilenius and I'm a solicitor representing the family of the man who met a tragic fate on this property.'

Olivia stood firmly in the doorway. 'Are you taking me to court?'

The man, the solicitor, seemed to ponder this for a moment. 'Why on earth would I do that?'

'I don't know,' said Olivia. 'It would fit the pattern of events today.'

The man placed his right foot on the next step. 'I don't want to take anyone to court. In fact I'm sure the matter can be resolved without getting the courts involved at all.'

'What matter?' Olivia caught herself asking, though she wasn't sure she wanted to continue this or any other conversation with the man.

'The matter of this unfortunate event. Getting to the bottom of it.'

'I don't know anything about it.'

The man looked at her. Olivia didn't know what to make of his gaze. It was hard to respond, not so much because it was aimed right at her but because it seemed to be missing something. The man's a lawyer, Olivia told herself, of course there's something missing.

'In the right company and after asking the right questions, we often find that we suddenly have the right answers. I have lots of experience of this. Good experience. Fantastic, even. So what do you say?'

Olivia leaned against the doorframe. 'About what?' she asked, genuinely perplexed.

The man smiled. Again it looked more like an athletic feat than an expression of a deep-felt sense of joy. 'About what I've suggested.'

'I'm not sure what you've suggested.'

'That we should talk.'

'It's not worth it. I already said so.'

'It might be worth it,' said the man and glanced back at his car. His gaze and smile returned with renewed vigour. 'We are prepared to pay ten thousand euros for information that leads us to the guilty party.'

Olivia felt the morning breeze against her face and hair, and looked at the man who was standing beneath her but who clearly wanted to take a few steps closer.

'Do you have a business card or something like that?'

'Of course,' said the man, raised his right hand to his jacket pocket and pulled out a small metallic case. He opened the case, took out one of the cards and handed it to Olivia. The card was made of quality material, the numbers and letters embossed on the front. The surname the man had given was one of three printed on the card, and in the lower left-hand corner was a golden company logo.

'I was just making some coffee,' said Olivia. 'Would you like some?'

◉

The coffee machine was spluttering in the kitchen: hissing, bubbling, wheezing as the water ran out and the machine could only gasp for air. The solicitor was sitting at the kitchen table, his back startlingly straight, his right hand on the table, his left somewhere out of sight. He looked around, his head moving slowly.

Through the window behind him the grey day was beginning

to take on different shades, a hint of blue and something lighter, perhaps a cloud penetrated here and there by the sun.

Olivia took two mugs from the cupboard and brought them to the table. She returned to the coffee machine, turned and looked at the man. His gaze shifted from somewhere near the cooker and fixed on Olivia.

'So you came home and found him dead?'

'Right there,' Olivia said as she pointed to the section of porch in front of the door and felt a shudder: a mixture of disgust, fear, confusion, annoyance. 'Of course, I didn't know he was dead.'

The man looked at the spot Olivia's finger had indicated.

'Tragic,' he said.

Olivia waited for the solicitor to add something, but he remained silent. She picked up the pot, poured coffee into the mugs. She hesitated, feeling uncomfortable dressed only in her dressing gown – after all, the man sitting across the table was in a suit – then thought how much more comfortable this was than sitting in front of Jorma Leivo in a swimming costume.

When exactly had her life become such that these were her only options: a swimming costume or a dressing gown? Because that's what had happened. That's the way it was. And at that Olivia came to another realisation and understood with the utmost, unshakeable certainty that she was desperate. That she had to come up with something. *Anything at all.*

Olivia sat down at the other side of the table and listened to the man's questions, which she answered as she had done many times before. She paid attention to the way the solicitor spoke. He sounded almost like the police. It was natural. She thought for a moment. The clarity she'd found only a moment ago was still there. Somehow it seemed to have combined with the morning breeze – cool and direct as it caressed her face. It hadn't disappeared.

Anything at all.

That's what she'd thought a moment ago.

Once the man had all the answers he required, Olivia spoke.

'The information that leads to finding the guilty party. How do you define that? You want the actual person? His name?'

'Preferably.'

'What about the money?'

The man looked at her and smiled. Olivia wasn't sure a smile suited lawyers. The smile seemed out of place given the rest of the man.

'Ten thousand euros.'

'You've already said that. But how do you deliver it? Cash, bank transfer, before or after?'

The solicitor paused for a moment.

'Does this mean you know who killed Ant— the victim, after all?'

Olivia shook her head.

'I was just thinking that if I were to find out and tell you, seeing as you represent the family, then there's no guarantee you would actually pay me. You would have the guilty party and that would be the end of the matter. Why would you pay me anything?'

'We are ... The family I represent is very honourable.'

'So am I,' said Olivia. 'But I still don't have enough money to sort out my plumbing. No matter how noble and honourable I am, I've still got no running water.' Olivia nodded towards the sink. A litre-and-a-half bottle of mineral water was standing on the counter. 'I even have to make coffee with Evian.'

The man looked at her.

'What I mean is,' Olivia continued, 'your word isn't really good enough.'

'I'm listening,' he said, and Olivia could see that he meant it.

Olivia leaned her elbows on the table. She was wrapped tightly inside her dressing gown. She could behave like this, operate like this: the clarity of a moment ago had reminded her of every euro she had spent on men – all that money, and now she had precisely nothing to show for it. Men had always taken her to the cleaners in the past. What if her luck was about to change, or if she could take destiny into her own hands and make her luck change?

'Let me explain,' said Olivia. 'I spent my entire childhood and youth in this small town. I came back a few months ago. Nothing has changed, except for the fact that nowadays it's called Palm Beach Finland. I've found a dead man in my kitchen, and my shed has exploded. Apart from that everything is as it always was. I know everyone. If I put time and energy into this, I'm sure I'll unearth something. And once I find something, I'll find out the rest. You can trust me,' she said and nodded again at the bottle of mineral water. 'If I don't find out what happened, there'll be no running water.'

The solicitor looked at her. Then he smiled again. No, it really didn't suit him. Olivia waited.

'You want to see the money?' he said.

Olivia shook her head, keeping her gaze fixed on the man's eyes.

'You don't want to see the money?' he asked.

It's as though inside this man there were two different men, thought Olivia. One came in the door in a stylish black suit with gold-embossed business cards and eager to negotiate with her, while the other was frightened of negotiations, almost as though he wanted the situation to run aground, wanted to take it all back. On the other hand, this pattern of behaviour suited about ninety-eight percent of all men. All the men she had encountered in the last thirty-nine years, that was.

'Let me make a suggestion,' said Olivia. 'You can take it or leave it. I've explained my situation. I need some money. As you can see.'

The solicitor's eyes moved towards the water bottle on the counter. Excellent, thought Olivia.

'I live here. I'm not going anywhere. You can always find me here.'

The man turned to look at her again.

'Ten thousand euros, up front, and I'll find you the guilty party.'

'You want the money,' he said.

'In cash.'

I'm dealing with building contractors here. Olivia decided not to say that out loud. It was none of the honourable family's business how she used their money.

'It's a large sum of money,' he said.

'By tomorrow,' said Olivia and stressed her words. 'I guarantee you nobody knows this town as well as I do.'

It was true enough. The solicitor knew nobody, but Olivia knew … lots of people. The man had placed both his hands on the kitchen table and relaxed his clenched fists. Olivia tried to read what was happening to his expression, but again his facial features seemed to blend into the background and the cautiously blue morning dawning outside.

'And what happens if you don't find the culprit?' he asked suddenly.

'I'll sell the house,' she said. 'I've already had an offer. Then I'll repay the money. See you tomorrow then?'

8

Falling in love, thought Jan Nyman as he gingerly sat on the bicycle saddle, is strictly out of the question. But taking a shine to someone, that's ... negotiable. It's negotiable because, with regard to the successful completion of his brief, it was decidedly advantageous. And if it happens naturally, so much the better. Nyman tried not to think about what would happen afterwards. The truth, the deceit, being found out, the emptiness, the loneliness, the next assignment. All at once, with all the trimmings.

If Nyman felt battered and bruised and worn out for other reasons, he could say the same about his rented bicycle. The bike, with five gears, drop handlebars that looked like a set of antlers, and a scratched grey-steel body, had been excellently repaired, but its cogs and proportions were oddly cumbersome, as though they were actively preventing him from pedalling and moving forwards. Which in turn...

You're talking about something else entirely.

Tuula's words.

Nyman reached his destination, jumped off, flicked the kickstand into place and left the bike standing. The petrol station building was a long low-rise building painted a light shade of green. Built in the 1970s, the proprietors seemed to have put a lot of effort into maintaining it. The paintwork was impeccable and floral curtains dotted with violets ran along the lower edges of the café windows. Nyman stepped inside, saw the person he had come to meet, and for a moment forgot all about Olivia Koski.

Muurla was in light summer attire, sitting at a table by the window and facing the room. Through the window was a view of the door of the carwash and behind that a hedge fluttering in the breeze. Nyman cracked open his can of lemonade, poured the fizzing drink into a glass and assumed a more comfortable position in his chair. The chair was hard. After the bike ride all chairs felt hard. Muurla looked like he was dressed for a fishing trip, right down to the lure hooked to his shirt pocket.

Nyman glanced around him. 'I've cycled eight kilometres.'

'No phones, you know how it is.'

Nyman decided not to point out that they shouldn't be meeting in public either. He took a sip of lemonade and realised quite how thirsty he was. Eight kilometres of bone-dry, grey country lanes – and it felt like it in his mouth and throat too. From the chair next to him Muurla picked up a plastic folder containing a pile of papers and photographs. He slid the folder across the table to Nyman.

'The guy in the kitchen. He's been identified.'

The rap sheet read like a tabloid newspaper: just as long, just as full of bizarre occurrences and events. It was hard to believe that one and the same man was behind it all. The thing the crimes all had in common was their pettiness – small enough to warrant a criminal record but not a stretch in prison. Just as noteworthy was how often the man had been caught. Judging by the list this must have happened in almost every instance. It looked like the man hadn't managed to pull off any of his stunts, not even a simple kiosk robbery, let alone any bigger crimes.

The man had been in prison only once. He had undertaken a money-printing scam by paying for a high-end laser printer with a forged credit card. His newly printed bank notes were tens on one side and twenties on the other. These he used to pay for a holiday for one in the sun, which he booked using his then-girlfriend's passport. Fair play, she was similarly dark-haired, gaunt and wore glasses, but still.

Nyman flicked through the rest of the papers.

Attempted shoplifting: an eiderdown jacket stuffed down the front of his jogging bottoms.

Minor narcotics misdemeanour: attempting to sell low-grade marijuana to two undercover narcotics investigators having lunch.

Selling stolen goods after a decidedly one-sided robbery: listing three hundred hammers on eBay, each item individually but all with the same user name.

Attempted robbery: threatening a taxi driver with an ice-hockey stick, seizing his bag of money then hailing the same taxi as a getaway vehicle thirty seconds later.

And the list went on.

Nyman gave him points for initiative and energy. He leaned back and thought about it. The petrol-station café smelled of fried eggs. They were the only customers. The man who had been standing behind the counter in a pique T-shirt and with thick golden bracelets had disappeared. From the speakers came the plastic sound of generic pop music as a female vocalist promised them that life could turn into a party at any moment.

Nyman took another look at the man's photograph. The name Antero Väänänen didn't ring any bells. Nyman replaced the pile of documents in the folder and slid it back to Muurla's side of the table. He was about to say what he thought of it all when Muurla spoke.

'The first summer was tough. I went on one of those singles' cruises. They had a game where you put your name tag in a big tombola, then they matched up two names and reserved you a table at the nightclub. So … my date's name is Teija. Quite a stunner but shy at the same time, talks in a whisper – which is a bit of a problem when you're in a nightclub. I miss half of what she says, but thankfully she's got her lips right up against my eardrum. And she doesn't mess about. We're sitting there talking and knocking back blue angels. Then she really goes for the kill, says maybe it's time we went up to her cabin. I suggest we go for a walk in the moonlight, seeing as the moon's shining and there's the sea and that. Out on the deck we start kissing, there in the shadows. She starts pulling me. It's a hot night. She's got strong hands, plays tennis, apparently. We get into her cabin, and I do my best. There's only so much you can do on a cramped bunk in the pitch dark. Once we're done Teija says she wants to sleep alone, says she hasn't been able to sleep with other people since her divorce. I take the hint and leave. When I wake up the next morning, I look out at the IKEA landscapes passing by and I think of Teija. It's done me good. I go down to the duty-free shop, buy a box of chocolates and head back to Teija's cabin. I remembered the number; I didn't have too many of those blue angels, too sweet for my taste, and I'm not sure there's much liquor in them anyway. The door's open. Teija is already packed and her suitcase is standing by the mirror, a battered old Samsonite from the nineties. The toilet door is ajar too. Teija is in there. She's got short cropped hair and there she is, having a piss standing up. I leave the box of chocolates on the table and wander off into the Old Town in Stockholm. Charming place, lots of history and good food. It was a start, the singles' cruise. I'd recommend something like that for you too.'

Nyman had been watching the swaying of the hedges outside. He turned and looked at Muurla. 'This guy wouldn't know the meaning of the words "professional crook",' he said and tapped the place on the table where the papers had been a moment ago. 'But it certainly begs a lot of questions.'

Muurla cleared his throat as he returned from the Old Town in Stockholm to the Finnish summer, to this table. 'What kind of questions?' he asked.

'The guy's been so busy he's probably never met a civilian in his life – in his adult life, at least. His human contact is limited to security guards, the police and the authorities. And when you read that, you realise something else too. Someone is protecting him.'

'Meaning?'

'There's a professional nearby. By his side, in front of him, behind him, who knows? Helping him whenever he gets himself into a jam.'

'A professional wouldn't touch a mastermind like this with a bargepole,' said Muurla. 'It's a dead end.'

'He might,' said Nyman. 'If he had to.'

'And what does that mean?'

'I don't know yet,' said Nyman. 'There's a limited number of people of interest. I've made progress with all of them. It's a slow business, as always. You have to wait for the right moment, for a situation to arise naturally. Right now I'm interested in Jorma Leivo.'

'What about the woman, Olivia Koski?'

Nyman looked out at the hedgerow, watched as the bushes fluttered against one another.

'Interesting,' he said and turned to Muurla. 'Jorma Leivo has renamed the place Palm Beach Finland. Do you know why?'

Muurla shook his head.

'Me neither,' said Nyman. 'But I plan to find out. The beach is as cold as a witch's tit. The rental chalets and other buildings look like they've just stepped out of an eighties discotheque. My chalet is called Tubbs. Jorma Leivo thinks the place is soon going to overtake Nice. I have the distinct feeling there's something I haven't quite understood yet.'

Muurla paused for a moment. 'When will we know more?'

'A few days, a week,' said Nyman quickly, and suddenly realised two things.

Naturally, the estimate he'd just given Muurla was pulled out of thin air. Furthermore, he had a number of thoughts regarding Olivia Koski, some of which had prevented him from telling Muurla what had happened. For instance, the fact that Olivia Koski might have recently blown up her own shed.

And as he remembered what he'd been thinking as he'd arrived at their meeting, the mental struggle he'd endured, Nyman thought of the difference between taking a shine to someone and falling in love with them, and how firm or flexible or wafer-thin the boundary between them might be. If you were to cross that boundary, was there any way of returning to the other side?

Nyman ran through a hypothetical scenario: Olivia Koski prepares the fire in the shed herself, douses the place in petrol, throws in a match, then sits down opposite him half an hour later, smiling and sipping her white wine. Nyman could see her brown eyes, hear her laughter, and he didn't care about the image of a blazing shed in the background. Why? he wondered. Why doesn't this bother me?

Nyman thanked Muurla, wished him a happy fishing trip, and returned to his bicycle.

9

Women, thought Chico. They were everywhere.

The thought, which at first had caused him joy and more often than not a faint tingling sensation, had now turned heavy, exhausting even. Women really did find their way into every facet of his life, and in one way or another every one of them had a surprise in store for him.

That morning it was Marjukka who had provided that surprise by informing him she wanted him to move out. How could someone do a thing like that after only one week? Even jobs had a trial period – so he'd heard – and that was often months long. He'd mentioned this to Marjukka, but she'd flown off the handle straight away: *Oh, so you work here now, do you? Doesn't much look like it to me, you don't lift a finger, you just lie on the beach all day, your face burned, then you come home stinking of petrol, probably careering around on a motorbike, having fun and games with some biker girl.*

Chico couldn't say he'd never so much as seen a motorbike, and he couldn't say that he and Robin had blown up a lawnmower and burned down an entire building. He didn't even say that living with Marjukka felt like hard work. Because Chico was a negotiator, he tried to steer the course of the conversation by suggesting a candlelit dinner at the beachside restaurant – if Marjukka could lend him the necessary funds, seeing as he was suffering from an acute lack of liquidity – but she wouldn't relent and instead started throwing his things around, first into the hallway, then out of the front door, and finally off the balcony. The last of these made Chico run outside. His Lidl underpants didn't quite fit his carefully cultivated image.

Now Chico was standing beneath a pine tree with a sports bag at his feet and his guitar case leaning against the trunk.

He was wearing far too much. It wasn't a particularly warm day, the wind was whipping in from the sea and he was quite near the shore, but he was wearing both a hoodie and a denim jacket because they didn't fit in his bag. Chico looked out to sea. Perhaps dreams are like waves, he thought, sometimes they are high, sometimes just little shimmers that only happen when it's utterly still.

It was thirty metres to the back door of the beach restaurant. The door was open. Robin saw him and started walking his way. He took a few calm steps, looked around, sped up and gathered pace, which made him stumble all the more. The terrain was uneven – the roots of the pine trees jutted from the sandy ground. Robin looked as though he was doing something particularly demanding. He finally arrived beneath the pine tree, and Chico could see his agitation.

'Nea's coming,' he said. 'She wants something.'

Chico couldn't help but return to the idea of women coming at him from all directions.

'What does she want?'

'She didn't say, just said she wants to meet us because we know people.'

'Who do we know?' asked Chico. 'Who do you know, for that matter?'

Robin looked at Chico. Chico realised that his tone of voice had been mean, frustrated. He knew things like that frightened Robin.

'Marjukka threw me out,' he explained. 'I'm a bit tense.'

'You can stay at my place,' said Robin.

Robin had offered this before, but Chico just couldn't bring himself to take him up on the offer. There were several reasons. One was that Robin was a bit too ... *laissez faire* for his liking. Chico didn't think it was right for two guys to sit next to each other on a couch watching TV together if one of them was only wearing a pair of underpants. But Robin simply stripped off his clothes if he was too hot.

'Thanks, Robin. I'll be fine. Did Nea phone you?'

'Yes,' Robin smiled.

'Why?'

'She wants to meet up, because we know—'

'Robin,' said Chico. 'Why did she phone you all of a sudden? You haven't told her anything, have you? You didn't mention anything about recent events, did you?'

Robin shook his head. Chico wondered what this was all about. It was difficult. He was a problem solver, but sometimes problems were … complicated.

'Nea's coming, let's go with her,' said Robin.

Chico looked towards the car park. Nea's sunglasses – a pair of aviators – were the most concealing item of clothing she was wearing. The mirrored surfaces reflected the sunshine in their direction. Her brown thighs were gleaming. Chico heard Robin make a low-pitched guttural sound and smack his lips. One day he'd tell Robin not to do that. But this time he asked simply:

'Where is she taking us?'

◉

Again they passed the bright, garish lights of the Palm Beach Finland signpost. Chico noted how seamlessly Nea's attire seemed to blend with the sign. It was as though the sheer surfaces, Nea's glowing skin and the sign's chemical coating had combined for a moment, as though the colours and shades strengthened and enhanced one another. It was like fireworks in the middle of the day, like a flashing music video. Then they turned, walked through the park, crossed another road and went downhill along the cycle path until they arrived at a narrow dirt track.

Chico was relieved he'd dumped his guitar and sports bag in the staffroom at the beach restaurant. This amount of exercise would have been impossible carrying all that stuff. The instrument and bag felt so heavy that it was hard to think of the weight in kilograms. Besides, today of all days, carrying his stuff around left him with the niggling feeling that people might ask how he was doing – a question to which even he didn't have an answer.

'What's happened to your faces?' asked Nea as they walked along the side of the cemetery.

Chico nudged Robin in the ribs and made sure his hand remained behind his back, out of sight.

'Nothing,' Chico replied quickly. 'Nothing has happened.'

He'd already forgotten all about it, all except the heat and exertion. The wind and the morning air had cooled his face, and a storm was raging inside him, distracting his attention from everything else. Their faces really looked burned. Or if not exactly burned, then certainly flambéed. That was the word Robin had used. Chico wasn't sure whether this was the sort of thing you should tell people. It didn't sound especially cool. *Oh, my face? It's flambéed.*

'You told Robin you wanted to meet,' he said.

Nea's sunglasses gleamed, her pouting lips gleamed, her face gleamed.

'A few weeks ago … the guy that turned up dead at Olivia's place,' said Nea, and Chico could see she'd chosen her words carefully. 'I wondered if you'd heard anything about it.'

Chico gave Robin another sharp nudge in the ribs.

'Why would we have heard anything about it?' he asked. 'Except what everybody else has heard. Everybody was talking about it, but not so much now. Hardly anyone's talking about it. I mean, it's still unsolved. Because nobody knows anything. Nobody's talking. Not a squeak.'

Chico stopped himself. That's enough, he told himself. Nea looked at him.

'I just thought, seeing as you two move in those circles.'

'What circles?'

'How should I put it?' Nea said and raised her hands, pulling her hair into a bundle on her head. Chico saw her breasts beneath her thin top. They were bigger than he remembered. Rounder. 'Rock 'n' roll circles. The underworld.'

Chico thought it best not to say that he'd been trying to find the town's underworld for the best part of thirty-nine years – and all he'd found was his one best friend, who right now was standing next to him, his brown eyes staring at a half-naked woman behind whom the gravestones rose and fell and the dead scurried around.

'No, I haven't heard anything, not from the underworld, and not from the rock 'n' roll crowd. Why do you ask? Have you heard something?'

Nea thought about what to say. Chico could see it. She had finished playing with her hair and let it fall back into place as she lowered her hands. She took the sunglasses from the bridge of her nose.

'I'm looking for the killer.'

'The killer's dead,' Chico snapped. 'You said so yourself.'

'I mean the killer's killer. The killer who died didn't get the chance to kill anyone. It's not that difficult.'

Chico had to think about this for a moment. Thankfully Robin seemed unable to do anything but stare ahead vacantly.

'I didn't know you were interested in the case. How come you're suddenly looking for the killer?'

'Why shouldn't I look for him?' asked Nea and turned to look at them. Behind her the birches in the cemetery swayed in the breeze. 'Why is it whenever I do anything everyone suspects I'm up to something? It was the same when I opened the food supplement shop. Everybody was like, who's going to shop at a place like that? Well, Robin came in every day and bought a large bag of protein powder, vitamins and minerals. Then he stopped coming in and the shop went bust. But that doesn't mean anything.'

Chico shook his head. Robin stared at the ground in front of him. Chico reminded himself that he was a problem solver.

'I don't suspect anything,' he said and hoped he could choose the right words. 'But, did you just come up with the idea one day? Have the police been asking anything? Or have you been in touch with the police?'

Nea gave him a quizzical look.

Fair enough, it isn't the police, thought Chico. It must be something else. But what?

Nea started walking again.

'Maybe we do know something,' said Chico.

That stopped her. Nea turned, looked at him and folded her arms: clench, thrust, display. The series of movements made looking at her breasts an entirely unavoidable course of action.

'I'm prepared to pay…'

The pause was long. Chico managed to pull his eyes away from her chest. He looked over Nea's shoulder; the sight of the headstones calmed him. It was hard to think about her gleaming breasts and their deceased neighbours at the same time.

'A hundred euros,' said Nea.

If Nea was prepared to pay to get to the bottom of this, that meant that … Nea must be getting something out of it. Money? Everybody was interested in money. But there was one thorny problem with this: Chico and Robin were the very people she was looking for.

'Five hundred,' said Chico, realising this was the surest way to move her suspicions somewhere else. 'Per head. That's a thousand in total. A thousand divided by two.'

Nea groaned, ran the pink tip of her tongue across her shiny lips and looked up at the sky. Chico realised he was witnessing something important.

'Okay,' she said. 'What do you know?'

She stuck her hands into her denim shorts. The pockets poked out beneath the shorts, the white tips peering out like mice against her tanned thighs.

'Where's the money?'

The words came out by themselves. It felt good. Chico was himself again.

'I'll pay,' said Nea. 'But I haven't got the money yet. I'll pay you later.'

Chico looked at Nea, then Robin, then Nea again. I'm the only sane one here, he thought. The thought gave him a good deal of satisfaction, and that satisfaction could be heard in his voice as he said:

'Pay us first, then we'll talk.'

10

There are plenty of us. I am not alone. Once word gets out…

Jorma Leivo checked the thermometer reading and gave a firm nod. To himself, as he was alone in his office, but also to some greater power that commanded the weather. Good work. The thermometer showed 13.5°C, the time was almost half past two, the warmest point of the day. Marvellous. Excellent. The Finnish summer. In an uncertain world, at least there was something people could rely on.

From the fridge in the kitchenette, Leivo fetched a can of energy drink and cracked it open. He gulped half the can of pineapple-flavoured juice as he carefully shuffled towards his desk. He stopped, looked at the piles of papers waiting for his attention, and emptied the can. An empty can in his hand and a pile of bills in front of him. His mood threatened to slip from triumph to irritation. It was beyond his control.

He needed an assistant, a secretary, a helper. Preferably three. That was clear enough. But not yet. There wasn't enough money coming in, but that would all change soon. The tide was turning.

Leivo sat down in his chair and turned to the window so that he could see a strip of the beach. Soon that beach would be full of people just like him, people that would finally understand their condition and seek out the optimal holiday experience. He craned his neck to see the lifeguards' tower. It was empty. He turned, found the rota on his desk and ran his finger along the paper until he found the right day and time. No surprise there, he thought: Korhonen was supposed to be on duty. And he wasn't.

They had torched the shed, thought Leivo. That was progress. He'd received a message on the phone he referred to as his operation phone. He didn't know what to think of Korhonen and his – what was the right word? – his partner, boyfriend, lover, but as long as they got the job done there was nothing to stop his plans from moving ahead.

Leivo looked at the empty watchtower for a moment. It was unlikely anyone would drown. There was nobody in the water.

11

Olivia Koski carefully placed a hand on the side of the sauna stove. It was warm. She turned her hand; it was black with soot. She looked around. All summer she had been telling herself that she would use one of her days off to tidy the shed and empty it out, to get rid of the old junk and do something with the building. *Problem solved:* it was her day off and the shed had well and truly been given an extreme makeover.

It didn't feel particularly good.

Olivia stepped cautiously, watching where she placed her feet. Her rubber boots had thick soles, but there were nails and sharp objects hidden beneath the mud and debris scattered across the yard. With each step came a crack, a crunch, a squelch.

Someone had burned down her shed. Before that someone had broken into her house and got himself murdered. Every time she started thinking about these things, every time she tried to work out what the hell was going on in her life, everything seemed to get more and more tangled. The more she thought, the tighter the knot became.

Last night, once she'd said good night to Jan Kaunisto – who was a nice, pleasant guy but who at that point in time was more of a distraction – she had tried to explain to the police that she was worried she no longer had any idea whatsoever of what was going on here, and asked straight out whether she needed some form of police protection and whether she was in imminent danger.

She didn't suggest the kind of thing she'd seen in films and on television. What was it called again? – when witnesses were given a new identity and relocated to a small town where somebody inevitably recognised them and they had to fight for their life and in the final scene, as the houses burned and the blood flowed, they were forced to shoot the bad guy who had driven them out of their home in the first place. Only then could they hug each other, regardless of any shoulder injuries sustained, and start to rebuild their lives.

Olivia wasn't quite that crazy. At least, she didn't think so.

But the police might have thought so. That was the impression she quickly got from them.

They started questioning her.

How do you know Mr Kaunisto? You can't think of any reason why the recent homicide in your house and the fire in your shed might be connected? Any difficult relationships recently? Have you been letting anybody live here? Do you know all your guests? Do you engage in any activities that involve fire, danger and strange men?

Yes, Olivia thought to herself, anonymous pyromaniacs really turn me on.

For God's sake, she'd replied, you're really asking me things like this? I ask you whether I'm in danger, you ask me whether I get excited at the thought of my shed burning down.

Olivia had lost her temper with them. Not entirely, but just enough. Enough for her body to start producing adrenalin, a protective shell, enough to spur her into action.

The conversation had continued for a while.

By the time the police explained that they hadn't meant it literally, it was too late. They had nothing to offer her. Olivia realised that. She'd had enough. And the annoyance was still there the next morning, making her wake up to the reality of her situation. It had made her think and act when Wilenius the solicitor had turned up to introduce himself and make his offer.

Olivia decided that if he really was about to offer her the ten thousand euros she needed to carry out the necessary plumbing renovations, she would get to the bottom of the matter. Abso-bloody-lutely. She had no other options. And there was another motivation too. That evening she had finally begun to realise – to accept – that the police considered her in some way suspect and maybe even guilty.

The thought made her livid. It brought together all her disappointments, all the times she'd gone against her best instincts: *Don't worry, I'll take care of it, I understand, maybe that's right, this time, I can do it.*

What a crock of shit.

Which reminded her what needed to be done first and foremost.

◉

Olivia spent the next four and a half hours in the old outhouse and its immediate vicinity. The work was sweaty, dirty, heavy. The outhouse hadn't been used for years. Luckily the original structure was sturdy, clearly built by someone other than her father or grandfather. She loved and respected them, but any outhouse they might have built would have collapsed under the pressure of the lightest of wipes – and not just of the building's surfaces

In recent years the small outhouse had been used as a storage space. There was so much junk everywhere that Olivia found herself wishing that whoever had burned her shed had burned this outhouse instead. Maybe not, though – now that the water was off for good. And anyway she had no idea what had been going through the arsonist's mind. They were sick people who, as the moustachioed police officer had insinuated, took sexual pleasure in starting fires. For whatever reason, burning the sauna offered greater pleasure than immolating the old privy.

Olivia emptied the back of the outhouse with a shovel. It was a peculiar mixture of decomposing matter – matter that had long since turned to earth – layer upon layer of old leaves (Olivia couldn't for the life of her understand how and why they had got there) and even some small pieces of junk. Once she'd managed to clean out the midden, she fetched a water barrel from the corner of the house, propped it in place and poured in some soil and a few spadefuls of old leaves. That was a start. She fetched some water from the shore and used that to wash the inside of the structure, giving every surface a thorough scrub. Eventually, at the end of her garden stood a relatively clean outdoor toilet...

...Where she was sitting with the door wide open – the smell of disinfectant was that strong, and she certainly wasn't expecting guests – when Jan Kaunisto pulled up in the drive on an old drop-handled Helkama. He looked her in the eyes from next to the charred ruins of the sauna, then looked down at his feet and seemed unsure what to do with himself or his bicycle. There he stood, still gripping the handlebars, as Olivia climbed off the toilet seat and walked into the yard. She was just resting, looking around, making sure she'd finished the job.

'It's all clean,' she said. 'Literally.'

Jan Kaunisto smiled, took that as a sign. He jumped off his bike and propped it on the kickstand.

◉

Jan Nyman looked at the woman holding the red bucket. Olivia's hair was tied in a loose ponytail, her T-shirt was partly stuck to her skin with sweat and her shorts were what might be called grandad-style. Her bare knees flashed above her black wellingtons. Nyman did his best not to show quite how pleasant it was to see Olivia Koski again. Well, *pleasant* was one word for it – Nyman hadn't even stopped off at his own chalet but had cycled straight out here after his meeting with Muurla. His legs were quivering with exertion.

'I was out cycling,' he said and gestured at his bike. 'And I was just passing.'

'On a dirt track that only leads to one place?'

There, thought Nyman. Straight to the point. Something had changed, he thought, and that something wasn't just to do with the bucket or the outhouse standing behind Olivia.

'Right,' Nyman admitted and cast a glance at the ruins. 'I just thought I'd pop in and see how you're bearing up.'

'The sauna and the shed have burned down. Someone died in my kitchen. I've just started using the outdoor toilet. Average day.'

Nyman was on thin ice, and he knew it. He had always been bad in situations like this, even with Tuula. She had always been telling him he didn't know how to engage with people, to encounter them. Perhaps it had something to do with the fact that he didn't know what those phrases meant.

'Sorry to hear that,' he said. 'Except the outdoor loo, that is. Good job you've got one.'

Olivia looked at him. Nyman didn't think she was trying to suggest he should leave, but she didn't seem overly enthusiastic at his presence.

'How's the windsurfing?' she asked suddenly.

'Cold,' he replied. 'I think I've made a new friend out of the teacher, though. Inquisitive fingers.'

Olivia looked as though she was thinking about something.

'When did you say you arrived here? At the resort?'

The question was direct, and Nyman could only think of two explanations. The first was that he, Nyman, had somehow become suspicious in Olivia's eyes, and that meant that Olivia Koski herself had nothing to do with the fire. The other explanation was, of course, that she had other reasons for asking.

'I had nothing to do with this,' he said and nodded at the ruins. 'I arrived yesterday, in the morning. I was in my chalet all evening, I chatted to my new neighbour then came to the bar, where I saw you. And I can honestly say that if I wanted to burn some of your property, I'd burn that old boat at the end of the yard, the one with a hole in the bottom.'

'It's a memento.'

'Then I probably wouldn't burn that either.'

Olivia seemed to inspect him. 'So why did you come here now?'

'I came to have a look,' he said. 'To make sure the fire had gone out properly, and if it hadn't, to help you put it out.'

Olivia Koski glanced at the ruins, swung her bucket and turned back to Nyman.

'The fire has gone out. But the coffee might still be warm.'

◉

They sat outside. Olivia was in bare feet, and Nyman noticed her toes rising and falling on the cropped lawn. A late afternoon by the shore, the soft glow of the sun slowly setting in the west, a hint of coolness in the air, the smells of nature: the sea, the trees, the plants, the flowers, the green lawn.

'You made coffee. Does that mean the water is on again?' asked Nyman.

'Mineral water, from the store. The plumbing company has given me a quote. Ten thousand euros.'

Nyman turned his head just enough to see the house. In the golden-red glow of the sun, it looked even more in need of repair. Ten thousand euros was just a sticking plaster.

'In the bar I got the impression you couldn't afford the renovations. So you *can* afford it after all?'

'Not yet.'

Nyman noticed how quickly Olivia gave her answer, how certain her voice was. He couldn't decide whether he should try and get a lengthier explanation out of her or bide his time. He didn't really have the luxury of either.

'Have you ever taken a real risk, Jan?' said Olivia, then turned and stared out to sea.

Nyman liked Olivia's eyes, but he liked her profile too. Did Nyman ever take risks? He took risks for a living.

'Depends how you define a real risk,' he said.

'A risk whereby you could lose everything you're trying to achieve.'

'That's quite a risk.'

'Have you ever done anything like that?'

Olivia turned back to face him.

Nyman shook his head. 'I try to avoid unnecessary risks,' he said. It was true, in its own way, once again.

He could see from Olivia's expression that she was expecting more.

'Maybe it's because I think life itself can be a pretty risky business,' he said. 'I mean, I've never understood bungee jumping or mountain climbing. Why increase your risk factor from what it already is? Everything we eat is dangerous, if you believe what you read in magazines that is; traffic can be fatal; every day thousands of people are diagnosed with cancer. Even going to work in the morning can prove a fateful decision. As for work – depending on what you do it can be very bad for your health.'

'It seems the life of a maths teacher is more dangerous than I thought,' she said.

'I just mean that life itself can be a risk.'

'So you think we shouldn't take risks?'

'I wouldn't say that,' Nyman replied, because there was something interesting going on here, both in the subject matter and the fact that Olivia had brought it up. 'Maybe the important thing is to know how big a risk you're taking, to make sure you're fully aware of the possible consequences. And if you're prepared to lose what you set out to achieve, then I suppose it's okay. Are you prepared for that?'

Olivia didn't answer immediately.

'What if you don't have any options?' she asked.

Nyman wanted to watch her more closely, scrutinise her reactions, but managed to hold himself back.

'Then it isn't really a risk,' he said. 'It's just something you have to do, without any prior knowledge of the outcome. Is that what this is about?'

He noticed that Olivia seemed to be watching him. Perhaps he was just imagining it. No, she really did look as though she was sizing him up, taking stock of him.

'But would you do it?' she asked. 'You haven't answered the question.'

Nyman looked away from Olivia's brown eyes. He could still feel her gaze on his face, he was sure of it.

'If my hands were tied,' he said. 'Yes, I would.'

Olivia shifted position, leaned back in her chair. For a moment they both stared out to sea. A swallow cut the sky in two. Nyman was going through the conversation in his head when Olivia turned back to face him.

'Tell me about your divorce. What was it like?' she asked, and Nyman couldn't tell whether it was just a note of curiosity in her voice or something more, something suspicious. And if it was suspicious, he assumed it must have something to do with his cover story. It felt … extremely disconcerting.

'Financially it was worth it,' he said eventually. 'My wife sold the apartment for a good price. She only told me about it as she slid the divorce papers across the table for me to sign. We were out having pizza. The pizzas had just arrived, steaming on the table in front of us. I can still remember what was on mine: walnuts, cherry tomatoes, gorgonzola and fresh rocket. It was a special offer.'

'What happened then?'

'I ate my pizza. I wouldn't recommend the combination.'

'I mean what happened then? To you?'

'Oh. I asked my wife – I suppose by this point she was technically my ex-wife – whether I'd done something wrong. She said yes, and asked me to pass the oregano. I signed the papers and the settlement appeared in my bank account.'

'Didn't your wife – your ex-wife – ever tell you what you'd done wrong?'

'Yes,' said Nyman. 'Many times. Many things: I never listened to her, I was never really there, always concentrating on work, not paying her enough attention; apparently I didn't encounter her as a person.'

It looked as though Olivia smiled. Either that or the light softened her features.

'What happened then?'

'I admitted she was probably right, because I wouldn't know how to encounter her as a person, whatever that means. As far as I was concerned I'd met her years ago in a bar. She said that's exactly what she meant. I paid for the pizzas, and rented the studio apartment where I still live.'

'Where's that?'

'On Pengerkatu in Helsinki.'

Nyman couldn't quite describe the expression on Olivia Koski's face. Something was going on in those brown eyes.

'Nice area,' she said.

'Very nice,' Nyman smiled and sipped his coffee. It was tepid. He drank it all the same.

'Do you ever eat at that Thai restaurant round the corner?'

'There are several, aren't there?' he asked.

'The one everybody knows,' said Olivia. Nyman noted how sharp her gaze was, though the rest of her body seemed relaxed.

'You mean Lemon Grass,' he said and stared back at her. 'Great coriander chicken.'

'That's the one,' said Olivia. 'You can't get decent Thai food round here. Which reminds me, I need to go to the shop. You can cycle with me if you like. I just need a change of clothes.'

Nyman watched as Olivia walked up the steps to the house, glancing back into the yard once she reached the door. It only lasted a split second, but he caught her gaze. Olivia Koski looked at him as though she were assessing something, calculating something.

12

Holma parked his car beneath the verdant trees outside a halal butcher's shop in Hakaniemi. Next to the shop was a kiosk. He stepped inside and bought a packet of ribbed condoms, a scratch card – in this life you always had to hope for the best – and a bottle of sugar-free fizzy orange. He tucked the contraceptives and his lottery ticket into his jacket pocket, opened the bottle of pop and looked around. The kiosk was bigger than it looked from the outside, a combination of café, second-hand store and betting shop. A television hung on the wall showing the results of various matches and competitions. Two men – both bald in strikingly identical fashion – were staring at the screen, their heads angled backwards, their gambling cards in hand. Holma thought of Antero. Antero was a gambling man. He played games in which the odds were always stacked against you. Holma gulped his fizzy orange and looked at the men. After a moment one of them sighed heavily, spun round in his chair and tore his ticket in half. He noticed Holma. Holma smiled back at him.

'Why do you play?' he asked.

The man looked at him as though he hadn't understood the question. His fifty-year-old face had lost its battle against gravity; his short-sleeved red-and-white stripy shirt bulged into an optical illusion around the stomach; his blue eyes stared at Holma, looking for something familiar.

'Who are you?'

Holma smiled.

'Why do you play?' he asked again.

'What's it got to do with you?'

'My brother used to play,' said Holma. 'I'm just interested.'

The man looked at him, shrugged his shoulders.

'You play to win, I suppose.'

'But you didn't win.'

The man glanced over at the shopkeeper, then back to Holma. 'Not this time.'

'What about last time?'

The man shook his head.

'The time before that?' asked Holma. 'When was the last time you won anything?'

The man was becoming irritable, Holma watched as he quickly shifted his weight to the other leg, shook his head and frowned.

'What's this about?'

'I'm trying to understand why people go out of their way to throw their money away. You know you're not going to win, but you still gamble.'

'I don't know.'

'That's your answer? You don't know?'

'You don't know either.'

'I know one thing. With absolutely certainty.'

The man looked at Holma. Something happened in his eyes. 'And you know who does win, do you?'

'I know who won't win,' said Holma.

'Who?'

Holma took a gulp from his bottle. In his own estimation, he was a person who naturally liked to help others. But sometimes there was simply nothing you could do. Holma glanced at the television screen, the list of forthcoming matches.

'Leverkusen,' he said.

The man turned. Slowly but surely. Holma took a few steps closer to him. They both looked at the rows of results on the screen.

'Away?' the man asked.

'Exactly,' said Holma. He could smell the man standing next to him: sweat, excitement, disappointment, the hunger for victory. 'I'd put a lot of money on it.'

◉

It was a windy afternoon, almost chilly. The blue of the sky seemed to deepen as Holma stepped between the tall, dark buildings rising up on all sides. A narrow road ran right through the western edge of the block. Holma walked along the left-hand side of the road, sunglasses over his eyes. The apartment he was aiming for was behind him. He allowed his eyes to scan across the courtyard, the parked cars, the row of windows in the building opposite.

A young student girl brought out her rubbish; the door of the bin shelter gave a crash that echoed round the courtyard. A man in a dressing gown was standing beside one of the doors smoking a cigarette. By the back door of a restaurant, a grocery-van driver was unloading a delivery, carrying boxes in through the narrow doorway.

Nobody moved the way the police moved, even when they were pretending to be civilians. Holma was sure he would be able to identify a police officer in a crowd of people anytime. The only risk appeared to be an apartment on the first floor of the building diagonally opposite his ground-floor apartment. There were two windows, and Holma had seen the figure of a man in both of them. It could have been chance, but if you knew how undercover drugs officers operated, the likelihood of it being merely chance dropped dramatically.

Fair enough, he thought. Given what I'm about to do, perhaps this is for the best. If and when everything goes to plan, people will think this was drugs related. Holma walked through the courtyard and out into the street, then went round the outside of the building, noted the tower blocks of Merihaka, and through the forest of houses could no longer see the building where he had been when he'd received the call that, in its own way, had brought him here now.

A holiday does you good, he thought. He felt free, he felt almost like he used to when he worked freelance – no boss, no time sheets, no weekly routines. His step was light, he didn't care about the summer breeze that cut through his silk suit. Now he understood why people liked holidays: new ideas and good, fresh thoughts came flooding into his mind. He made sure the switchblade was tucked out of sight beneath his belt by his lower back.

He crossed to the other side of the street. He was about to walk into a Chinese grocery store but realised that he didn't need any Chinese groceries, so he turned at the steps and remained standing on the pavement outside the store. In the middle of the road, between the lanes of traffic, was the door to an underground parking lot. It swallowed cars from the surface and spat them out onto the road again. Holma focussed his eyes on the front door of a light-yellow building across the square.

He shouldn't have known, but he did know. This made him suspect that quite a few other people knew too – even the police maybe. The drugs trade was like that: before long everybody knew about it. Thankfully the dealer was generally the last person to know about it. There would be plenty of cash in the apartment.

Holma recalled the conversation. At first he'd been surprised, almost taken aback at Olivia Koski's demands. He hadn't imagined anyone would take his offer so literally or that they would ask to see the money upfront. Ten thousand euros. Then he'd changed his mind: this could be fun, and wasn't that the point of a holiday? And so he had agreed with Ms Koski – he'd duly noted that she wasn't married – that he would come back tomorrow morning, show her the ten thousand euros in cash, and in return he would get information about who had murdered his dimwit of a brother. He would let Ms Koski keep the money for as long as it took him to find and punish Antero's killers. Once he'd taken care of them, he would return and reclaim his money, and depending on how Ms Koski dealt with the news, he would either use the ribbed condoms or do the deed without them.

Holma thought for a second. The dealer knew him. The only risk factor was the police. If they were watching the apartment, they would see him. If they weren't watching the apartment, there was no problem that couldn't be solved with a switchblade. Holma crossed the road at the pedestrian crossing and rang the doorbell. He waited for a moment, then rang again.

Eventually a man's voice came through the intercom. 'What?'

'A word,' said Holma.

'Who is this?'

Holma said who he was working for.

'I don't owe him a penny.'

'This is something else. More important. It's to do with you.'

'What?'

'Come on. I'm outside. Open the door.'

Silence. With junkies, paranoia and greed would always win the day, Holma counted on that. The door buzzed open. The most primitive instincts had triumphed again.

Holma listened to the sound of the stairwell, inhaled its air. He heard nothing, couldn't smell any perfume, cigarette smoke, food aromas or anything else. No movement, no people. He arrived at the door of the apartment, adjusted his jacket and rang the doorbell as briefly as he could. The door opened.

The man was about Holma's age, stocky and unwashed, a wannabe biker in a leather waistcoat. Moving quickly, Holma shoved the man deeper into the apartment, stepped inside and without hesitation sunk the switchblade into the man's neck. Holma yanked the knife towards himself, snapping the oesophagus and the carotid artery on the other side. He took a step back and watched as the man squirmed in the narrow entrance hall, blood spurting all around as he knocked into the walls on both sides, fell to his knees and died on the floor.

The apartment comprised two rooms and a kitchen. Everything in the apartment was covered in the same layer of grime as its inhabitant. The blinds were closed in all the windows. The living-room couch was so filthy that Holma would only have sat on it for a substantial fee. He took a pair of latex gloves from his jacket pocket and got to work. He examined the bedroom first. Judging by the piles of clothes across the floor, a woman lived here too – or was at least a frequent visitor. Holma turned over the mattresses and emptied the wardrobes, looking for a drawer, a loose section of wall panelling or something similar. The bedroom turned up a blank.

The dirty dishes in the sink looked like they'd been there since the war. The smell was like that of an underground cellar. Holma opened the drawers and cupboards, emptied everything onto the floor. He found a packet of macaroni from the Gorbachev era, but not what he was looking for. He rummaged through the kitchen cabinets and structures, feeling with his hands where his eyes couldn't see.

He returned to the living room. The only new and clean piece of furniture was an enormous flat-screen television. It was typical of crackheads. They watched gangster and action films, and eventually they started believing they too were gangsters and action heroes, behaved like it and either ended up in prison or took a switchblade in the jugular. Holma's attention turned to the sofa.

Could it really be this simple? He realised he'd left the sofa until last because it was so repulsive. Even he had his weaknesses. He walked up to it, lifted one of the cushions, threw it to one side to reveal a microwavable pizza – or more specifically a biomass that resembled one. He picked up another cushion. This one was heavier and lumpier than the first. As soon as he lifted it up, he knew he'd struck gold.

Holma transferred the money into a canvas bag he pulled from his jacket pocket. There was well over twenty thousand euros. It was a lot, but it meant the wannabe biker was only a mid-level crook. Which, of course, was the main reason he had come to serve as Holma's cash machine. Holma left the assorted capsules, pills and powders stuffed inside the cushion.

In the hallway Holma checked he had everything: the knife in a ziplock bag in his trouser pocket, the money in the canvas bag, and a latex glove on his right hand, which he used to open and close the front door.

13

Olivia Koski made sure that Jan Kaunisto really did go on his way. He jumped on his rented Helkama, which he'd left outside the supermarket, and pedalled off between the cars to the other side of the car park before cycling the wrong way down a one-way ramp to the road below. Olivia saw him go. Not staring, but as she stood there locking her own bike, taking the shopping bags from the basket attached to the carrier at the back, out of the corner of her eye she watched as his blue-green flannel shirt disappeared between the houses.

A maths teacher. Good-looking, attentive, able to laugh at himself. And somehow, not really there. Perhaps Jan's ex-wife was right when she'd talked about him not being present. Maybe he simply didn't know how...

If the story he'd told was the truth, she reminded herself. She'd been following Jan Kaunisto, her interest growing through the course of their conversation, and planted a carefully considered trap when the opportunity arose. As if she could ever have forgotten the coriander chicken at Lemon Grass. It seemed he hadn't forgotten it either.

Olivia stood by her bicycle a moment longer, dropped her shopping bag back into the basket, jumped on the saddle and pedalled off in the same direction that Jan Kaunisto had taken only a moment earlier.

The fact was, she did know a lot of people in this town. She had dismissed the thought; perhaps she hadn't wanted to think about how well she knew this town, or how well the town knew her. Not all of her memories were good ones, and the less pleasant memories related to her mother and how she had been treated.

Olivia's mother was ahead of her time, as they say. A manic-depressive artist trying to bring 1920s Paris to a small Finnish seaside town.

Unlike her mother's mood swings, which were clear for all to see, her artistry was a matter of interpretation. She painted only rarely, and even then it was without a brush. To put it discreetly, she used her body parts. Olivia's father was her mother's primary patron – an anonymous admirer that her mother talked about as she dreamily stared out to sea, a glass of red wine in her hand – and after buying the paintings he would send them with only the recipient's name and no return address all over the world, generally to people who had at some point thrust their business cards into her father's hand. Olivia found out about the scam just before she turned ten. Her father, who had seemingly loved her mother more than anything before or after, asked Olivia to keep it their little secret. And she did – for a year and a half. Then her mother died. Olivia never really found out what her mother had died of. An illness, her father said. An accident, her relatives said. A strange case, said a family acquaintance who visited from time to time.

The latter was the closest her mother had had to a friend in the entire time they had lived here. Olivia hadn't remained in contact with Miss Simola after leaving town. She either didn't know or couldn't remember Miss Simola's first name. But she knew where she lived: one of the furthest buildings high up on the hill in the district of Hiekkala.

The district was awkwardly built on a steep hillside, and looking from below it seemed as though the main entrances to the houses were in fact on the upper floor. Miss Simola's house was situated almost at the top of the hill, and beyond it began a stretch of unkempt woodland, which everyone called a protected area of natural beauty but was anything but. There was so much vagueness in this town, she thought, that it was hardly surprising somebody could just turn up and rename the place Palm Beach Finland. It was an indication of just how strange recent events had been that Olivia hadn't batted an eyelid at the new name.

The roads in and around Hiekkala were either up or downhill. Cycling this way, they were all uphill, and very steep. Olivia pedalled halfway up the hill, jumped off her bike and pushed it the rest of the way up. How did Miss Simola get up here? She must have been more than seventy, she must have been…

Miss Simola looked like Miss Marple in the TV drama. So much so that Olivia expected her to burst into prim, cricket-lawn English at any moment. But she did not. Miss Simola's leather brogues, her tweed skirt and white lace blouse were all immaculate, her hair was grey, just as curly as it always had been, perhaps even curlier on top, where her fringe rose in a grey, Elvis-like tsunami sweeping all before it. Olivia would have remembered her eyes anywhere; they were dark brown, like a pair of soaked almonds.

Miss Simola gave Olivia a vigorous hug, asked how she was doing (in Finnish), didn't listen when Olivia answered, and informed her that if Olivia had come to talk about her mother, she was ready. She had understood Liisa, and Liisa had understood her, and that, back then, and in a place like this, friends were few and far between, and for that reason they were all the more valuable. Miss Simola stressed that she was prepared to talk about anything. Quite literally. She could talk about everything now, and she did so, directly, face-to-face. She clearly relished the opportunity to talk. Especially about love between ladies.

'But Liisa wasn't very keen on gardening … not the type of gardening I like to indulge in, anyway,' Miss Simola added, as non-chalantly as if she really were talking about watering the hydrangeas. 'Not even a very well-tended *lady garden*.' Her eyes twinkled. 'But I didn't hold it against her.'

Olivia explained that this wasn't quite the reason for her visit.

Miss Simola kept her arm gently round Olivia as she guided her through to the veranda. Olivia felt awkward, but only for one reason: the woman's arm was only slightly longer than Olivia's forearm. Miss Simola was barely five feet tall, and felt so slight next to Olivia that it seemed she was being walked through the garden by a doll.

The garden was small and overgrown, as though all the flowers, bushes and various sprawling trees of a larger garden had been crammed into a small cube, which had then been shaken and opened only at the top. Olivia had to look directly up in order to ensure that she was still part of the same world.

They sat down on the veranda's white iron chairs, and Olivia could feel on her skin that here within the garden, sheltered from the wind, it was much warmer than elsewhere in the town; here there was a hint, a promise perhaps, of tropical weather. At the same time she found herself hoping that Jorma Leivo never found his way out here. He would doubtless rename the place Everglade and set alligators loose in the bushes.

'I imagined you'd come one day,' said Miss Simola.

'I should have come and said hello when I first got back.'

'It's understandable. You probably don't have many good memories of this place.'

'But of you, I do,' said Olivia. 'And you look ... wonderful.'

Miss Simola leaned forwards slightly, and said, her voice hushed: 'I'm expecting company.'

'I'll only take a minute of your time.'

'I didn't mean that. I'll always have time for you. I've been thinking of you.'

'Really?'

'Especially when they found that thief dead in your house.'

'Thief? According to the police he might have been a sexual predator who got into an argument with his accomplice.'

'Nonsense, dear. He was a thief, plain and simple. Nothing more, nothing less. The whole matter seems nothing but a confounded mess. Men behaving badly, if you ask me.'

'I am asking you, actually,' said Olivia.

Miss Simola waited a moment, her eyes fixed on Olivia. Olivia could see a smile descending from her eyes and reaching her lips, her cheeks.

'You don't trust the police to get to the bottom of things?'

'I do, I think. But yesterday I got the impression they suspected me of something. If not of killing that man, then of something else. It felt quite unpleasant. And then...'

Olivia thought for a moment. No, she wouldn't mention the offer of ten thousand euros. Or was it an agreement? Maybe not, not before she had the money. Perhaps this was the no-man's-land between offer and agreement.

'It's just that…' she began and saw that Miss Simola was listening. It felt good. 'I remember my father used to say that nothing happens round here without Miss Simola finding out about it.'

'You want to get to the bottom of it yourself,' said Miss Simola, her intonation not rising at the end of the sentence. It was not a question.

Olivia stared at the woman's brown eyes.

'You remember our house. It needs renovating from top to bottom. I've starting using the outhouse again, because there's no running water. Yesterday my sauna and shed burned down. I don't know what's going on. I don't want to sell the house. It's all I have. I'm going to renovate it, if it's the last thing I do.'

Miss Simola didn't speak, clearly waiting for Olivia to continue.

'One way of doing that is to find out exactly what happened. It would help me move on.'

'You said you don't want to sell.'

'Under no circumstances.'

'But someone's made an offer?'

'Yes,' said Olivia. 'Jorma Leivo. My boss. The man who…'

'Palm Beach Finland,' said Miss Simola. The name sounded far more appropriate, more fitting, pronounced in Miss Simola's thick Finnish accent. 'I know the man. You're thinking of him?'

'In what sense?'

'As the person who killed the man in your kitchen? I didn't mean as husband material.'

Olivia shook her head. 'The police told me Jorma Leivo spent that evening in his own restaurant, eating and mingling with the customers, offering everyone ice cream and taking selfies, apparently. I heard this the last time I was interviewed, and I asked the police whether Jorma Leivo was a suspect. And that's the problem, I suppose. All logical explanations have been examined and discarded. That must be why the police have stopped investigating.'

'The police never stop investigating,' said Miss Simola. She sounded suddenly different.

'That's what it looks like,' said Olivia. 'First there were the local police – the big one with the moustache who was friendly at first but who yesterday seemed to read something into my every word; and the other one, who wouldn't stop staring at me. Then came the physicists – I call them physicists because they had identical pairs of glasses, shirts and jackets, and they were always measuring things, places, time, and the way they spoke was terribly officious: "In your own words, how would you describe your hallway at 23:51 hours on the evening in question?" One of them, the one that did most of the talking, had a buzz cut that made him look at least twenty years younger, meaning he looked like he'd just got out of Sunday school. I liked them both, they were pleasant enough, and I told them the whole story. They measured everything again, the things they'd already measured, and I thought we were close to a breakthrough. Then the next day they disappeared, and I haven't heard from them since. So in that sense...'

'The police never stop investigating,' Miss Simola repeated, her voice now stern.

Olivia couldn't quite read her expression. She decided to wait. Miss Simola looked around. As though someone was hiding in the garden listening. It wouldn't be surprising. These bushes could hide a legion of spies. But maybe not, after all.

'Have you noticed anyone following you?'

Again Olivia shook her head. Perhaps Miss Simola was suffering from the type of dementia that made people paranoid. As if anyone would want to waste their time following Olivia, who knew nothing and had done nothing.

'No,' said Olivia. 'There's no reason to follow me.'

Miss Simola appeared to weigh up this assertion, then visibly relaxed. The curiosity returned to her eyes. Somewhere among the

greenery a bird chirped; judging by the sound and location, Olivia
assumed it must be a small bird, one that could easily land in the
palm of her hand and start singing.

'And what about love?'

'What about it?'

'The clumsy, hairy, slightly smelly type,' Miss Simola smiled.
'Men.'

'I've been engaged twice, married once. Nice guys for all their
faults. I lost all my money. It all happened a while ago.'

'And you haven't met anyone since?'

As if by itself, an image appeared in Olivia's mind in which she
was drinking coffee opposite a man she had only just met. When
she thought about it honestly, she enjoyed the man's company and
felt some degree of attraction towards him. Why not? she thought.
Indeed, why not?

'A maths teacher,' said Olivia, and was taken aback at the certainty
in her voice. 'He's nice, handsome. We've only just met. I don't really
know what to think about it. Perhaps there's something there.'

'That sounds good. It's never too late, you know.'

'Thank you.'

'I didn't mean your age.'

'I think I did,' said Olivia and decided she could be as direct as
Miss Simola. 'I'm thirty-nine years old. I feel as though if I give in
over the house, I'll never be able to stand up for myself again. And
if I don't do this, I'll never do anything. There it is, take it or leave
it, forever. A final chance, that's what it feels like. A chance to show
what I'm made of. Something like that.'

Miss Simola was about to say something when the bright, shrill
sound of the doorbell pealed from within the house. Miss Simola leapt
to her feet and smiled. A ruddiness appeared on her cheeks, making
her look considerably younger. Just as her body language had changed,
her posture sharpened and her hands came to life: in an instant Miss
Simola had adjusted her hair, fixed the position of her skirt and blouse,
stretched her fingers and clasped her hands together across her chest.

'My guest,' she said. 'You can leave through the gate at the bottom of the garden if you'd rather not meet the mayor's widow.'

Miss Simola looked as though she was about to rush to the door on the other side of the house.

'I left my bike down there; the garden gate is perfect.'

'I'll be in touch if and when I hear something. Now that I know you're looking into the matter. And you're always welcome here,' said Miss Simola and was perhaps about to add something when the doorbell rang again.

'Bye then.'

'Goodbye, Olivia dear,' said Miss Simola and shuffled off in her leather brogues.

⊙

Jan Nyman watched from behind the bushes as Olivia Koski left the red house a different way from how she had arrived. Nyman had positioned himself further up the hill, looking down diagonally at the house, giving him a view of the front door too, where an elderly lady in an attractive light-grey tweed suit and shiny, laced black-leather high heels was waiting for the door to open. After a small diversionary move, Nyman had decided to follow Olivia Koski. He had cycled in one direction for a short distance, checked to see whether Olivia or anyone else was behind him, then turned and headed in the direction he had come.

He had quickly caught up with her. Following her uphill had been hard going as the paths were narrow and winding and varied greatly in height. The situation had eased considerably once Olivia had entered the house and Nyman had been able to pass the building and climb further up, deep into the woods and the cover of the trees. Of course, the relief was relative. He was plagued by mosquitoes, a horsefly bit a chunk out of his neck, the branches and undergrowth scratched and tickled his legs. His bare ankles made him feel uneasy. He was convinced he could hear the surrounding Lyme disease whispering his name.

The front door opened just as Olivia Koski jumped on her bike and began freewheeling downhill. Nyman's eyes followed Olivia long enough that he missed what happened at the front door. The door closed quickly. Nyman thought for a moment. Olivia Koski must have had a reason for coming all the way up here. Nyman didn't know who lived in the house. There was no mention of this address in any of the reports he'd seen. And that made the location of particular interest. Nyman made a quick decision. He would catch up with Olivia again, somewhere, somehow. He had to look into this house and its occupants.

Nyman made his way from the woodland to the edge of the bushes, then, remaining in their shadows, moved down to the gateway through which he had just seen Olivia leave the property. The gate was unlocked. He silently lifted the catch and the gate opened without creaking. His first sensory observation was the simultaneous scent of a thousand flowers. It was as though he had walked into a fairy tale. The garden was dense, green, and exuded primitive life force from all directions. Nyman watched his step, afraid that he might step out of the bushes at any moment and give himself away. He caught a glimpse of the house's red wall, changed direction and moved towards the building, crouched as low as he could. He came to a stop behind a large fern-like bush, listened to the birds, their chirping becoming all the more intense as evening drew in, and cautiously rose to his feet.

He saw two old ladies, both grey-haired and stylishly dressed. They were on the veranda, standing in the garden, sheltered from the outside world, and kissing. Fervently. The woman who had arrived a moment ago had pulled the other lady's skirt up higher in order to get a better grip on her buttock, which she clenched like dough, gripping and releasing, allowing the flesh to relax, plump and ruddy, and fill her hand again.

This she did again and again. Carefully, scrupulously, clearly with a firm grasp of technique.

The woman then helped the other lady to place her right leg on a white iron garden chair, lifted up her skirt – not quite over her ears but to her armpits – and gently pushed her between the shoulder blades. The woman, who must have been the age of Nyman's mother, bent forwards and mooned in Nyman's direction. He averted his eyes and stared at the ferns, or whatever genus they belonged to.

When he looked up again, the other lady was crouching behind the lady bending over, and pressing her face and presumably her mouth toward the dark gulf between her legs. Everything happened rather slowly, perhaps because of the ladies' advanced years. At least this was Nyman's initial interpretation, which he instantly realised was a rash conclusion. The ladies' lack of hurry had more to do with skill and the precision of their movements, that and the fact that later in life we are able to value each individual moment in turn. The lady in the black shoes was clearly good with her hands. And eventually everything was as it should be, everything in the optimal position. The final result looked and sounded very successful indeed.

After a few seconds, he concluded that this probably had nothing to do with the investigation whatsoever.

He retraced his steps back to the gateway, the birds guiding him with their song. The flowers smelt heady and the setting sun seemed to gild the horizon with melted copper.

14

It wasn't the first time in his life that Kari 'Chico' Korhonen found himself in the situation of having nowhere to go. On this particular evening the thought felt especially unfair. Moreover, the feeling had now assumed a new colour, a hint of finality, of irreconcilability. It was like cold liquid coursing through his body, from his neck, along his spine and finally to his knees and ankles. Chico tried to shake off the sensation, tried to throw it from his hands and fingers, kick it from his feet. But it wouldn't budge, would not fall to the sand with a splat.

The sky above him had darkened, layers of pink and gold gathered along the horizon, flashed by blue and violet. To his right his accursed cheap guitar lay in its case, to his left a sports bag full of clothes rested on its side, and Chico almost felt like leaving them there and running howling into the sea. He didn't normally consider himself a self-destructive person, he wasn't on suicide watch, someone that had to be guarded in case he harmed himself. In Chico's experience, life and the world around him took care of that for him. He didn't need his own actions to add to the hurt. And as for his current situation: he was homeless, penniless, workless, all at once. What had he done to deserve that?

Chico looked at the shore, a place where he had spent more or less his entire life, in one way or another. Today it went by the name of Palm Beach Finland. The name didn't matter: there was always the same number of people (too few) and they always looked the same (frozen stiff). Chico tried not to think of how many summers he'd spent on this beach in his capacity as lifeguard, ice-cream vendor, beach volleyball umpire (though he had no understanding of the rules), Mr Beach (he'd spent an entire summer wandering back and forth along the shore in nothing but tanning oil and a pair of Speedos, answering tourists' questions; when he'd won first prize in the Mr Beach competition he'd understood the word 'exposure' to mean something rather different and a bit more glamorous), and everything in between, and despite his best efforts to avoid it, he came to the conclusion he'd been here twenty-four summers in a row. And that meant it was nineteen years since his encounter with God.

God.

The word of God.

Chico, the young Chico, had been sitting on the beach in the early hours, strumming his acoustic guitar beneath the starry sky. The beach was deserted, so Chico had decided to start a small bonfire, which crackled and kept him warm in the chill of the night. In those days he was a poet too. He wrote scraps of lyrics in notebooks and read them aloud to his various girlfriends. His golden youth. Those were the days, my friend.

He was sitting by his bonfire, his legs crossed on a blanket, quietly playing and singing, putting together a new song that didn't yet have a name, that didn't really have any words, when he noticed a man standing just inside the light of the fire. Chico stopped playing and initially thought it must be one of the local drunks – Tamminen or Holopainen – but the man was dressed differently, and the closer Chico looked at him, he saw that everything else was different too. His shoes were sturdy, a cross between boots and walking shoes; his jeans were dark blue and sat snugly round his toned legs; his white T-shirt seemed almost moulded to his body. On anybody else they would have looked like ordinary clothes, but Bruce Springsteen had brought them together in a way that changed everything: they became a uniform, something so cool, so desirable that just thinking about it gave him a wincing pain in his stomach because the clothes shops were shut and he couldn't run off and get them for himself. Bruce looked like a god, which of course he was. Chico wondered whether Bruce had been doing a gig in Finland that evening. But it was a rhetorical question – if he had, Chico would have been in the front row. It's a good thing Chico had read that Bruce was a down-to-earth kind of guy, someone who enjoyed mixing with normal people, walking down the street, minding his own business. So it was entirely conceivable that Bruce was simply on vacation; he happened to be in town and decided to pay a visit, just like that.

'*Dancing in the dark?*' Bruce asked him.

'No,' said Chico, but added a few words once he'd recovered from the initial shock. 'I don't dance. I'm just playing my guitar, writing a new song.'

'*I'm on fire,*' said Bruce.

'It just feels like that. It can get pretty warm by the bonfire.'

'*I'm goin' down.*'

Chico sensed that Bruce wanted to sit down. He laid out an extra blanket. Bruce sat down. In the glow of the bonfire, he looked even more mystical, more valiant, more like a rock god. They sat for a moment in silence. The bonfire crackled. Bruce gazed out at the dark sea.

'*The river?*'

'No, the Baltic Sea.'

Again, silence. Chico realised he too ought to say something, that the least he could do was ask Bruce how he was doing. Chico asked and Bruce thought about this for a moment.

'*Glory days,*' he said, looked as though he changed his mind, then added: '*Better days.*'

Bruce looked at him. Chico couldn't understand why he wasn't more nervous, why he wasn't completely freaking out. The situation felt so natural.

Bruce nodded at him and the guitar. '*Born in the USA?*'

Chico shook his head.

'No, I'm local,' he said. 'From round here.'

Chico realised Bruce was still staring at his guitar. Chico placed his left hand on the fingerboard, and at that moment the perfect song title appeared in his mind, bright, almost ablaze, like the fire roaring between the two men. He began strumming 'Beach Princess', though the song wasn't quite ready yet. From out of nowhere came the certainty that this was the song he was meant to perform. It was semi-autobiographical, based on Chico's own experiences – the references to work notwithstanding – and, besides, this was his Bruce Springsteen song, not a cover or a pastiche, but strongly influenced by The Boss. Chico translated the lyrics into English as he played:

'I'm so lonely, I'm a working man,
I work so hard every day and in the evening I have a beer,
I come to the beach and I see you,
Beach Princess, can I say something,
Beach Princess, let me touch you,
Beach Princess, don't run away,
Beach Princess, don't call your brother,
He's too strong and his fists hurt my face,
In the morning I go back to work,
I work so hard all day and put ice on my wounds
And I dream of you,
Beach Princess, can I say something,
Beach Princess, let me touch you,
Beach Princess, don't run away,
Beach Princess, I didn't steal your bikini.'

Chico stopped. The song was ready. He didn't know where it had come from. He looked first at his guitar, then at Bruce.

'*She's the one,*' said Bruce quietly.

Chico nodded. Bruce had understood everything, he knew what Chico meant, knew what he was singing about. Bruce started to smooth the crinkles in his T-shirt. Chico realised Bruce was about to leave. Bruce stood up. Chico's eyes followed him.

'Where next?' he asked.

Bruce looked at the bonfire, almost with a note of sadness. '*Streets of Philadelphia,*' he said.

And with that Bruce disappeared from the light of the bonfire, somewhere beneath the stars.

The next morning Chico had woken up beside the cold bonfire, both hands wrapped tightly round his guitar. There was sand in his mouth, he was shivering with cold and his head was pounding, but it didn't matter. He had a mission, he'd found a calling. Apart from Robin, he told only one other person about that encounter – one of the other lifeguards who these days washed vegetables for a living at a hippie commune on an island in the Turku Archipelago. It was a mistake. The story was just getting started: Bruce, the bonfire … and he was halfway through 'Beach Princess' when the eco-warrior stopped him and said, You didn't build your bonfire out of those planks from the old boathouse covered in noxious paint, did you? The ones you're not supposed to burn because the fumes can cause hallucinations and if you breathe in enough of it, brain damage even? Chico fell silent, forever. The most significant night of his life belonged to him and him alone.

Now, as he looked at the place where that fire had burned, where God had stood, he realised with utter clarity that he would have to act quickly before the fire went out for good. The embers were still glowing faintly, but Chico was filled with a sense that time was of the essence.

⊙

Robin had trouble understanding two things. First, that Nea was in his apartment at all, and second, what she was talking about. At that precise moment they seemed essentially like one and the same thing, as Nea had started talking the moment she stepped inside.

And there she now stood, her lips moving, there in Robin's living room, right there in the middle. Her dark-blue stretch-denim jeans were tightly fitted, and Robin could see the camel toe. It was awful. He tried to concentrate and keep his eyes firmly focussed on Nea's gleaming, tanned face. That wasn't easy either. She was beautiful, more beautiful than ever, at her most beautiful, right there in Robin's living room, between the old, black leather sofa and the new flat-screen TV, twirling on the grey tufted rug that used to belong to his Aunt Hilkka.

Only a moment ago Robin had been lying on the sofa watching his favourite show – each character better, each gag funnier than the last – when the doorbell rang. Robin was in his underpants, because in the summer the evening sunshine turned the room into a furnace, and Robin knew of no better way to cool off than the chill of the leather sofa against his bare skin. Of course, the sofa soon began to warm against his skin, turning first tacky with sweat, then sticky and eventually slippery, but the momentary relief was worth it.

Robin had walked to the front door, droplets of sweat running down him, and guessed it was probably Chico at the door. He looked out of the kitchen window and experienced something akin to a heart attack. Nea. Robin pulled on a pair of tracksuit bottoms and a jacket from the coat rack. Now he found himself sitting on the sofa in a windcheater and a pair of work trousers covered with paint, oil and grease stains from mending the roof and fixing his scooter. He felt altogether hot, bothered and filthy.

'What has Chico ever done for you?' asked Nea.

Robin thought about this.

'I always get to come along for the action.'

'But what do you get out of it?'

Again Robin thought about this.

'He's my mate. You don't always have to get something out of mates.'

'But what kind of mate just lets you come along for the action, though you never get anything out of it?' said Nea, and spun around, and again Robin's gaze left her face and wandered considerably lower down. 'If you don't get anything at all?'

'What am I supposed to get out of it?' he asked and mustered all the willpower he could to hoist his gaze back to those mesmerising eyes.

'Robin,' she said. 'I've been offered ten thousand euros if I can find out who murdered that guy in Olivia's house.'

Robin thought about this.

'Ten thousand euros,' he said. 'This afternoon you offered us a thousand. Split in two. A thousand divided by two is five hundred.'

'That's what I told Chico,' she nodded. 'But I've had second thoughts. Let me explain again. I need somebody I can trust, someone who knows everybody. That's you. Think about it. You work in a restaurant! You see everyone, you know everyone. Chico's a bum. He thinks he's a great guitar player, but he's not. Where does he play? What does he play? I've never heard of any of his bands. He came by my store one day to put up a poster. Endless Cowboys, or something.'

'Endless Cowboys is one of his bands, country-rock fusion. Then there's Endless Enemas, that's the heavy stuff. There's even Endless Plato, which is more poetic, chilled out. I've never heard them live, and I don't know where they do any gigs, but Chico told me.'

Nea cast her hand in an arc through the air, wiping clean an imaginary board.

'Whatever. We're different, Robin. We're ambitious. I've seen the way you cook, the way you painstakingly put those dishes together; you're so precise you're like a stamp collector. In a good way. I work out twice a day. We can do this. Chico can't. Ten thousand euros, Robin.'

'It's a lot,' he said, and he really meant it.

And he thought his head might explode, thought about how in the restaurant kitchen he only ever saw the backs of the familiar vegetable delivery people and the waiting staff as they hurriedly carried dishes out of the kitchen. He wiped sweat from his brow and chin. His sleeve felt rough – after all, the coat was made of thick fabric, designed to withstand the chill of October. If Robin had ever heard of the phrase *cognitive dissonance*, he would have been trying to process its meaning right then. He looked at Nea and wanted her so much that he felt a searing cold at the bottom of his stomach.

He certainly couldn't say no to ten thousand euros. Or was it five thousand because there were two of them and ten thousand divided by two was five thousand. But even that was almost exactly five thousand more than he had at the moment.

But more than anything, what was threatening to send his head spinning off his shoulders and causing him a certain amount of anguish – not least because it was also the key to Nea's favours – boiled down to the fact that he knew perfectly well who had killed the guy in Olivia's house: he had.

Wait a minute.

He – and Chico.

Chico.

It wasn't an easy thought.

Robin looked at Nea.

'It's a lot of money,' he said, his voice audibly hoarser than usual.

'It's enough for us to get out of this place,' said Nea and looked at him.

Us. Something welled up inside him. He was closing in on something he'd always dreamed of. And he remembered something that now seemed dangerous. In his apartment he still had the wooden pasta fork that he'd swiped from Olivia's kitchen. It had been hanging by itself on the wall, and Robin's hand had grabbed it almost instinctively, automatically. But now it might be in the wrong place because … Robin didn't know what to think about all this: Nea's suggestion, Chico, and in particular the pasta fork with the long wooden handle. But perhaps it all had a meaning. What that might be, and how, and in what order things might happen was still unclear. The overall picture was painfully blurred and out of focus.

'I'm going to be a personal trainer,' said Nea. 'What about you, Robin?'

He gulped. He knew what he wanted. But there were so many things in his way. It wasn't an easy question to answer. He did his best to look pensive. That bought him some time. He guessed a solution would appear in its own time. That's how things worked in the restaurant kitchen. If he ran out of an ingredient, he simply switched it for another, and nobody ever knew the difference. But this time the solution remained hidden; the kitchen cupboards were bare. The situation continued. Robin sat on the sofa, Nea's thighs right in front of him.

And at that moment, the very thing he yearned for yet feared the most looked like it was about to happen. Nea approached him, sat down next to him on the sofa, placed a hand on his thigh. Robin stared at her long, shiny red nails against his tracksuit. The room was unbearably hot. Rivulets of sweat were tickling his back. He focussed on her fiery red nails and found himself imagining what it would feel like if she used them to scratch his sweaty back.

⊙

Chico didn't want to venture inside. He sat on the park bench and tried to imagine the sight: Robin half naked on his couch, his mouth drooping open, comedy sketches on television, men in women's clothing, shouting, wild applause.

Chico leaned forwards, propped his elbows against his knees and glanced again towards the familiar terraced house in the distance. Robin's flat was at the end of the terrace. The lights were on, so he was definitely at home. Chico was in no hurry. His old friend would wait faithfully. He might not be the sharpest tool in the box, but at least Robin was reliable.

Chico grabbed a bite of his last hot dog. It was lukewarm. He'd bought five hot dogs at the stand on the street, but they didn't taste right. He had the same arrangement with the owner as he did with the pub: he bought stuff that was a bit old at a knock-down price. Five extra-long hot dogs for one euro. These had most definitely passed their best-before date. The sausages tasted of last summer. Chico carefully placed a spoonful of mustard along the last hot dog and lobbed it into his mouth. His mouth was full of mustard, but the sausage still had a stale, mushroomy taste, and the texture was tacky and slimy. He swallowed. The hot dogs were on their way to his stomach. One less thing to worry about. Which didn't mean there weren't still plenty of other things on his mind.

Chico sighed and stood up. The wind caught his hair. The evening was dark. He couldn't spend the night out here on a park bench. He tried to explain to himself that Robin was a childhood friend and that nudity was perfectly natural and, besides, this was only going to be a temporary, one-night arrangement. Again. But the thought of all the unpleasantness kept him standing on the spot by the path watching the house…

As its front door opened.

Light escaped from the apartment, spilled out into the yard, and into the light stepped Nea.

Chico would have recognised her anytime, anywhere. Nea? He couldn't begin to imagine what she might be up to at Robin's place. Chico stared at the ensuing theatre as Nea blew a kiss to someone – it must have been Robin, as he lived alone – jumped on her bike and pedalled off in the direction of her own house.

Chico stood by himself in the darkness for a moment, then picked up his guitar and sports bag and began walking towards Robin's house. The front door had shut, of course. Chico was walking slowly under the weight of his assorted belongings. He rang the bell and heard footsteps, more animated than usual. Robin opened the door. Shirtless. He looked … disappointed, perhaps. Surprised, at least.

'Chico. Hi.'

'Hi,' Chico replied and knew straight away that he shouldn't mention Nea unless Robin brought up the subject. He didn't know where this certainty came from, but the matter was absolutely clear. 'You said I could crash here.'

Robin didn't answer immediately.

'I guess so,' he said eventually.

Neither of them moved. They stood at the door.

'What's up?' asked Chico.

'Not much,' said Robin. 'I was watching TV.'

Robin's eyes were fixed on the floor between them.

'A night in front of the box? Okay,' said Chico. 'Anything good on?'

'Yeah.'

Robin continued to stare at the floor.

'What?' asked Chico.

Now Robin looked up at him. He was clearly confused. 'What d'you mean, what?'

'You said there's something good on, I asked what. What's on the box? What were you watching before I rang the bell?'

Robin tried to avoid eye contact. What was it Chico had thought only a moment ago? Robin might have been a few cans short of a six-pack, but he was still faithful and trustworthy. Chico took a firmer grip on his guitar case.

'Alright if I bring my stuff in?' he asked.

Robin didn't say anything, but opened the door wider and took a step backwards. He turned. Chico stepped inside into the bright light of the hallway and almost dropped his guitar case. Robin's back looked like he'd been wrestling with tigers.

15

Holma counted the money. Again. Twenty-five thousand, two hundred and forty-five euros. More than he'd thought. He gathered the notes into a pile, moved it to the middle of the table, and in the early-morning light he saw not only the pile of banknotes but a world of possibilities. Naturally he'd already been able to think about things on his drive through the night.

A holiday fund. Gambling chips. Bargaining chips. And fun, for sure.

Money made people go crazy. The sum didn't really matter. The most important thing was how quickly and easily you could hoard it. Whether it was ten cents or a million euros. Nothing excited people like the thought of winning the lottery. This Holma knew from experience. He'd spent years visiting people who had become blind. Some for a shorter time, some longer. Once he had helped open their eyes, eventually they had all woken up.

Holma counted out ten thousand euros. That would go to Olivia Koski – for the time being, until he'd had a chance to deal with whoever had killed Antero. Holma dreamed of a long, extravagant meeting with that person, an event that would require some planning and a suitable location. He would find one.

This left just over fifteen thousand on the table. Holma thought of those brown, firm buttocks, glistening with sweat, and thought of how much use he had for them. If he lent Olivia Koski ten thousand, he could lend Nea the same amount. The sense of competition would be interesting for many reasons, from the perspective of Holma's own amusement but first and foremost with regard to results. Which of them would be able to lead him in the right direction the quickest?

He laughed.

His laughter was cut short.

Holma thought of the man who had rented him this chalet. The man who owned this place. Holma hadn't listened to half of what the man had said, but the general gist had been about his desire to expand. Expand his business, grow it. Holma knew plenty of men like this, or at least he had in the past. Men whose businesses were on the verge of taking off. Men for whom Holma had provided a parachute of his own when their upward trajectory suddenly – or not so suddenly – came to a halt. Holma couldn't remember the owner's name, though they'd shaken hands. It didn't matter, he thought. He would introduce himself again. It was only natural, seeing as he had a business proposition of his own.

Once he had shaved and dressed – tight black jeans, a yellow pique T-shirt, a pair of golden Asics trainers – he picked up the bundle of notes, placed it inside the microwave and pressed the door shut. Not a very safe place as stashes go, but there couldn't be many criminals wandering the streets in a place like this. Holma made the bed, brushed his teeth, opened the door and stepped out to the porch.

The morning was cool, but someone was sitting on the veranda outside the neighbouring chalet. The man from next door had introduced himself, but Holma couldn't remember his name. He had a habit of forgetting insignificant people in a hurry. If they were of no use to him, why store them in his head? It took up capacity that he could put to better use. This morning's aphorism: Remember that the sun will rise when … the sun…

'Morning,' said the man next door.

When Holma looked at him more closely, the man looked like a tramp. His hair was long and tousled, his stubble was on the verge of turning into a fully-fledged beard, a faded brown T-shirt, and on top of that a red-and-white checked flannel shirt hanging open and slightly askew. How could someone like that be on holiday? And where had he come from? Since when had the job centre started sending the long-term unemployed on beach holidays?

'Morning,' Holma replied and gave a smile. 'Up early?'

'Windsurfing lesson starting shortly. I'm learning to surf. It's only my second lesson.'

Perhaps the tramp was here for some much-needed rehabilitation. But rehabilitation from what exactly? General dishevelment?

'Aren't they two different things?' asked Holma. 'Surfing and windsurfing?'

The tramp looked at him. There was something familiar about him, Holma thought. But what was it?

'As far as I've understood,' said the tramp, seemingly not in any hurry to respond, 'in Finland they mean the same thing: windsurfing. Regardless of which one you're talking about. But it's a good point. Surfing needs waves, so you can't really do that here. Well, you could, but it would be pretty boring. Because we don't get big waves.'

You've got to be kidding me, thought Holma. The guy's not exactly Einstein, is he? Holma smiled again.

'But there's plenty of wind in Finland,' he said. 'So…'

The tramp nodded.

'It's windsurfing. Do you surf yourself? Wind or the other variety?'

'No,' said Holma.

'Canoeing?'

'No.'

'Beach volleyball?'

'No.'

'Swimming?'

'No.'

'Probably wise,' the tramp rambled on. 'Yesterday the water was so cold you could—'

'I have to get going,' Holma cut him off before he sprained his frontal lobe. He gave the man a final smile. 'Happy surfing.'

The man smiled, and Holma saw in him what he'd seen a moment earlier. Something about his demeanour, his eyes, his body language – he just couldn't put his finger on it. Holma stepped from the porch straight into the pine forest, felt the earth beneath his feet, turned and left.

◉

Jan Nyman watched his neighbour disappear. He set off on foot, leaving his car – a shiny black BMW – parked behind the chalet. Nyman was in two minds. His surfing lesson was about to start, that much was true. However, he was in no hurry to get to his lesson, and any sense of urgency drifted further away every time he recalled the feel of the instructor's hands on his backside, the muscular fingers inching their way ever closer. It can't have been pedagogically sound. But even that wasn't the real reason for his hesitation. He was trying to decide whether or not to break into his neighbour's chalet.

Nyman had deliberately spoken slowly, trying to delay the man with questions. He wanted to see how the man reacted. And he'd reacted just as Nyman had expected: he had become impatient. In situations like that people often inadvertently revealed something more about themselves. Nyman hadn't picked up on anything this time. On the other hand, his direct questions and the man's answers had demonstrated a lot. It seemed the man had come to Palm Beach Finland on holiday, but wasn't interested in any of the activities on offer. If you own a seventy-grand car, Nyman asked himself, and you're not interested in any of the activities on offer at a beach resort, would you come to the erstwhile Martti's Motel to rent a cheap cabin and do absolutely nothing?

The answer was so clear that Nyman walked over to his kit box and took out a lock-picking set and a pair of disposable latex gloves.

He walked to the road and looked in both directions. Nothing but cool light, a breeze through the trees, echoes of a life far away. Nyman returned to the chalet. The lock was the old Abloy make, and he had it open in thirty seconds. Nyman stepped inside and closed the door behind him. Castillo looked just like Tubbs, and vice versa. The design and equipment were identical to those in his own chalet: bunk bed, kitchenette, dining table, chairs placed around it, wardrobe, mini bathroom. The man was tidy: the bed had been neatly made, his shirts were all on hangers, the few items on the table were in a meticulous row. Nyman pulled on the latex gloves and got to work. First he examined the furniture, moved the items, picked them up and put them back again, looked underneath them. He felt the bed, the mattress, the sheets, pillows, glanced under the mattress. He examined the wardrobe inside, outside and behind. He rummaged through the pockets of the two jackets and one pair of trousers. He opened the fridge to find it stocked with foods high in protein: quark (mostly raspberry-blueberry flavour), eggs, seven packets of fat-free minced beef, fat-free cottage cheese and – somewhat surprising given everything else in the fridge – a packet of the cheapest salami you could find in the store. Nyman closed the fridge door, looked through the cupboards, opened the drawers making sure to check beneath the liners and round the back, crouched down to peer under the sink and examined the rubbish bin, which revealed that the food in the fridge was no departure from the man's usual eating habits. He stood up and went to the window, couldn't see anybody. He lay on the floor on his stomach, raised his head just enough to let his eyes gaze across the floor, beneath the furniture, around the skirting boards. He rolled onto his back, scrutinised the ceiling and everything rising upwards, paying particular attention to the bedframe, the kitchenette and the points where the units were bolted to the wall. He stood up, took a chair and climbed onto it so he could check above the cupboards. Then stepped down, put the chair back in its place at the dining table and went into the bathroom. He lifted the toilet lid, put it back down again, checked both with his hand and eyes behind the toilet bowl, went through the contents of a toiletry bag and found a bottle of expensive shampoo, expensive deodorant, mid-price shaving gel and a brand-new razor. No medicine or anything else that might have had a name on it. He checked beneath the sink, inside the microscopic shower unit, and let his eyes run along the edges of the walls and flooring, but nothing looked loose or as though it would provide a suitable hiding place. He returned to the main room and stood right in the middle. A rule of thumb: have you opened everything that can be opened, moved everything that can be moved? Nyman slowly looked round the space from one item to the next, checking that he knew what was inside it, beneath it or above it. He did this carefully and methodically, and eventually his eyes came to rest at the kitchenette. Had he tried every handle, opened everything that could be opened? Yes … No. He walked towards the microwave, opened it and saw a pile of cash inside. He pulled out his phone, took a picture of the money, returned his phone to his pocket and looked more closely at the microwave. The only cash in the chalet was stored in the microwave. Nyman turned and walked again to the window. Still quiet, deserted. He returned to the microwave and eyed the money. From the kitchen drawer he took a plastic spatula, stepped slightly to the side and cautiously prodded the pile. No ink booby traps, no electric shock, and seemingly no other security precautions. Just a large pile of cash inside a microwave. Nyman picked up the bundle and estimated its value. At a glance, he'd say about twenty-five thousand. Nyman placed the money back inside the microwave, closed the door and glanced round the kitchen once more before leaving. He opened the front door, took off his gloves and stuffed them in his pocket. He stepped onto the porch, hopped past the steps and onto the ground, and filled his lungs with fresh morning air. It was cool and clean, like the first breath after a long dive.

Nyman committed the BMW's registration number to memory and returned to his own chalet. He sat down at the dining table, brought his iPad to life with a click and did a search. He got a hit. The BMW was registered to a holding company whose name was a collection of italicised letters. Nyman searched for the company's name and again came up with several hits. The company was a few months old and hadn't provided any information about its business model. The CEO was listed as one Esa Koljonen – the name the man next door had given. Nyman searched for the man's name – both on the search engine and the police's own database – but couldn't find anything. The circle came to a close. Nyman leaned back in his chair, looked out of the window and saw the corner of the next-door chalet.

It seems Castillo has a mildew problem too, he thought.

◉

The resort's office was a bright-blue box-shaped building, and on the roof was a miniature version of the sign for the beach. In front of the entrance, on both sides of the door, palm trees had been planted. The soil around the trees looked dark and churned. There was something strange about the palms themselves, but Holma couldn't work out what.

Holma stepped inside and immediately located the owner by sound alone. The man was on the telephone. Holma looked around. The man was by himself. Holma walked right into his office, shut the door behind him and sat down in a chair across the desk. The man watched him, his expression quizzical. It was understandable. Holma gestured and nodded to indicate that as far as he was concerned the owner could continue his conversation. The man continued talking the way Holma had heard so many men talking before him.

'It's probably been sent to my junk-mail folder … Our accountant has been a bit ill lately, so things are backlogged … Cancer of the kidneys. But he's on the mend now … Of course, money isn't everything … But of course, we'll … To the front of the queue, yes indeed, I'll make a note of it right away.'

Holma looked at the man, who didn't seem about to make a note of anything at all.

On the wall behind the man was a framed poster of a woman in an itsy-bitsy bikini, standing in a suggestive, tilted position on a long sandy beach and smiling next to an autograph in felt-tip pen. Holma didn't recognise the woman, whose significant breasts seemed to test the strength of the flimsy laces tied around them, and he couldn't make out the autograph either. He did manage to read the short text scrawled in black lettering across the blue sky: *To Jorma With Love.* That's right, thought Holma. The man's name was Jorma Leivo.

Leivo eventually brought his phone conversation to an end. He picked up a cotton handkerchief from his desk and wiped the sweat from his brow. Holma didn't think it was warm in the room.

Leivo looked up and smiled. 'Sorry you had to wait,' he said. 'It seems all our customer service officers are busy at the moment. Everything all right with the chalet?'

'Yes,' said Holma.

'Are you here to ask about the many other things we provide here at Palm Beach Finland? Would you like to buy some extra services?'

'Extra services?'

'A tennis course, perhaps,' said Leivo. 'Tennis coaching is on offer today. Our instructor almost won Wimbledon. I know him person-ally, so I can get you a good price. I'll throw in racket rental on the house. A genuine Wilson, none of your cheap knock-offs. Tested by professionals, you know, but otherwise brand new – well, an old lady used it once. In an hour I think she managed to hit the ball three times. Two and a half, to be precise. Had a heart attack. A weak arm but an iron grip. We managed to protect the racket while we prised her hand open. New tape round the handle, good as new, not the slightest whiff of granny odour. The court is the best surface around, the same stuff they use at Roland Garros. I've got a mate who's visited France, and he told me as much. Big wine drinker, makes the stuff at home. Well then, shall I put your name down?'

Holma had been observing Leivo throughout his monologue. A bright-green shirt, hands rhythmically gesticulating, ruddy face, unruly white hair sprouting at the side of his head, and those blue, red-rimmed eyes. He looked like a burned-out maestro.

'Put it down in the same place where you made note of that final demand,' said Holma. 'Right at the front of the queue, where you put that last caller.'

Holma watched as Leivo's expression changed.

'I'm kidding,' he said. 'I'm not here to register for a course, and I don't want to buy any extra services.'

'What's this about?' asked Leivo. This was now the voice of an altogether different man.

'There's no shame in finding yourself in financial difficulty,' said Holma and took the box of business cards from his pocket, opened it and handed one to Leivo. 'We all have cash-flow problems now and then. Well, not me personally, but I know people who do. And I also know, no matter what the problem, there's always a solution.'

Holma decided not to add that sometimes that solution was terminal. Leivo didn't say anything. He read the card, turning it in his fingers. Holma watched as the card's embossed golden insignia flashed in the sun.

'I like this place a lot,' he said and looked up at Leivo. 'And the investors I represent think along the same lines. We see this as a possible investment prospect. We've been thinking about the sum we'd like to invest. My client operates on a cash-only basis.'

Again, Holma decided not to add that his client was lying in a Helsinki hovel with his throat slit.

'But there's one thing we're concerned about,' Holma continued. 'Which, I'm sure, we can solve and control. I'm referring to the reputation of this place.'

Leivo cast a curious look at Holma. His expression was more open than a moment ago. The whiff of money had changed things. People suddenly became friends. Not friends, perhaps, but something even better: allies who were prepared to sell out their friends.

'A while ago a homicide occurred here, an event that has cast an unfortunate shadow over the entire community,' said Holma. 'To my understanding, the case remains unsolved. My client strongly believes that if this case were to be solved, providing, if you will, some form of closure, the whole matter could be wiped away and we could all start with a clean slate. Who knows what Palm Beach Finland could then become?'

Leivo seemed interested. He turned the card in his hand and read it aloud: 'Vanamoinen & Siltakari.' Leivo nodded, impressed. 'Capital Ventures and Investment Portfolios.' Leivo pronounced the words in a thick Finnish accent. Holma considered this a good sign.

'That's right.'

'And you are?'

'Markus Komulainen. A company representative.'

'Right, of course,' said Leivo, and by now his voice had reverted to the teddy-bear tones he had used when presenting the tennis course. 'Potential. This place has plenty. And let me be frank, it's no wonder Palm Beach Finland is already being compared to the likes of St Tropez. We're about to acquire some extra land too, which we're going to use to build a luxury area for the more discerning customer. Just a few plots still to snatch up – well, only one, actually – and there will be no stopping us. There will be a helipad, a new marina. I can show you the designs, I've got them over here…'

Holma raised a hand to stop him.

'First things first,' he said. 'The homicide.'

Leivo looked at him. Holma couldn't quite read his expression.

'I don't think it's a problem,' said Leivo. 'People die in beach resorts all the time.'

'We are prepared to pay ten thousand euros for information leading to the arrest of the guilty party.'

Leivo fell silent. This is what it would take, thought Holma. Leivo cast his eyes down at the desk in front of him and seemed to notice it was covered in papers, presumably unpaid bills. He looked pensive. Then he placed both hands on the desk and looked up at Holma again.

'Ten thousand euros?' he asked.

'In cash,' said Holma and paused slightly to allow the sum to burrow its way into Leivo's understanding. 'Let me stress that this is just an initial step, but a necessary step nonetheless. After this, anything is possible. Things here could really take off. I promise you that. But first let's make sure the resort's reputation is restored and this unfortunate matter is cleared up once and for all. And there is another reason why we are approaching you in this manner.'

Leivo stared at him, motionless.

'It's to do with your position in the community,' said Holma. 'You know a lot of people, you hear all sorts of things. You interact personally with almost all the tourists that come and go. You can ask around.'

Leivo said nothing. It didn't matter, thought Holma, he'd already made himself clear. There was nobody, nobody at all, that an easy ten thousand euros wouldn't spur into action – making them do something, anything. Holma stood up.

'You know where to find me,' he said and stepped out of the office.

16

Now there's a surprise, thought Olivia Koski. This morning her swimming costume felt almost as though it fitted properly. It still didn't look good, and the text emblazoned across it seemed all the more absurd, but in some way the garment itself felt lighter, easier to bear. Maybe, thought Olivia, it was because she now knew all of this was temporary. And how did she know that? She … just knew. More to the point, she had decided to make sure it would be temporary.

In the morning light she looked at herself in the mirror and wondered how much it took for people to really learn things. How much did it take for a thirty-nine-year old to look herself in the mirror and know with certainty that from now on everything was going to be different? In her case it had required two catastrophic relationships, the death of her mother and father, a murder, an explosion in her shed, the incineration of her sauna, the water suddenly cutting off – and a curious maths teacher. Olivia had realised it later the previous evening as she'd said it out loud to herself. Jan Kaunisto was funny and fascinating, she'd said. In all honesty, when was the last time she'd met an interesting, funny man who hadn't started complaining about his dire financial situation – temporary, of course, and purely circumstantial – on their second date? Olivia smiled and caught a glimpse of her smiling face in the mirror. It felt good. So good that it looked good too.

Olivia pulled her tracksuit and hoodie over her swimming costume and tied her trainers. She looked in her bags, double-checked that she'd packed a change of clothes. She went down the steps and walked to her bicycle. She always left it in the yard unlocked, and there it was now, the remains of the sauna behind it. She thought about the solicitor's proposition. She had told him she'd be at home until nine in the morning, then at work on the beach, so she would be easy to find: she would be in the watchtower, of which there was only one. He could bring the ten thousand euros to either place, as long as it was in a neat package. The solicitor said he understood, assured her he was always discreet when it came to money.

Olivia placed the bag in the basket tied to the rack at the back of her bike, secured it with a bungee cord and jumped on the saddle. It was a cool, beautiful morning. She inhaled the sharp air and remembered that Jan Kaunisto's windsurfing lesson was about to start. There was something comical about it. Not in the laugh-out-loud sense. In the sense that she felt it beneath her sternum rather than in her cheeks.

Olivia recalled what Miss Simola had said about the police always continuing their investigations. The reason Olivia had previously dismissed Leivo was because just by looking at him he was too obvious a suspect: he talked the way all salesmen talked, lying if not with every word but at the very latest by the end of each sentence. What's more, Leivo had put in a pathetic, offensively low offer on Olivia's house and land, and in that way almost put himself forward for an identity line-up. What's more, on the night of the murder Leivo had been sitting in his restaurant eating ice cream and managed to stain the front of his white shirt, and there were photographs to prove it. Given all this, Olivia found it impossible to suspect him. It all seemed too easy.

But Miss Simola wasn't one for idle gossip. Olivia remembered her as a woman who followed her own path, who said what she meant and meant what she said, and seeing her again after all these years hadn't remotely changed that impression.

Very well, she thought. Let's assume it is Leivo after all. He doesn't get his own hands dirty, but … But what? Leivo sends someone into her house, then someone else to kill the first guy. No. Leivo hires two men who end up having an argument while they are doing … what exactly? Nothing had been taken except her old wooden backscratcher, so this definitely wasn't a burglary. Which, in any case, would have been completely futile. Apart from the house itself, Olivia didn't own anything of worth, and there was nothing in the house of any monetary value except, maybe, her mother's paintings. They didn't normally count, as sad as it sounded. So this whole scenario, in all its absurdity, went as follows: Leivo hires a person or persons to go into her house and fight until one of them dies.

It didn't sound very plausible. Not that Jorma Leivo was going to displace Stephen Hawking as the greatest mind to bless the universe anytime soon, but the sheer insanity of a plot like that would be too much for anyone. And yet, it was these unexplained events – the death and Olivia's renewed fear – that Leivo took such pains to underline every time he got the chance. Olivia wanted to talk to Miss Simola again. Even if she didn't have any answers, Olivia felt as though Miss Simola guided and supported her thoughts. They had only spoken for a few minutes, but in that time an old channel seemed to have opened up and Olivia found it easy to talk. And because of that she saw everything more clearly.

The bike juddered along the knobbly dirt track. Olivia caught sight of the sea, its blue, shimmering surface, which at first glance seemed infinite but which was cut off along its other edge and disappeared from view. As with everything else, even infinity had its limits: from this point you can go no further.

Olivia glided past the resort's sign. The brightness, the garishness of its colours, seemed to stick to her clothes, though she passed it quickly, as though she was trying to escape the screaming shades of pink and neon green. Again she tried to fit Jorma Leivo into the picture.

First a mysterious death, then the sauna burns down. There was always something very clear and explicit about burning down a sauna. If you want to get a Finn's attention, if you want to tell your compatriot something vital and important, you burn down his sauna. Then he'll get the message. It lets him know, more effectively than anything else, that you have stepped on his turf, that you don't respect his territorial integrity, and that nothing between you is sacred. It's a declaration of war. But that was exactly the problem.

What war? Whom exactly was Olivia supposed to rise against? More to the point, who was on the battlefield? If we assumed that Jorma Leivo still wanted to get his hands on her land, did he really need to declare all-out war and attract everyone's attention – not to mention getting the police and the fire department involved? Wouldn't that just make everything more difficult? It didn't seem like a particularly clever way of advancing Palm Beach Finland's business concerns.

Olivia propped her bike against a tree and locked it. The beach had once been a safe place, but this summer lots of people had reported petty thefts: lunch vouchers and other small items taken from a handbag; someone's sandwiches had disappeared from their picnic basket; and one visitor was convinced that someone had taken her poodle's collar while she was swimming, explaining that she'd bought a studded black leather collar from abroad, that the dog had been very attached it and had howled with shock after the attack. Olivia expressed regret at the dog's distress but couldn't for the life of her imagine who would want to steal a collar the size of a wristband from a poodle – or why.

She arrived at the bright-yellow tower, climbed up a few steps and threw her bag inside. The beach itself was deserted, but further afield there was plenty going on: to the left four people playing beach volleyball, and to the right, in the shallow water just off the shore before the seafloor began its steep drop, an instructor was teaching three students to windsurf. One of the students was Jan Kaunisto.

Olivia recognised him easily. He was wearing a rented wetsuit with the silhouette of a white palm tree printed on the back. He fell over and climbed back onto his board, hoisted the sail upright, fell, climbed, hoisted … Jan Kaunisto looked like a determined man.

Olivia took off her hoodie and hung it on a screw protruding from the wall of the watchtower. She bent over and was about to slip off her tracksuit bottoms when she heard a voice behind her.

'Nice view.'

Olivia spun round, her trousers at her ankles. The solicitor. So he'd turned up after all.

The man's eyes slowly rose from her groin to eye level. What was that all about? Was this what evolution had come to? Did one caveman say to another, hey, there's pussy round here somewhere, I think the rest of the women must be nearby? Olivia looked the man in the eye. He smiled; the smile spread across his face quickly and remained fixed in place. Olivia continued getting undressed, took off her trousers and hung them on the screw. She turned to look squarely at the solicitor.

'As we agreed,' he said and held out a small paper bag.

Olivia took the bag. The name of a renowned fashion house ran along one side. This was the kind of place where people bought handbags and scarves, but when Olivia quickly peered inside she saw that the bag contained a bundle of banknotes. It might even have been exactly ten thousand euros; it was certainly a lot. She wasn't going to count the money there and then.

'Ten thousand euros,' said the solicitor. 'And there's more where that came from.'

'I'll bear that in mind,' said Olivia.

'But only once we see results,' he said. 'And we want quick results. If we don't get any, we expect the funds returned to us. With interest. This is a matter we wish to be very clear about, so allow me to remind you. People forget about interest. As if money didn't cost anything. As if there was such a thing as free money. There isn't.'

Every time the man stopped talking, he smiled. And he did so now too. But quite what he was smiling at, Olivia wasn't sure, because he rarely said anything funny or amusing. On the contrary, his voice was so soft, bland and neutral that he couldn't possibly say anything ending in a punch line, and besides, his intonation always seemed to fall in the wrong places.

'I'll be in touch,' said Olivia.

'When?' the man asked immediately.

Naturally, this was a question to which there was only one correct answer.

'Soon.'

Olivia had imagined the solicitor would leave after receiving his answer, but instead he pushed his hands into his pockets, took a few steps forwards, stood next to Olivia and stared out to sea. Olivia had to turn around. They stood next to each other. She could sense the man next to her. She saw Jan Kaunisto clambering back on his board, pulling the sail up again, perhaps glancing towards the shore before finally getting the sail into position and bobbing off towards the open sea.

'So the tramp really is windsurfing,' said the solicitor.

Olivia had no idea what he was talking about.

'It makes me angry,' he continued. 'You pay your taxes, and this is what you get. Some hippie on holiday, windsurfing all day and growing a beard. And for what? Now he knows how to windsurf. Good for him. Hey man, have a tan on the house. There he is, surfing away, learning a few clumsy moves for a couple of days, then he'll go home, sit down on his sofa feeling energised and get up next summer. If he gets up at all. Because it's too cold here, and the collapsing sails will leave him traumatised. At some point a psychiatrist will turn up and explain that we shouldn't remind the frostbitten windsurfer of his sail collapsing, we should give him a hug and tell him he's special just the way he is, that he should be allowed to recover emotionally before going back in the water. Adults are like babies. They stretch out their podgy hands whenever they want something but can't quite reach it. Then they burst into tears.'

Olivia said nothing.

'Do you know what I'd do?' he asked.

Olivia shook her head.

'I'd make people compete with each other – for real.'

The man took the stairs down to the sand, said something over his shoulder like *We'll talk soon*, and strode off with long, purposeful steps.

Olivia counted the money. She sat in the watchtower and counted to ten thousand. Well, two hundred. Two hundred times fifty euros. Olivia did the maths in the safety of the bag, put the banknotes back in their place, folded the brown, shiny bag into as tight a parcel as she could and placed it at the bottom of her bag beneath her other things. She had the money. Perhaps the man who'd given it to her wasn't the most pleasant that Olivia had ever met – but since when were men with money pleasant? They were obsessed with themselves, loved the sound of their own voices, and they were deathly dull. Just like this solicitor, who appeared to know everything about subjects from windsurfing to social policy. The more money they had, the more they imagined they were capable of original thoughts – thoughts that deserved to be shared with others, thoughts on every subject under the sun. But they had money. So keep your mouth shut, she told herself, do what you've promised and do not – and in this respect the man had hit the nail on the head – do not behave like a baby ever again.

And her next move: Jorma Leivo. That was the most logical explanation. Miss Simola was right, and she always knew what she was doing. Olivia thought for a moment. She looked out to sea. Windsurfers. The maths teacher, the pleasant Jan Kaunisto, who turns up in town just before her sauna burns down. What would Miss Simola have to say about that? Olivia could guess.

But first she had a plumber to call.

17

Copulating old ladies, twenty-five thousand euros in cash stashed inside a microwave, the sauna burning down – not to mention that before all of this a body had turned up in the kitchen. And everything, every detail, related one way or another to that woman.

Jan Nyman's thighs were trembling from the adrenalin rush as he waded out of the water and onto dry land. Yes, he was cold again, so cold he was shivering, but he felt a languid sense of satisfaction. From the windsurfing, that is, and absolutely nothing else.

As he'd climbed back onto the board for the umpteenth time, he'd glanced back to the shore and seen Olivia and his next-door neighbour standing side by side, almost touching. Why had this man come to meet Olivia Koski? The man with twenty-five thousand in his microwave.

Nyman saw that Olivia Koski was smiling. He admired her tanned arms, her figure. He felt a familiar tingling in the bottom of his stomach, the instinctive eruption of happiness every time a woman came into view, then immediately afterwards a sensation as though he'd been thumped in the diaphragm with a blunt implement, as though something had been poured into his mind to spoil the thought. Nyman got a grip on the emotion. It had been a while since he'd last experienced it.

Jealousy. That's what it was. Surely not?

Don't be ridiculous, Nyman told himself and concentrated on trying to walk in a straight line.

Who could have imagined windsurfing was this demanding? His legs were quivering, his arms were numb, hanging like wooden blocks at the side of his body. He realised he was trying to give a good impression of himself as he walked across the sand towards Olivia

Koski, which was difficult given the stiffness of his thighs and the softness of the sand. He knew he was wobbling.

He was a policeman, he reminded himself, and this woman was as much as suspect as a person could possibly be without concrete evidence; his attraction was a way of getting close to her – nature's way of creating tension between them, tension that would build into trust, intimacy. That was it. Nothing more. He would not go any further and certainly wouldn't…

'I was wondering if you'd like to join me for dinner this evening?' Nyman said as soon as they'd exchanged greetings.

Olivia Koski stood upright, leaned her head to one side, as though she was about to say something sarcastic – no, something surprising. And that's what happened. Both what she said and the speed with which she said it took him aback.

'Actually,' she said. 'I was thinking the same thing. It would be good to talk.'

Nyman was speechless for only about a second and a half, but Olivia noticed it. He could see it in those brown eyes: a flash of realisation, of recognition.

'Shall we say eight o'clock?' asked Nyman.

'Let's do that.'

Did Olivia smile or was it just the light?

'As far as restaurants go, I'm not really…'

'It depends what we want to eat,' Olivia nodded. 'And how fancy you want to go. If we want good food, maybe we should look further afield. I know, I'm terrible when it comes to promoting the virtues of Palm Beach Finland, but I just think … If you're prepared to go a little way out of town, there's a nice fish place. Not a restaurant as such, more a kind of barbeque, a few tables and lots of landscape, but there's fish on the menu every day and the menu changes depending on the catch. So I can't tell you what's on offer, but the food is always excellent.'

'Sounds good. But you said it's further away. I don't have a car, and…'

'We'll cycle,' said Olivia. 'You like racing around on that old thing, don't you?'

Again, those eyes.

'I'll rent it again,' said Nyman. 'Apparently I like bikes that are too small for me.'

'Let's meet at the end of Shore Street. And remember to wrap up warm. The place is right by the sea, and as you know...'

'*It's the hottest beach in Finland*,' said Nyman like a TV anchor.

'You're getting the hang of this,' said Olivia Koski. But to Nyman's disappointment, this time she didn't smile.

⊙

Nyman returned to his chalet to change his clothes. The long-sleeved flannel shirt felt soft and warm. He ate breakfast in the beachside restaurant; he ordered six fried eggs, placed them on a long, curved slice of squeaky cheese and tucked in. His intention wasn't to gobble it all in one, but Christ, he'd broken into the chalet next door, spent an hour windsurfing and asked a suspect out on a date on only a glass of apple juice, and his hands were trembling from lack of food. He wiped egg yolk from his fingers and the corner of his mouth, spread a thick layer of marmalade on a slice of crisp, golden-brown toast, and washed it down with a second cup of black coffee. After that he walked to the bike rental shop.

In front of the shop he looked at his phone, not because he wanted to call someone – there was no one to call. He looked at the time. Olivia Koski would still be in her watchtower for hours.

Nyman jumped on his bike and cycled through the quiet town in a matter of minutes. He pedalled to the top of the hill and felt his thighs fill with lactic acid for the second time that morning. A moment later he was freewheeling downhill. The trees and undergrowth seemed to change. Spruces, sandy soil. He turned on to a dirt track, pedalled for a few more minutes and came to a fork in the road. He took the narrower, more difficult path.

A moment later he began to catch glimpses of Olivia Koski's house through the trees. Nyman stopped, walked his bike into the woods and left it behind a large boulder. He walked through the woods to the edge of the property and came to a stop. The yard was empty, the house looked quiet. He waited for a moment then began walking towards the building. He went round it from the side facing the woodland before arriving at the front. Before him were the charred remains of the sauna, and behind them, further off, the blue glimmer of the sea, although it was now grey. Clouds hid the sun from view, and the trees along the shore swayed in the wind.

Nyman took the steps up to the veranda, pulled his lock-picking set from his pocket and opened the door. He pulled the door shut behind him and stood there listening for a moment. He was slightly ashamed of what he was doing – he felt a wave of disgust – but this was the nature of his job. He opened the glass door in the porch. It creaked, making Nyman start; the sound was loud, its frequency one that would carry some distance. So everybody who stepped through this door made their presence known. Nyman kept a hold on the handle. He couldn't quite work out what this might mean, but imagined it must have some significance.

He took a few cautious steps across the floorboards. Their faint creaking was nothing compared to the door. Halfway along the hall was the door into the kitchen. Nyman stepped inside and stood right in the middle of the room. He recalled from photographs where the body had been found, but he wasn't here to reconstruct a crime scene. He turned and looked outside.

The windowpanes, smashed during the original altercation, had been replaced. Outside the clouds must have parted because the kitchen was flooded with fresh sunlight. The yard was clearly on a lower level – from down there you would only be able to see the head of anyone standing inside, if that. Nyman turned and saw his shadow reflected on the wall. He turned back, focussed his eyes in the middle of the yard, turned, and again saw his shadow on the wall. An interrupted trajectory. Whatever that meant.

Time to move on.

Nyman walked through another doorway. This lead into the living room, which was larger than his entire studio flat. On the back wall, the only wall without any windows, was a painting about three metres tall and a metre and a half wide. It was a powerful image: red and black swirls, and right in the middle of the painting was a red pattern on a black background that Nyman couldn't make out at all. It vaguely resembled … something. He walked from the living room into a smaller room with a long dining table and cupboards with glass doors. The stairs were situated between the smaller room and the hallway.

Now Nyman went upstairs, arriving at a small landing with one door leading out to the balcony and giving access to all the other rooms. There were three bedrooms. Nyman could see straight away which one was Olivia's. He stepped inside and immediately sensed that he was in the wrong place. The sensation was powerful. He felt it spread through his body like a minor electric shock. He'd never experienced anything like it before. Never with regard to a suspect. All the same, Nyman tried to take an inventory of items in the bedroom, or more to the point, to see whether there was anything in the bedroom that didn't belong there. The problem with a house this size was that he simply couldn't rifle through every cupboard and drawer, every nook and cranny. It was more about what he could see and what he couldn't, and about finding a balance or imbalance between the two. In this respect the bedroom was neutral. In other respects it was not. As he returned to the door Nyman realised what had been bugging him. Olivia's scent. Bugging him was perhaps the wrong turn of phrase. Quite the contrary. And at the moment Nyman saw himself as exactly the kind of pathetic panty thief that only has the guts to step into a woman's bedroom when nobody is watching – who leaves his mark on her bed and disappears into the night with sticky hands. It wasn't the most uplifting of sensations.

The two other bedrooms were simpler cases. The first one had a bed that hadn't been made up and an empty bedside table, and was clearly being used as a guest room, while the other one served as a library with shelves, a desk and a laptop computer. Nyman didn't switch on the laptop. It was too easy to detect whether someone had used it, and, besides, most people signed into their computers with a password. He wondered whether Olivia was on Facebook. Probably. Definitely. Nyman was not. After all, who was he? Who would have wanted to be his friend? And why were thoughts like this suddenly whirring through his head?

As he walked down the stairs he recapped his main conclusions. Nothing had aroused his suspicions, nothing suggested Olivia Koski's guilt or innocence. He hadn't learned anything new. Except that in this case things might actually be exactly the way they seemed and he really was a pitiful, lonely wanker.

He walked round the lower floor once more, this time in the opposite direction: the dining room, the living room, the bathroom – with no running water; the kitchen, hallway, porch – and came to the same conclusion as he had upstairs. He opened the front door and stepped onto the veranda. He carefully closed the door behind him, took the few steps down to the yard and thankfully managed to take a few steps towards the garden before he made out the sound of a motor and tyres against the gravel. A few seconds later a car pulled into view.

A police car.

18

The phone rang and Chico woke up. He'd been asleep in Robin's bed. Next to Robin, by the looks of it. That hadn't been the situation in the early hours when he'd moved into the bedroom. Robin had been snoring on the couch, soft sighing noises emanating from some part of his body, and Chico had realised there was only one place in the apartment where he would be able to lie down before starting to feel queasy.

But before that…

Chico followed Robin inside. Robin turned, began backing up towards the couch and sat down at the far end, all the while keeping his back to the wall. But Chico had already seen it. It looked like a cat's scratching post. Chico sat down in a twenty-euro armchair that was so rickety, it felt as though it might collapse at any moment.

'So you were watching the box,' said Chico, determined not to mention Nea. 'What happened to your back?'

Robin looked at him as though he had no idea what Chico was talking about.

'Been thrashing yourself in the sauna again?' Chico asked. 'Where did you go?'

'A sauna … nearby…'

His best friend was lying to him. Why?

'Good soak?'

Something flickered in Robin's eyes. 'Hot.'

'You haven't heard any news?' asked Chico.

Robin shook his head, seemed to think of something and pointed at the television. 'There are new characters on tonight.'

The phone continued to ring. Robin's flayed back was on his left, and on his right was the window, light filtering through the blinds and falling onto the bed. There was something unpleasant about this lighting, the sensual interaction of light and shadow – something inappropriate. Chico stood up, snatched his jeans from the back of the chair and found his phone. He didn't want to pick up the phone but its trill insisted he did so. Chico looked at Robin, who was fast asleep. Chico answered and Jorma Leivo asked where he was. Chico told him. Jorma Leivo explained that either Chico would meet him in thirty minutes in the same place as last time or he would meet the police considerably sooner. Chico plumped for the thirty-minute option.

◉

Jorma Leivo was waiting at the quarry when Chico arrived. The sky was cloudy. Chico was wearing the same clothes as the day before, including the grey Led Zeppelin T-shirt. He felt grey in many other respects too. Even the surface of the small pond looked grey. Jorma Leivo, however, exuded energy and bright colours.

'We're going on the offensive,' he said. 'We're going to increase the pressure. I mean, *you're* going to increase the pressure. You and your boyfriend.'

'Robin isn't my boyfriend.'

'You sleep together. You just told me.'

'We were just sleeping. And it isn't what it looks like. Nothing is.'

Leivo seemed to ponder Chico's last sentence. Chico didn't know where the words had come from.

'For your information,' Leivo continued, 'I've been offered ten thousand euros for your head.'

Chico tried to put the pieces together in his mind. For some reason everybody seemed to know more about what was going on than he did. Jorma Leivo didn't wait for a reply.

'That means I expect you to give me results worth ten thousand

euros – and more besides. That's my price; for that amount I'll keep
your little secret – I won't tell anybody you're the one who killed that
guy in the house.'

Chico thought about this.

'We didn't kill him. I know it looks like we did, but we were
actually trying to help him. It's the truth. We only wanted to clear
his head. He was so bloody angry, probably because someone threw
a rock at him. And listen, you're every bit as guilty as we are. We
wouldn't have gone down there if you hadn't paid us.'

'There's no evidence of that. None whatsoever.'

Chico stared at Leivo and thought. Leivo's expression suggested
he was confident he was in the right.

'And where's your partner in crime?'

'In bed,' said Chico. 'Asleep.'

Leivo looked at him for a moment, then shrugged his shoulders.
'And you're awake. Good. This might yet come to something, if you
two would just pull your fingers out and remember what's in store
for you if I don't start to see results.'

'We torched her shed too,' said Chico. 'You can't say we haven't
tried.'

'That was too much,' Leivo sighed. 'Too obvious. You've had the
police and the fire squad round there twice now. You were supposed
to make things difficult for her, unpleasant. You were supposed to
cause a little bit of distress, not get the authorities involved. You
might as well have exploded a neutron bomb in there. Use your
brains.'

'We've tried,' said Chico and realised what that must sound like.
'I mean, we have been using our brains, but something unexpected
always happens.'

'This is your last chance. It's Thursday today. By Monday, that
land is mine. In other words, she'll have accepted my offer. It's your
business how you make it happen. This is an ultimatum. Do you
know what that means?'

Chico shook his head.

'You don't know what an ultimatum is?'

'Yes,' said Chico and stopped shaking his head. 'But what can we do?'

'You can start by thinking what I could do with ten thousand euros.'

They stood facing each other for a moment. Sand, silence, two men. Chico thought of the static Western in which Clint Eastwood held a cigar at the corner of his mouth for two and half hours and eventually killed everybody.

Jorma Leivo was like a lost colour chart in a world of grey. He turned and walked back to his car. Chico clipped on his helmet, jumped on the back of Robin's scooter and watched as Leivo's SUV trundled up the side of the quarry, black smoke belching from its exhaust pipe. The vehicle disappeared from view, and suddenly everything was silent. A swallow swooped along the wall of the quarry, back to its nest.

Chico couldn't say where the hunch came from, how it took root in his mind, but he realised then, with unflinching clarity, that he wouldn't spend a single second thinking about what Jorma Leivo might or might not do with ten thousand euros.

⊙

It took quite a violent shake to rouse Robin. He blearily listened to Chico's explanation of what had happened at the quarry.

'That's not fair. It's not Leivo's money,' said Robin.

Robin looked like an animal roused from hibernation. An animal that needed a shave. There was a stiffness to his voice that Chico hadn't heard before. Robin repeated himself, and Chico nodded. Though Robin looked like a creature more at home in the woods or the savanna, he sounded as convincing as the hero in an action movie. The kind of action hero who, in the most impossible situation, says, *We're gonna pull through this*, and the viewer believes him wholeheartedly.

They sat in Robin's living room, Chico in the precarious armchair, Robin on the couch. Shirtless. It was light outside, though still grey, and Chico had opened the blinds, yet for some reason the room refused to open up. To Chico it felt as though they were stuck in a freezer container. And he didn't know why Robin wasn't at work. He wasn't going to ask. The same instinct that prevented him from letting on that he knew Nea had visited and ravaged Robin's back (Chico couldn't bring himself to envisage the event any more than he could the factors leading up to the mauling) now made him hesitant about everything else too.

'It's so wrong,' said Robin.

At least Chico could say something about this. 'What if Leivo doesn't get the money?'

'He will, if he grasses us up.'

'And if he doesn't?'

'But he'll get ten thousand—'

'Robin,' Chico interrupted. 'What if he doesn't drop us in it *and* doesn't get the money? What if we stop him?'

'How much?'

Chico was beginning to lose his cool. 'How much what?'

'How much should we stop him?'

Chico hadn't thought about this. 'I guess if we decide to stop him, we'll have to do something that stops him from…'

'Ever…'

Chico saw a change. Robin propped his elbows on his knees, leaned forwards. Chico shrugged his shoulders.

'I guess,' he heard himself saying.

Robin nodded. It was a determined, physical nod.

'You see, yesterday…' said Robin, his voice now that of someone who makes decisions for a living. At least, that's what Chico thought such people might sound like. 'I saw this thing on TV.'

19

Sitting in her swimming costume, Olivia Koski crossed her right leg over her left and explained to Jorma Leivo that she had begun to reconsider his offer.

'I think I'm in danger,' she said. 'I've been thinking about our conversation since my sauna burned down. I'm out at the end of the peninsula all by myself...'

Olivia used her brown eyes to her advantage and showed plenty of leg. Jorma Leivo was a man, after all. Though his taste in women was probably more in line with those who appeared on a tyre calendar, he had the same hormones as all the others of his species. Hormones were democratic: once a certain limit had been exceeded, a man would run after almost anything at all.

'But I'm concerned about two things,' she continued. 'First, there's the offer you made: it's far too low.'

'I think it's quite realistic,' said Leivo. 'But let's consider it an opening bid, something we can come back to if both of us agree.'

'Of course,' said Olivia. This man's like a boomerang, she thought. No matter how things start, they always end up benefitting him. 'The second thing I'm worried about is what happened at my house. The homicide. The dead man in my kitchen.'

'What about it?' asked Jorma Leivo. 'Him?' he quickly corrected himself.

The office was silent. Olivia was certain she could still smell the fresh pink paint on the walls. The former scouts' summer cabin had undergone quite a transformation, with its new plastic palm trees and other tasteless paraphernalia. Next to Leivo's desk was an advert for sun cream and a tower of tubs. It didn't look like many of them had been sold.

'I want the matter resolved before I move out, quite simply because it's my parents' house – it belonged to my mother and father…'

'The police looked into it,' said Leivo, 'and they came to the conclusion that it's impossible to resolve.'

'That's why I've come to talk to you.'

Leivo thought about this for a moment. Olivia kept her eyes fixed on him.

'Of course, I don't know anything about it,' he said, trying to avoid eye contact. 'But if those are your terms…'

'It's one of my terms.'

'One of your terms,' Leivo continued seamlessly. 'If that's one of your terms I can employ a very reliable person to look into the matter. If we agree that it will lead to the sale of the property. The person in question is, shall we say, a master detective by any standards, worked with Interpol and the rest of them. But I don't understand how…'

'Finding out who did this will bring me peace of mind,' said Olivia. 'And once I have peace of mind, I'll be better placed to consider your offer, which we can discuss separately.'

Leivo seemed to think about this. At least, Olivia hoped he was thinking about it. She hoped she had started the ball rolling.

'How should we get to the bottom of this?' Leivo asked eventually. 'I mean, how precisely?'

Olivia shifted position, slowly uncrossed and crossed her legs.

'I want to know who he is and where he is,' she said. 'That's a must. But, between you and me, I don't mind if that information goes no further. In fact, we can agree that it stays within these four walls. What's important is to find out what happened. I don't know if you can imagine what it's like to be a woman living in a remote house all by herself. It's frightening. Especially, as you said, if this is only the beginning of a larger crime wave.'

Leivo's face lit up as he remembered what he'd told her. 'Exactly,' he said and looked pensive, or at least he did a good job of pretending. 'Who knows what kind of serial killer might be on the loose? And with that in mind you're absolutely right that this case needs to be investigated thoroughly. We agree on that. I'll put my best man on it.'

'Who is he?' asked Olivia.

Leivo was twiddling a biro in his left hand. At her question the pen stopped still.

'He operates anonymously.'

Olivia nodded. 'Undercover? I understand.'

'How are things at the beach?'

Olivia thought for a moment. 'Fifteen minutes ago it was grey and windy. There were maybe two dozen people out in total. Quite a few sunloungers still free.'

'How many?'

'How many are there altogether?'

'The brand-new sunloungers…' he said, a hint of pride in his voice. 'The white ones with the turquoise shades … there are sixty of them. A hundred and twenty in total.'

'I'd say there are about a hundred and fifteen free.'

Leivo glanced at Olivia. 'Word hasn't got round yet. We need a boost.'

Olivia said nothing.

'A marketing campaign, maybe,' said Leivo. 'Once people know what this is all about, they'll choose us. Often all it needs is a little push. I've been thinking of different marketing slogans we could use: *Frugal families save on sunscreen. Forget the language barrier once and for all. Sun and sand only a six-minute flight away.* If you imagine that a jet plane travels at eight hundred and fifty kilometres an hour, then the journey from Helsinki is about six minutes. Of course, disembarking is a bit of challenge, but we're going to fix that soon. And my favourite for our transatlantic clientele: *Florida without the face-eating junkies.* I saw that on TV. It's a bit edgy, I know, and maybe it's not appropriate at the moment, what with a murderer on the loose, but for the future, once we get to the bottom of the case. Then there are slogans for the Thai market: *Diarrhoea only from your own cuisine.* And for our European customers: *Finally – a beach that's one hundred percent sunburn-free.* And how about: *Leave your melanoma at home.* These still need a bit of tweaking, I know, but as you can see we're holding all the cards here. I wouldn't have put money into this place unless I knew it was the best business venture in the world.'

Olivia sat in silence. She was beginning to understand things, to see things clearly, both figuratively and in reality. Leivo, sitting across the desk, was sweating profusely. Talking this much had turned him red in the face. It seemed the slightest exertion made him hot and bothered.

'Sounds good,' she said, and in some ways this was true. When it came to Palm Beach Finland, Leivo appeared to be deadly serious. That meant he might be prepared to go very far indeed to shore up his own interests. 'I'll wait to see what your investigation turns up.'

Leivo gave a start. He had clearly been carried away by his own slogans.

'You won't need to wait long for that. I guarantee you things will start to become clear sooner than you think.'

◉

Olivia's legs were trembling as she walked across the sand. She was startled when she noticed it. She had done what she set out to do: she had got the investigation under way. And straight away she'd heard more than she'd expected. Leivo said he'd sunk all his money into this place. That said a lot. He didn't need to think of anybody but himself. Olivia had sunk all her money into her house. And what was she prepared to do? The answer was simple: whatever it took. Her thoughts made her shiver.

The wind had dropped slightly. The clouds were parting. A typical summer's day.

She arrived at the lifeguards' tower. Leivo's words were spinning through her head. Olivia had carefully played the role of the damsel in distress; she hadn't said anything specifically untrue, though she had embellished the pure, unadulterated truth somewhat. When you behaved like that, it was worth bearing in mind that the person across the table might be doing the same. Or worse.

And Leivo had a dream.

Those dreams seemed dangerous.

Olivia climbed into the watchtower. She looked at the beach, the sea, the people. Ultimately everybody was looking for something. And that's what had happened to her too. She'd been walking through life with her eyes closed, doing the things she assumed she was supposed to do or what other people had asked her to do. Then she had woken up. She couldn't be the only one. The older you are when you wake up to your dreams, she thought, the more vigorously you pursue them. The more desperately. Because with every passing day there's simply less to lose.

She tried to guess Jorma Leivo's age. Fifty-five, perhaps. If she, at the age of thirty-nine, was prepared to do everything she'd managed to achieve so far that day, what did that say about an easily agitated man in a Sonny Crockett outfit who'd sunk his last dime into a failing beach resort?

Olivia took a deep breath.

She would continue her investigation. She wasn't afraid. She would not shun her own dreams or those of others. She'd survived before, and she would survive this too. Jesus Christ, she lived in a house with no running water and where a man had recently been murdered; she had survived the strange deaths of her parents, which had so fascinated the entire village; she had survived two men who had taken her to the cleaners; and yet here she was. Slightly cold, that went without saying, but otherwise ready for anything.

She didn't believe Leivo, and at the same time she did. When it came to Palm Beach Finland, it was easy to imagine that Leivo believed his own words. On the other hand, she didn't think that he would hire the best man possible to undertake their little investigation. He almost certainly didn't know a man like that. A man like that was hard to imagine.

Olivia laughed.

Even more incredible was the notion that a detective could work undercover in a place like Palm Beach Finland. The idea was utterly inconceivable.

Many things happened, had happened and would happen in the future, but that wasn't one of them.

20

Nyman liked the police station. Situated in a wooden building, it was small and quiet, and the windows in the interview room looked out into the park. The park wasn't especially big, but it was well looked after: the flowerbeds were in neat, straight rows bursting with yellow, blue, violet and pink, the tidily mown grass glowed a vivid hue of green and the elms invited people into their shade. The room itself was oblong, the ceiling high. The walls were white and empty. Opposite the door was a window, in the middle of the room a birch-veneer desk with four chairs, three of which were currently occupied. The police officers were sitting in a row on one side of the table, Nyman on the other. The floorboards creaked whenever they moved their chairs or adjusted their positions.

In other circumstances Nyman would have enjoyed the situation. But the phone call he'd had with Muurla a moment ago only made him feel more insecure. That sense of insecurity was heightened by the clock above the door and the slow progression of its hands.

Upon arriving at the station, two matters were at the front of his mind: he must make a phone call to Muurla and he must get to his dinner date with Olivia Koski. The call to Muurla was granted, as Nyman had first asked the officers whether he was suspected of a crime and whether this was an official interview. No, came the answer from the front seat of the car, they only wanted to chat to him, so Nyman knew this was only an informal conversation. That made things easier from Nyman's perspective. In that case, he replied, it's probably alright if I call my colleague to let him know I won't be able to spend the afternoon with him.

Once they arrived at the station, the officers courteously left the room for the duration of his phone call. Muurla picked up right away. Nyman explained where he was, apologised for calling and said that his phone was about to run out of battery. He spoke quickly.

'I'm in a hurry. Olivia Koski mustn't find out that the police picked somebody up outside her house this afternoon. We need a media blackout. Effective until further notice. Other than that, things can wait. This is a perfect opportunity. I want to talk to these local officers. But there's one appointment I've got to keep, so make sure I'm out of here by seven thirty.'

Nyman gave a brief description of the wooden building, the park, the silence and the friendliness. Then he waited.

And eventually Muurla spoke: 'Reminds me of the nudist colony I found in Ibiza last summer, when I decided to broaden my—'

Nyman interrupted him. 'Sorry, I haven't got time for this. I'm at work and…'

'Right,' said Muurla and again paused before replying. 'We've got a problem.'

Nyman waited.

Muurla continued. 'You've asked an investigator from the fraud office to look into the accounts of certain persons who are not directly under investigation.'

'You weren't supposed to know about that.'

'Neither was the head of the fraud office, or his boss, or *his* boss.'

Nyman said nothing.

Muurla continued. 'As you know, what you've asked for is completely illegal. Everyone here is treading carefully after what happened with a few cases in the narcotics department. Now all requests for information under the radar have to been double- and triple-checked.'

'That means all our investigations would be a matter of public record, which kind of goes against the whole undercover idea.'

'I know. But my hands are tied.'

'In what way, exactly?'

'You're on your own. If you decide to continue.'

'Excuse me?'

'There's nothing I can do. I can't hold things up at that end. I can't even contact them without first reporting the matter here and asking for permission. And once I have permission, there's nothing I can do without blowing your cover. And if I blow your cover, the investigation will be over as far as you're concerned and you'll have to come back to Helsinki.'

Nyman looked out of the window. He didn't need time to think. Muurla fell silent too. Nyman understood what that meant. He was on his own.

'I'm going to continue,' he said and ended the call.

◉

Murder. That's what this was all about. Forget all the initial niceties and the 'friendly chat'. The senior constable already seemed familiar. Grey moustache, metallic-rimmed glasses, blue eyes. Beside him sat a dark-haired man with a ruddy face, significantly younger than his colleague, who was taking notes for both of them. Nyman remembered this man too, from Olivia's yard. On that occasion he had observed keenly, stared even, without saying much.

'It's a busy yard,' said the senior constable. 'It's like Central Station, people in and out, dead or alive. What were you doing there this afternoon?'

'I believe that's between me and the owner of the property.'

The officer shrugged his shoulders. 'It's just a question,' he said. 'This is just an informal chat. Were you on foot?'

'I cycled some distance, then started walking. It felt better, and you see so much more. It's a beautiful peninsula.'

'Why didn't you cycle down to the yard and enjoy the view from there?'

'It's a bit embarrassing.'

'Don't mind us, we've heard it all.'

'It's to do with my backside.'

The deputy looked up from his notepad. 'We're listening,' he said in a soft voice.

'I've taken up windsurfing, and I haven't cycled in a while. My muscles are aching in places I didn't even know existed. Even sitting down feels like being punched. I couldn't sit on the saddle a moment longer.'

Both officers looked at him.

'Let's assume that to be the case,' the senior constable said eventually. 'There are a few other matters…'

Nyman also wanted to get on to the subject of the homicide. He wanted to find out, by reading between the lines, exactly what these officers thought about it – hear the things they hadn't written in the case file.

'Let's start from when you arrived here,' said the senior constable. 'How do you like the resort's new look?'

'I suppose I'm getting used to it.'

'What does that mean?'

'I'm thinking of staying on a bit longer.'

'People to kill? Saunas to burn down?'

'I did neither of those things.'

'You're living in one of the chalets, yes? Alone?'

'Tubbs, the bright-green one. And yes, I'm there by myself.'

'On the night of the fire, you said there was a witness who could place you elsewhere, earlier that evening.'

'My neighbour. Drives a BMW. Why do you assume it was an outsider?'

'I beg your pardon?'

'Couldn't it be a local behind these crimes?'

'Are you one of these wannabe detectives?'

'Absolutely not. What's wrong with local crooks?'

'Cruelty, that's what,' said the deputy. 'We haven't seen this level of cruelty and malice.'

The senior constable looked at his deputy.

'That happens sometimes,' said Nyman before the constable could get a word in. 'Things get out of hand, as it were.'

The constable turned to look at Nyman. 'You say you're a maths teacher.'

'That's right.'

'Where?'

'Nowhere at the moment. If I get a call, I'm always ready to teach. But surely cruelty itself doesn't rule anybody out? As far as I know, crimes of this magnitude are generally rare.'

'We know everybody round here,' said the deputy. 'The ones with brawn haven't got any brains. And the ones with brains, they're war veterans. The youngest is eighty-seven years old and in round-the-clock care. And as for people my age – those who haven't already moved away and who don't work for the council – well, the less said the better.'

The constable nodded and straightened his back. 'If you ask me, they're a bit too stupid,' he said. 'There are a couple of guys we might have considered, but we can't think what would motivate them. These guys can barely change their underpants without a financial incentive. It would take one hell of a dictator to get them off their backsides.'

'I might know who you mean,' said Nyman. 'I think I saw them on the beach; am I right?'

'That's where they tend to gravitate,' said the deputy. 'It's a force of nature.'

And just as Nyman was beginning to think they were making progress, the senior constable leaned forwards and stared Nyman right in the eyes.

'And that brings us to you. An outsider.'

And so the game of cat and mouse continued. It continued going round in circles for hours: Nyman didn't make any progress in his own investigation and couldn't help the police in theirs. All the while he was conscious of the passing of time. He took a deep breath and tried time and again to bring this lengthy, entirely voluntary conversation to a natural end. But there seemed to be no end in sight. Every now and then one of the officers went to the bathroom, fetched a drink, read through his notes, his colleague's notes, and returned to something they'd already discussed hours ago.

The closer the clock came to half past seven, the more agitated Nyman became.

And finally the clock reached half past seven.

Nyman had to get away.

He had a murder to investigate.

He had a date.

21

Jorma Leivo closed his eyes and again saw the other side of the world. It was hot there.

Leivo recalled his own discomfort: the tingling in his nose and cheeks, the slow but no less agonising sunburn on his arms and legs, the shirt clinging to his skin, his underwear rubbing and chafing against his groin, loose on one side, ever tightening on the other, gradually working its way deeper and deeper down his crevice before eventually turning into a wet rope that he had to disentangle from his body whenever he visited one of the filthy public toilets. Toilets where there was never any soap, leaving his hands unnaturally sticky and odorous. It was bad enough when he was eating and made him feel distinctly uncomfortable shaking hands with new acquaintances. He couldn't bring himself to apologise, saying the gunk between his thumb and forefinger probably started life in his pants.

Was there a single tourist destination in Asia or southern Europe where he hadn't felt uncomfortably hot and bothered? No. He had always set off with great expectations, trying to convince himself that this time things would be different. But things were never different. It was always the same. Until just over a year ago, on a particularly clammy day to the east of Phuket, his skin positively sizzling with sunburn, and he felt like he'd been driven into a corner, when he experienced nothing short of a religious awakening.

The moment was so clear that Leivo would have praised the Lord for giving him this business idea, if he had been one of the faithful, like his mother, who only a month before had passed away in the presence of Jesus. His mother was a cleaner by profession, and even after retirement she had continued working for the church in a voluntary capacity. Her jobs included making sure the altar in their brand-new place of worship was kept spotless. And so one morning, as she was dusting the holy accoutrements, his mother had stumbled or somehow misjudged her body weight and, unaware of an inherent design flaw in the cross, set in motion a chain reaction ending with the Lord himself falling down from his tall plinth. Perhaps she had seen it coming, and perhaps she had tried to catch the falling bronze statue, but it turned out the Messiah weighed more than a tonne and Leivo's mother had ended up crushed beneath the body of Christ, legs and arms akimbo.

The business idea that Leivo hit upon on that tropical, white sandy beach was simple: what if you could have all of this, palms and everything, but without all the unpleasant parts? Without this heat, for one, which he found utterly unbearable. Without having to change your clothes three times a day, without roasting your skin, without suntan lotion that stings your eyes. That same evening, once Leivo had returned to the air-conditioned sanctuary of his bedroom, opened a bag of crisps and sat on his bed to flick through the myriad TV channels (fair play, tourist hotels did this best: the endless stream of TV channels, especially those that showed reruns of the old classics), Leivo had come across an episode of his favourite show of all time and had the second revelation of the day. The theme music and the opening credits descended on the room like an omen. His favourite show from all those years ago. This couldn't be coincidence. And with that, the two ideas collided, combined, became one. He jumped up from the bed, spilling bright-yellow energy drink across his pyjamas in the process, switched on his computer and started searching for holiday resorts for sale in Finland. He found a grand total of one.

Leivo had invested every last penny of his inheritance in the property. Almost every penny. He still had enough left over to buy Olivia Koski's unique strip of land. After that he would have enough collateral to offset new loans and take the next step. He was taking a considerable risk, but couldn't help thinking that he was following his destiny. Why else would his mother have given him two lives:

first as the happy-go-lucky Leivo, and now as the proprietor and manager of Palm Beach Finland? Besides, his inheritance came with great responsibility. In the eyes of his mother, Jesus and the bank, the one thing Jorma Leivo could not afford was failure.

He opened his eyes and looked at the papers in front of him.

It was a challenging scenario.

Olivia Koski had said she was prepared to sell the property if the matter of the homicide could be brought to a conclusion. But if it happened too easily, the price would still be a problem. Even if Leivo were to hand Olivia Koski the two good-for-nothings, he still might not be able to acquire the plot for himself. That meant he still needed the pair of idiots: to make life at the house uncomfortable and to make Olivia Koski even more desperate. On the other hand, there was the offer of ten thousand euros from the suave investor (the *Executive Investment Manager*, according to his business card) for the identity of the culprits. That would help him make up the difference between his naturally low initial offer and Olivia Koski's presumably much higher asking price. It might just be enough. He needed both; he needed everything. He needed the Chuckle Brothers as part of his plan, then, in order to hand them over – twice; both to Koski and the investor and to whatever fate awaited them. He needed ten thousand euros and a lower asking price.

Jorma Leivo cracked open a can of energy drink. He took a long sip.

It was quite a puzzle. But Leivo guessed he was already through the worst of it. He had guts. He was the founder of Palm Beach Finland. And Palm Beach Finland was something that soon the whole country would thank him for; something for which he would be remembered.

22

Chico had to find a beer. A fresh beer, not the same swill he usually drank, clouded with plankton and other small creatures, but real beer, frothing like a brook – beer that clears your thoughts and steadies your nerves. Chilled beer from a real tap. He downed half of his pint in one go and lowered the glass to the counter. Just as he'd feared, it instantly started feeling expensive. It *was* expensive: six euros fifty. For one measly pint. What was this stuff made from? Liquid gold collected by maidens straight from a mountain spring while unicorns watched over them? It felt as if this too was a plot in which someone else was pulling the strings. Chico didn't want to think about it. Life was mostly a string of disappointments, and he already had plenty of other things to think about. Chico carried the rest of his pint to the table in the corner where Robin was waiting for him.

Chico had to admit that in some miraculous way Robin seemed to be taking control of matters. It was bewildering. Where had Robin suddenly found the determination, the strength of character, the new vocabulary? Words like *perspective*, *regaining control* and *procedure*. He looked at his old friend and wondered whether this really was his old friend at all. Robin had always opened his mouth before engaging his brain, letting out a stream of consciousness that sounded like random material on a cassette, and had a habit of repeating things with a surprising degree of accuracy. But the things he was talking about now, Chico had difficulty following, and it wasn't just because of the words. Robin looked as though he was chairing a meeting. And even more unheard-of, he wasn't drinking beer.

'Protein, caffeine, creatine,' Robin explained the contents of the bottle in front of him. 'Before my workout.'

'Workout?'

'It's hard work.'

Chico shook his head. 'I don't know.'

'You said yourself: what if he doesn't grass us up – ever? This is a preventative measure.'

Again. Another new term.

'It's a bit … final.'

'Not for us. Nature will take care of the rest. We just … prepare the food and someone else will eat it.'

Chico looked at the man sitting across the table, a man he no longer knew at all. 'That sounds even worse.'

Robin gave a melodramatic shrug. 'I thought you wanted to be a rock star, I thought that was your dream.'

Chico drank his beer. It wasn't nearly worth six fifty.

'I want…' he began but didn't know how to continue – with anything. He felt like he'd already given everything. And now he was being asked to give more. 'I'm just not sure this is the path we should…'

'I bet Springsteen wouldn't think like that.'

'Springsteen is hardly sitting in a small-town bar, just shy of forty and with no money to his name, wondering how to take out his boss.'

'Or maybe he is. And there you have it. You said it yourself. Bruce is the boss. He's already got rid of all the other bosses.'

'He didn't kill them.'

'How do you know?' asked Robin and again sounded like a complete stranger. Chico recognised the rhythm of the speech, but couldn't say who it belonged to. 'Maybe Bruce saw an opportunity and grabbed it. Maybe he realised that sometimes you've gotta do what you've gotta do. And maybe Bruce hasn't told the whole truth about how he got his career off the ground. Of course, he's not going to blurt out that he was involved with the Jersey mafia, he's not going to let on where he found the money for his first real guitar. They have *omertà*. The law of silence. How much do you bet Bruce is a hitman? Think about it. He's got the perfect alibi. Constantly on the road, travelling from one town to the next. And nobody would bat an eyelid if they saw him moving around at night. Everyone's, like, *Hey it's Bruce, everybody's buddy, probably coming home from a gig.* And he is – but it's not the gig they think.'

Chico stared at Robin. Robin sipped his protein shake.

'Robin, Bruce is not a hitman.'

'You believe what you want.'

'I've read his autobiography…'

'Right, his *auto*biography. Who's going to write, *Oh, by the way, I killed a rival singer last week.* Think about all the drug killings, the overdoses, a private jet falls out of the sky, a car plunges down a ravine, a rival rock singer dies inexplicably. Suddenly Bruce is in New York or Los Angeles at the same time, strutting around, muscles bulging, always ready to grab the mic. Coincidence? I think not.'

Chico shook his head. 'This is…'

Robin leaned forwards. 'This is your last chance. Guitar or no guitar. Do you want to spend the rest of your life roaming around that miserable beach?'

The final question was phrased in a way that Chico knew only too well. It hit the exact spot – the place that was the seat of all his frustrations and about which he had poured his heart out to Robin all these painful years. It was just about the only sensible thing Robin had said that evening, but it was the crux of the matter, the only reasonable question Chico could have asked himself.

Do you want to be on that beach for the rest of your life? Answer: no.

He wanted a fresh start, one last chance. The one he thought he'd already had, but which … he might be about to get again. Robin was right. He still had an astonishing ability to find clarity amid the confusion.

And there was another, more pressing factor at play too: Jorma Leivo was going to sell them out. So why shouldn't they sell him out first? Chico finished off his pint.

'Let's get the spades,' he said.

PART THREE
RESULTS

1

Jan Nyman had no other option but to interrupt the senior constable. Nyman raised a hand, slowly but firmly, as if to ask a question in class. The constable understood the sign, slowed his words and eventually stopped mid-sentence.

'Yes?'

'May I go to the bathroom?' asked Nyman.

Nyman couldn't imagine there was really anything to think about here. He was silent, and looked the senior constable in the eye.

'Very well,' he sighed eventually. 'Leo can go with you.'

Nyman looked at the deputy. Leo seemed uncomfortable.

'The more the merrier,' said Nyman.

Leo's already reddened cheeks now looked as if they were on fire.

'Leo,' said the constable. 'Use the staff bathroom.'

They stood up. Nyman was first to walk through the door and remained standing in the corridor. Leo, the young constable, passed him and ushered him onwards. Nyman followed him. The old wooden floorboards creaked cosily with every step. Nyman noted that the sound was quite distinct. They arrived at a doorway at the far end of the short corridor. The staffroom ahead of them stank of stale coffee, and the bathroom was situated behind a round dining table. Nyman realised why the constable had told them to use this bathroom; the public bathroom was in the foyer, right next to the front door. This, however, was at the back of the building, with no possible escape route

Nyman stepped into the cubicle, locked the door and did his business. He flushed the toilet, washed his hands and dried them. He took his phone from his pocket. The battery had died. Nyman sighed. He placed his hands on the lock and the handle and rattled them back and forth in different directions. The door did not open, but the sound of the ratcheting was just right. Nyman paused. He was sure he could hear footsteps behind the door.

'Leo,' he called through the door.

'Yes?'

Leo's voice sounded like it was very nearby; he must have been standing directly on the other side of the door.

'Leo, the door's stuck.'

'How?'

'I don't know. I'm not a locksmith. Go and get help.'

'Help?'

'Can you open the door from that side?' Nyman asked and tightened his grip on the lock and the handle.

Leo tried the handle. 'It's locked.'

'I know that, Leo. Fetch a screwdriver and open the lock from that side.'

'I don't know…'

'The lock is jammed. I can't stay in here.'

Silence.

'I'll have to ask Reijo.'

Nyman said nothing. He gave the handle another rattle and waited. Eventually he heard Leo's footsteps walking away from the door. Then he heard the creaking of the floorboards. Leo was in the corridor. Nyman opened the door and stepped outside.

From the staffroom, the only possible direction was the way they had come in. Nyman quickly crept to the doorway, glanced into the corridor and saw Leo's back at the door to the interview room. Nyman jumped across the floorboards to the door on the other side of the corridor and landed right on the threshold. The frame was made of strong material and didn't make a sound. Leo remained where he was, and Nyman slipped into the room.

This was clearly an office for two people. There was one window. Nyman moved the framed photographs of children and teenagers from the windowsill, gripped the handle and carefully pulled the window ajar. The window frame made a noise that sounded like the dying gasp of an ageing opera singer. Nyman yanked the window fully open. He heard the creaking of floorboards, the thud of footsteps, shouting.

Nyman jumped. The rosebushes tore his shins. He clambered through the bushes, millions of tiny thorns lacerating him on the way. The thorns were strong and as sharp as tacks. The pain brought tears to his eyes.

'Where do you think you're going?' Nyman heard Leo's voice behind him.

Nyman thought better of saying he had a dinner date with a potential murderer. He finally emerged from the bushes and broke into a run. He was an experienced runner, but the thorns had affected his legs. They were on fire. Nyman glanced behind him. Leo dashed out of the main door, and Nyman instantly saw that Leo could run too.

Nyman crossed the street, tried to get his bearings and choose the best possible route. The asphalt road turned into a dirt track. Even if his phone hadn't been out of battery, he didn't have time to check the map. Nyman realised he would be no match for Leo once they were on flat ground. Nyman ran as fast as he humanly could, and still it seemed as though Leo was gaining on him with every step.

This was an area of detached houses. Wooden houses with lush green gardens. Nyman headed off the path and into one of the gardens, ran between the rows of currant bushes and hurdled across a fence. Garden upon garden. A trampoline. A playhouse. A barbeque. A ride-on lawnmower the size of a tractor. A barking dog. A trampoline. A playhouse. A barbeque. A quad bike. A barking…

Just when he thought he'd managed to lose Leo, he heard the deputy approaching again.

Nyman dipped beneath a row of apple trees and arrived in yet another garden. In the garden was a wooden house – and Nyman saw that the porch door was ajar. He ran to the door, opened it, stepped inside and quietly pulled the door shut behind him, all the while keeping his eyes on the garden.

Leo burst from beneath the apple trees just as Nyman had a moment earlier. Nyman imagined that Leo would continue running, but he didn't. He slowed before the next garden, stopped and looked around.

Nyman tried to steady his breathing. And, once he had, he heard it: he wasn't the only one panting. He carefully turned around.

On the screen of the laptop that had fallen to the floor, a curvaceous blonde woman was engaged in what seemed like mortal combat with a black man of substantial endowment. The tempo was frantic, the voices of the actors ecstatic. But this X-rated Grand National wasn't the only thing waiting for him in the porch.

Behind the computer, slumped in a cosy dark-blue armchair, a boy of about fourteen sat with a look of terror on his face, his right hand still clenched around his glistening fire-red joystick.

Nyman looked the boy in the eyes as calmly as he could and raised his right forefinger to his lips. Everything's all right, he gestured to the boy with his left hand, let's take it easy. Nyman couldn't tell whether the boy registered any of his hand signals.

Nyman carefully peered out into the garden. Leo was standing on the spot, glancing back the way he had come, then to the sides.

He looked back at the boy. Nyman wished the boy would release his grip and maybe even pull up his trousers, but he seemed frozen stiff, in every possible way. Nyman hoped he hadn't caused the kid any lasting trauma. Youth can be a delicate time. Nyman was about to whisper to the boy that there was a blanket within reach, but he didn't have time. What the boy did next was utterly incomprehensible.

'Mum!' he screamed. 'Mum!'

Nyman shook his head and looked out into the garden. Leo was approaching.

Nyman locked the door, ran through the house to the front door – and naturally couldn't see a sign of Mum anywhere. He opened the door, closed it carefully behind him, and found himself on the street again.

He crossed the road, arrived at another garden: more currant bushes, a pile of firewood and a dartboard with a picture of an obnoxious celebrity pinned to the top. Nyman climbed over the mesh fence and tried to make his way forwards behind the bushes, trees and hedges, but realised almost at once that it was impossible.

He saw the police car on the street. It was moving slowly, gravel crunching beneath its tyres. The senior constable was driving.

Nyman had to change direction. He circled the house, climbed on top of a slatted wooden fence, and from his vantage point he saw the main road.

A few gardens, a dirt track and a narrow strip of thicket later, he was standing at the main road with his thumb in the air. Nyman was a typical Finnish man, and thus asking for help was the last thing that would normally enter his mind. But now his thumb had risen all by itself.

It was the eighth car that finally stopped. Nyman ran up to the small grey Volvo. He opened the passenger door and leaned inside. Behind the wheel sat a burly man in his fifties with a broad smile, his face so suntanned it had turned the bright red-brown colour of pine trees in the evening sun. The man had short hair, metallic-rimmed glasses, a brown waistcoat whose every pocket seemed stuffed to the brim, and a flannel shirt.

'Where you heading?' he asked.

'I need to get to Shore Street,' said Nyman.

The man clearly thought about this for a moment.

'Yes, I'm driving down that way. But I'll have to stop at the petrol station.'

Did Nyman have any choice?

'That's fine,' he said. The most important thing was to get away from the road, to safety, and head in vaguely the right direction. He sat down. The car set off. There was a pungent whiff inside the car. Fish, he realised. Nyman glanced at the back seat. Boxes of lures, reams of fishing line, a detached reel. In the footwell was a net.

'Where is the petrol station?' he asked.

'Just down the road, right by the police station.'

Nyman said nothing.

'I'm Matti.'

'Jan.'

'Car break down, eh?'

'I only got a lift one way.'

They drove back towards the area through which Nyman had just sprinted. The now-familiar gardens flashed past in reverse order. Nyman was going back to the starting line.

'Listen,' he began 'I don't mean to be rude, but I've got a very important meeting and…'

'I understand,' said the man. 'I'll take a shortcut.' And straight away he turned the car.

Nyman recognised the street. It was the one with the house he had just run through. Maybe the teenage boy had finally managed to release the grip on his crank. If not, he really would need his mother.

The police car came into view at the other end of the street. It must have either reversed or driven round the block.

'Can I put the seat back?' asked Nyman. 'I'm a bit allergic to fish.'

'To fish?'

'I think so. I feel dizzy. Anyway, I think I've eaten quite badly today.'

'Fish?'

'No, I don't eat fish. With my allergy and everything…'

'Even trout? You allergic to trout?'

'Even trout.'

'Herring?'

'And herring.'

'What about grilled perch?'

'That too.'

'Fillet of whitefish?'

'Whitefish is a … fish too.'

'Smoked salmon?'

'Can I just put the seat back?'

The police car was getting closer. Nyman pulled the lever at the side of the chair. The mechanism reacted painfully slowly. It felt as though he was in a slow-motion film while everything else was speeding up. Nyman decided to slide down the seat as far as he could. He realised Matti was more than a little bewildered.

'You must be feeling pretty rough. Never seen a man squirm like that. Shall I drop you at the doctor's? It's right opposite the police station.'

Was there anything round here that wasn't in the immediate vicinity of the police station? thought Nyman.

'No thanks,' he said. 'I'll be fine, if I can just rest a little.'

The passenger seat was finally as far back as it would go. By now Nyman was almost crouching in the footwell And not a moment too soon. As he slid below the dashboard, he could just make out the interior of the police car. All he could do was stare at the car ceiling and hope for the best.

'Well,' said Matti. 'Looks like Reijo Pitkänen in that squad car. I could ask him—'

'I'm really in a quite a hurry. Very important meeting.'

'Of course.'

In some respects, thought Nyman, this was the longest car journey he had ever undertaken. From his hideout in the footwell, he saw Matti wave a hand and guessed they must have passed the police car. A moment later, they turned. Nyman remained where he was.

At the petrol station, Nyman raised the back of the seat, not fully but just enough to see out of the window. If anyone noticed him, he hoped he might look like a child. At least at a quick glance. Matti took an age to fill up the tank. What were the odds that the one car to pick him up was almost out of petrol? He sat facing the police station. He could see the spot in the rosebushes he had jumped into and then struggled his way through. His legs were still sore. Eventually Matti replaced the petrol nozzle with a clank. Nyman imagined they would finally set off. Matti knocked on the window. Nyman rolled it down.

'Something to drink? If you're feeling woozy?'

'No, thank you. I'm a little late…'

'That's right.'

Matti walked round the car and sat in the driver's seat. He fastened his belt and looked as though he was gradually getting used to the idea that he was in the car again, taking back control. Eventually he started the car and they got under way. Nyman didn't dare say anything. He wanted to keep a low profile.

'What's your line of work, then?' asked Matti.

'I'm a maths teacher.'

'You're joking?' Matti exclaimed. 'Me too.'

Nyman looked at Matti. What were the odds that he'd get in a car that was almost out of petrol and whose driver was a real maths teacher, a profession Nyman was doing his best to fake?

'What grade?' asked Matti.

'What do you mean?'

'What grade do you teach?'

'Primary…'

'Primary school, right. I'm in high school myself. Further maths is my thing. What do you think about the new curriculum?'

'Quite something,' Nyman answered cautiously.

'Oh yes, you can say that again.'

And with that Matti started talking. It was a good thing. It gave Nyman the chance to concentrate on remaining as invisible as possible while also constantly keeping an eye on his surroundings. They would soon reach Shore Street. Nyman said he could get out anywhere and that if they bumped into each other again, Nyman would buy him a pint by way of thanks. Very nice of you, replied Matti. Nyman thanked him once again, got out of the car and closed the door. He caught sight of the clock on the wall of the bike rental shop. It was eight o'clock sharp. He was just in time. It felt incredible. He would even have time to rent another bike.

Nyman turned in a full circle.

Olivia Koski was nowhere in sight.

◉

Olivia heard the sound of some kind of chains being dragged through the pipes, listened to the sound of hammering and heard Esa – the owner and director and, as he had explained a moment earlier, the only regular employee of Kuurainen & Company – busily pottering in the bathroom.

She looked at the wall clock. She was late. She walked up to the bathroom doorway. On the bathroom floor was a small monitor, on top of the toilet bowl a meter with which Esa was taking various readings. The taps in the shower had been removed altogether.

'This will all have to be replaced. It's a much bigger job than I'd thought.'

'What does that mean?'

'I thought we'd manage with a few strategic patches, but there's nothing here that still works properly. You don't use this, I hope.' He looked at the toilet. 'Nothing moving in here. You'll end up with floater after floater.'

'There's an outhouse at the end of the garden.'

'Excellent. The good thing about the natural method is size isn't a problem. You could eat Wiener schnitzels for a week, and even if nothing moves for a while and everything comes out at once—'

'So, the renovation,' Olivia interrupted him. 'I'm going to need one.'

Esa nodded. He was still on his knees on the floor. He was a short man, and now his eyes were level with Olivia's waist, a fact that made her feel distinctly uncomfortable.

'It's going to be a big one,' he said. 'Nothing can drain away, and there's no water coming in. Everything will have to be replaced. The mains pipe leading up to the house is new enough, so we can leave that, but as for everything in and out of the house … right up to the septic tank, which at the moment looks like the final days of Waterloo, if you get my drift.'

Olivia knew what was coming next. She waited. She didn't have to wait long.

'We'll have to reassess the budget.'

'You gave me a written quote,' she said.

'And we can do the renovations outlined in the quote at that price,' said Esa, still speaking to her waist, to a point slightly south of her navel. Olivia didn't want to take the thought any further. 'But it would be a bit pointless, because even after that you'd still have no running water and no working toilet. I didn't realise the situation was this bad. So bad that a simple repair job inside the house won't be enough. The situation has changed. When I gave you the quote, you still had running water and the toilet worked. Now you have neither.'

Olivia looked at the man kneeling on her bathroom floor. There was something metaphorical about it. Either that or it reminded her of something. How come every time Olivia thought she'd finally got through something, another surprise appeared from a different direction?

'Am I wrong to think ten thousand euros won't be enough?'

Esa shook his head. He looked as though he'd just heard the most outlandish suggestion in the world. He could barely speak.

'What ball park are we talking about?' she asked.

Esa stopped shaking his head. And when they finally appeared, the words flowed from his mouth like the clearest, purest water from a sparkling new tap.

'Twenty-five thousand.'

◉

As Olivia furiously pedalled her bike into town, she imagined she propelled it forwards with pure rage. She turns every stone, draws up contracts and gets her hands on ten grand, which is supposed to fix everything, only to discover that it's not enough, not by a long way. Damn it. Fuck it. Fucketty buggering bollocks. Twenty-five thousand euros. She already had ten thousand, but now it seemed that was merely a down payment that would only cover removing the old piping and strengthening existing structures before fitting the new plumbing. In other words, the money she had at the moment was only enough to buy her a gaping hole in the ground. Brilliant. She tried to think affectionately of her father, but now it was really difficult. The man who had sat in that same bathroom and taken at least twenty thousand dumps without a care in the world, the rusty fruits of his regular bowel movements now falling at his daughter's feet. Quite literally.

Olivia knew she would soon regret these thoughts, but she was far too agitated to give a shit.

Twenty-five thousand euros.

She had ten thousand. Which wasn't yet technically hers.

The other fifteen thousand. Where would she get that?

Olivia steered her bike onto Shore Street where she saw a few people eating and drinking in the bars and restaurants. High season. Right. Palm Beach Finland hadn't quite yet attracted the promised throngs of tourists. How could she find a sum of money like that round here?

Olivia was hot and bothered. She'd wrapped up warm, knowing only too well how quickly the temperature by the sea could plummet, how cold it eventually became once the sun set and the wind, which you hardly noticed at first, starting tugging at your clothes and stinging your skin before chilling you to the bone. At the end of the street she saw Jan Kaunisto. The sight reminded Olivia of what she was doing – what she should do regardless of her plumbing; of what was necessary, especially when it came to this man. And what do you know? All of a sudden she wasn't so hot and bothered after all.

She approached the man who had come here to learn to windsurf. Olivia smiled. Jan Kaunisto smiled back at her and raised a hand from his handlebars.

The maths teacher.

The maths teacher who couldn't count.

2

As soon as he gripped the spade, Chico's breath became instantly shallower. It was the same feeling he had when he placed his electric guitar round his neck, as though he held the key to another dimension in his hand. Chico didn't know whether that was a good or a bad sign right here, right now. The excitement and the spike in his pulse had absolutely nothing to do with physical exertion. They hadn't started that bit yet.

Evening was gliding gently towards night, daylight slowly fading from the sky. They had been waiting for a good while, at times standing near the back wall of the chalet, at others sitting in the folding wooden chairs on the patio. Leivo lived in his chalet all year round. Crockett used to be rented out, just like Tubbs, Castillo and all the others, though it was situated apart from them and stood on its own. Leivo had painted it a bright turquoise, and around it erected a low white fence, the purpose of which escaped Chico. It didn't keep people away and didn't keep anything inside. In any case, the chalet looked like part of a film set. This was partly due to its size – it was small – and also because the sign above the door reading Crockett made it look more like a bar or an old village store.

Robin looked like he was in the zone. He was sitting in a wooden chair, holding his spade upright in his left hand, and seemed to be gazing out to sea. Once Robin had explained the plan, Chico had asked him if he was sure he'd thought of everything. It was a genuine question. Robin had simply looked Chico in the eyes and handed him a spade.

The first part of the plan seemed perfectly plausible. The choice of location was excellent. Crockett was situated far enough away from everything else and it was relatively close to the disposal site.

The disposal site – another of Robin's terms. The thickening darkness was on their side too. The few outdoor lights along the shore were far away too, so the element of surprise would work like a dream. They had very little to carry; in addition to the spades and balaclavas only a torch and a length of rope. They'd left their phones at home, because Robin had said they could be used to track their movements. The phones were waiting next to each other on Robin's couch.

Chico found it hard to comprehend the transformation that had taken place in Robin. It must have had something to do with Nea. Chico sat down in the chair next to him and looked at the sea. He could make out fewer and fewer details – the sea became an empty field as the waves merged into the dimness. Chico held the spade in his lap, resting it on his thighs. It weighed about the same as his guitar. Maybe that was a good thing. It kept his thoughts focussed, gave them a meaning.

Life had brought him here so quickly.

A few crazy steps, and here he was.

All he had done was grab an opportunity the way people always tell you: passionately; give it everything you've got. Then the very thing Chico thought always happened to him had happened. An outside force had messed up his plans and steered them off course, in a direction whose ultimate goal was the opposite of what he'd set out to achieve. It was like standing in front of a mirror, holding up your right hand and seeing your left hand rising. The moral of the story appeared to be that if he wanted to succeed at something, he should first start by ruining his chances. The results could hardly be worse.

Chico snapped out of his musings.

The sound of a car. Getting closer.

As agreed, they both stood up, took a few steps towards the chalet, stood tight against the slatted wall and pulled on their balaclavas.

The car sounded exactly as it should: Leivo's SUV wasn't new – it didn't have that peculiar hum that new engines make. This was the sound of a good-old diesel engine. The car's front lights now embraced the chalet as if to gently push it towards the sea. A moment later the engine sounded as if it was coming from inside the chalet. That meant it must have reached the gravel-covered parking spot on the other side. The motor stopped, the lights went out. They waited for the sign. As the car door opened, they moved.

Chico went round one side of the chalet, Robin the other.

They moved at the same speed. Chico saw Robin step from behind the opposite corner just as he appeared from his own. The plan worked perfectly. And Leivo did exactly as Robin had said he would. He turned in the direction of the first person he saw. It was Chico.

Chico was only a few steps away from Leivo, and had already raised the shovel to shoulder height.

And at that moment, everything changed.

Chico had expected Leivo to look terrified, or at least vaguely surprised, for the microsecond it took Chico to swing the spade in his direction. As Chico saw it, Leivo should have been frozen, perhaps not consciously expecting the blow, but his body bracing itself for the impact.

But that's not what happened.

In the faint light, Leivo's expression was not terrified. It was something else, as was the change in his body position. Chico was startled. He glanced past Leivo at Robin, who was moving slower than Chico had expected. Chico brought his eyes back to Leivo, and Leivo's gaze fixed on the spade in Chico's hands. Again, Chico hesitated for one, crucial second.

Leivo, however, did not hesitate. He removed something from his jacket pocket and held his hand in front of Chico's face. And just as Chico realised what was happening, his eyes seemed to burst into flames. He screamed, he had to let go of the spade. He heard a thud, which he assumed meant that Robin had got within striking distance. Leivo huffed and puffed and let out a volley of curses, so the blow couldn't have been very accurate. Immediately afterwards Chico heard Robin shouting and howling in pain. Perhaps Leivo had managed to set Robin's eyes on fire too.

Chico fumbled for his spade, eventually found it and staggered to his feet. He could see nothing but thick mist and blurred shadows. He lashed out with the spade but didn't hit anything. Then he heard the same thud as before, and again Leivo bellowed. Robin had hit him again. Leivo continued to swear like a trooper, but this time his diction was markedly less clear than before. Chico tried to see where Leivo was. Robin had struck him with the spade twice now. One blow should have been enough, thought Chico. He lashed out. Something shattered, presumably glass, and the spade scraped against the bonnet. He'd hit the car. With this is mind, Chico tried another direction. He took a few steps forwards before he felt a fist in his stomach.

He couldn't breathe and couldn't see anything in front of him. Chico was furious by now. He raised the spade and began swinging it wildly. A window smashed. Again, he was too close to the car. He heard noises that sounded like ... wrestling. Roaring, panting, the thud of the earth. He did everything he could think of to regain his sight: pressed his eyelids shut, blinked, squinted, forced his eyelids open again. Eventually, right in front of the chalet, he saw a writhing mass on the ground. Leivo and Robin were struggling. Chico dashed forwards but realised he couldn't use the spade because he couldn't see who to hit. He threw the spade to one side and dived onto the thrashing pile of bodies.

Using his hands Chico worked out who was who. Just as Chico was about to get a grip on Leivo's neck, he realised he was now wrestling with his boss alone. And Leivo was a ferocious opponent, strong as a bear. Chico lost his grip, Leivo turned him over. He could feel Leivo's hands at his throat. Leivo was strangling him. Chico tried to shout out. Leivo growled. Chico thrashed his legs about and tried to turn over, but Leivo's fists were like the hardest steel. At that moment Chico knew he was going to die.

Then he heard a thud.

Leivo began to slump across him like a burst balloon. He let out a long, loud, low-pitched fart, which puttered into the evening

darkness like a small motor. It seemed to last an eternity. A voice
bubbling from deep within Leivo revealed that they finally had a
result. Chico started to breathe hungrily, regardless of the fact that
the air with which he filled his lungs stank of sulphur, a mix of eggs
and rotten herring. Leivo wasn't dead; he lay there, his moist breath
puffing against Chico's face. The unconsciousness must have been
deep and dark.

Chico's hands were weak, his body feeble.

Once he had steadied his breathing, he managed to croak out a
few words: 'Move. Him.'

'I can't,' said Robin as he coughed and spluttered somewhere
further off. 'Jesus, that stinks.'

'I'm underneath him.'

'Hold your breath.'

'I can't. He's strangling me.'

'How can shit smell that bad?'

'Because there's a lot of it. Help.'

'You can't exactly put it back in.'

'Will you just help me?'

Robin walked over, and together they managed to roll Leivo to
one side. Chico climbed to his feet, staggered a few steps, vomited.
It hurt his throat more than Leivo's hands. Robin appeared beside
him. He threw up too.

They leaned against their knees.

The worst was yet to come.

3

The food was divine. Whitefish grilled whole on an open fire, the flesh falling from the bone. New potatoes boiled in water with just enough salt. Crisp, fresh salad, green and earthy, a taste of summer. A vinaigrette with a hint of mustard and lemon – not a thick, ready-made one, but one that was perfectly fresh and invigorating and made the tongue tingle.

Nyman didn't doubt himself any longer, the way he had on the long, silent bike ride along the scenic route Olivia had chosen, steal-ing glances at each other and exchanging quick smiles, perhaps to make sure the pace was suitable for both of them. Nyman knew he had made the right decision. He was close. Experience told him that. Olivia Koski wiped the corner of her mouth with a napkin and asked him what he thought of the food.

'Much better than I dared to hope,' he said.

'That's good to hear. And how was your lesson today?'

Olivia brushed her long chestnut hair from across her face. All the better to see him, perhaps.

'I don't know. Something happened this morning, and I think I finally got the hang of it. It didn't feel like such an unnatural activity anymore. That moment when the board obeys your commands and the sail stays upright and pulls you in the right direction … I don't know. I'm almost looking forward to the next lesson.'

'What made you want to learn how to windsurf?'

Nyman shrugged his shoulders. It was all Muurla's idea.

'Just got it into my head, I suppose. I didn't really give it much thought.'

Nyman looked at the landscape. They were sitting outside the restaurant in the furthest corner of the patio. To his left was the sea, to his right a dusty road with darkened woodland along both sides. Diagonally above them was a faint lantern that lit Nyman's face but which left Olivia, sitting across the table, in shadow. In this light her brown eyes looked like lumps of coal.

'You woke up one day and said, *I know, I'm going to learn how to windsurf.*' Olivia smiled. 'You hadn't decided before you got here?'

I found out by text message, he thought.

'No.'

'That's spontaneous,' said Olivia. 'I could probably do with being a bit more spontaneous. I should do something wild. It looks like fun.'

'What do you mean?'

'You seem like such a relaxed guy, that's all. It's great. You suddenly decide to take a holiday in a strange little town, you head down here, start windsurfing, meet the locals. Do you do that everywhere you go?'

'What do you mean?' asked Nyman before realising that was the second time he'd asked that question. This wasn't going the way he'd planned.

'I must be really unclear, if you need to ask what I mean,' said Olivia, her voice soft and friendly. 'I'm sorry. All I mean is, from where I'm sitting, it looks like you're having a really pleasant summer.'

'True,' said Nyman and guessed eating so quickly must have dulled his senses. The fuller the stomach, the slower the mind. 'Like I said, divorce and a change of job. Sometimes it's good to let your hair down.'

'A change of job?'

'Yes. Didn't I mention that?'

Didn't I? he asked himself, and realised he'd not told Olivia, he'd told the local police. He'd said he was between jobs, because there was no job from which he could legitimately claim to be on holiday.

'You just said you're a maths teacher,' said Olivia. Her eyes were so hidden in shadow that Nyman couldn't read her expression. But her voice was soft, almost a whisper.

The nearest diners were one table away. A grey-haired man, a dark-haired woman, both wearing woollen jumpers and thick scarves to fend off the evening chill. Wise, thought Nyman, who, despite all the warnings, was wearing far too little.

'That's right,' said Nyman, by now keen to steer the conversation away from himself. 'At the moment I'm not teaching anywhere, temporarily or full-time. But I'm ready to teach again as soon as a job comes up.'

'Addition? Division? Derivatives? I never liked those. Percentage calculations have come in handy. Everyday life is full of mathematics. We have to count everything. Time, money, calories. But why am I telling you this? You know all this already.'

Nyman watched Olivia. She was somehow…

'Do you teach secondary or high school kids?' she asked.

What did Nyman remember about high-school maths? All he could remember was that he'd done the minimum possible. And it hadn't gone very well. The wisest thing would be to say he taught primary-school children. He couldn't remember much about that either, but didn't imagine it was very complicated. He didn't have a chance to answer though.

'Can I interest you in dessert?' Nyman heard a voice beside him. He looked up. The waiter began clearing their plates and stood waiting for an answer. He was a broad-shouldered, dark-haired man. Nyman looked at Olivia.

'Of course,' she said.

'Yes, of course,' said Nyman and glanced at the waiter.

The waiter nodded, walked off. There was only one dessert on the menu. Handy. Nyman couldn't remember what it was, but it hardly mattered. As long as it's sweet, he thought, he would like it. He poured the rest of his beer from the bottle into the glass, took a sip, and decided he'd had enough of the mathematics talk.

'What about your day?' he asked Olivia as he placed his glass on the table.

'You should know,' said Olivia. Her voice soft and friendly. Still.

Nyman didn't want to ask *What do you mean?* a third time. Perhaps in the light of the lantern his expression was suitably bemused.

'We met down at the beach, remember?'

'Ah, that's right,' he said.

'I was there all day, standing in for Chico. He called in sick.'

'And who is Chico?'

'The lifeguard. Looks like Patrick Swayze. He'll tell you that himself in case you don't notice.'

Kari Korhonen, thought Nyman. The man with his hand down his pants at every opportunity.

'What's he like?'

'Chico? Why do you ask?'

Nyman was certain Olivia was smiling a little. Her hair covered her face now more than before.

'Just curious,' he said. 'I've seen him down at the beach and…'

'With me, perhaps?'

What *did* Olivia mean? Did she think Nyman might be jealous, was that it? He *was* jealous, but that was irrelevant. Well, maybe not entirely irrelevant. Relevant in that everything is linked to everything else. Nyman tried to muster an expression that said, *Goodness, you've hit the nail on the head.* Which was true, of course. And that seemed good enough for Olivia.

'He's … Well, to be perfectly honest, Chico is … Let's say he doesn't pose an imminent threat to the theory of relativity. But he's a nice guy, I suppose. Friendly when he wants to be. Not the most hardworking of people, and he very often has a cold. Even in the summer. Especially in the summer.'

Nyman had heard this sentiment repeated twice in quick succession. The police might have suspected Korhonen if only the man had an iota of gumption. To Nyman, this particular character trait made him the perfect suspect. He always liked rooting for the underdog.

'Does that answer your question?' asked Olivia. 'Are you happy with that?'

Nyman didn't get a chance to respond. The desserts arrived. Rhubarb pie and homemade ice cream. The spoon felt cold to the touch. Nyman didn't know how to phrase his next question without bringing up the subject of jealousy again.

'I noticed my neighbour from the resort was at the beach today,' he said as though he was talking about a good friend. He didn't have any of those. 'I would have recommended the windsurfing course, but he'd left before I got the chance. And I haven't seen him since. I would have told him to come down to the beach in the morning. It's never too late to get started. He seems like a sporty guy. He might enjoy a spot of windsurfing.'

Olivia's expression changed. Nyman was certain of it.

'You should ask him,' she said.

Olivia said no more on the subject. Nyman thought the rhubarb pie needed some coffee to wash it down. And he sensed there was something going on between Olivia and his neighbour. But what?

'I guessed he must have had some questions about the beach,' said Nyman. 'But maybe not.'

'He came to tell me about everything that's wrong with society.'

'And what is wrong with society?'

'Drifters like you, apparently.'

'That's the biggest problem?'

'It really seemed to bug him.'

They commented on how the pie melted in the mouth. Nyman suggested coffee, and they ordered.

'Doesn't it worry you, not having a job?' she asked suddenly. 'Though I remember you said you came into some money when your wife sold your apartment. So I guess you can spend all summer on holiday and surf to your heart's content. But what about the future?'

'I've been thinking of taking some time out.'

'You mean taking even more time out?'

'Maybe I want to do something else altogether.'

'And maybe mathematics isn't your field at all,' said Olivia. 'Maths teachers generally know how to count.'

Olivia continued eating her pie, slowly raising the spoon to her mouth, and looked as though she was savouring it, relishing the melting, creamy vanilla ice cream. Nyman wondered what she might say next. Olivia waited until her mouth was empty.

'You can make one mistake,' she said. 'Everyone makes mistakes. But surely a maths teacher doesn't make mistakes all the time.'

'I'm in holiday mode.'

'That may be so. But you're not a maths teacher.'

Nyman tried to make out what Olivia Koski was thinking, but it was futile. He could only see the waiter approaching with a pot of coffee and two cups, the dark evening, the adjacent couple, the lantern and the long shadows. He heard a phone ringing. Softly at first, but as Olivia Koski picked up her handbag, the sound grew louder. The waiter arrived and began pouring the coffee.

Olivia looked at her phone, excused herself and left the table.

⊙

Olivia recognised the number. The timing was strange. She stepped away from the six tables on the patio to a small knoll where she could see both the patio and the blackened sea. In the golden light of the lanterns, the waiter was pouring Jan Kaunisto's coffee.

Jan looked as though he hadn't noticed Olivia's departure. Olivia didn't know what to make of him: he seemed genuinely interested in her, but something wasn't quite right. Olivia had tried to catch him off-guard and surprise him, but Jan always seemed perfectly calm and collected. And a moment ago, when Olivia had said out loud that she didn't think he was a maths teacher, he'd simply said he was in holiday mode.

Olivia recognised the caller's voice too. Indeed, the voice was so recognisable that she could envisage the grey moustache above the man's lip. The caller introduced himself all the same: Reijo Pitkänen, senior constable with the local police. Olivia listened and asked if something had happened.

'To be honest, I don't know,' said the constable. 'That's what I'd like to ask you, Ms Koski.'

'Ms Koski?'

'May I call you Olivia?'

You called me Olivia when you thought I might be sleeping with a pyromaniac, she thought. Olivia was fine, she replied.

'Good,' the constable said in such a neutral voice that it could have meant anything at all. 'And may I apologise if I seemed a little unfriendly the last time we met. It wasn't my intention. Sometimes it's part of the job. I'm calling because we stopped by your house this afternoon, thinking we would inspect the area around the sauna. When we arrived, there was a man wandering around your garden.'

'Really?'

'The same man you were with the night the sauna caught fire. Or when it was deliberately torched.'

Olivia looked back towards the restaurant. Jan Kaunisto was sipping his coffee and slowly but surely working his way through his rhubarb pie.

'He said he'd come to visit you,' the constable continued. 'Naturally, we asked him why, and he said that was between you and him. Which it is, of course – if, indeed, he is telling the truth.'

Olivia continued staring at the patio. Jan had turned and was now looking in her direction. He pointed a spoon at his plate and nodded in approval. Olivia was sure she could see him smiling. When he smiled he was even more handsome than usual.

'I'd like to ask,' the constable continued, 'is that the case? And if it's not the case, have you noticed anything out of the ordinary around the house?'

Jan poured himself more coffee and glanced again in Olivia's direction. With the forefinger of her left hand, Olivia indicated she would only be a minute. She thought of the ten thousand euros. Damn it. Why was it that every time she was about to achieve something in her life, there was always an insurmountable moral obstacle in her way? All she wanted was a bathroom with running water, to go some way towards correcting generations of neglect. Now Olivia was convinced that Jan Kaunisto was the man the solicitor was looking for. That's why she'd suggested they take the scenic route; there were more people out and about.

Jan Kaunisto fitted the timeline of recent events: he had arrived in town just before the fire, which had exploded as though a bomb had gone off. That's what the fire chief had said. Olivia didn't know much about fuses or timer devices, but she imagined putting one together couldn't be all that difficult. Then there was the way in which Jan had got to know her, instantly making her acquaintance and sticking to her ever since. And now he was asking about other people in her circle. And he most definitely wasn't a maths teacher. Of that she was absolutely certain.

The only thing Olivia didn't understand was why Jan would return to the town after killing a man in her house. There might be an explanation for that too: if you're twisted enough to murder someone, then you're twisted enough for anything, right?

Olivia had to do what had to be done. Jan had made his own bed, and now he'd have to lie in it. Besides, the solicitor had already given her the ten thousand euros in order to establish the identity of the killer. Olivia had given her word. Before that she'd promised herself that she would do everything in her power, anything at all, to raise enough money for her renovations. Nothing about this felt right or good, but that didn't mean that her decision couldn't be either of those things. She had learned this the hard way; sometimes you have to make a decision that feels bad in order to bring about something good.

But back to the matter at hand: anything out of the ordinary?

If you thought the events of the last three weeks were the new normal, that this was what her everyday life had now become, then in that respect nothing out of the ordinary had happened.

'Everything at the house seemed fine,' she said. 'If you don't count the massive renovations.'

'That's right,' said the constable. 'I mean, a little touching up will do the place good. One more thing. If you hear or see anything, you'll let us know?'

Olivia turned, stared into the dark woods.

'I can't see anything.'

They bade each other a pleasant evening and ended the call. Olivia took the solicitor's card out of her pocket, dialled the number and waited. The call went straight to voicemail. Olivia left a message and began walking back towards the dessert, the coffee and Jan Kaunisto.

4

The moving operation was infernal. Leivo must have weighed about 220 pounds, and dragging him through the undergrowth was hard work. Chico and Robin pulled him by the arms, which they had hastily tied together. It was hard going, and every time they stopped to take a breath, the wind whipped around them making them feel ill.

They had two options: either pull or deal with the nausea.

In fact, now that Chico thought about it, this part had been curiously absent from Robin's plan. Chico hadn't given it a second thought either. He had concentrated on one location, one task at a time, and completely forgotten about the transitions from one place to the next. As he slogged through the woodland, he realised that this same problem had been an issue with all of his previous plans too. He had never appreciated that between all the really important events, there was the dirty work, and the majority of his life was precisely that.

The thing he had always dreamed of – standing in the spotlights with a guitar over his shoulder – was nothing but the blink of an eye, a fleeting image that, once it faded, left him there in the pine grove dragging a heavy load. If that was what had to be done at all. The thought made him feel both grateful and restless. The feelings joined, causing him considerable confusion. Perhaps he should thank Robin for all this. He didn't know.

But here they were that summer's night, in the shelter of the pines, by the sea – and soon in the second phase of their plan.

They each pulled with one hand, carrying a spade in the other. Leivo's eyes had been bound in case he regained consciousness. They had tied a rag across his mouth too so he couldn't shout out. But

Leivo tried neither of these. When they slowed enough and the scratching of the dry undergrowth ceased, Chico heard the sound of Leivo snoring. It had a calming effect. Peculiarly enough.

They pulled Leivo over a flat stretch of rock and made their way down to the sand. They hauled their load towards the water's edge and started digging. It was extraordinarily hard work. Slow and arduous. Using their spades, they measured Leivo as he lay outstretched, and each time had to accept that the hole still wasn't deep enough. Chico had to stop every few minutes to catch his breath. His arms were aching, burning, his palms were chafed and bleeding, and he couldn't straighten his back. To Robin's credit, though, he worked with hitherto unprecedented vigour – and without taking a break. From one moment to the next his spade struck the ground and raised up again, as precise and effective as a piston.

Finally the spade measurements showed they had reached the required depth. Chico helped Robin up to shore level. There in the moonlight they stood next to their pit. Leivo was still snoring on the other side. The sea was tickling the edge of the pit. Chico looked at both ends of the beach. Empty, deserted. This area of Palm Beach Finland was a conservation area, and even in the daytime it wasn't very popular. The strip of sand along the shoreline was closed off on both sides by woodland.

Once again they gripped Leivo by the arms and hauled him to the edge of the pit. They turned him over, carefully pulled his legs to the edge and slid him in. First his feet disappeared, then his shins; his knees buckled … and it was then that Chico realised they had a problem. He stopped Robin and explained. If they simply threw him into the pit, Leivo would slump to the bottom like jelly.

Robin had an idea. They tied the rope beneath his armpits, and Robin took the role of brakeman: he slid Leivo into the pit and held him in an upright position. Perhaps upright was a rather optimistic term. Leivo's heavy head slumped against his chest and his body looked limp.

Once Leivo's shoes reached the bottom of the pit, Chico took hold of the rope and Robin started shovelling. Filling the pit around Leivo went quickly; with every spadeful Chico had less to hold in place. It was a relief because his arm and back muscles were screaming in agony.

It wasn't their intention to bury Leivo entirely. Oh no – because this plan was a stroke of genius. Chico was prepared to admit it now that the job was almost done. All they were going to do was dig a pit that would solve all their problems.

Robin filled the pit until the sand was up to Leivo's shoulders. It was time for the finishing touch. This needed a degree of precision. Robin dropped to his knees and started using his hands. He told Chico to do the same. Chico hesitated. He didn't want to go anywhere near Leivo. It didn't feel right. But Robin insisted and Chico relented. He picked up handfuls of wet sand and packed it round Leivo's shoulders and pressed it against his neck. Not too tightly – this was a precision operation. This had to work. It absolutely had to…

Chico was on Leivo's right-hand side when Robin said he wanted Leivo to see the rising tide. Robin grabbed the rag tied round Leivo's eyes and pulled it off.

Leivo's steady breathing stopped. His eyes opened.

They opened and widened. He looked to the sides. Chico looked at Leivo. Leivo looked at him. The distance between their eyes was less than a metre. Chico realised he had taken off his balaclava because digging had been such hard, sweaty work. At that same moment, Leivo realised enough about what was going on that he started bellowing wildly.

Thank god there was a rag in his mouth too.

Chico could have fainted with shock. He imagined Leivo leaping out of the sand. It didn't happen. He remained where he was. As did Chico. He and Leivo looked one another in the eye until Chico finally managed to tear his eyes away and stand up.

Chico staggered behind Leivo. Leivo's head was thrashing against the sand, his hair now even more dishevelled than usual, jutting in all directions. There in the sand, the wobbling tufts of hair made the head look like a possessed pineapple. Leivo's snarling sounded like a lion, a dog and probably a prehistoric creature of some description.

Robin whispered that someone would have to fetch the spades from next to Leivo, and because Chico had already been seen, he should get them. Chico looked at Robin. They were both backing away from Leivo and the sea. They stopped. A moment later Chico realised that he should have known what was going to happen next, though it seemed impossible. He knew Robin was right and agreed to go – if only because it was the fastest way to get them off this beach.

Chico approached Leivo again.

One of the spades was right in front of Leivo. More specifically, it was right in front of Leivo's head – buried up to his neck in sand Chico found it hard to think of Leivo as a whole entity; he was, rather, a malevolent ball in the sand – which for now was suddenly still.

Chico pulled the spade away from Leivo and walked round the back of his head to the other side. He thought he could grip the other spade quickly round the shaft; that way it would be easier to carry. But Chico could not make eye contact with him again. He decided to stare at the sea, reach out his hand and grab the spade. He crouched down, stretched out his hand, gazed up at the moonlight reflected in the mirror-like sea and felt...

Leivo's teeth.

Leivo bit him.

He bit harder than any dog had ever bitten anyone. Either the rag pulled over his mouth had slackened or Leivo had managed to spit it out. It didn't matter, thought Chico as Leivo's teeth sunk deeper and deeper into the back of his hand. Chico tried to yank his hand free, but Leivo had a firm grip. Leivo growled, and Chico could see his entire head was tensed. The pain coursing through Chico's hand was dizzying. He shouted out, though they had agreed only to speak in whispers. Robin stood on the spot. With his free hand Chico tried to push Leivo's head to one side – but where could it go? They had just buried him right there in the sand. Chico couldn't think of any other course of action but to hit him. He struck Leivo twice on the forehead. It felt wrong, wholly unfair.

Robin finally started approaching, but it took him an age to reach them. Leivo was like a Doberman. Chico's eyes were watering, this time with tears of pain.

Robin knelt down behind Leivo and began lifting the knot in the rag. Once he had the rag in position, he began pulling Leivo by the ears. Chico had to close his eyes. Finally, after an excruciatingly long time, Leivo bellowed, from pain perhaps, and opened his jaw just enough for Chico to pull his hand free.

Chico staggered backwards and jerked to his feet. He was waving his hand in the air; it felt as if some part of it was broken or at the very least severely damaged. Chico watched as Robin reattached the rag in Leivo's mouth and tied the knot behind his neck. Leivo resisted, but Robin was strong and deftly kept away from those gnashing teeth. Leivo's head thrashed and wrenched, and a terrifying snarl came hissing through the rag. The movement slowly calmed and eventually stopped. Leivo appeared to have lost consciousness again.

Robin stood up, picked up the spades and headed into the woods. Chico followed him, trying to calm the pain throbbing in his hand in the cool of the evening air. They stepped into the cover of the trees, taking a different route from before. Then Chico remembered something important that they hadn't talked about. At least, he couldn't remember them talking about it.

'Wait,' Chico said to Robin's back.

Robin stopped and turned slowly. Chico couldn't really see his expression; the moonlight was like white gold, it lit them well, but here among the trees the shadows were nothing but a thick, impenetrable darkness. Chico turned his back to Robin and looked towards the shore.

In the moonlight, Leivo's head looked like a small object washed up on the sand. Chico thought about the view, and it felt as though something was missing. Something essential, he thought, something he couldn't quite put his finger on. Then he realised. He turned back to Robin, and just as the words came from his mouth he saw the spade getting closer.

'Is there even a tide here...?' he began. At the same time he both did and didn't feel the blow as the spade came into contact with his temple. There was a dullness to it, and Chico was certain he could almost taste it: metal, blood, damp sand.

In fact those tastes awaited him on the ground, which gently softened his fall. Chico's final thought was that this really was an excellent plan. Except for the fact that it was based entirely on something that didn't exist: the tide. At least, it didn't exist here, he thought. It never had.

Robin might not be the brightest of the bunch, he thought, but at least he was a friend you could trust. Or was he?

5

'Everything okay?' asked Nyman as Olivia returned to the table and sat down. Nyman realised he'd almost finished his rhubarb pie, while Olivia had barely tasted hers.

'Sorry?' she asked. 'Oh, the phone call? It was about the house.'

Nyman could see that Olivia was watching him expectantly. She was clearly more alert than a moment ago.

'Nothing bad, I hope,' he said.

'Today I found out the renovation is going to be much bigger than I'd previously thought.'

'And a bigger renovation means a bigger bill?'

Olivia said nothing. She didn't touch her pie. Nyman allowed a few seconds to pass. He tried to examine Olivia's expression more closely. It was serious, yes, but now it was also somewhat agitated.

'You're very interested in my financial affairs,' she said. 'I've noticed that. Well, I haven't got any money. You're barking up the wrong tree. I'm skint. You won't get any money out of me because I don't have any.'

Nyman placed his spoon on his plate. He wiped the corner of his mouth on his napkin and leaned back.

'I don't want your money,' he said. 'Even if you did have some, I'm not interested in that.'

Olivia stared at him. Nyman noticed that Olivia was still clutching her phone. It seemed rather late in the evening for a call about the renovations to the house. Nyman didn't believe this explanation for a second. Judging by the change in Olivia's body language, he guessed the caller must have been the senior constable.

He could see this situation from the perspective of Muurla, his superior and operation coordinator. From Muurla's point of view, it might be more interesting to let Nyman operate on his own. Police units often did this to undercover agents, pushed them deeper and deeper and watched to see which ones came back up to the surface and what kind of results they got. Nyman didn't consider this at all unfair; he had always accepted it as part of the job. What's more, there was another side to this scenario, and that side had been signed off only a few hours earlier: now there was nothing holding him back. He was free to operate in ways that earlier would have been out of the question.

'You're not after money?' asked Olivia.

'No.'

'Well, I suppose it's understandable,' she said. 'If you had more than two euros, you wouldn't be able to count them properly.'

'There's no need to get personal.'

'For God's sake. In the short time we've know each other you haven't managed to do a single sum correctly. You've counted everything wrong: the surfboard rental times, my theory about men, everything. I just said I don't think you're a maths teacher. I'm sure of it.'

They stared at each other. Nyman listened to the chit-chat of the couple at the table next to them. He couldn't make out individual words, but he could hear the tone of voice, the closeness. Thankfully the waiter was nowhere nearby. Nyman placed his napkin on the table, tucking it beneath the edge of the plate. He thought for a moment. The house has to be renovated; she cannot afford it; a body is found in the kitchen; the sauna burns down; money suddenly starts to appear.

Nyman leaned forwards and spoke in a quiet, friendly voice. 'Olivia,' he said. 'Is someone threatening you?'

Olivia looked at him in the same way she had the first time they'd met at the rental store: eyeing him up, taking stock of him. Nyman started to shiver. It was a purely physical reaction; he was wearing far too little. The proximity of the sea is deceptive: at first the air is fresh and pleasant, but when the cold finally hits, you realise it has been cold all along. For some reason the realisation is delayed.

'Who's asking?'

'I am.'

'I heard that. I just don't know who *you* are. To answer your question: maybe. I don't know. Are *you* threatening me?'

Nyman realised how much Olivia affected his physical sensations. He felt the attraction. Besides the shivering, it was foremost in his mind.

'I don't think so,' he said and instantly regretted his answer.

But what else could he have said? If Olivia was involved in something illegal, then of course he was threatening her. But if she was innocent, then the answer was…

'That's comforting,' she said. 'By the way, the police are on to you. I know you were snooping round my house today.'

'I thought so,' said Nyman and realised that he would finally have to tell her what was going on. But what was holding him back? The very same Olivia Koski, whom he suspected. Nyman thought he knew what would happen when he told her he was an undercover police officer. It would lead Olivia to the only logical conclusion: that Nyman had tried to get close to her by lying, cheating and pretending to be someone else. It wasn't an ideal starting point for any further romantic involvement. And romantic involvement was exactly what Nyman hoped might happen, if and when he was completely honest with himself. He had reached a turning point in his life. He would soon turn forty, so perhaps this was the moment.

'Who are you?' Olivia asked. Her voice had changed.

'I'm not a maths teacher,' said Nyman and decided to take the greatest risk thus far. 'I'm a police officer.'

'A policeman?'

'Yes.'

'A policeman called Jan Kaunisto?'

'Not exactly.'

'Not exactly?'

'Jan Nyman.'

'Can you prove it?'

'Yes.'

Olivia's eyes gleamed like hard glass.

Nyman held out his hands. 'Well, not right now. I only have a passport in the name of Jan Kaunisto with me at the moment. But I can prove it later. I just need a little time. And a few answers. From you.'

It was hard to read Olivia's expression. The harshness had spread across her face. She looked down. Nyman couldn't say how long she sat in that position – four or five seconds perhaps – but when her position changed, a look of disgust had appeared on her face. Olivia picked up a piece of pie between her fingers and threw it at Nyman's face, hitting him directly between the eyes. She stood up.

'Who do you think you are?' she asked. Her voice was agitated, hurt.

'If you're innocent, I can most definitely help you.'

'Innocent?' Olivia almost shouted.

The neighbouring couple turned to look at them. A few quick glances before returning to their own conversation.

Nyman remained seated. 'If you haven't done anything—'

'Wait a minute,' Olivia snapped and raised a hand to cut him off. 'Just a minute. Let's assume for a moment that you really are a policeman…'

'I am.'

'Whatever,' she nodded. 'You suspect *me* of something? And what might that be?'

Olivia was waiting, he could see that. He couldn't think of any option but to continue on the path of honesty.

'Murder. Manslaughter. Arson. Or at the very least accessory to those crimes.'

Olivia's hand remained in the air. The harsh glare of her eyes was fixed on him. He heard the rush of the sea, not so much the crashing of individual waves, but the presence of the sea. Were the lanterns moving in the wind? The shadows on Olivia's face seemed to lengthen and shorten in turn. She lowered her hand, gripped her glass and chucked the remainder of her wine in Nyman's face. Nyman took his napkin from the table and wiped his face. She'll soon run out of things to throw at me, he thought. She's already used the wine and the dessert. Unless she turns to the crockery. Even that was preferable to her leaving. Nyman finished wiping his face. Olivia took several deep breaths. She looked like she was making a decision. Eventually she pulled out her chair and sat in silence. Nyman gave her some time.

'I suppose this explains a lot,' she said eventually. Her voice was steadier now, but there was still a note of pure, incandescent rage. 'Like how you knew to ask about the sauna when there was a fire in my yard, how you just happen to turn up everywhere, always so interested in my affairs, in the men around me. You've been playing a role.'

There it was.

'It started like that,' Nyman heard himself saying, and once he'd said it, he guessed he could say more too. 'But it changed. It changed the moment I met you.'

'What changed? You mean after that you only suspected me of arson?'

Olivia placed her hand on the table. Nyman wanted to touch it. The distance between the tips of their fingers was about twenty centimetres.

'I became interested in you, more than as a ... suspect.'

'Did a woman ever hear anything more touching?'

Nyman was no longer sure of anything. Rather, he was sure of many things, but now things were even more starkly divided into those about which he was certain and those about which he wasn't, and most things didn't seem to fit together very easily at all and...

'A friend recently told me the police never stop investigating.'

'With serious crimes that's the case,' he said.

'Now you're talking like a policeman.'

'I am a policeman.'

'I should have listened to her.'

'If you're innocent, you have nothing to—'

'When were you thinking of telling me you were a police officer? And what did you think would happen when you told me?'

Nyman didn't know. This situation was new, something he'd never experienced.

'Did you imagine I'd shrug my shoulders and say, *That's okay, it doesn't matter?*' Olivia continued. '*That's nice, now I feel safe after a little bit of spying and snooping and lying?*'

'It's not exactly an ideal start.'

'Start!' Olivia blurted. Her expression turned solemn. 'I'm sorry. The start of what?'

Something happened to Nyman, something that hadn't happened in the course of his entire career. He blushed. His cheeks burned. Why wouldn't the sea breeze cool them? He felt as though he'd been found out in many ways, as though many layers had been peeled off him at once. He, who had hung out with hardened criminals, spent evenings with them, taken a sauna with them; he, who had remained calm even when a knife was pressed to his throat and he'd been asked directly and perfectly calmly who the hell he was. The situation was so completely different. That was it. A turning point. Olivia Koski.

'The start of a relationship?' she asked. Her voice was now so prickly that it seemed to shoot darts into Nyman's sensitive skin.

'I don't know if I'd use that word, it's a bit corny,' he replied honestly. 'I thought we could get to know one another.'

'And who would I be getting to know?' Olivia asked, clearly in disbelief. 'The person you might have been or the person you claim to be now? I have to say, if those are the options, I should think twice before going on a date with you again. And another thing: why would I have murdered someone in my kitchen and why the hell would I burn down my own sauna?'

Nyman didn't know the answer to either of those questions.

Two mutually exclusive options lay before him: get to the bottom of this or prepare for full-blown catastrophe.

6

Robin's head was buzzing and crackling, small explosions popping one after the other. Just as he was trying his best to forget things – especially what he had just done – his synapses began frantically forming new connections. Time after time he saw Chico's expression, felt the thud running from the shaft of the spade and into his wrists, his fingers, his fingertips. No matter how much he shook his arms, he couldn't get rid of the sensation.

Robin was half running, half walking. In the moonlight everything seemed still, frozen. He felt himself hurtling through the landscape.

And time and again Chico's face appeared in front of his eyes. Robin was sure Chico must have seen the spade approaching, that he'd had just enough time to realise Robin was about to hit him with it. That felt even worse than the actual thud. His best friend. But, he thought, Chico would understand; eventually he'd understand how important this was. Chico wasn't the only one with dreams. Robin had dreams too. They might not have been the same dreams of rock stardom as Chico, but they were just as important, just as big.

Robin thought perhaps he should send Chico a letter and explain everything, but – as he passed the enormous sign for Palm Beach Finland, which, in the moonlight, seemed to have lost its neon glare – he realised the idea was impossible: he hadn't written a single letter in his life, and besides, Chico didn't have a permanent address. If Chico ever decided to join Facebook, Robin could send him a friend request. No, even that seemed wrong.

In any case, from Chico's point of view there was still plenty to be happy about. It was summer, so he wouldn't freeze to death in the woods. And he had work until the autumn. Or did he? What would happen to Palm Beach Finland? Robin didn't want to think about it, but his brain wouldn't obey his orders. Again he saw Chico's face just before the steely kiss of the spade. It was weird, but the expression wasn't surprised or remotely angry or enraged. On the contrary, Chico looked as though he accepted his fate, as though he had finally … arrived. But what did that mean? They hadn't arrived anywhere; they had dug a pit for Leivo and walked off. And that's when Robin did it, thwacked his best friend round the head with his own spade.

Was it possible for your brain to go into overdrive? Robin couldn't slow down his thoughts. He did everything he could: he tried counting to ten, but when he reached the end two more words appeared – *ten thousand* – and that didn't cool him down at all. He tried to move his thoughts to the next matters that needed his attention. He tried to phrase what he needed to say, how he planned to explain what was going to happen next. The result was that the buzzing and crackling grew stronger.

He arrived outside the familiar block of flats. He had to stop and look at his hands. Why did his hands still feel like he was carrying a spade? They were empty. They were also black from all the digging. His clothes, his jeans, T-shirt and trainers, all looked like he'd been rolling on the ground for hours. Which was true, of course, but it was unfortunate. Robin realised he should have gone through the whole plan first, from start to finish. Then he might have thought about bringing a change of clothes. But maybe his clothes were unimportant. If things went to plan, he would throw them to one side very shortly.

The tingling sensation spread from his stomach to the rest of his body. This was followed by a fever moving in the opposite direction. It felt somehow inappropriate as he loitered behind the bins. He could feel his breath becoming shallower. He realised his breath was becoming heavier too, almost rasping. He stopped himself. With that he stepped out from behind the bins and stood beneath a large birch tree.

He wanted everything to be just right. He wanted to find the right

words, because this was an important moment, and important decision. He went through everything again and looked up to find the
right window. He saw a faint pink light. That meant Nea was at home.

⊙

Holma didn't like surprises. And now there were plenty of them.

For a quarter of an hour Nea had been bouncing up and down,
stark naked, on his lap where he sat in the armchair. First she was
facing him and then, when he realised she had no intention of
shutting up, he turned her round and listened as she said, among a
million other things, that she might be a little in love with him and
that she'd already hired an undercover agent of her own who would
take care of this business for them and that Nea had used the ten
grand to tease him. Holma didn't know what to think.

On the other hand, he liked Nea.

Her back was tanned and muscular, gleaming with sweat, her buttocks were like soft hemispheres urging him to grab hold them, and
the only hair on her body was on her head. And Nea was good at her
job, if a little absent-minded.

Her nonstop talking ultimately determined their speed. Her buttocks rammed against Holma's hips until the tempo slowed a little as
she began to explain something else, and once she got near the end of
each topic, she stopped moving altogether and just sat in his lap until
finally, when Holma's sweat had all but dried, she came to another
completely unfathomable conclusion on the subject. Then everything
was quiet for a moment – a moment during which Holma didn't quite
know what to do: he was underneath, and in this position his only
job – the only job of all men in this situation – was to provide a firm
platform for the action at hand. Then, as he worried that his gallant
warrior might pull back and shrink, things got going again, this time
with a new topic providing a new monologue. To Holma, the best
part was when Nea was gathering her disparate thoughts – the people,
events and times associated with them. The tempo was passionate,

and everything felt natural. But a moment later things became more complicated again. Holma found it hard to concentrate, he felt as though he was being abused both mentally and physically. On neither front were matters brought to a clear conclusion.

It was as though he was involved in some form of rear-guard action, but at this point he didn't dare speculate as to who was going to win the battle.

Holma knew perfectly well what had caused Nea's verbal diarrhoea and what had made her throw the few items of skimpy clothing she was wearing into the corners of the room. Ten thousand euros inspired people. That's life. He'd learned that the human mind is simply programmed that way. He had also learned that when someone comes into possession of ten thousand euros they very quickly start counting in both directions at once: Think of everything I can buy with this and – above all – how can I get my hands on some more?

Holma enjoyed seeing people's expressions when greed lit them up like a lamp. It made their faces narrow and taut, and caused the same kind of primitive reactions as lust and hunger: the shallowing of the breath, heightened salivation, audible swallowing, and eventually – and best of all – action before thought.

With the exception of Olivia Koski, that was. Holma had tried to see whether anything changed in Olivia Koski when he'd handed her the bag of money – but nothing did. He couldn't get over her lack of reaction. She had behaved as if she'd simply picked up a pay check. Holma wondered whether he'd offered her too little. Should he have given her more in order to make a bigger impression?

Just then he realised that Nea had stopped talking. That gave Holma some space. He tried to take control of the situation and increased the tempo again, both with regard to physical and mental exertion. If he had understood correctly, Nea had told someone (or several people) about the ten thousand euros, and that meant she'd told them about him. The thought didn't please him. What pleased him least of all was the idea that Nea had outsourced the work to a subcontractor. In that case, what did he need Nea for – beyond the next three minutes? Nothing at all was the answer.

He thought of the book he was writing. Not physically writing, of course, as he didn't consider that a sensible use of his time. Great authors dictated stories to a secretary or some other bespectacled person, who did the boring job of writing everything out, dotting the i's and crossing the t's, and taking care of other menial tasks that zapped his creative juices. The book was certainly going to include a section on leadership. He was a natural leader. When you lead, lead. Excellent, he mused. That's the stuff. That sounded like something out of the leadership textbooks he'd read in prison.

By now Nea's tempo was dizzying, her hips heaving up and down like a sewing machine against Holma's lap. Holma's mind zigzagged around; it inspired new thoughts. You are born a leader, he began, so think carefully about how you are born. Holma felt a tingling both upstairs and down. He was reaching his climax in every respect.

Clench and spasm. Clench and spasm. There. Good.

He pulled Nea against his body, thought about how his forthcoming book would be received, he imagined the sensation would be much like this, only many times greater, because this was a book aimed at everyone in Finland, and that meant the feeling would be five and a half million times as great. Perhaps not this specific feeling, but still.

Holma looked at the shoulder blades in front of him.

Every company gets rid of workers it no longer needs. In the bathroom or the kitchen he was sure he would find something to make sacking this particular employee all the more enjoyable.

Holma stood up, almost throwing Nea from his lap, then walked into the bathroom and pulled the door behind him. He didn't pay attention to what she said. Something irritated, disappointed, no doubt.

A leader, Holma thought as he turned on the shower, listens only to himself.

7

Love or murder? Nyman guessed these were his two options.

Either he could continue his murder investigation or he could try to fix his relationship with Olivia Koski. The two options seemed to cancel each other out.

Nyman was convinced that in the soft light of the lantern his face was shining like fresh paint. The sensation made the situation all the more unpleasant. Olivia was sitting with her back to the lantern. The moonlight wasn't bright enough to reveal what was going on in those dark eyes. Nyman could only think of banalities with a vague ring of truth. *I want to help. If you've got yourself into trouble, you need to tell me about it.* And heaven forbid: *I think I'm in love with you.*

'I'm prepared to believe you,' he said eventually.

'*You* are prepared to believe *me*? How has that ever been up for discussion? It's you that's been lying about everything.'

'Not everything,' he said. That sounded bad, so he continued. 'In fact, I haven't lied about anything. I've just left some things out or deliberately used ambiguous turns of phrase or explained something from a perspective that isn't necessarily my own.'

'So in other words, you lied.'

'I was doing my job.'

'That's what you call it?'

'If needs be.'

'What else do you call it?'

The moment of truth.

'I like you.'

'In an ambiguous sense or from a perspective that isn't necessarily your own?'

Nyman sensed an element of understanding in Olivia's voice. Of course, the tone was still angry and thorny. But maybe there was hope.

'If I'd known I'd find someone like you here, I would have come without the murder.'

'How flattering. You really know how to charm the ladies.'

'It's true,' he said.

Olivia was silent.

'I told my friend about you,' she said eventually. 'The one that said the police never stop investigating. She could see I was interested. She encouraged me. I wonder what she'd say now if she heard you were both interesting and a cop.'

'What do you think she would say?'

'Maybe she'd tell me to be careful.'

'And?'

'If I'm still interested in you, she might encourage me to see where things go.'

'I hope she'd say the latter,' said Nyman.

'What about the murder?'

'I'm convinced you didn't do it.'

'Of course I didn't. But what are you going to do about it?'

Nyman shifted position, propped his left elbow against the armrest. 'Is there someone who wants something from you?' he asked. 'Right now?'

Nyman couldn't say what changed in Olivia's expression, but something did; it was small, barely perceptible.

'You mean apart from the undercover policeman stalking me? I don't know if anyone wants anything from *me*, but there has been some interest in my property.'

'From whom?'

'Jorma Leivo. Mr Palm Beach Finland himself. I'm sure you've met him. He wants to buy the plot – for a pittance.'

Why was there no mention of this in the case file, Nyman wondered?

'Did you tell the police about this at the time?'

Olivia shook her head. 'No, because it doesn't matter to me. It's irrelevant. The place isn't for sale. Not now, and not in the future. Period.'

Needless to say, Jorma Leivo hadn't mentioned the matter himself when he'd been questioned. Nyman recalled Leivo's highfalutin talk of development models, a rambling monologue that required careful attention in order to understand what on earth he was talking about.

Nyman had another thought. 'What about the guy that looks like Patrick Swayze?'

'Kari Korhonen,' said Olivia. 'Everyone calls him Chico. But he wouldn't…'

'What's his relationship to Leivo?'

'Frightened.'

'In what way?'

'I guessed it from the way he talks about Leivo. The last time I was talking to him, he shuddered at the mention of Leivo's name.'

'Really?'

'Leivo is his boss, of course,' said Olivia. 'And when it comes to Chico, work-shy is putting it mildly.'

Nyman thought about this.

'Anyone else? Has Chico got any close friends?'

'One. Robin, he's a cook at the beach restaurant. Chico and Robin are childhood buddies. They're inseparable. Like brothers – in their mental capacity too. When we were kids we used to say they're not really thick as thieves, they're just thick.'

'That's cruel,' said Nyman.

'I don't know how I could apologise without him finding out.'

For a moment they sat in silence. Nyman wondered how this too – the friendship between Chico and Robin – had never come to light, though he thought he knew the answer. Someone had doubtless given them instructions as to what to say. And if Chico was afraid of whoever was calling the shots, he would surely do as he was told. Furthermore: because the dead man wasn't a local and, it appeared, hadn't been in cahoots with any of those previously mentioned, it was obvious that no connection would be apparent there either. Until now, as Nyman began to see everything in the light of new information. The whole series of events might be a combination of two separate lines of enquiry that had been pursued individually: it was a combination of pure chance and ambitious planning, and both schemes rested on the fortunes of a bunch of bungling amateurs. That was, if hearsay and the criminal history of the deceased man were anything to go by.

Nyman looked at Olivia, her long dark hair, her chestnut eyes. Her face was in shadow, ready to speak as sharply as was needed. Love or murder? Nyman knew the answer.

'Maybe I'm the one who should apologise,' he said.

◉

Jorma Leivo awoke with a snort. He felt as if he had the worst hangover he'd ever experienced ... ten thousand times over. His head ached as though it had been drilled both inside and out. He felt so wretched that he couldn't even move his legs. Or his arms. Or turn in this uncomfortable bed, this uncomfortable position. Or ... He couldn't move anything. He was hot and cold at the same time. His eyes stung when he tried to open them. There was something stuck in them, but what? There was a strange taste in his mouth, as though he'd been eating a meal of sand and raw meat.

He remembered. Jorma Leivo opened his eyes.

He saw the sea, gilded in the moonlight. He turned his head as far to the right as he could, as far to the left as his neck would allow. Nobody. Of course. Around him was what he called the old beach – a pointless conversation area, the perfect location for a water theme park and shopping mall.

Using his tongue he pushed the rag from between his teeth, wiggled his mouth and jaw and shook his head. It took a few minutes, but eventually he managed to loosen the rag completely. He shouted out. Or rather, he tried to shout out. His mouth was so dry, so rough with sand, so ... traumatised that he couldn't make a sound at all. The only sound he could muster was a low-pitched growl. How loudly can a man growl? Jorma Leivo realised the answer was: not very.

He had to think.

He was clearly stuck. That much was obvious. A significant setback. But he was Jorma Leivo, and he had survived worse. He had survived wives, bankruptcies and combinations of the two. He would get through this. He steadied his breathing.

A quick look at the facts: the pair of clowns he'd hired to do his dirty work had taken him by surprise. They had buried him on the beach, and Leivo understood why. Their intent was to get rid of him at high tide. Except that there was no tide round here, high or low. In that respect the duo's actions were a continuation of before. Everything they touched blew up: they killed the wrong guy or didn't kill the guy when they were supposed to. But all of that aside – because he was an optimist at heart and preferred to see opportunities instead of threats – he admired the passion, the fire, the open-mindedness with which they got to work. It was impressive.

It was impossible not to admire passion like that. And what he was now experiencing – with his whole body, no less – was quite a feat. Leivo had always thought the pair lazy and cack-handed. He admitted, first to himself, then to the glistening moonlight, that he had been wrong.

The boys had shown him what they were made of.

◉

Jan Nyman thought long and hard, hesitated, but eventually took the plunge. He lowered his hand to the table and took Olivia's hand in his. She didn't pull away. I have apologised, he thought. He had made clear who he was, what had happened and what had led them to this point, both concretely and figuratively. To this moment, right here. This touch.

Nyman looked Olivia in the eyes and felt approximately thirty years younger than he was. Perhaps things like this really did happen in real life: you find yourself holding someone by the hand and it feels just like the very first time, long ago, when the touch opened up a world inside you, a world to which the other person's hand held the key, that boy or girl in the school playground that you secretly fancied; then thirty years later you realise the feeling is still there and that it means more than everything that happened in between.

Olivia Koski remained silent. Nyman couldn't read her expression, and he no longer wanted to. He tried all the same: Olivia looked as though she had come to a decision. Nyman noticed he was hoping the decision had something to do with him, hoping it was affirmative. Only someone truly in love thinks like that, he admitted to himself. Nyman hoped he wouldn't have to break the silence. But what could he do? He was still a police officer. He might be in love, he might even be sure that Olivia Koski hadn't murdered anyone or burned down her own sauna, but he still had a case to investigate. Eventually he had to say it. He was a police officer.

'Can I call you?'

'For what?'

'The way people call one another. You know.'

'Why do you ask? Are you leaving?'

'Actually, yes,' he said. 'I have to. But I want to see you again.'

Olivia was silent for a moment.

'Call me,' she said. 'I assume you have my number.'

Nyman couldn't tell whether her tone was neutral or whether it carried a hint of a smile. He was in a hurry. The bike was calling his name.

Nyman freewheeled down the hills, swerved round the corners and headed right into the centre of the small town. He passed the Palm Beach Finland sign, which in the moonlight looked as though it might just be real, in every sense. Amid the rush of adrenalin and feverish thoughts, the notion made Nyman stop. For a split second it even made him doubt himself. Did Jorma Leivo know something that nobody else did? He undoubtedly knew a lot, but it probably had to do with this perplexing beach resort. Nyman felt as though passing the sign took longer than the laws of physics allowed.

Nyman pedalled hard. He could already see the SUV parked outside the chalet in the distance. Good, he thought. Leivo was at home. Nyman jumped from his bike and glanced at the vehicle. The windows had been smashed, the paintwork scraped, and the small white fence had been kicked over. The chalet was dark. Nyman saw a pile of sand behind the car. In the sand were two sets of foot-prints, and between them a series of drag marks. Nyman had seen things like this in Afghanistan. Back then it had meant only one thing. Someone was being moved, either wounded or against his will. Nyman followed the marks.

At times he lost the tracks in the woodland, the undergrowth barely visible in the faint light, but he quickly picked them up again as the terrain became sandy. He walked through the small woodland and came out at a stretch of beach he hadn't known existed. He saw a ball by the water's edge.

The ball was whistling.

◉

Nyman had nothing to drink. He hadn't expected to find a thirsty head whose speech he could barely make out – presumably because its mouth was so dry. In the moonlight Nyman ascertained that Leivo had been struck over the head at least once. He came to a number of other conclusions too; primarily – and this Nyman was able to say with some degree of certainty – that Leivo had not buried himself in the sand. And it was this that made his behaviour all the more curious. At first Leivo was snapping and growling, but when Nyman explained that he was in fact a police officer and that eve-rything would be fine, Leivo's demeanour completely changed. He even smiled, let out noises that sounded almost like little laughs.

Nyman was standing right by the water's edge. He placed his feet where the sand was still firm and crouched down. Standing so close to the buried head made him feel awkward, queasy. The difference in height was too much. Leivo seemed like the shortest person Nyman had ever met. He crouched down further. Now he could make out the words. Nyman asked who had buried him in the sand.

'A couple of mates,' Leivo whispered. 'It's a joke.'

'You call this a joke?'

'A practical joke. It's not the first time.'

'Where are your mates now?'

'Bring a spade.'

Nyman looked around. The empty beach, the silver sea, the woods – now darker than ever. Leivo was obviously lying. Nyman looked at him. He didn't appear to be in any imminent danger. His hair fluttered in the soft night-time breeze.

'I'll find one soon,' he said. 'If you tell me who left you here. And why.'

Leivo stared at the water and remained silent.

'You're up to your ears in sand,' Nyman said, stating the obvious. 'I'm the only person on this beach.'

Leivo said nothing. Nyman allowed a few waves to wash against the shore.

'This is madness,' he said. 'And you know it. Who? Why? Tell me and I'll dig you out.'

'I'm fine,' Leivo whispered. 'I'll wait for my friends.'

'There's nobody here. Nobody ever comes down this way. I didn't even know there was a beach here. This must be part of the conservation area. I saw a sign further up the road. If the worst comes to the worst, it might be days before someone ventures out this way.'

Leivo glanced up at Nyman. Waves gently rippled against the shore. Leivo was clearly thinking things over. Nyman shifted his body weight from his left leg to his right. Crouching was taking its toll on his legs. It was in his heart and knees that he most felt the onset of his fortieth birthday, he thought.

'I suspect that neighbour of yours,' said Leivo.

So much for his mates. So much for a practical joke. Nyman thought of the man with the BMW.

'Why did he bury you here?'

'Wants to get his hands on this place.'

'This place?'

'Palm Beach Finland.'

'Why would he be after Palm Beach Finland?'

'This place is the future.'

Very well, thought Nyman. This wasn't a subject he cared to pursue any further.

'Did you see him?'

'I didn't see anything.'

'What makes you think it was him?'

'He offered me money. I didn't take it.'

Nyman thought of the twenty-five thousand euros he'd seen in the microwave. He might be on to something.

'Then what?'

Leivo glared at Nyman. He looked angry now.

'Then the friendly policeman finds a spade and digs me out of here.'

Nyman turned. It was a beautiful night. The breeze was nothing but a barely perceptible caress; the moonlight cast its silver beams over all the shapes and forms he could see: the flat beach, the twinkling sea, the trees standing perfectly still, Jorma Leivo's head – especially his head. It was like a peculiar, living work of art. Nyman thought of the man Leivo claimed had done this. The man with all that cash.

'How long have you been here?' he asked.

'Hard to say. Can't see my watch at the moment.'

Good point.

'Not for long,' Leivo whispered. 'It was after ten when I got home.'

Nyman went through the meetings and conversations he'd had with the BMW man. If he was prepared to do this, he was prepared to…

Nyman thought of Olivia. Then he stood up. He was in a hurry.

'Are you going to fetch a spade?' Leivo whispered.

Nyman glanced down at Leivo. There are no tides in Finland. It was a calm night, relatively warm. Nyman ran back towards his bike. He wasn't certain, but it was perfectly possible that behind him Jorma Leivo had started growling again.

◉

Robin tried to shake the sand from his shirt, but it was hopeless. Perhaps it wasn't even necessary. He had the news they had been waiting for. He had done what he'd been asked to and, as far as he understood it, what she desired. Robin breathed deeply – in, out, inhaling the stale air in the darkened stairwell – and rang the doorbell. Nothing happened. He could see the lights, so Nea must be at home. Robin was about to ring for a second time when he heard the inside door opening. A moment passed. Robin realised someone was looking at him through the peephole. Then the door opened.

The little boats inside Robin's head were still slowly puttering towards the harbour. And now their volume increased. Nea was wearing tracksuit bottoms and a hoodie and looked … as though she'd been working out.

In the small entrance hall, the light was behind her, but Robin could still see the woman standing in front of him. Her face was gleaming, her hair was tousled, her lipstick patchy, the make-up on her face smudged. Then he heard the shower.

The bathroom door was behind Nea. Robin didn't understand what was going on. He had so much to say, and in his imagination this situation was completely different. For some reason he had assumed he'd be given a hero's welcome and that he would be able to tell his story in his own time, as though they were sitting round a bonfire, Nea hanging on his every word. But now … this was difficult, complicated. His brain refused to cooperate.

'All that's left of Leivo is his head,' said Robin and realised he was gasping for air. 'The money is ours.'

Nea looked at Robin as though he was from outer space. Robin could do nothing but step inside, close the door behind him and carry on explaining the situation.

'Chico's got a job now,' he said. 'And getting hit with a spade never killed anybody.'

This was all going horribly wrong. Nea looked like she was about to burst into tears.

Robin didn't know what to do. Just then he heard the sounds of showering. That's right. Splashing, movements beneath the shower-head. He peered into the living room and saw a black blazer hanging over one of the dining chairs. If things had been popping in Robin's head before, now there were full-on explosions. Huge, dizzying explosions. The pink room became the molten heart of a volcanic eruption.

'You bitch,' he gasped.

The words startled Robin too. Nea shouted something, slapped him on the face. Robin staggered backwards and his body, exhausted from the digging, was too tired to keep him upright. He fell. The hallway was narrow. Robin fumbled for something to hold on to, but what he found was a tall, full-length mirror, which came tumbling down with him. The mirror shattered as it struck the floor, though Robin held on to its crumbling frame.

At that moment the bathroom door opened.

A man. A man wearing a white helmet. No. Shampoo. A thick lather of shampoo.

His furious face, furious voice.

The man lunged at Robin.

He took a step forwards but seemed to slip. Robin held on to the broad frame and lifted the mirror, which, with its jagged edges, now looked like a sheet of sheer ice. The man dived towards Robin as he lay on the floor. Robin realised he needed to remove the mirror from between them.

Everything moved. The mirror glinted, the mound of shampoo approached.

Then everything stopped. The upper corner of the mirror had disappeared and the sharpest shard of glass awaited the man's throat. At the same time, the lower edge of the frame made sure the mirror's position was stable.

The shard sunk deeper into the man's throat. The man made a noise that sounded like the mating call of a large water bird. Eventually the shard came to a halt as the corner of the frame began to split apart. He stopped and knelt above Robin. Robin could see the man's head twice, reflected upside down in the glass. His frozen blue eyes betrayed a look of confusion.

Dark blood began to flow across the glass of the mirror. It moved slowly, like maple syrup across a slanted waffle.

◉

Nyman approached the row of darkened chalets. The black BMW was gone, but Nyman was taking no risks. He stood in the shadows, listening. He heard the same as he had heard at the deserted beach a moment ago. A humming, a combination of wind, sea, trees, distant sounds carrying in from the village. He was about to take a step forwards when he heard something. It was a faint sound, and disappeared almost at once. He couldn't say what it was. The crunch of gravel beneath tyres maybe, but there hadn't been the noise of an engine. Nyman waited for a moment, but the sound didn't return. He walked to his own chalet.

There was nobody waiting for him with a gun. Why he had even imagined such a thing, he didn't know. But instinct told him it was possible. He took the steps up to the porch and tried the door. It was as he had left it.

He stepped down again, looked around and walked towards his neighbour's chalet. As he approached the porch he noticed the front door. On the side with the handle it was fractionally loose from the doorframe.

Nyman walked up the right side of the steps to avoid making

them creak. He looked for a section of the porch where the boards were firmly nailed to the structure beneath. The wood didn't make a sound. He approached the door, pressed his back against the wall and tried the door. It was open. Nyman glanced at the lock: no signs of forced entry.

Nyman allowed the door to swing fully open. Inside, all he could hear was the low electrical hum of the mini fridge. He waited a moment longer and peered inside. Nobody burst through the door, nobody lunged at him. He cast his eyes across the interior of the chalet. Nobody.

He stepped inside. His eyes quickly became accustomed to the dimness. The moonlight outside was powerful, forcing its way through the smallest chinks in the woodwork. Again Nyman looked around. With the exception of one T-shirt, everything was as it had been previously. The T-shirt was over the back of a chair, drying perhaps. Other than that nothing had changed. Nyman thought for a moment.

He walked to the small kitchen, took the dishcloth from across the tap and, using it to cover his fingers, pressed the button to open the microwave.

It was empty.

8

Robin was afraid. More afraid than he'd ever been before.

He revved the engine and accelerated. He drove well over the speed limit through the nocturnal black-and-white world, his heart and mind throbbing, and wished for one thing only: that he would get there in time. He ran the rest of the way, darting between the pines, jumping over rocks, at times almost flying. Finally he arrived.

Chico was lying on the ground among the trees, curled in a foetal position, his hands between his knees. He looked like a little boy. Perhaps exactly the same age as when they had first met and become friends, when they had founded their secret club that didn't accept any other members. Not then, and not now.

Robin fell to his knees beside his friend. He felt tears running down his cheeks. This was worse than anything that had happened before. The uncertainty. The fact of what he had done. The thought of what he might have broken.

'What happened?' Chico mumbled as he turned to face Robin.

Chico squinted his eyes as though he was trying to focus. 'Robin,' he said.

Robin could feel his chin trembling. He tried to stop it, but it wouldn't obey his will. He said nothing, he was choking so much it felt as though there was an apple lodged in his throat. He felt his chin moving, felt the tears streaming from his eyes as though someone were wringing out a cloth.

Chico sat up. He raised his left hand and gingerly touched his temple. 'You hit me with a spade.'

'I lost it,' Robin stammered.

'Let me guess. Nea.'

'I just … lost it.'

Chico lowered his hand. He propped himself up, shuffled towards a tree and rested against the trunk. Robin watched him. Chico avoided eye contact and remained quiet.

'I think I lost it too,' he said.

Robin didn't know what he meant.

'I thought I could be like Bruce Springsteen,' said Chico. 'But I can't, Robin. There's no way. It wasn't meant to be. And I never met Bruce.'

'You didn't?'

'No, I was hallucinating. That's why I never told you where and when I met him. I just said, *Sure, I've met him*. And you believed me.'

'Because you said so. Because you're my best friend. And because I trust you.'

The woods were perfectly still. The wind had died down, its hush quietened. Robin was sitting on the ground opposite Chico.

Chico looked up. 'Your best friend?'

'By a mile,' Robin nodded. 'I've never had a better friend than you.'

'How many friends have you had?'

Robin stared at the shrubs, the darkened woods. Again tears came to his eyes.

'I'm sorry, Robin. I didn't mean to be cruel. But you hit me with a spade. I'm a bit pissed off.'

Robin looked up. He saw Chico smiling.

'You're my best friend, Robin.'

Robin wiped his eyes and nose. He chuckled. The thing he had feared most looked like it wouldn't happen after all. Chico laughed too. Robin leaned forwards and hugged him. That opened the water-works once and for all. He felt Chico patting him on the back. It felt good. After a moment they let go of one another and stood up. Their heads turned towards the beach.

'We can't leave him there,' they said together.

They picked up their spades and started walking.

⊙

'Come closer,' Jorma Leivo whispered.

Chico tried to hear what Leivo was saying. It was hard because his voice didn't carry very far. Chico didn't dare get too close. His palm still ached, and Leivo's teeth marks were imprinted across the back of his hand.

'You won't bite?' said Chico.

Leivo shook his head. Chico and Robin looked at each other and knelt down in front of him.

Leivo looked first at Chico then at Robin. 'Good work,' he said.

Chico wasn't sure he'd heard right.

'Full marks for initiative, innovation, willpower and speed,' Leivo continued in a whisper.

Chico glanced at Robin. He nodded at Leivo's words.

'This final act was the only drawback,' he continued. 'But I'm happy to see you.'

Chico gave Robin another glance. Robin shrugged his shoulders.

'You're not angry?' asked Chico.

'On the contrary. I'm impressed.'

'If we dig you out of here…'

'I'll hire you. I've been thinking about this. Together the three of us could do things we can't do by ourselves.'

Chico said nothing. Jorma Leivo looked at each of them in turn. Chico gripped Robin's arm, pulled him to his feet and led him to one side. Chico turned towards the sea. Robin realised he should do the same. The view was at once dark and glistening.

'Do you believe him?' asked Chico.

'I think I'm going to need a new job.'

The answer took Chico by surprise. Not because of what Robin said or thought, but because of how the words affected him. Only a moment ago he had realised – inevitably and decisively – that as far as he was concerned the Bruce Springsteen train had already gone. It had left the station so long ago, there was grass growing between the tracks. He just hadn't seen it. Chico didn't know whether it was the result of recent events, the spade blow, or what he'd just confessed to Robin, but in all respects he felt lighter. Sometimes dreams were so heavy that they became too much to handle, like a stupid, unopened hundred-kilo rucksack, its straps chafing and throttling him. And he realised that letting go of your dreams was almost like getting out of prison. Which naturally brought him back to the here and now.

'I think I'm going to need one too.'

◉

They dug and Jorma Leivo talked.

To be fair, Leivo only whispered and spluttered. Chico and Robin dug and kept their guard. Chico listened carefully to Leivo, trying to hear whether his tone of voice changed or whether he stopped talking and his expression altered, but such a moment never came. And when Leivo's arms were finally free, they shook hands to seal their new partnership. Freeing up his hips and legs seemed to move more quickly, as the atmosphere was so very optimistic.

Leivo's admiration for them knew no bounds. He liked the idea of the ambush, their start-up entrepreneurial spirit – he stressed that the country needed innovative pioneers like him, them and Palm Beach Finland – and said he admired their ability to work quickly and, above all, their flexibility so that when it turned out that Plan A wouldn't work, they seamlessly moved on to Plan B. Real entrepreneurs, he repeated. That said, he reminded them that from now on all plans should be cleared with him first, because the devil was always in the detail. Leivo was talking a lot, thought Chico, considering his voice was more a mutter than anything else.

Leivo's limbs had stiffened in the sand, so Chico and Robin had to pull him out of the pit. They hauled him onto level ground and helped him to his feet. Leivo was between them, his arms round their shoulders, the three of them stood in a row, the pit in front of them. It was deep and black. Chico was sure he'd done more physical work in a single night than in his entire life. And it felt good, though every conceivable muscle ached, his palms were chafed and his head throbbed in time with his racing heart. But he had done something, he had…

'You need to fill the pit,' said Leivo and removed his arms from around them.

Chico was about to let Leivo stand by himself when Robin tightened his grip.

'One thing,' he said.

They waited.

'We might need that pit.'

They waited.

'It was self-defence,' said Robin.

◉

They lifted the body out of the boot of the BMW and folded it in two at the bottom of the pit so that the layer of sand on top would be enough. It was a metre thick, which Leivo said was the official minimum. These venture capitalists can sometimes get pretty aggressive, Leivo explained, they might talk nicely but in reality they're nothing but hostile squatters who don't spare a thought for long-term success of a business the way a committed shareholder should. Chico didn't have a clue what Leivo was talking about, but he decided not to ask any further. Chico realised he was enjoying this. He enjoyed working with Robin and liked the clarity with which Leivo took control of events. Leivo was a changed man, he thought, his attitude to them had changed though he was still their foreman, as it were. But he was a foreman who valued his own men.

They flattened the earth with their spades and sprinkled a layer of fresh sand on top. Finally the place looked as though nothing had happened there at all. They picked up their spades and walked off. Leivo again stood between them and raised his hands. He hugged them tight against his shoulders as they walked towards the woodland.

'Chico, Robin,' he whispered looking at them both in turn, 'I've got a feeling this is the beginning of a beautiful friendship.'

◉

Jan Nyman was sitting in his chalet, at the table in the light of the moon, waiting for his phone to come to life. The world was so quiet that his breathing sounded like a car approaching then speeding away again. Jorma Leivo might have been lying. It was entirely possible. Likely, even. But Nyman had to be sure.

Finally the phone deigned to switch itself on. Nyman quickly found Olivia's number and called. Olivia picked up.

'Everything okay?' he asked.

'You mean apart from the fact that you ran away from our dinner date?'

'Sorry about that,' he said. 'I thought I made it clear I—'

'I'm just teasing.'

'Right.'

Nyman thought about what to say next. He heard the rush on the phone, steady and distant. Olivia must have been outdoors. In the yard, perhaps, looking at the night-time sea, gilded in the moonlight.

'So everything's fine?' he asked.

'Very.'

'Good night.'

'Good night. Jan?'

'Yes?'

'Thanks for an interesting evening.'

'Thanks...'

Olivia had already hung up.

Nyman swallowed, feeling slightly awkward, but calmed himself with the thought that Olivia was safe.

So what was still niggling at him?

Those two.

The surfer and his mate.

Nyman knew where Leivo was. He had tried to get hold of his neighbour the mystery man. But what about the other two?

Nyman tapped his phone and thought about everything Olivia Koski had told him. He switched on his iPad and opened the documents, did a few searches. Kari Korhonen had no fixed address. It seemed that Robin, however, lived across the bay. Pedalling hard it would take him barely ten minutes to get there.

Nyman returned to his bike, set off through the town and completed the journey in seven minutes. The final section was a stretch of badly lit dirt track. Nyman slowed a little, he didn't want to damage the bike. The mudguards rattled. He wasn't sure if it was his fault, whether he'd treated the old rented bike too strenuously. He slowed his pace even further and jumped from the saddle in good time before the corner of the terraced house.

The apartment was dark. Either the cook was asleep or he was somewhere else. Nyman plumped for the latter. He looked around, and once he was sure he couldn't see anybody and that the only lights were in windows that didn't look directly onto the forecourt, he took the lock picks from his pocket and walked up to the front door.

The lock was an Abloy Classic, the easiest model to pick. Nyman was inside in two minutes. He stopped in the hallway and listened. Silence. He stepped further inside, treading on the rugs so that his trainers wouldn't creak against the laminate. Nobody. Nyman began to feel as though he was walking through a post-apocalyptic landscape, as though he was in a disaster movie in which a lone survivor tries to find a way out of a deserted town.

He quickly established the basic layout of the apartment, noted the places where you might hide something, anything at all. He took another breath and listened. When everything was quiet and nothing moved, he pulled on a pair of latex gloves, closed the blinds and switched on the lights.

The first things he saw were two mobile phones next to each other on the leather couch. He looked at them for a moment, running through various possible scenarios. He tried the phones; both were in working order. Both required a password. He returned them to the couch. This might be of interest. Or it might not. If the phones had been left here on purpose, that might mean that their owners wanted to make their movements untraceable. Be that as it may, that wasn't why he was here.

Nyman got to work.

He was quick and thorough. He went through the bedroom, the living room and the small kitchen. He found nothing. The microwave he left till last. There was no money in this microwave. At the back of the microwave was a sausage that had gone through several rounds of heating and now resembled a charred twig. Nyman returned the mummified sausage to where he had found it, gave the place another once-over, and asked himself: have you pulled, pushed, moved and lifted everything you can?

He ran his eyes round the room, the furniture, the corners, the shapes. He was about to answer his question with a yes, but suddenly changed his mind.

Nyman went to the dishwasher, opened the door and almost gagged at the smell – glasses rimmed with rancid milk. This machine certainly wasn't overused. He held his breath, looked through the contents and froze almost instantly.

Nyman turned, searched through the cupboard for a freezer bag big enough and grabbed the object he had found. He wrapped it in the bag, tied the corners of the bag, walked through to the living room and stood beneath the overhead light. He carefully examined the object, one millimetre at a time, and felt his heart skip a beat when, on the surface of the object, so clear that it could have come straight from the pages of a textbook, he found a set of bloody fingerprints, five in total. And as if that wasn't enough, there, on the worn wooden surface of the object resembling a fork, was an engraving.

SAMUEL KOSKI, read the text on the handle.

⊙

Olivia Koski let her bike glide silently through the night. Sometimes that was enough, she thought: all you have to do is enjoy the ride. Keep calm, sit upright, and steer. And eventually you arrived at your destination.

She came to a turn in the road and caught a view of the beach resort. She was far away and couldn't make out the details. The moon gleamed above everything like a night light. She saw the shores of Palm Beach Finland, the enormous sign, the office, the beach huts and, further off, the chalets. The moonlight softened the worst glare of the colours, but they were bright all the same.

It was the warmest night so far that summer. It felt as though there had been a turn in the weather, as though that turn had occurred only minutes earlier. The wind had calmed, taking a well-needed break, and somewhere a giant thermostat was being turned up. You could feel it. Even the rippling of the sea was different.

Olivia stood still. Here she was. After all this.

In the end everything had happened very quickly.

When Jan Nyman left the restaurant, she had followed him. She couldn't automatically take him at his word; she wanted to know what was true and what was going on. Nyman had disappeared into the woodland near Jorma Leivo's chalet. Olivia waited. After a while she noticed a familiar car appearing from the opposite direction. Olivia walked her bike deeper into the cover of the trees. From her vantage point she saw that, behind the wheel of the BMW belonging to the man claiming to be a solicitor, was not the solicitor but Robin, who stopped the car by the side of the road and … wept. Robin sobbed, gasped for air and blew his nose. A used handkerchief flew out of the opened window and fell right at Olivia's feet.

Olivia guessed something serious must have happened. And if the man behind the wheel wasn't that strange man but a weepy Robin, then … Olivia remembered what the man had said as he handed her the ten grand: *There's more where that came from.*

The man might have been lying about everything else, but he wasn't lying about that.

Olivia had located the money in a matter of minutes. It had taken her the same amount of time to break into the chalet. The door was locked, of course. But Olivia had noted in the past that in all his renovation work Jorma Leivo was more interested in aesthetics than structural integrity. The chalet was glowing with a fresh coat of bright paint, but everything else was old, including the windows. She remembered a trick she'd seen as a child. She positioned herself in front of the window, placed her hand on the side of the window that opened and gave a sharp push. The single-pane window frame was made of soft, cheap materials. Olivia pushed again. And again. And again. The frame started to move, with each shove it loosened further. In the moonlight she saw the handle move. She put all her body weight into one last shove, and the window opened with a crack. The sound wasn't particularly loud, but Olivia waited a moment longer. When she didn't hear anything, she climbed inside, closed the window behind her and looked around. For a moment she felt a sense of despair, then told herself to think like a man. Where would a man hide the money? she asked herself. A few misses, then bingo. Only her departure left a small blemish. She imagined it would be okay to leave by the front door, and that's exactly what she did, but from the outside the lock seemed somehow faulty. You could only lock it with the key. She had to leave the door ajar.

Olivia took the bag from her back and peered inside. She hadn't yet counted the money; she didn't want to do so right away. She ran her fingertip along the thick bundles of cash and estimated that there was more here than in her initial down payment of ten thousand euros. After a spot of haggling, she guessed this would be just enough for a full-scale plumbing renovation.

She closed the zip and slung the bag over her shoulder. She gripped the handlebars and placed a foot on the pedal. A moment later the bike was moving again, gently gliding forwards, and all Olivia had to do was keep her feet on the pedals and steer in the right direction.

She thought of the promise she'd made to herself. Never again would she allow a man to mess with her finances. This was a promise she was determined to keep. And she would keep another promise too: she was going to renovate her house.

She wondered how Jan Nyman might fit into that scenario.

The bike rolled gently onwards. Olivia smiled.

◉

Robin wanted to drive. Chico knew this. Robin took responsibility. It was a new quality. Chico could see the changes in Robin with his own eyes. He was growing both inside and out: he stood more upright, his gaze had gone from drifting and submissive to determined and self-assured without appearing brash or arrogant, his speech was more concise and generally more sensible, the words new and precise. And it had all happened since Robin sat down in the driver's seat.

The BMW sped through the ghoulish night with the two quiet, dirty men inside. Robin kept to the speed limit, just to be on the safe side. Leivo had given them a job, said he needed a shower and a change of clothes before a meeting in the morning. With them.

They turned off the highway. Gravel pattered against the chassis. They drove along a darkened road lined with spruce trees. When they arrived at a junction, they took an even narrower dirt track. Eventually they turned off that too. The slip road was steep and familiar. The BMW's front lights illuminated the bottom of the quarry as Robin gradually slowed the vehicle. The surface of the pond was like black ice. Robin drove the car right to the water's edge.

The pond wasn't very big, but it was deep. Chico had once heard that it was created the way you sometimes saw on TV: the ground suddenly sunk away and fell into the depths below. He didn't know whether that was strictly true or not, but right now it hardly mattered. Most important was what the pond could swallow up.

Robin turned to look at Chico. In the light of the dashboard and the moon, his face looked like the face of a grown man. It wasn't the face of a giant baby or a forest creature; it was a man's face. Chico said nothing as Robin shifted the automatic gearstick to P and left the engine running as they stepped out of the car.

Chico left the door open and walked to the back of the car. He was standing a few metres away when Robin reached inside and shifted the gearstick to D. Robin jumped back, away from the car, just as it jolted forwards.

The BMW crept into the water like a large black beetle. It seemed to swim upright for a few metres then to turn on a sharp axis, and soon it looked as though the car dived underwater head first. The rear of the car bobbed on the surface, and for a moment it seemed as though it might remain in that position. Water frothed around it, something hissed, and the sound of frantic bubbling came up from the deep. Eventually the lights went off and the dive sped up, and soon the BMW disappeared altogether. The bubbling was steady and continued for some time. That stopped too and the surface of the pond gradually calmed again. There was only Chico, Robin and the moonlit quarry.

Chico couldn't take his eyes from the dark surface of the pond. They had sunk the BMW. They'd done what had to be done. Chico realised that only recently they wouldn't have been able to do it, not after sitting on its leather upholstery and feeling the power of its huge engine. They would have kept the car, though it would have caused them no end of problems. They would have been unable to resist their own instincts. But now they had done just that.

And Chico realised that something else had sunk too. Something heavy pressing down on his shoulders. He remembered something he had noticed while sitting in the passenger seat: the numbers flashing on the dashboard.

'Robin,' he said.

'Don't worry,' said Robin. 'The spades went down with it.'

'I wasn't thinking about the spades. But, good. I was thinking about the time. It's three o'clock.'

'So?'

'It's the twelfth of July. It's my birthday. I'm forty years old.'

Robin turned.

'Happy birthday.'

'Thanks.'

'How are you going to celebrate?'

Chico thought about this. He looked at Robin, then the surface of the water.

'I think I'm celebrating now.'

'Will you be long?'

Chico knew what Robin meant. They had to get going, they had a long walk ahead of them.

The length of the return journey didn't matter, thought Chico, and neither did the exertion.

Not when the journey was right.

9

Jan Nyman imagined that one day Muurla might actually turn into the item of furniture that he so resembled. In a matter of days, Muurla had acquired a tan, which further enhanced the impression of an antique English divan.

Muurla was sitting behind his desk, Nyman in the plastic chair on the other side. Outside it was the first real summer's day of the year and Nyman was wearing only jeans and a T-shirt.

Nyman had travelled to Helsinki by bus, taken a commuter train to Tikkurila and walked from the station to the headquarters of the National Bureau of Investigation. He'd made the most of the summer's morning. The sun rose in time with his steps, its beams were soft and warm, the sky cloudless and light blue in such a way that no painting could ever do justice. The grass on the empty plot next to the station was fragrant. The leaves of the trees danced in the gentle breeze.

Nyman placed the plastic bag on the desk along with the initial report, which he'd hurriedly written up on the bus. Nyman assumed that because he could see the bloody fingerprints on the shaft of the backscratcher, Muurla must see them too. In any case, Muurla was looking at the bag and the wooden object inside it, so Nyman began to speak.

'Some things we can prove fairly easily,' he began. 'And others we can't, unless someone starts talking. Nobody has spoken up so far, and I don't think that's going to change. But, this is basically what happened. These two genii – the surfer and the cook – their names are in the report – are hired or somehow recruited to disrupt the life of Olivia Koski, either to make Koski agree to sell her house or for some other reason. They go to her house; they either do or do not know that there's already somebody else inside, but nonetheless decide to act. At the moment, I assume they threw a stone through the window, and the stone struck this guy, Antero Väänänen. That explains the broken windows and what happened next. We didn't find any stones inside the house, but it would have been easy to remove them. Be that as it may, Väänänen was hit, and these guys decided they would have to finish off the job. I'm not entirely sure about this. There could be other reasons. But the two guys enter the house, and there's an almighty fracas, as we can see from the photographs. Things go badly for Väänänen. One of these guys, or both of them, steals this wooden item here. I don't know why. It belongs to Olivia Koski, it's a … tool used by her father and grandfather. Most importantly, it's covered in fingerprints and lots of blood, presumably Väänänen's. I'm convinced the fingerprints belong to the cook. The cook and the surfer do everything together. I'm also fairly sure they were responsible for burning down Olivia Koski's sauna. I wouldn't be surprised if it turned out they had bought or procured fire-starting equipment earlier that day. At present I don't know whether the sauna building has any more than insurance value, because in the wider picture we're investigating a homicide. In the report you'll see where to find these guys, and I've emailed you pictures of where I found the wooden implement. At this point I'm going to hand the investigation over to someone else, but here's everything you need.'

Muurla was still staring at the item on the desk. 'What about the woman?'

Nyman nodded, though Muurla didn't so much as look up at him.

'Olivia Koski. She has nothing to do with Väänänen's death.'

'Are you sure? You got close to her?'

Nyman thought for a moment.

'She has nothing to do with this.'

Muurla looked up, his eyes staring straight ahead. They sat for a moment in silence.

'You said these two guys were recruited. If this woman didn't hire them, then who did?'

'My guess is Jorma Leivo, the proprietor of Palm Beach Finland. I've got no proof. And I doubt he'll ever come clean. He's a hard-headed man. In one sense, I take my hat off to him. I encountered him under circumstances in which a lesser man would have confessed to absolutely anything. He was buried up to his neck in sand. But when I went back to the spot to find him, he wasn't there. Maybe it really was all a big joke, as he told me. There's a determination about him. But, as I said, I don't have any proof of his role in events. As you know, I asked the fraud department to look into Leivo's financial dealings. You and I both know that was illegal, and that if something had turned up it would have been inadmissible in court. But I did hear that there was nothing untoward in his accounts. Leivo came into an inheritance some time ago and invested all the money in his Palm Beach Finland project. I don't know if we'll ever be able to link Jorma Leivo to any of this. Maybe it's not the end of the world. The most important thing is that we know the identity of the people who killed Väänänen, either accidentally or on purpose.'

Muurla seemed to accept Nyman's explanation. All of it. Muurla's eyes returned to the pronged wooden implement on the table.

'Toys can really spice things up, you know,' he said eventually. 'It was a dreary time for me before I met Leena, but when she finally opened that suitcase she kept beneath the bed—'

'Sorry to interrupt,' said Nyman. 'But there's something else.'

Muurla looked at him. His expression revealed that his mind was elsewhere, engaged in activities of a wholly different variety. Nyman waited for him to return to the here and now. You could see it in his eyes as they focussed again.

'I want a holiday,' said Nyman. 'Well, not so much a holiday. I need some time off.'

'How long?'

'Until the sea freezes over.'

Muurla stared at him. Nyman remembered what he'd said to Olivia. The same things he had said to his ex-wife. He'd said he didn't have any dreams.

He'd thought about this on the journey back to Helsinki, the only passenger on the bus as the empty landscapes flashed past in the opposite direction. The fact that he didn't have dreams didn't mean he didn't desire things. And for the first time in his life, the object of his desire was clear. For all its simplicity, the feeling was baffling. This is what it must feel like when people decided to work to make their dreams come true. At that moment, he thought, that blink of an eye, the moment when a dream turned into a concrete endeavour, there was something so primitive and clear, so powerful that it didn't stop at turning dreams into action. It changed a person, and it did so well before the dream was near to becoming a reality. After all, wasn't that what dreams were for – to change us? Because surely our lives will never change if we don't change ourselves first.

And there was no time to lose.

'On what grounds?' asked Muurla.

'I want to learn to windsurf,' said Nyman. It was true. It wasn't the whole truth, but in and of itself, it was the truth and nothing but.

'I thought you didn't like windsurfing.'

'So did I,' said Nyman, then, after a short pause, he added: 'I couldn't have been more wrong.'

FIVE WEEKS LATER

Jorma Leivo held the drawing in front of his face. He held it at the end of his outstretched arm, brought it up to eye height and tried to fit it into the landscape. Yes, he said to himself.

He was standing on a boulder in the stretch of pine forest between the shore and the conservation area at Palm Beach Finland and gazing out towards the furthest edge of the beach. He lowered the drawing a little, saw the old quayside, the handful of boats and the clubhouse at the small sailing club. He raised the drawing again and saw something altogether better.

The drawing depicted a pink flamingo which, once it was completed, would stand almost thirty metres tall. The flamingo's head would house a deck with panoramic views opening up to Helsinki and, on a clear day, all the way to Estonia. The deck would also be the starting point for the longest, highest and best water slide in Finland, which would twist and turn through the bird's body and wind its way round the flamingo's legs. There could even be two water slides – one for the smallest in the family, and one for real daredevils. The flamingo's body would provide more opportunities to take in the view and let your hair down. Right in the middle, Jorma Leivo had drawn a cocktail bar in true *Miami Vice* style. The décor would be colourful: Florida-chic, white leather sofas, cocktails with sunhats, straws and sparkling fans. The drinks would have appropriate names, such as Sonny's Special, Rico's Arrest, Castillo Cool. Leivo had already drawn up the preliminary recipes: for Sonny, a stubbly, smoky whisky; for Rico, a heartening rum; for Castillo, a pure, ice-cool vodka. Customers could drink as much as they wanted, as a lift would run up and down the bird's straight leg. Its raised leg and outstretched webbed foot would be the perfect place for a diving board.

There would be no direct access from the cocktail bar, but the diving area could feature a bar selling energy drinks too.

Leivo squinted, sharpened his focus.

The flamingo would be a landmark too. The kind of landmark that this age, this country needed. Courage, innovation, open-mindedness. It would be visible from afar, even from planes cruising above the Baltic Sea. Leivo had never understood the Finlandia Hall and other supposed national monuments. Where was the originality, the ingenuity, the ability to think outside the box? Where was the life, the joy, the colour? Jorma Leivo only had to lower his hand and turn his head slightly, and he got his answer.

It was only eleven o'clock on a Saturday morning, and every single one of the hundred and twenty deckchairs was occupied. A game of beach volleyball was in full swing. And further in the distance, new chalets were being constructed, eight in total. A queue of the smallest customers wiggled in front of the ice-cream stand. Jorma Leivo had been right. Word about Palm Beach Finland was getting around.

It was almost 16°C, the breeze cooled the air and the weather forecast said it was getting colder. Maybe even hail by the end of the week. Excellent, he thought.

He gazed again at the thronging beach. Then he turned and raised his drawing again. He thought for a moment, then slowly lowered it. The masts of the sailboats appeared first, then the clubhouse gleaming with a fresh coat of white paint, the white hulls of the boats, and finally the jetties along the quayside standing in the path of progress. A dozen or so boats were moored along the quay. Three or four members of the boating club were refusing to sell their waterfront properties. They weren't many in number, but their resistance was all the more adamant.

Leivo raised the drawing again. He looked at it. Three or four boaters apparently believed he shouldn't be allowed to realise his dream and lift the country out of the doldrums. It was wholly unacceptable. Those three or four boaters would change their minds. At the very latest by the time…

Leivo took his phone from his pocket. He looked at his drawing one more time and selected the right number.

◉

Chico was restringing his guitar, and he was doing it with care. After last night's performance, the guitar was like a wheezing flu patient: it had lost its voice and seemed exhausted. Chico had played hard. He had given his all.

Playing hadn't felt this good for a long time. While he was playing, he no longer wished he was somewhere else, no longer dreamed of bigger and better venues, let alone absurd things like the famed tattooed English woman with the gleaming breasts who had plagued him for years – not because Chico really desired her, but because she had never really existed. Like most other things that had commanded his thoughts over the years. It was as though he had forgotten all about what he held in his hands: a guitar.

And if he had a guitar in his hands, all he could do was play, not think about what playing might or might not bring him.

Last night, after finishing his thunderous, rollicking encore, he received the kind of applause he'd always wanted. Strong pairs of hands clapped vigorously in a genuine wave of exhilaration.

Chico was tightening the upper strings as Robin's head appeared in the doorway.

'I talked to Nea.'

Chico looked at his friend, a friend who in recent weeks had surprised him on more than one occasion. Robin seemed to have a grip on more new things all the time. Chico had no idea what had made such an impression on Nea that she wanted to marry Robin as soon as possible. He guessed it might have something to do with the body laid to rest in the old beach, but he didn't know the details, and Robin didn't provide them. It didn't bother Chico. There was so much else to talk about. Like the fact that Robin was now Chico's manager.

'She's spoken to Leivo,' said Robin, and sat on the bed.

Chico took his left hand from the guitar's neck. 'And?'

'He's going to get us out of it. We'll get the best lawyer money can buy. The lawyer said there's every chance we'll get off with involuntary manslaughter or even just a public-order offence. Because we're first-timers, it means we'll be out by next summer or the one after that at the latest. Apparently it's the same lawyer who got that back-passage rapist out in three weeks.'

'What did Leivo say?' asked Chico.

'He said there are a few boaters that need the wind taken out of their sails.'

Chico thought for a moment. 'That probably means something else too.'

'I told him we like working.'

'True,' said Chico. 'Especially together.'

'Bro,' said Robin.

They high-fived, clasped their hands in an arm-wrestling grip and finished off with a fist bump.

For a moment they were silent.

'You've got a gig tomorrow at the open prison,' said Robin. 'There'll be a captive audience. It's a fresh crowd. Drink drivers, junkies. They like a good party.'

Chico looked at Robin. 'How did you organise that so quickly?'

'I told them we'd have a barbeque too.'

'What are you going to cook?'

'Anything. I'll spread everything with my special marinade. It's so good you could grill a toilet roll in it.'

'True.'

'It's called the Bruce Springsteen Barbeque.'

'Again?'

'You're at your best when you sing Bruce. You really know how to channel The Boss. It must be because you've met him.'

Chico shook his head.

'But I—'

Robin raised a finger to his lips and gave a *shush*. 'I've already told everyone. Your first number is 'Working on a Dream'.'

◉

Jan Nyman put down his bucket, sat down in the two-seater garden chair and looked towards the house. The old place looked as though it was being pulled in all directions at once: up, down and to the sides. The pit at the side of the house was large and gaping, sections were missing from the side of the building, and, inside, the bathroom was nothing but an empty space with an enormous hole in its freshly laid concrete floor. The renovations were still on schedule. Nyman knew exactly why that was. He looked away.

It had been another comfortingly chilly day. Bright, but chilly. When the sun and its beams were reflected at this angle, the sea looked like it was sloping away, becoming steeper. And if you squinted your eyes and allowed your imagination to run wild, you could imagine the whole world slowly turning upside down. He knew a few things about that too.

Nyman had been working since seven that morning. It had just gone five o'clock in the evening. The remains of the burned sauna had been removed and taken away to make room for new foundations. That was Nyman's first job. He couldn't remember everything he'd done since. The days and tasks all seemed to merge into one.

'Having a break?'

Nyman turned. Olivia was standing behind him holding a large hammer.

'Does that thing mean I'm not allowed?' he asked, nodding at the tool in her hand.

Olivia pointed with the hammer. 'Those planks need to be carried behind the new foundations and covered with tarpaulin.'

'In a minute,' said Nyman and looked out to sea.

Nyman could sense Olivia behind him, both physically and mentally. It had been like that since the beginning. He'd noticed it as soon as he returned. Now he could almost feel the cool steel of the hammer behind him, swinging in Olivia's hand like a metronome. He knew without looking.

'How about,' he began. 'How about I don't get up or carry anything ever again?'

Olivia was silent.

'What if I just sit here and watch you at work, enjoy the summer, learn to windsurf? What do you say to that?'

She didn't answer.

'I bought that board you recommended,' he said. 'I don't know what's happened, but it seems to obey me now. Either that or it's called a truce. I noticed it yesterday. It wasn't pulling me in different directions anymore.'

A few seconds, then Nyman felt it on the top of his head.

Olivia's lips.

She walked round the chair and sat down next to him. Nyman looked to the side. That profile: the long, regal nose, the sharp, thin lips, the brown eyes, raised cheekbones and dark hair. Nyman could have looked at Olivia for hours, or at least until the end of the dwindling light on this wistful summer's evening.

'Perhaps that's enough for today,' said Olivia.

'What about Esa?'

Nyman could hear Esa drilling and banging something at the other side of the house.

'Esa will finish once the job is done.'

Nyman looked at Olivia. Her expression gave nothing away.

'Besides,' she said. 'He's being paid as the job progresses.'

'Right,' said Nyman.

He hadn't asked. He had never asked Olivia how she suddenly had enough money to pay for the renovation. He didn't ask whether she was aware that a man who had visited the beach resort and suddenly disappeared had been keeping a wad of cash in his microwave, a sum of money almost exactly the same as the amount for which Esa Kuurainen had agreed to complete the plumbing renovation.

Nyman had his suspicions, but he allowed them to fade and disperse, just as he had the thought of how he had first met Olivia Koski. In fact, the latter was far more painful to process. Yes, he had been doing his job, but still. Again he allowed the thought to drift further off, let it float up to the fluttering boughs of the trees to be carried somewhere across the sea by a greater wind.

'Leivo has been very friendly these past few weeks,' said Olivia.

Nyman said nothing.

'After he made me lifeguard supervisor and gave me a pay rise, he's even started asking for my advice. He did so again yesterday.'

'Really?'

'I was about to go home when he turned up on the beach and asked what the president of the boating club – who's a good friend of Miss Simola – likes to do. He said he was thinking of what to get her as a birthday present.'

'Really?' he said again. He listened closely.

'Yes. And before you warn me or patronise me, I know how to look after myself.'

'I know that.'

Nyman was more concerned about the implications this might have for himself. He hoped it didn't mean what he thought it might. He'd been serious about what he said to Muurla. He wanted some time off. Which meant toiling round this house from morning till evening, which felt better than anything had for a long time. Better than almost anything.

'I'm on morning shift tomorrow,' said Olivia.

Nyman turned and placed a hand on Olivia's tanned, muscular shoulder. He ran his fingers across her bare skin. The warmth of her skin travelled from his fingertips to the bottom of his stomach.

'Then we should get to bed early,' he said.

Olivia smiled, brushed the hair from her eyes and let it fall, casting a shadow across her face. It was an impressive gesture that Nyman was only too pleased to watch.

'Get to sleep, you mean?'

'I mean get to bed.'

Olivia leaned over and kissed Nyman. How he loved the touch of those lips, so warm, so hot, so cool, so heavy, so feather-light.

'Esa will be in the bathroom for a while yet,' said Olivia.

'Let him. We can go upstairs.'

'The bedroom is right above the bathroom.'

'We'll be quiet.'

Olivia placed a kiss on Nyman's cheek and whispered in his ear. 'When was the last time you were quiet when I did this?'

Nyman felt her tongue against his skin.

If he'd been able to dream, he would have dreamed of this. But he didn't have to.

This was real.

ACKNOWLEDGEMENTS

Palm Beach, Finland is my seventh published novel. By the time you read this, I will have published my eighth novel, *Little Siberia,* in Finland, and *that* book will be published in the UK in 2019, marking my sixth English translation. Ahem. The point is, I didn't get here all by myself. Of course, I wrote the books – the texts are all mine, every single word – and the stories are very much a product of my imagination, for better or worse. But I did get more than a little help from a few friends along the way.

My previous novel (the sixth overall, if anyone is counting), *The Man Who Died*, felt like a turning point in many ways. After writing five very dark books – albeit that they all differ from each other, ranging from the dystopia of *The Healer* to the icy north of *The Mine* – I started to feel that I needed to change things up a bit. Well, more than a bit, to be honest.

As a result, my eight (if we're really keeping count) books can be roughly divided into two groups: the very dark ones and the ones with a healthy (or unhealthy) dose of black humour in them, flavouring the *noir* proceedings. I feel I've been very fortunate to have been able to change my direction in this way. And I feel even more fortunate to have had the support to do so.

First, I want to thank my literary agent, Federico Ambrosini, for his invaluable and incomparable support and feedback. I am very grateful to have him in my corner. And on the subject of agents, I want to extend my gratitude to each and every person at Salomonsson Agency, Stockholm. Thank you.

I wish to thank the amazing Karen Sullivan, my UK publisher. She is a fearless independent publisher and an inspiration for anyone and everyone working with books. She works harder than anyone I know. Karen, from the bottom of my heart, thank you.

My most sincere thank you to Jaakko Launimaa, the editor of this book (the original Finnish version, that is).

Thank you to my supremely talented translator, David Hackston. Finnish is not an easy language, but you make it seem so. I'm privileged to be translated by you.

Thank you to West Camel for your steadfast and careful editing of the English version.

I want to thank my mother and father for giving me the love of books and early encouragement with writing. I have the best job in the entire world, and that wouldn't be possible without the bookshelves in our home a long time ago.

Finally, I wish to thank my beautiful, wise wife, Anu. None of this would be possible without you. You are my heart and my home. Thank you for everything.